A LESSON IN LOVE ...

"I won't let you go under," Oliver said. Allegra shivered in the cool Carribean surf, then gripped Oliver's arms. As his steady strength and cool commands placated her terror, she yielded to his protection. She clung to him with absolute faith.

Oliver was so moved by the trust in her wide, violet-blue eyes, he couldn't resist the temptation. Slowly, still treading water, he pulled her closer, held her tighter, touched his lips to hers.

They were all alone in the ocean, their bodies tugged apart and bumped together by the waves. For a moment, Allegra felt her whole being almost ache with uninhibited desire, fed by Oliver's kiss, by the feel of his lips on her skin. She abandoned herself to the vibrant sensations rippling over her as relentlessly as the sea ...

A TASTE OF HEAVEN

LAURA SIMON

BERKLEY BOOKS, NEW YORK

FOR HILDA

I would like to thank the following people for their gracious help in gathering the information for this book: Arthur Perez at Krön Chocolatier, New York; Sir Willy Branch, Dougaldston, St. John's, Grenada; Cyril Stephen, St. John's, Grenada; Miss Abraham at the Grenada Public Library, St. George's, Grenada; Arnold and Royston Hopkin, *Blue Horizons*, Grande Anse, Grenada; Mrs. Betty Mascoll, *Morne Fendue*, St. Patrick's, Grenada; Selwyn Humphrey at the Grenada Cocoa Association, St. George's, Grenada; Frances Kay Brinkley, Carriacou.

A TASTE OF HEAVEN

A Berkley Book / published by arrangement with
the author

PRINTING HISTORY
Berkley edition / December 1989

ISBN: 0-425-11873-8

Chapter
One

"*You* are Cecil's daughter?" His tone was blunt. And incredulous.

Allegra felt a flush rising beneath the damp and wilted collar of her traveling dress. She was hot, tired, and increasingly doubtful about this impulsive trip to the Caribbean in search of a father she had never met. When she had left Connecticut two weeks ago, on a dismal, early autumn day, the idea had seemed inspired, the perfect escape from the bleak New England winter ahead, and from an equally bleak and predictable future. Now, standing in the office of James Forsythe, Esquire, facing two astonished men in their shirt-sleeves, she wished, after the fact as usual, that she had thought this out more thoroughly. She didn't even know which of the men, each in his early thirties, was the solicitor who handled the affairs of her father's estate, L'Etoile.

"*You* are Allegra Pembroke?" he demanded again.

Allegra managed to nod, miserably aware of her frazzled appearance, of the flustered color creeping up her neck and disappearing into the cloud of honey-blond curls springing heedlessly from the knot in which she had tried to restrain them. Suddenly awkward, as she always was when her impetuous nature pitched her headlong into circumstances that collided with convention, she found herself studying the wooden floor beneath her nervously shifting feet. Tongue-tied and stiff, she felt the flush deepening.

She had no idea of how attractive a picture she presented. Though only average height, her slender build and the energy apparent in her posture gave the illusion of her being much taller. The silky curls, springing wildly from her coiffure, also added inches to her stature. They framed a face that just missed classical perfection by the scattering of a few golden freckles across her forehead and down her nose. Her expression defied perfection, too. Wide eyes, almost violet-blue, seemed too eager and too curious to reflect the docile disposition so desirable in a woman.

"Can't you speak?" The voice was more suspicious now. "How do we know you are Cecil's daughter? Where did you come from?"

Allegra looked up for an instant, snatching a glance at the tall, lean man questioning her. He couldn't be Mr. Forsythe. Although certainly assured, he hardly seemed lawyerly. His thick, black hair had scarcely seen a brush today, let alone a pomade. And while his accent was educated English, hiding just a hint of a Scottish brogue, his deep suntan and exceedingly casual attire bespoke either a disdain for form and fashion or an out-of-doors career. Not only jacketless, he was collarless and tieless as well, with his shirt open at the neck and his sleeves rolled up above his elbows. A pair of royal blue braces embroidered with tiny yellow stars held up his trousers, whose barely pressed legs ended at well-worn canvas tennis shoes.

"Yes. Yes, I can speak." The words came stuttering out before her eyes swept down again. His eyes were dark sea-blue, improbably fringed with long, black lashes. "I came off the *Creole Prince*. From New York."

"Right." The single syllable was pronounced dryly, emerging from a mouth that seemed perpetually ready to grin, despite his brusque tone. "As she is the only vessel over fourteen feet to make port in two days, and, as it seems highly unlikely that you have been hiding in the hills, that much is obvious. Perhaps my question should be . . ."

"Hush, Oliver," the second man interrupted, finally overcoming his astonishment and struggling courteously into his jacket. "Will you never learn to keep a civil tongue in your head? You are behaving like a proper Tartar." The heather and mist of the Scottish highlands were much more evident in this man's accent, as they were in his fine red hair and fair complexion, neither treated kindly by the tropical sun.

"You must forgive us, Miss Pembroke," he said, addressing

himself to Allegra and hurrying to set out a chair for her comfort. "It's just that Cecil, uh, that is, your father would have had us believe that you were scarcely out of the cradle. We had you pictured as a wee lass."

Allegra lifted her eyes again and was relieved to see a smile on the Scotsman's face. Relieved also that this man, by process of elimination, must be her father's solicitor, she collapsed into the proffered chair. Not knowing quite how to respond to his comment, but not wanting to be so rude as to make him appear wrong, she explained, "I was little, once." Realizing how simpleminded that made her sound, she hastily added, "But I'm not now."

"Quite so," murmured the man called Oliver, undaunted by Mr. Forsythe's reprimand. He resumed the position he had been in when Allegra had entered, tipped back in a chair, feet crossed on a desk, arms crossed on his chest.

The red-haired man shot his friend another quelling glance before dragging his chair over by Allegra and sitting down again. "Your father can be a bit vague with dates and details," he told her. "So we really shouldn't be so surprised." He paused a minute, his sunburned brow puckered in sudden thought. "Actually," he said more slowly, assembling an idea as it occurred to him. "We should have been able to calculate for ourselves that you were no longer a babe. If we put all of Cecil's tales in order and added them together, it would only make sense that you would be a full-grown woman."

This time Allegra was completely at a loss for a response and could only, as before, manage an awkward nod. James Forsythe twisted in his chair to face the lounging man behind him. "You know, Oliver," he said, counting on his fingers, "it's been almost six years since Cecil came to Grenada. He came in November of '87 and bought L'Etoile from that French planter, Le Ciel, in April of '88. I recall that most distinctly because I'd only just arrived myself."

"Hmmm," Oliver admitted, tilting his head toward the ceiling as he did some addition of his own.

"And we are quite certain he was at least three years in Madagascar growing peppercorns because he uses that experience to illustrate the idiom that bad luck comes in threes: His crop was ruined three years in a row by flood, fire, and—what was the third?"

"Stampeding cattle."

"Ah, yes. How could I forget the story of the Blind Brahma Bull? We're also fairly sure that he spent two years in Shanghai trading silks and spices because that tapestry hanging in the gallery at L'Etoile took two years to weave. Remember the story of how he pulled a warlord's son out of the Yangtze, and the man had the tapestry made for him in gratitude?"

"Right. After Cecil refused to accept his daughter as a gift, instead."

The Scotsman gave Oliver an impatient tsk, indicating that certain episodes should be edited for feminine ears, then glanced back at Allegra apologetically. Far from being offended, however, Allegra was listening with awe. Her doubts vanished and the eagerness with which she had embarked on this journey returned. Her father was just as she had hoped and imagined him to be, gallant, romantic, and, above all, adventurous. She leaned forward to hear more.

Slightly startled to see her blushing timidity replaced by a radiant expression, the lawyer turned back to his friend and continued his enumerations. "Let's see," he said. "Uh, yes. He was in California for quite a while. Didn't he cross America on the first transcontinental train? In '68, was it?"

"'Sixty-nine, Jamie." Oliver answered his friend automatically, but his gaze, removed from the ceiling, was fixed on Allegra. "May 1869." He too was taken by the change in her. He recognized in her face, surrounded by the undisciplined curls, the same spontaneous spirit he enjoyed in Cecil, and his initial disbelief and suspicion vanished. In fact, he suddenly realized how much he was attracted to her. Everything about her was appealing, from her engaging appearance to her unexpected, and unchaperoned, arrival in Grenada. Even her inexplicable awkwardness was a refreshing contrast to the studied moves of the young ladies he had met in London.

"Yes, yes, '69," Jamie said. "He tried panning for gold, but discovered only that he was a wee bit late and a great deal disinclined for that means of making his fortune. Then he got involved in the fur trade to Alaska, didn't he? It seems to me that lasted some time."

"Yes, until he went to Sitka," Oliver responded, turning back to Jamie, his face breaking into its promised grin. "Cecil hates being cold. He claims it's a reaction to the dampness and gloom of Pembroke Hall. Those old English manors are impossible to heat."

"Well, it's all there, then," Jamie said, waving his hands through the air in judicial summary. "Add in the odd stint on the tea plantation in Ceylon and the coffee estate in Java, plus a few seasons buying cocoa for a firm in Amsterdam, and it only stands to reason that his wee babe in arms should be fully grown." A frown pulled at his pleasant face as another thought struck him. "I wonder if Cecil himself realizes how much time has gone by?" he asked speculatively.

"He wrote," Allegra offered quickly. Then, thinking of the small stack of infrequent and unanswered letters tucked under the chemises and next to the diaries in her mother's bureau, she added, "Sometimes." A knowing snort from Oliver made the color leap into her face again, and she resumed her scrutiny of the tightly twined fingers in her lap. This unusual man had a disquieting effect on her, due as much, she suspected, to his strong, striking features as to his direct manner and unvarnished remarks. She had never met anyone who was quite so candid.

"I'm certain he did," Jamie said, smoothing over his friend's appraisal of Cecil's consistency as a correspondent. "I had one or two remarkable letters from him, myself, last year when he went home to England. Your father has an amazing flair with a pen, a true gift for words. I've often told him he should put all his tales on paper. It would make a marvelous book." Allegra looked up, again grateful for the lawyer's tactful intervention. The reassuring smile he gave her loosened her twisting fingers.

"That may be," Oliver said practically, dismissing Cecil's artistic talents and returning to his more commonplace qualities. "But I find it odd that your father isn't here to collect you, Miss Pembroke. That he never told Jamie or me of your intended arrival I can only attribute to his sense of drama. I'm sure he meant to surprise us. And he may be well satisfied that he succeeded; we are thoroughly astounded. However, once having set the stage, it is unlike him to miss the performance. Even given his peculiar notion of time, I can't imagine Cecil forgetting as important an appointment as this."

"Oh," Allegra said, her hands clamping together again. "Well." Her head tilted to one side and she examined the molding above the wide-open window. After a few moments of utter silence, she spoke. "Actually, he doesn't know anything at all about my arrival. It only just occurred to me to come." Oliver's feet swung off the desk and his chair thudded forward. "After I discovered his whereabouts quite by accident," she finished, her eyes moving to study the framed certificate claiming James Andrew Forsythe to be a graduate of the University of Edinburgh.

"Oh, fine," Oliver said flatly. "Not a single act, after all, but an entire play."

"Do you mean to say, Miss Pembroke," Jamie asked, ignoring Oliver and leaning forward in sudden earnestness, "that you have come all the way here from New York, twenty-five hundred miles alone, on *chance*?" His voice was serious, but not censorious.

Allegra finally turned her gaze away from the wall and looked squarely at James Forsythe, Esquire. Her wide eyes were honest and innocent. "Well, yes," she answered with equal earnestness. "Except that I've come from Connecticut."

From behind her came the sound of Oliver's chuckle. "Well, Jamie," he said, amusement enriching his voice. "No need, in the end, for your figuring. If we had any doubts, we can lay them aside. There can be no surer proof that this is Cecil's daughter."

However he intended them, his words went straight to Allegra's heart. She couldn't think of any finer compliment than to be irrefutably associated with her father. He was a gentleman and an explorer, a man who lived by his imagination and his resources, always seeking something extra out of life.

If she tended to exaggerate his adventurous spirit, it was due, perhaps, to the newness of his presence in her life. As she had admitted to Mr. Forsythe, she had only just discovered his very existence. Neither her mother nor her grandfather had ever talked about him, answering all her questions with the brief statement that he had been carried off by the flu when she was six weeks old. She hadn't even known his name. Until a few weeks ago. Rummaging aimlessly through a bureau drawer, she had come across her mother's diaries and the small bundle of correspondence underneath them. From the twenty-six-year-old memories, the occasional letters, and her own fertile imagination, she had finally assembled her family history.

Cecil Pembroke arrived in New York City in 1867. At age twenty-four, he was fair of hair and full of charm; his finely wrought face appealed to everyone he met. The second son of Sir Arthur Pembroke, a country squire with wealthy holdings in Sussex, England, Cecil could look forward to little, if any, inheritance. Fresh from the university, and still attached to his father's purse strings, Cecil was in search of a glorious future.

Within days of his arrival he fell madly in love with Miss Amelia Bromely, a young lady every bit as beautiful as he was handsome, and in town for a visit with her maiden aunt. Within weeks of his arrival, over the objections of both their widowed parents, they were wed.

Amelia's father, the sober owner and headmaster of an unexceptional boys' school in a small Connecticut town, voiced stern disapproval of his son-in-law's lack of occupation. Sir Arthur, on the other hand, demonstrated his displeasure with his daughter-in-law's ordinary American lineage more forcefully. He cut off Cecil's quarterly allowance, plunging the newlyweds into immediate poverty. The appearance, nine months later, of a baby girl caused still more complications, though Cecil, with characteristic optimism (and in keeping with the fashionable penchant for Greek and Latin names), christened her Allegra.

Soon, however, Allegra's demands for food, attention, and dry diapers put further burdens on the already strained relationship of her parents, and on the delicate state of her mother's health. Less than a year after she left her quiet Connecticut home, Amelia returned there to recover and to raise her child. Alone.

Cecil disappeared into the wide world beyond, promising to find a situation, to create a secure home, and to come back and retrieve them. Over the years letters arrived irregularly, attesting to his sincerity of purpose, if not to his perception of passing time. Finally, in 1889 came a letter from Grenada describing L'Etoile. It was a cocoa estate he had purchased, eight-hundred acres of tropical splendor. The great house, high on a hill with views of the Caribbean Sea, was nearly complete, a beautiful and graceful home for his beautiful and graceful family. He wrote rapturously of their reunion.

By then, however, it was twenty years too late. Amelia did not have the irrepressible spirit that Cecil had, the vitality he had passed along to their daughter. Her one disastrous attempt at finding adventure and romance had cured her forever of the desire to venture beyond the familiar borders of her father's home and standards. To everyone who had asked, including Allegra, she had said her husband had died of the flu soon after their baby was born. She had stopped writing in her diary and had tucked Cecil's few letters into a drawer.

It was there that Allegra had found them in early autumn, 1893. Her mother had died several years before, offering little resistance when a summer cold had developed into pneumonia and had carried her away. Allegra had mourned her, missing the soft and gentle light Amelia had cast, but otherwise continued her somber existence unchanged. It was only after her grandfather's death in August that the relentlessly regular rhythm of her life had altered. Suddenly, utterly alone in a house that had always seemed too small, in a town where she had never felt entirely comfortable, she had combed through years of collected possessions in an unconscious search for direction.

The discovery that her father was alive, very much alive, had filled Allegra with unbounded excitement. It hadn't only been the fact that she now had a family where minutes before she had been an orphan. It had also been the fact of just who Cecil was. The more she had read, the more sure she had become: She had found not only a father, but also an explanation of herself.

All her life Allegra had repressed the bubbling spirit within her, deemed indecorous in a young lady. "Sit on your hands," her grandfather had constantly instructed her as an exercise for stilling the physical and mental energy propelling her. Her mother, more subtle as was her nature, had presented Allegra with a gilt-edged guide to etiquette for her fifteenth birthday. ". . . be always employed in something useful . . . avoid extremes . . . be temperate in all things . . ." She had made fervent resolutions to change, to become more complacent, but even these vows had been too impassioned and, inevitably, had failed.

Try as she might, Allegra couldn't help wishing for something more: more exciting, more important, more grand. She wanted to do something. To be someone. For as long as she could remember, she had wanted the sum of her life to be more than a tedious accumulation of years. Reading Amelia's early infatuated diary entries and Cecil's accounts of his adventures, she recognized the same desire in her father. Except that while she had scarcely dared dream about it, fearing rebuke, he was realizing it.

Cecil and L'Etoile had become a symbol, a goal. They stood for a way of living she had always yearned for but had never had the courage to define. Now, with her father alive, Allegra had gathered that courage. She had assessed her dreary prospects, had anticipated the oncoming raw winter, and had made a typically impulsive, optimistic, and, probably, improper decision. She had bought a steamer ticket for Grenada and had set off for a bright, fulfilling future, centered around Cecil.

Oliver laughed again. "You two are definitely cut from the same cloth," he said, shaking his head in amazement. "Only I daresay the tailor used magic carpet rather than sensible serge. I can just imagine the fellow coming upon a bit of flying rug and saying to himself, 'Hey, ho, I think I'll use this pretty piece for Cecil Pembroke and daughter.'" His black brows arched a moment over his remarkable eyes. "You know," he concluded, "that sounds like the name of a genteel little business in Knightsbridge or, perhaps, an elegant shop on Bond Street. Pembroke and Daughter. Or, as the French would say, Pembroke et Fille."

His tone might have been teasing, but it wasn't sarcastic. Allegra detected a genuine affection for her father in his words and again felt a warm glow spread through her. Her reaction was inspired not only by the man's kind words, but also the man himself. Although she could practically feel her grandfather's ghost stiffening in horror at Oliver's presumption, Allegra found herself fascinated by his assured informality. She had just begun to relax and to frame a reply when he interrupted her thoughts and threw her off-balance again.

"It's a pity you are dining with old Johnny Hooper tomorrow night," he told Jamie, "or you could come with us to L'Etoile in the morning. I'll wager you won't want to miss seeing Cecil's face when I bring him his daughter along with the post."

"Oh, no," Allegra blurted out before Jamie could answer. Both men turned to look at her. "I mean to go to L'Etoile today. Right now. From what my father wrote, the estate is only ten miles from the port. If you will be kind enough to give me directions, I will hire a carriage." Though her voice was polite as she had been taught, her fascination for Oliver was suddenly tinged with alarm at the way he was taking over.

"Ridiculous," Oliver answered brusquely. "A carriage is a ridiculous means of transportation in Grenada, unless you are making social calls in town. And even at that, you are better off on your feet. One of my cargo schooners is loaded and ready to go. We'll sail up the coast to Gouyave tomorrow morning, then it's just a short ride by horse to L'Etoile."

"I don't ride," Allegra said faintly. Her alarm was growing. When she had imagined this adventure, no thoughts of horses or freight boats or audacious strangers had crossed her mind. "Really, a carriage will do nicely."

"I'm afraid my friend is right, Miss Pembroke," Jamie broke in, tossing another stern look at Oliver. "A carriage trip to L'Etoile is not at all a pleasant experience. Those ten miles will seem more like fifty. The roads here are in a wretched state. Not only do they twist and turn around the coastline and climb and fall over mountains, but they are sadly rutted or washed out or rendered impassable by mud slides. I feel sure you will be more comfortable going by sea."

"Surely then there's some public conveyance, today," Allegra responded desperately. "A ferry, perhaps?"

"There's nothing," Oliver replied, again unchastened by Jamie's glare. "And only a fool would put to sea today. There's a squall brewing; who knows how nasty it will be? It's still the rainy season, after all. We'll go tomorrow."

Allegra made one last attempt to free herself. "Please don't feel obligated to escort me," she said. "I just came here to get directions to L'Etoile. I have no intention of taking you out of your way."

"You won't be," Oliver returned easily. "That is precisely where I am going. Tomorrow."

"It is?" Allegra asked, half curious, half suspicious herself.

"Och, Blessed Heaven!" Jamie exclaimed. "We've been sitting here gaping and gabbing like country bumpkins and we've never even introduced ourselves. I beg you to forgive our atrocious manners, Miss Pembroke. I'm James Forsythe, your father's solicitor and friend. And this chap who dresses like a pirate and seems ready to carry you off over the horizon is really quite a respectable gentleman. Permit me to present Mr. Oliver Mac-Kenzie, your father's partner in L'Etoile."

For a stunned moment Allegra was silent, then she echoed, "My father's partner in L'Etoile?"

"Ahhh," Oliver said, tipping his chair back once more. Amusement tugged at the corners of his mouth again. "I can see that there are some surprises in this for you, too. Yes, I'm your father's partner. He offered to sell me half interest in the estate three years ago. As I liked L'Etoile very much, and I liked Cecil even more, I accepted. It's been a satisfactory arrangement for us both."

"I see," Allegra murmured, suddenly seeing quite a bit more than he described. She saw how foolish she had been to abandon the life she knew on the strength of a nearly five-year-old letter. In the intervening years her father had found a partner. He wasn't sitting all alone in the house that he had built, waiting for wife and daughter to make it a home. He had found a partner. Perhaps he had even found another family and had new children to delight him. Disappointment filled her as thoroughly as the glow of happiness had only minutes before.

The image she had been willing away these past few weeks, the image of her grandfather's disapproving face, came rushing forward to reproach her. She knew he would have advised against this trip; he had told her time and again to be more circumspect, to consider her actions more carefully. As she felt the deflating weight of chagrin, she realized he was, as usual, right. In a subconscious effort to mend her ways, to make up for her lapse, she straightened in her chair and adopted such a prim air, even her most conservative critic would have been satisfied.

"We'll secure lodgings for you at the St. George's Hotel for tonight," Jamie said, unaware that Allegra was undergoing a change, if not of heart, then of spirit. His was an easy nature: If his schedule didn't fit the circumstances, he would make a new schedule. He was always surprised to discover that most other people, in the same situation, would instead seek to alter the circumstances. "It's not particularly grand, but it's clean, and Mrs. Douglas, in whose charge it is, is a dear lady."

"Oh, no, I couldn't," Allegra said, with such a show of refined dread, Grandfather Bromely would have nodded his head in pride. "I couldn't possibly stay the night in a hotel alone. It would be most unseemly." She lowered her eyes delicately and smoothed a fold in the beige linen duster she wore for traveling. With the zeal of the newly reformed, she failed to see the incongruity of her refusal to spend the night, unchaperoned, in a lodging house after having passed most of two weeks on a steamer from New York in exactly that state. When she adopted an attitude, she adopted it wholeheartedly.

The discrepancy between her current words and previous actions did not go unnoticed by her audience, however. Although it had Jamie temporarily stumped for a reply, it disgusted Oliver.

He had little patience for the pomp and protocol of polite society, and picked his friends and associates accordingly. He got along well with Jamie, because of the red-haired lawyer's easygoing outlook. Jamie had given up a good opportunity to practice law in Edinburgh, choosing instead the mellow pace of the tropical colonies with their numerous opportunities for leisurely escape.

Oliver was disappointed to see the irresistibly eccentric spirit, which had identified Allegra as Cecil's daughter, suffocated by the stiff codes of convention he despised. He decided that despite the enchanting first impression she had made, despite her corkscrew curls and her incredible violet-colored eyes, she was really very ordinary, after all. She had the staid manners and starched posture of a thousand other young ladies of her age and class. The keenness of his disappointment caught him by surprise, upsetting his usually steady temper. Always a direct man, his words now carried much more bite.

"You should have thought of that before you left Connecticut," he said unfeelingly. He set his chair down with a resounding thump and got to his feet. "Even more unseemly than passing a night in a perfectly respectable hotel would be to blow out the sails or snap a mast and end up awash in Grand Roy Bay. Or hanging onto a timber on the beach in Venezuela. We'll go tomorrow."

"I shall go today," Allegra replied. Although she was determined to correct her impulsive actions by conducting herself with utmost propriety, Oliver's harsh tone had an unsettling effect on her. She stood up and said, her voice slightly quavering, "I wouldn't dream of asking you to imperil either yourself or your vessel on my behalf." She found it necessary to study the stars on his braces rather than face the force of his dark blue eyes. "I shall hire a carriage to take me to L'Etoile. I feel sure Mr. Forsythe exaggerated the difficulty of the drive out of concern for my comfort, but I shall bear up."

"Such a display of fortitude is noble, Miss Pembroke," Oliver snapped before Jamie could stop him, "but completely misplaced. Mr. Forsythe did not exaggerate one iota the difficulty of the drive, whether your comfort was uppermost in his mind or not. If anything, he failed to emphasize the danger of such a journey in this season. When that storm hits, as it surely will before you reach L'Etoile, the road will become a nightmare. It may even cease to exist at times. If you are set on making the trip overland, it, too, should be postponed until tomorrow."

Having embarked on a course she was sure represented behavior her grandfather would approve, Allegra could hardly retreat. Besides, the more Oliver insisted to the contrary, the more unaccountably adamant she became. Jamie tried to mediate, his thin, freckled hands patting the air placatingly, but his diplomatic words went unheeded. In the end, it was Oliver who conceded, not because he believed Allegra was right, but because he knew she would try to reach L'Etoile today, one way or another. He was sure she would be safer with him than with anyone else, and he had an obligation, however onerous, to protect her. After all, she was Cecil's daughter.

"Very well," he finally capitulated. "We'll go. But I promise you, it won't be a pleasant jaunt."

Jamie let out an imperceptible sigh of relief. Despite the fact that his profession depended on controversy, he had a distinct aversion to it. "Good," he said with an encouraging smile. "That's settled, then. While you get under way, shall I go around to the telephone company and call Cecil? I know you thought to surprise him, Oliver, but perhaps Miss Pembroke would feel more reassured if her father came to meet her at the pier."

Oliver looked at Allegra for confirmation of this idea before answering, cocking a black eyebrow in question. After a moment, Allegra nodded, again unable to speak. As before, her emotions were in total disarray, her recent avowal to act with decorum at odds with the renewed thrill Jamie's remark created. In her anxiety to complete her journey, she had temporarily forgotten its object. Now, the thought of her father waiting to welcome her as they sailed up to the dock stirred her imagination.

Stepping out of the law office a few minutes later, those stirrings were intensified. The colors, the sounds, the sights and smells, even the heavy heat that assaulted her senses vividly reminded her of the reasons she had fled Connecticut. Half walking, half trotting down a precipitously steep lane in the tropical port city of St. George's beside an intriguingly handsome Scotsman, she was again excited to be engaged in an adventure.

A small black girl in bare feet and a blue calico gown walked by, balancing on her head a basket filled with shiny green, oval-shaped fruits. Allegra glanced sideways at Oliver, but dared not disturb him to ask what they were. "Mangoes," Oliver answered unemotionally. "They are in season just now." He didn't even turn his head. Allegra gulped and nodded.

A scarlet curtain fluttered in the doorway of a weather-stained wood house. Through the unshuttered opening drifted the aroma of roasted coconut. Across the way, a woman poked her head out from an upstairs window, her features mysteriously shaded by the green-and-white striped tin awning above her. In the lyrical accent of the West Indies, she called to her friend passing below. "Pearline, Pearline La Salle. Watch me. Where you been?"

Her friend slowed her leisurely stroll, tilted up her turban-wrapped head, and called back, "What is it? I just stepped out to come back." Consumed by curiosity, Allegra twisted her neck to follow the dialogue. Though he didn't slow his pace or acknowledge her interest, the beginning of his usual grin was edging out the scowl on Oliver's face.

They turned the corner by a two-story building whose bricks were painted yellow and whose raised mortar was painted white. Its tall windows were outlined by a geometric pattern of blocks, and its roof, way above, bore flat red fish-scale tiles. As Allegra lost sight of the two women, she reluctantly turned around again; then stopped short with a gasp of delight. "It's so lovely!" she exclaimed at the view in front of her.

They were at the harbor, or the Carenage, as it was called, a wide, deep, horseshoe-shaped expanse of dark blue water pressed against the walkway hugging it. Dozens of schooners and sloops, freighters and fishing boats, sailboats and rowboats, all built of wood and all painted bright colors, lay tied to the cleats in the walk, singly, doubly, even rafted five deep.

Around the walk ran a road, and around the road stood building after building made of brick and stone and stucco, pale pink and white and royal blue, green and beige and butter yellow, massive buildings, warehouses, and feed stores, wholesalers and hardware suppliers, Hubbard's and Huggin's and Otway's and Wm. Steele. Some had elaborate wrought-iron grates over rectangular windows, some had scallop-edged tin awnings; some windows were narrow, some semicircular, some enlarged by a balcony. All were big, bold, and beautiful.

And beyond the buildings, above the Carenage, the rest of St. George's rose on high hills covered with palm trees and flamboyant trees and with lush, green vegetation crowding around pastel painted houses. "It's perfect," Allegra said softly.

"Mmmm," Oliver answered, not wanting to agree with her on any subject, but unable to keep the pride out of his voice.

For a moment, Allegra forgot about the tension between them as her eyes traveled around the half-moon harbor, absorbing it all. A muscular youth sat on an upended beer keg, chopping conch out of pearly pink shells. A donkey, dwarfed by its giant load, trotted by so close its bulging burlap bags brushed against her sleeve. The earthy odor of nutmegs remained in its wake. "I love the colors," she said, almost to herself. "I love the red roofs."

"It's the law," Oliver replied practically. "After a severe fire in 1775 the legislature passed a law stating that all construction must be of brick and all roofs must be of fish-scale tile. It came as ballast in the ships from Europe. Although," he added, after a moment's pause to scan the scene himself, "that law didn't prevent another fire from wiping out nearly a third of the city in 1792. A ship laden with rum, tied right there where that yellow and blue fishing smack is sitting, burned to the waterline and took St. George's with her. They started taking the law a trifle more seriously after that."

Allegra tore her eyes away from the fascinating sight, remembering her recent resolution. "What was a whole ship full of rum doing here?" she asked primly. "Surely such a small little island as this has no need for so great a quantity of spirits."

"Good God!" Oliver exclaimed, disgusted. "Don't tell me you are one of those damned temperance people, as well." The natural good humor in his face was fading again. "For your information, Miss Carrie Nation, that rum was not for *import* but for *export*. In those days, the economy of Grenada revolved around sugar cane and its derivatives, rum being one of them. At the time of the fire, there were 125 sugar estates here and more than 100,000 gallons of rum were shipped abroad that year, much of it considered to be the finest in the world. Even today, with the sugar industry all but replaced by cocoa, there is some outstanding rum distilled here. It's as smooth as the best French brandy."

"Oh," Allegra said, much abashed. In truth, she had never tasted rum, having sipped only a very occasional glass of sherry, but her mother had seemed quite sure that demon rum not only caused most of the world's troubles, but also signaled a coarse and vulgar character.

"What's more," Oliver added, affronted, "Grenada is not so

very small. It is twenty-one miles long and twelve miles wide. And half a mile high. It's as big as it need be."

"Oh," Allegra said again, even more subdued. Her gaze dropped to the black tarred road, soft and sticky beneath the Caribbean sun. She could feel the heat through the leather soles of her boots. It was trapped inside her clothes, too, making the layers of linen hot and heavy and the mutton sleeves of her dress hang limp.

"Come along," Oliver said briskly. "We're wasting time. My schooner is just down the way. Across from that warehouse with the bright green trim."

Allegra looked to her left, in the direction he was pointing. She immediately identified the building by the patterns of green blocks around the windows and the giant doors. And by the sign swinging from a wrought-iron post above them. STAR SHIPPING, it stated. INTERISLAND FREIGHT. TRANSATLANTIC COMMERCE. OLIVER MACKENZIE, PROP.

She sneaked a glance at Oliver in surprise and awe. In Connecticut, businessmen of such stature wore worsted-wool suits with gold watch chains stretched across high-buttoned vests. They wore bowler hats on their heads and neatly trimmed moustaches under their noses. They would never be seen in public dressed like Oliver MacKenzie, Prop. in a shirt of admittedly fine fabric, but so weathered and soft some of its pinstripes had faded. Still, there was no denying the sense of confidence in his bearing. Or the esteem of his peers. Almost everyone he passed called out a greeting, friendly, affectionate, full of respect.

Allegra looked back down the Carenage, picking out the schooner that was to carry them to Gouyave. It was about sixty feet long and sat gracefully in the water, its cedar-planked sides painted a clean white, its rails and square center cabin painted blue. Along the bow, in big red letters, was its name: *Miss Lily*. Allegra felt an inexplicable stab when she read it, wondering who the namesake was.

Oliver leaped easily on board and turned to help Allegra, but she stood fast on the walk. "I have my trunks in the custom shed," she said, looking across the harbor to the piers where oceangoing vessels docked and where official entry offices stood in a collection of colorful buildings.

Oliver made a noise with his tongue against his teeth, a very

West Indian exclamation of disgust. "Trunks?" he asked. "Just how many trunks have you come with?"

"Only three," Allegra answered, suddenly feeling that it was a great deal too many.

"*Only* three?" Oliver shook his head. "And probably not a sensible frock in any of them."

"*All* my clothes are sensible," Allegra retorted, thinking of the sturdy tweeds and practical poplins her mother had always selected.

"Not for this climate, they aren't. Not if they look like that." Oliver nodded toward her duster, hopelessly crushed and darkened by a huge damp streak down her back. Allegra blushed and quickly closed the offending garment. Oliver's tone was so frank, it seemed indecently intimate. Somehow it made her feel as if she were wearing nothing, rather than too much.

Either Oliver didn't notice her embarrassment, or he was indifferent to it. He shook his head again. "You can wear what you please," he said. "But you'll have to wait until tomorrow for your trunks. It will take too much time to retrieve them now If we're to have any chance at all of beating the squall, we'll have to get under way immediately."

"But I can't leave them here," Allegra protested, concerned. "All my things . . ." Her voice trailed off. She realized how silly she sounded, but those three trunks contained not only the wardrobe of which Oliver already disapproved, but so much else as well. Her books, her pictures, her mother's diaries, some embroidered sheets, her grandfather's silver, and a worn but still smiling doll that had kept her company for years. "I must have them," she insisted.

Oliver started to argue, but then thought the better of it. In the time they would waste debating the matter, one of his men could be across the harbor in a bumboat, and halfway back with the trunks. "As you wish," he said briefly, then handed her on board. As he turned away to issue instructions to his crew, he decided that his first image of Allegra had been an aberration, a mirage, and that his subsequent assessment was more accurate. She was just an ordinary woman with rigid opinions, too much luggage, and an arrogant disregard for weather.

Very little conversation passed between them for the rest of the journey. Oliver installed Allegra in the cabin, an eight-by-eight wooden box with a wooden door both portside and starboard, two wooden benches that doubled as berths, and four wooden shelves that held some rolled up charts, some mismatched teacups, and a battered shortbread tin. She inspected the shelves, tested the benches, then wandered restlessly out on deck. If Oliver noticed her, he ignored her, busying himself by the big wheel in the stern.

By the time they got under way, her trunks finally stowed in the hold, the storm that Oliver had prophesied seemed a real possibility. The hazy sunshine disappeared in a sky that looked like polished steel and ominous black clouds crept over the horizon. But Allegra was unworried. She remained on deck, relishing the cooler air and the breeze from the sea. For once, she didn't care about her unraveling coiffure in her relief to escape the heat of St. George's. She stood with her back to the foremast, watching the green, steep shore glide by and eagerly anticipating the reunion with her father.

The wind hit suddenly, cracking against the canvas sails and heeling the schooner on its side. It wrapped the linen duster around her legs and tore at the tight lace neck of her dress. Tortoiseshell hairpins flew out of her bun; her curls seemed to straighten as they streamed away from her head. Her knuckles turned white as she clung to a cleat on the mast, her whole body straining to stand upright. Looking back toward the cabin, she wished she were within the comparative safety of its walls, but she was afraid to release her grip on the groaning mast to cross the open deck. All romantic images and adventurous visions left her mind. She thought only of hanging on.

For what seemed like an eternity, she watched the shoreline go past, no longer gliding, but heaving and bucking before her eyes, her vision blurred by the wind. All of Grenada seemed to rise sharply from the sea, sometimes leaving a slash of white or black sand at its base, sometimes surging, in vine-covered cliffs, straight out of the waves. The schooner pounded and crashed, sending geysers of spray over the bow. The right half of her duster was soon soaked. Water trickled along her scalp and ran in rivulets down her face, making her lips taste salty when she licked them with a dry tongue.

"Come, Miss," a voice shouted in her ear. Startled, she craned her neck around toward the source of the sound and saw the face of a black sailor only inches from her own. "Come, Miss," he shouted again. "Hold fast to me."

For a moment, Allegra just stared at him, hardly comprehending what was happening. Then, making up her mind, she let go of the mast and lurched into the sailor, holding onto his arm for all she was worth. Braced against the wind on wideset bare feet, he led her to the lee of the cabin, opened the door, and shoved her in. Allegra sank gratefully and gracelessly onto the wooden bench and stayed where she landed for the remainder of the trip, feeling a bit frightened and very foolish for having insisted on coming.

It was only when the schooner righted itself and seemed to stop, when she could hear the ratchety sound of sails sliding down the mast, when she felt the vessel bumping against a pier, that she struggled again to her feet and regained some of her excitement. This was the moment she had been waiting for, the moment when she would meet her father and have him open the door on a new and wonderful way of life. As she fidgeted with her snarled hair, that excitement grew until it blotted out her recent doubts. It didn't matter that Cecil had a partner, the unusual Mr. MacKenzie, or even, perhaps another family. She was still his daughter.

Heart thumping, she opened the cabin door and stepped back out into the wind. It was not as overpowering as it had been when they were under sail, but it still attacked in fierce gusts, undoing in a second the hasty hair repairs she had made. While her hand flew reflexively to her disheveled curls, her eyes anxiously scanned the scene before her.

A long cement pier, just wide enough for a fully loaded donkey cart to pass, connected the rocking schooner to the tiny town of Gouyave. On one side was a beach made of round black rocks, made smooth by their incessant rolling in the sea. On the other side was a beach of pure white sand, overhung with wind-whipped palm trees. Bordering both beaches were small houses, all made of cedar planks, and all standing off the ground on wooden legs. Underneath the houses were piles of fishnets beside brightly painted fish boats, assorted fish traps, and an occasional pig or chicken. The window shutters were all closed against the imminent storm, but more than one door stood open, a curious onlooker leaning against its frame.

In the hard-packed dirt plaza at the head of the pier, a few workmen milled around, amiably speculating on whether they would unload the cargo today or tomorrow. From out of the two-story block building by the edge of the road marched the local constable, resplendent in the gold-braided uniform that had been designed for his slightly larger predecessor. Down the dock ran two small boys, the knees of their cotton pants much patched, happy to welcome home their sailor papa.

But no one among the crowd gathered to greet the *Miss Lily* looked remotely like the man Allegra imagined her father to be. Disappointment tightened her throat.

"I know Cecil's memory of appointments is lamentable," Oliver said, suddenly quite close behind her and speaking above the wind, "but one would think he could remember, for three hours, the arrival of a daughter he hasn't seen in twenty-five years." His tone was brusquer than usual, expressing the annoyance he felt with his partner for his lack of punctuality and with his passenger for the harrowing voyage he had just made on her behalf.

The instant he said it, though, he was remorseful. Tears welled up in Allegra's eyes and hurt was apparent on her tired face. "Perhaps he never got the message," Oliver said more sympathetically. "The telephone system has only recently been extended to the estate and it is constantly going out. Either that, or else the line is so full of clicking and hissing, it is impossible to hear what is being said. More than likely, Jamie couldn't get through." Once again, hope illuminated Allegra's face. It astonished Oliver how deeply that light touched her.

His irritation returned, however, when he tried to organize the last leg of their trip. Allegra didn't know how to ride, and was in no mood to learn. Gouyave, though a pretty little village, definitely lacked the amenities of St. George's, and there was not a carriage or buggy to be hired or borrowed. The best Oliver could come up with was a knock-kneed donkey and a traditional Grenadian cart, narrow and crude, with high sides and big wheels. After Allegra climbed awkwardly into the back, he seized the lead rope and they started for L'Etoile.

From the first minute, Allegra was again grabbing desperately for support. The rickety cart, buffeted by the relentless wind, bounced into every hole in the barely tarred road. Shortly north of the small collection of houses that was Gouyave, the road veered away from the sea and up into the hills. There it gave up every pretense of being paved, becoming instead rich red earth.

The road twisted and turned, always rising, with very few level spots and no gentle views. For a while, it wound through a seemingly impenetrable forest of strange trees, then it cut along the very edge of a precipice that plunged into a dramatic deep chasm. Even the open areas offered no relief, showing enormous expanses of ever more threatening sky. Tall trees, with roots hooped above the ground, bent and swayed as the wind screamed around them. Coconuts came crashing to earth only inches away.

Allegra was more than a little bit frightened now. Exhausted both physically and emotionally, she could no longer bear the violence of nature and the bluntness of her companion. For the first time, she began to wish she had never left Connecticut.

And then the rain came, emptying an almost black sky. It poured more ferociously than Allegra had ever felt it, instantly soaking her layers of linen, pounding at her skin, obliterating the tears streaming down her cheeks. She could hardly make out Oliver only a few feet away, struggling to guide them up the steep road. Torrents of water raced down the ruts, snatching at the wheels and catching the feet of the donkey. They seemed to make no headway, slipping back on the slick, sticky clay each time they tried to move forward. Miserable and afraid, Allegra could only bend her head and pray this would soon end.

The sheets of rain were just starting to ease when the cart came to a complete halt. Allegra looked up, her heart leaping in hope, but she saw nothing that appeared to be shelter. She could see Oliver more clearly now and was shocked by the harsh look pulling at his features. Following his grim gaze up the treacherous road, her eyes came to rest on a big tree stretched across the road. Blown down by the wind, the tree blocked the way. Its muddy roots reached pathetically into the air; its leafy branches were splayed out on the ground.

Then her heart, which had been so full of hope only a moment before, seemed to stop, frozen with dread. Through the blur of rain and the confusion of branches, she could see the bodies of a horse and a man, trapped beneath the heavy tree trunk. They were very still.

In an instant, she was out of the cart, stumbling and tripping up the road behind Oliver. Suddenly oblivious to the still-raging storm, she fell to her knees beside the body of the man. He lay on his back, his head twisted at an odd angle. Sky-blue eyes stared up at her; the pelting rain plastered blond hair to his fine fore-head. A trace of blood, washed to the palest pink, stained full, faintly smiling lips. She knew exactly who he was, exactly what had happened. She didn't need Oliver to tell her, but he said it anyway.

"It's Cecil." His voice was hoarse. "Your father is dead."

Chapter
Two

"Dear Lord, please take this soul into the glorious embrace of heaven," the voice intoned. "Let him dwell for eternity in the midst of Thy splendor..." Allegra lifted her face, as if to catch a glimpse of the puffy clouds of paradise. All she saw was a blue sky, clear, hard, and hot, the unblinking sun directly in its center.

There was little evidence today of the terrifying storm. The fierce winds had died to a barely detectable breeze; the raging rivers in the rutted road had disappeared into the red earth. A six-foot hedge of hibiscus was bursting with brilliant scarlet blooms; bright blue and white windflowers bordered the path. Even the sea, once so dark and menacing, now glistened blue and green and deep purple, only a rhythmic ripple disturbing its surface.

The quickly constructed coffin being lowered into the freshly dug ground was the only reminder of yesterday's savage monsoon. Just the coffin and the somber crowd in the cemetery on a hilltop near Gouyave: women in rustling black dresses and shadowy veils, men in black suits, some people sobbing, everyone sad. Allegra stood between Jamie and Oliver, overwhelmed.

She struggled to focus her thoughts, to comprehend what had happened, but it was all so bewildering, so cruel. It had been a miracle to have her father appear suddenly in her life, to have him spring into it holding out hope and promise for her future. And it had been a macabre joke to have him killed minutes before meeting her, to have the hope suffocated, the promise unfulfilled. She had come over two thousand miles to find him, from a continent to an island, from a country to a colony, to a different climate, a different culture, a different world. She had come to find him and, through him, herself. Now that she was here, he was gone. Forever. Despite the throng of people, despite her father's solicitor on one side of her and his partner on the other, Allegra felt more alone than she ever had before.

She had wept when her mother had died. She had ached with sorrow, feeling Amelia's absence in every corner of her consciousness. When her grandfather had passed on, she had cried as well, missing even his austere presence in her life. But no tears came now. There was only a numb void where grief should have been. She had come to find her father, and now that he was lost, so was she.

"He was a good man who sought only happiness for himself and others . . ." the preacher droned on. Allegra forced her attention to his sermon, straining to find in his words some clue, at least, to her father's identity, and thus to her own. She hoped desperately to hear a solution to her present predicament, to be told what direction to follow. Reverend Smythe, whose years in the tropics had dried his skin to parchment, could have been eulogizing any member of his Anglican congregation. She looked away from him.

"He's almost through jabbering," Oliver muttered, seeming once again to sense what she was thinking.

Allegra gave a barely perceptible nod of acknowledgment, her loneliness oddly eased by his low-pitched growl. She turned her attention to the people crowding around the grave, filling the aisles of uncut grass, obscuring tilted headstones from view. They were still arriving, climbing the steep hill to the cemetery, fanning themselves against the heat and the exertion. They were black and white, planters and laborers, coming from all over the island to pay their final regards to Cecil.

Through her confusion came a trickle of wonder. Because of the heat, even more intense than usual, the funeral had to be held almost immediately, yet hundreds of people had stopped what they were doing, and had journeyed over torturous roads or by water to be here. They had come to pay tribute to her father. Her wonder increased; surely this was a far greater testimonial than Reverend Smythe's sermon.

"It's over," came Oliver's terse words, interrupting her musing. She glanced quickly at him and then at the minister, feeling an edge of panic when she realized that everyone was staring at her expectantly. She froze, not knowing what was happening.

"Toss your flowers on the coffin," Jamie whispered, giving her elbow an encouraging nudge.

Allegra took a few hesitating steps to the brink of the grave and released the three lilies she had been clutching. She watched them land on the rough-cut mahogany lid, wondering what she should do next. Again her unasked question was answered as she felt Oliver by her side. He pulled her hand through the crook of his arm and guided her down the path to the carriage waiting on the road.

For the rest of the afternoon, either he or Jamie were always close at hand as she stood for endless hours on the veranda of L'Etoile, principal player in a scene that was becoming increasingly surreal. Amid this strange setting she accepted condolences from total strangers for a man who had been a total stranger. The heat, caught inside her linen suit and beneath her layers of underwear, conspired with the exhaustion of her long trip and her almost sleepless night to practically paralyze her.

As if underwater, she heard the voices of one person after another greeting her in the accents of the West Indies or England or Scotland. She heard Jamie and Oliver make the introductions and explain who each person was, and she heard the hollow sound of her own voice respond. Only gradually did she realize that with every new person, a portrait of her father was emerging.

"He was a lovely man," Mrs. Smythe, the desiccated wife of the desiccated minister, said wistfully. "So well bred. When he attended my Thursday afternoon teas, he added such elegance to the party. A true gentleman. I'm so sorry."

"Yes, ma'am. Thank you, ma'am," Allegra murmured, picturing her father, a Wedgwood teacup held artlessly in his hand, charming and aristocratic.

"Miss Pembroke, I would like you to meet Col. Horace Woodbury," Oliver said. "Colonel Woodbury has an estate in St. Mark's Parish and has lived in Grenada since retiring from Her Majesty's Service six years ago. He came here at almost the same time as your father."

Allegra held out her hand to a compact man with a debonair moustache and the air of a confirmed bachelor. "You must have felt a kinship," she said politely.

"Eh?" the colonel questioned, suspicious of the emotional tie she intimated had existed. "Kinship? A healthy competition, more likely," he said heartily. "Of course, I did have a bit of the advantage, having spent thirty years in the colonies. Know my way around, so to speak. Never did see the like of Pembroke, though. Dove right in. Read everything in print on growing cocoa. Learned all there was to know. Had this place running like a top in no time. Never saw anyone so keen on the subject.

"Beastly weather, eh, MacKenzie? Thought that storm yesterday would break this heat spell, but it's just made it worse. My sympathies, Miss Pembroke," he concluded, wheeling away, leaving Allegra to picture her father as a man full of energy and enthusiasm.

"Allow me to introduce Mr. Martin Briggs, Miss Pembroke," Jamie said. Allegra turned to meet a slender smiling man whose dark complexion and broad features indicated black ancestry. "He owns several cocoa holdings in St. Patrick's Parish and serves as the magistrate in Sauteurs, as well."

"And your father's teammate at cricket," Mr. Briggs added with a graceful bow. "He was a capital bowler. Utterly tireless. I recall one match, several years ago, when he stood out in the sun from morning till dusk, bowling the ball with naught but some tea and a few cucumber sandwiches to sustain him. And at day's end, he attended a fete at Grand Anse, dancing half the night away. He was always a favorite with the ladies, being so fair and fine and so light on his feet. He shall be missed by everyone."

"Yes, he shall," Allegra agreed, smiling over Mr. Briggs's tales of the handsome, dashing father she would never know.

"My dear, you have my *deepest* sympathy," a squeaky voice said. Allegra turned again and nearly overlooked a diminutive woman whose white hair was screwed tightly in a bun and whose straw hat was stuck full of feathers.

"Mrs. Potter, Miss Pembroke," Jamie said. "She is our unofficial ornithologist and botanist. I believe she knows every bird on the island by its given name."

"And I've never had anyone ask me so *many* questions about them as your *dear* father," Mrs. Potter chirped. "He was *fascinated* by everything around him, whether it was birds or animals or people. He could never ask enough questions on any subject. And *ideas*. My dear, he had more ideas than the library, I'm sure. They were like fireworks in his head, each one setting off the next. He positively *delighted* in hatching new ideas. We would have the *jolliest* outings, just chattering like blue jays the whole time." She stopped and gave an unexpected sniff, a tear rolling down her cheek. From up her sleeve, she produced a handkerchief and blew her nose delicately. Trying once more to talk, but failing, she shook her head sorrowfully and turned away. As Allegra watched her flutter off, she pictured a picnic dominated by her father's curiosity and imagination.

So it went for the remainder of the day. Allegra met dozens of people, heard dozens of anecdotes. There was only extravagant praise. Very few people hinted at the flaws that Jamie and Oliver had alluded to, however affectionately, yesterday. The glowing picture of her father grew larger and brighter, reinforcing the image she had created in Connecticut. By the time the crowd diminished, her head was buzzing.

"You look entirely undone," Jamie said sympathetically. "You must come and sit down; you've been on your feet for hours." He led her, unprotesting, to a large wooden planter's chair, stuffed full of chintz-covered cushions. Allegra sank down gratefully, the full force of her fatigue suddenly weighing on her. "And you've had no chance for food or drink," he continued kindly. "Let me fetch you something before it is all carried away." He nodded his head toward the dining room where long tables bearing the remains of platters of food and bowls of punch were being cleared.

Just the thought of eating made Allegra feel ill, and she shook her head weakly. "Thank you, but no," she murmured. "I couldn't." The next instant a glass was thrust into her hand.

"Drink it," Oliver commanded. "You've had no nourishment all day. In the tropics, you can't forget to take in fluids or you'll become dehydrated and faint. And the last thing we need on top of this day is a swooning female."

Allegra looked at the glass in her hand. It was full of an orangy pink, opaque liquid that left a little froth around the rim. "What is it?" she asked, interest momentarily overcoming her exhaustion and her usual alarm at Oliver's brusque manner.

"Fruit punch. It's an island specialty made with mashed banana and grapefruit juice and anything else that's in season. I would guess that this brew has guava and paw paw juice, too. Drink up," he repeated. He watched until Allegra took a tentative sip, then obviously finding it refreshing, a large swallow. With a satisfied nod, he turned his attention to Jamie.

"You'd best be off," he said. "You don't want to be tracking down the road to Gouyave in the dark, and it lacks just a short while until sunset. It would be better, too, if the *Miss Lily* could clear the pier in daylight. You'll have the light of a half moon to guide you into the Carenage, which should be enough for Arthur Fergusson, but he won't be happy having to set sail before moonrise. Everyone else bound for St. George's has already gone down."

Jamie nodded, sending a lock of thin red hair sliding across his forehead and making him look suddenly weary, too. "I'm away," he said, then bent to pat Allegra's hand. "You've nothing to worry about, Miss Pembroke," he told her reassuringly. "I feel confident that you are your father's only heir, but first thing in the morning I'll cable the office of his London solicitors. He kept his will there, although from all he has told me, he meant for his entire estate to pass on to you."

Allegra looked up, stunned. "His heir?" she repeated, disbelieving. "I am to inherit L'Etoile?"

"Only half interest," Oliver corrected instantly. "The other half is still, very definitely, mine."

Shaking her head, Allegra refrained from saying aloud the thought that leaped most immediately into her mind, that the *whole* of L'Etoile seemed very definitely his. Although she had felt, from the moment she had first discovered her mother's diaries, that she had inherited her father's ungovernable spirit, it had never occurred to her that she might inherit his property, as well. Now that she was here, with the unaccustomed heat and the unnatural exhaustion pressing against her, the idea seemed even more preposterous. L'Etoile rightly belonged to Oliver. Or to Jamie, or even to Mrs. Potter. It belonged to all of Cecil's friends and admirers, people who, like him, had adapted to and thrived in the tropics with its dramatic weather, wild jungle, and bright sea.

She shook her head again. "It doesn't make sense," she said, more to herself than to the two men in front of her.

Oliver arched his eyebrows in surprise. "A great deal in this world doesn't make sense," he said, seeming to suggest her remark was among those things that didn't. "Nonetheless, that's the way it is. Come, Jamie, I'll walk you down the drive. Excuse us, Miss Pembroke."

"It doesn't make sense," Allegra repeated, hardly noticing they were gone. It had made sense that she should inherit her grandfather's house and school; no matter how uncomfortable she had been in them, they were part of her life. The neat, white clapboards enclosed all of her memories; they had housed her mother and her grandfather, the only family she had ever known. But it didn't make sense that she should inherit L'Etoile. Although she had come to Grenada searching for something different, something exciting and adventurous, she had also come searching for her father. Without him, the estate was simply foreign and strange.

Even the architecture was unlike any she had ever encountered. While she would have found it delightful if Cecil were there to inhabit it with her, all alone, she didn't know what to make of it. Painted faded pink and powder blue and trimmed with white curlicues, the two-story wooden structure seemed more like an overgrown birthday cake than a home. There wasn't a pane of glass anywhere to be found, only long, louvered shutters on the windows, and wide, two-panel shutters on the doors. There were arches and awnings and eight pointy peaks on the roof. There were polished plank floors, painted plank ceilings, and white-washed walls with lots of rose-colored moldings and trim.

Still suffering from shock and from mind-numbing exhaustion, Allegra didn't really see the house; she only absorbed impressions of its huge size and airy texture. But she observed enough to realize that it was a world away from the small, self-effacing home in which she had grown up. It was even a world away from what she had imagined L'Etoile to be: more on the order of an antebellum plantation in Georgia, replete with white columns on the portico and English antiques in the parlors. It was a world away from anything familiar, and at the moment, Allegra wasn't sure she had the fortitude to inherit an unfamiliar world.

With a deep sigh, she forced herself from her comfortable seat on the front veranda and entered the house, meaning to take more notice of the details. All she ended up doing, though, was wandering through the open gallery and immense dining room and out the double doors to the veranda on the back. It wasn't very wide, but it ran the length of the house and was encompassed by a railing made of white gingerbread balusters and a powder blue banister. It looked out on a yard that dropped so sharply, the tops of the tall trees were barely at eye level. Allegra sat sideways on the banister, her back against a supporting post, watching the sun sink through the feathery fronds and fat-fingered leaves of palm and paw paw trees toward the navy blue sea beyond.

When Oliver found her a few minutes later, he paused before announcing his presence, taken by the sight of her. With the fading sun catching on the curls springing out of her bun and illuminating her clear, soft skin, she made a lovely picture. Despite his crisp and logical manner, Oliver was not a cold man. On the contrary, he was greatly moved by genuine emotion, and he was moved now by the vulnerable expression making shadows around Allegra's remarkable eyes. He forgot his secondary assessment of her as he felt again his original attraction.

"You should have your portrait painted in that position," he said. "You look like part of the landscape."

Startled, her hand flying up to her throat, Allegra looked around quickly. "I didn't hear you come in," she said. Then, as his words sank in, her hand dropped and a pink tint crept across her cheeks. "I don't feel like part of the landscape," she said dolefully, leaning her head back against the post. "I feel the very opposite, as if I am completely out of place, as if I were one of Mrs. Potter's birds who took a wrong turn while migrating for the winter."

Oliver sat on the banister facing her. "You've had a difficult time of it," he said solicitously. "I'm sure that nothing is as you expected it to be, least of all the loss of your father. Undoubtedly, that colors all your reactions. Things would have seemed quite different if he were here as you planned. You're in shock; so if you're trying to find the sense of the situation, don't."

Perhaps it was the mellow light that the sun left behind as it slid into the ocean, or perhaps it was simply the welcome sympathy in Oliver's voice that touched a chord in Allegra. Whatever the cause, she felt the numbing fog she had been in all day lift, and found herself freely confessing her feelings.

"It's useless, my trying to find the sense of it all," she said, breaking a leaf off a small palm in a pot by the post and twisting it around her finger. "Because there is no sense to be found. I came to Grenada to meet my father." She threw the mangled leaf over the banister and looked earnestly at Oliver. "All my life I'd been told he was dead. Then, suddenly, I found out that he was alive, that he had a wonderful life, full of adventure and excitement. I had twenty-five years to catch up on. I wanted to talk to him, to ask him questions, to listen to his answers. I wanted to watch him. To be with him." She paused, then said more softly, "I wanted to have him be with me."

She looked away and pulled another leaf off the palm, wrapping this one around her finger, too. "But what did I get instead?" Her hand waved out over the yard, sweeping over the landscape of exotic trees and flamboyant flowers. "L'Etoile. I got his cocoa farm. What good is that to me?" She sounded not bitter, but woebegone. "What am I to do with it? I don't know the first thing about raising cocoa."

"I can't answer for the rest, but I can tell you about cocoa," Oliver said, a hint of a smile forming in the corners of his mouth. "The *first* thing about cocoa is that it is grown, not raised. And we generally refer to the land as an estate, not a farm, although there are some Englishmen who are fond of calling their holdings plantations or 'cocoa walks.' Beyond that, however, it really isn't necessary for you to know anything about it.

"The majority of estates in Grenada have absentee owners who are probably every bit as ignorant on the subject as you. Many of them have never so much as set foot on their land. They hire solicitors and the solicitors hire overseers and the overseers run the works. Every so often they send a report back to England, and any profits are automatically shifted to their bank accounts in London. So you see, owning a cocoa estate, particularly half interest in one where your partner is on the premises, is quite a painless activity."

His voice grew more serious as he continued, "I understand that losing your father before you ever got to know him is a terrible disappointment. But you needn't let the responsibility of your inheritance add to your distress. Jamie and I will look after your share equally with mine. There's no reason for you to extend your visit. You can go home as soon as you are ready."

Allegra shook her head sadly. "No, I can't," she said.

"Why not?" Oliver was puzzled. "I can assure you that your affairs will be in safe hands. Cecil felt no hesitation entrusting his interest in the estate to us."

"It isn't a question of trust," Allegra said hastily, anxious to correct a wrong impression. "I feel quite sure that you know *exactly* what you are doing. Always," she added ruefully. She looked down at her lap, again twisting the piece of palm in her fingers. "You see, I can't go home," she said, "because I have no home to go to."

"What?" Oliver's question was direct and demanding.

Allegra still didn't look at him as she repeated, "I have no home to go to." Forcing her fingers to stop fidgeting, she made herself say the words, "I sold it before I came. I meant to start a whole new life with my father."

A long, low whistle escaped Oliver's lips. "You don't do things by half measures, do you?" he asked, partly in amazement, partly in admiration. More wryly, he went on, "Forgive my pedestrian inquiry, but I would like to know where your mother and your grandfather were when you made this, um, shall we say, rather spontaneous decision."

"They're gone," she answered briefly, squirming where she sat like a schoolgirl caught reading romances behind her geography book. It was an all too familiar sensation, one she had felt over and over all her life as she had been made to explain her madcap actions. "Mother died three years ago, and Grandfather passed away in August." Her face fell lower still as she added, grudgingly, "You may say it was an impetuous decision. Grandfather would have called it that."

Oliver laughed. "I'm sure he would have," he said, remembering the stories Cecil had told about his father-in-law. "And at the risk of sounding hopelessly unspirited, I would have to admit I'd agree with him. What could possibly have motivated you?"

Unable to meet his gaze, Allegra hunched her shoulders. "It was a novel I read once," she answered. "By Miss Lorna Lockhart." Her voice was almost monotone as she explained. "It was about an orphaned girl who inherits the house of her nasty guardian. He had always treated her abominably, making her scrub the floors and sweep the ashes, so the house held only bad memories."

As she got more involved in the story, Allegra's voice grew stronger, and she lifted her eyes. "She couldn't bear to stay in the house any longer," she recounted, "so she sold it for more money than she had ever imagined and went off to live in Italy. It changed her whole life. Inspired by the wonderful art she saw all around her, she began to paint and eventually became a famous artist. And married a handsome man who turned out to be a very rich duke." Her voice faltered again when she saw the amusement on Oliver's face. "It was a good book," she finished lamely, looking down once more.

"Undoubtedly," Oliver agreed. "Although I might be reluctant to recommend it as a guide for one's life. Was there no one but Miss Lorna Lockhart to advise you? A relative? A friend of the family? A solicitor?"

For a moment Allegra said nothing, but Oliver waited patiently for an answer. Finally she admitted, "There was William Browne. My grandfather charged him to look after his estate, but in America he is called a lawyer, not a solicitor."

Oliver nodded, accepting the variation in terminology. "Whatever he is called, I can't imagine that any responsible legal counselor would support your decision," he said. "Didn't he caution you against selling your property right away?"

Shrugging again, Allegra said simply, "I didn't tell him until after it was sold."

"Didn't tell him?" Oliver repeated in astonishment. "If he had been doing his job, he shouldn't have needed to have you tell him, he should have known it himself. From what Cecil has said, this town of yours isn't all that large. Any conscientious solicitor, sorry, *lawyer*, would know everything that is going on. He'd hear every door open and every dog roll over. Either William Browne is blind, deaf, and dumb, or he is incompetent. He wasn't being attentive."

"Oh, he was *very* attentive," Allegra responded quickly, perhaps a bit too quickly. She lifted her head when she said it, but let it drop back when she saw the look Oliver was giving her. Hot color flooded her face again.

Eyes narrowing in speculation, Oliver folded his arms across his chest. "Tell me, Miss Pembroke," he said slowly. "How does it happen that a woman as attractive and refined as you has neither husband nor fiancé to help you with these matters?"

This time Allegra remained silent, the flush on her cheeks deepening, caused as much by his backhanded compliment as by her embarrassment at his utterly impertinent question. His lack of manners left her at a loss for words.

The same could not be said for Oliver. With more curiosity than courtesy, he probed further. "Surely you've had proposals," he said. "I've never been to Connecticut, but I can't believe that the men there are so wanting as not to perceive your charms." When Allegra didn't respond, but only sat perfectly still, her chin suddenly taking on a determined set, he pushed harder. "Well?" he asked.

"They are not wanting," Allegra snapped, her head jerking up defiantly. "They are dull!"

The grin that had been hovering around the edges of his mouth burst across Oliver's face. "Ahh," he said. "That is a definite problem. What about the lawyer? William Browne. Is he dull, too?"

"Yes," Allegra started to say, then instantly corrected herself and said, "No. No, he isn't. He is a very nice man. Really he is. He has a degree from Yale. He's reliable. And well-respected." It was almost as if she were reciting by rote.

"Sterling qualities," Oliver murmured.

"They are," Allegra said feebly. Her shoulders sagged. She sounded defeated, her momentary defiance gone.

"If he is such a paragon, why didn't you marry him? Why did you run twenty-five hundred miles to escape him?"

Allegra sat bolt upright, her mouth popping open in shock. "Really, Mr. MacKenzie!" she gasped.

"Really, what, Miss Pembroke?" Oliver knew that he was overstepping even his own relaxed rules of conduct, but some unnamed emotion made him pursue the issue. "If the life he offered you was so estimable, why didn't you accept: Why are you in Grenada with three steamer trunks, which, I now realize, must hold much more than some unsuitable frocks?"

Allegra stared hard at him for a minute, but when his dark blue eyes didn't waver, she abruptly turned away and watched as the sky had become orange and pink where the sun had been. "Because," she finally blurted out.

Because despite being intelligent and hardworking, William was also unexciting. Because despite his deep devotion to her, he lacked romance and passion. Because despite his unimpeachable credentials as a pillar of the community, his life was completely predictable. Because there was something about his conservative, safe approach to all situations that made Allegra automatically and unreasonably want to do just the opposite of what he suggested.

She had been almost engaged to him, after years of rejecting his suit. And the suits of other equally respectable, equally uninspiring young men. She had been almost ready to give in, not out of love, but out of resignation, worn down by her grandfather's lectures to make a sensible, secure future for herself, and by his rather transparent tactic of making William the administrator of his modest estate.

She had almost convinced herself that a marriage to him would make her comfortable and content, if not wildly happy. In addition to his law practice, he ran his family's business, a large, well-established apple orchard and cider mill. He was polite and considerate, and dealt efficiently with the piles of paper work Allegra found unintelligible.

She was almost ready to accept his proposal when her aimless search through her mother's bureau had unearthed the old diaries. Now, no matter what else happened, it was impossible for her to contemplate marriage to William. She didn't know where else she could go, but she could never go back to him.

Brief though it was, Oliver seemed satisfied with her answer. Intuitively, he had guessed what she hadn't said. For a few minutes he was quiet, reflecting that the impetuous spirit she shared with Cecil was considered by society to be eccentric in an English gentleman, but was condemned, by that same society, as unacceptable behavior in his daughter. Not for the first time he marveled at the hypocrisy of people.

"It's been a very long day," he said, rising from the railing. "I feel thoroughly played out, so I can imagine that you must be on the brink of collapse. I suggest we seek relief in sleep, a good, sound, early night's sleep. Everything will be easier to cope with tomorrow. You should postpone any decisions until after you've rested." He paused, then added, the humor back in his voice, "Even then, you might be advised to think things through at least three times, just to make sure you've come to the proper conclusion."

As he spoke, Allegra also rose from the banister and took a step forward, an easy fluid motion. Then his penultimate word hit the recesses of her mind and struck lifelong reflexes. Proper. It turned her limbs stiff and her movements awkward, as always happened when her education and her instincts collided. Proper. Her mother and grandfather had drummed it into her conscience as time and again they used the word to describe desirable behavior. And, more often than not, to chide Allegra for actions that failed to meet that impeccable standard. Proper. She froze where she was, automatically checking herself for error, searching for her breach of etiquette.

Suddenly conscious of the silent house, completely empty except for herself and the extremely attractive man in front of her, she stammered. "Oh, no. This is most unthinkable. I'm unchaperoned; I can't possibly spend the night here with you. It will ruin my reputation. It isn't proper."

As if in physical horror of the prospect, she turned quickly to flee. Just as she pivoted, a speckled chicken passed through the house on its belated way to roost. At exactly the wrong instant, Allegra's ungainly flight crossed the hen's hurried path. The bird let out a loud squawk, and Allegra went flying, her arms flailing for balance.

She felt Oliver's arm around her waist, catching her almost in midair and easily setting her back on her feet. And then the arm remained. It held her so near to him, she could feel him breathing, could smell the scent of salt air and spices that seemed to cling to him. Her own breathing was suddenly irregular, keeping erratic pace with her pounding heart. Although she was vitally aware of his strength, it was not the sure circle of his arm that kept her close. An unknown force rushed through her legs, weakening them, making her powerless to move.

Almost as if in a dream, she could see Oliver's free hand come up, could feel it cradling her chin, gently lifting her face toward his. She could see his eyes, with their improbable fringe of lashes, and she could see his mouth, wit lurking in its corners. Then her own eyes fluttered closed and her lips were covered by a long, luxurious, sensuous kiss.

For several seconds nothing else existed. There was only the touch of his lips pressed against hers and the warm feel of his fingers on her skin. A sensation of deep, unbounded pleasure spread through her body, a sensation that intensified as he pulled her, slowly, closer to him. For several seconds she was profoundly, passionately, unaware of anything else.

Then an image scurried across the edge of her mind, an image of a leather-bound book with raised gilt letters along the spine that read, "Decorum." Right after the image of her fifteenth birthday gift came that of her grandfather's disapproving visage. Faster and faster flashed the tight-lipped, sober-eyed faces of citizens of her town, of William Browne and Reverend Dodge, of Mrs. Bartlett, the first Selectman's wife, and Mr. Humphrey, who had the dry goods store, and even Asa Gibbons, the emaciated man who swept their chimney.

With a gasp, Allegra twisted sharply out of Oliver's arms.

"How dare you?" she demanded, her voice made husky by interrupted desire. "How dare you take such liberties? You've forced your attentions on me in the most common manner, in utter violation of good breeding and good taste." The more she talked, the more she worked herself into a state of moral outrage, repeating all the prim phrases she had ever been taught.

"Really, Mr. MacKenzie, your conduct has been exceedingly unprincipled. Not at all what I would expect of a gentleman. It simply is not done. First you interrogated me in a most unseemly mode, completely indifferent to my sensibilities, and then, and then . . ." Her voice broke as she remembered what came next.

"And then what, Miss Pembroke?" Oliver asked, disgusted. He had been merely amused when Allegra had expressed alarm at being alone with him in the huge house. Considering their preceding conversation, he hadn't taken her seriously. Now he concluded, as he had yesterday in Jamie's office, that the occasional glimpses of Cecil's delightful spirit were like so much smoke, vanishing in the air. Today's disappointment at that discovery, however, went quite a bit deeper than yesterday's. "You were saying, Miss Pembroke? 'And then . . .'"

"And then you," she gulped, her cheeks very pink, "and then you took advantage of me," she finished, desperately rallying her self-righteous air.

"Wrong, Miss Pembroke," Oliver replied crisply. "I did not take advantage of you. I kissed you. I may have taken advantage of the situation to do so, but at no time did I take advantage of you. Moreover, I did not force my attentions, or anything else, on you. I kissed you and you seemed willing to accept it. If you now decide it was unwelcome, kindly tell me so. Do not plague me with boring little sermons about my breeding and my taste. I had enough of that type of starched behavior during my years in England to last me a lifetime. I certainly don't need to be badgered by it in my own home."

Such directness was more than Allegra could take in her present state of emotional chaos and physical exhaustion. It required too much effort to separate long hidden feelings from long taught facts. Near to tears, she choked, "You are being extremely unkind, Mr. MacKenzie. All I ask is that you supply me with safe shelter. It seems a slight request."

"All you ask, Miss Pembroke," he corrected, "is that I vacate my home—a house with seven enormous, widely spaced bedrooms—to accommodate some ridiculous notion you have of respectability." He paused to glare at her and to hear whatever stodgy reply she had. When he saw, however, that she was close to hysteria, he capitulated.

In part, he gave in because if he didn't, she would probably do something impulsive. But he also gave in because he was not at all, as she accused, indifferent or unkind. Although he would have liked to deflate her puffed-up attitude, he couldn't ignore her genuine distress. Still annoyed, he stomped off to sleep in one of the sheds, leaving her good reputation unsullied. As he went, he wished the reliable, respected, Yale-educated William Browne were here to take this woman off his hands. Despite her protests to the contrary, he decided that she would make Mr. Browne the perfect wife.

Allegra stumbled up the stairs to her room feeling oddly unvictorious, rather defeated and alone. Through the open louvers of her windows came the unfamiliar scents and sounds of the tropical night. Crickets, many decibels louder than those in Connecticut, split the silence of the great house. Despite the heat still trapped against her skin, a shiver went down her spine as she fell into bed.

Chapter
Three

It was late morning when Allegra woke, her exhaustion having ultimately overcome her uneasiness with the night noises. So solidly had she finally slept that when she opened her eyes, her mind was momentarily blank. She wondered where she was and why the heavy maple footboard of the bed she had slept in all her life had sprouted gracefully spun mahogany posters, a gauzy white canopy, and sheer, fluttery curtains. She became aware of the heat beneath her long-sleeved nightgown and of the bright slats of sun shining through the louvered windows. Recent events came back in a rush.

Kicking off the sheet and hiking up her nightgown, she propped herself against the pillows to think. She found her situation a little less frightening this morning, a result, no doubt, of her long, deep rest, but the same set of problems remained to be solved. Plus a new one: Oliver MacKenzie.

Even as she told herself that her father's partner was an ill-mannered boor, an insensitive oaf, a flush that had nothing to do with the Caribbean sunshine spread over her body. She unconsciously lowered her gown as she remembered the indescribable thrill she had felt at his touch. Despite a half-hearted attempt to turn her thoughts away, the memory of his lips on hers brought back the same exciting sensation.

She had never felt that way before, never felt the force of her emotions melt her limbs. It wasn't that she hadn't been kissed before; on four separate occasions hopeful suitors had expressed their ardor. Each time, the hastily applied peck had left her unmoved. She had tried to summon more enthusiasm for William Browne's attentions, thinking that her lack of feeling was some flaw in her nature. But when his kiss had come, squashing her nose and pinching her lips, it, too, had left her cold. There was no comparison between the clumsy caresses of her Connecticut swains and the heart-stirring, blood-racing embrace of Oliver MacKenzie.

As if seeking an escape from the disturbing memory, Allegra twisted back and forth against her pillows. When the image would not meekly recede, she shoved aside the mosquito net and jumped out of bed, trying to purge it with movement. She pulled open the shutters, letting in such a burst of light it made her blink. Pleased with this distraction, she yanked open the double doors that led out onto yet another veranda. The breeze that wafted in was welcome. Too embarrassed to step outside in her nightclothes, she stood on tiptoes, peering beyond the railing at the front yard.

Brilliant pink and purple and orange bougainvillea twined over an arched iron entry gate, the hundreds of papery blossoms nearly obliterating the maze of delicately wrought stars. A wide brick wall, bordered by arrangements of potted plants and huge pink shells, came up to and continued around the L-shaped house. Out on the lawn, tethered to a comfortable bench in the shade of a lime tree full of round, yellow fruit, a white goat neatly nibbled the grass. Behind it, an ixora bush stood, its pompons of tiny red flowers yielding nectar to a thumb-sized hummingbird. Set beneath a relentlessly blue, completely cloudless sky, the riotously colorful, somewhat whimsical scene made Allegra smile. She was beginning to like it here, after all.

Turning back into the room, she felt much better. With every moment that passed, with every new sight or sound or scent that stimulated senses refreshed by sleep, she was quickly concluding that she was going to stay at L'Etoile. "If my father thought enough of me to leave me his estate, the least I can do is accept it," she reasoned as she splashed herself with water in the adjoining bathroom. The excess landed on the tiled floor, draining away down the center.

It was plain Cecil had built the house with pride, blending tropical beauty and English comfort and his own unique taste. Drying her face, Allegra admired the details: the palm frond fretwork in the half-moon panel over the inside door, the artless cluster of ribbons holding back the mosquito curtain, the simple pine armoire painted pink with green faux vines. Bright and beautiful and smelling of fruit and flowers, the room was an extension of the view beyond the veranda. Tears welled up in her eyes as Allegra realized that L'Etoile itself was the most significant clue to her father's character. He captured the essence of the island, she thought. He captured the color and light and movement, and recreated it indoors. He knew how to *really* see.

With that thought, a mental picture of Cecil emerged, one that had been gaining clarity and magnificence ever since she'd discovered his existence. Using equal parts of what she had heard, read, or seen, and what she wanted to be true, Allegra assembled an image of her father. "He was very handsome," she decided, her memory of the pale man lying tragically in the road reinforced by the descriptions in her mother's diary. "As well as utterly charming and well-bred," she continued, relying on the reports of Mrs. Smythe and Mrs. Potter and a host of his friends.

"He was curious and intelligent and his sense of adventure was unrivaled." His own letters had told her that and were corroborated by Jamie's tales and Colonel Woodbury's remarks. "And he was honorable, loyal, and courageous," she threw in because those traits seemed to go hand in hand with the others. "But most of all," she thought, as she dabbed away her tears and hung the towel back on its rack, "he was a man with an extraordinary imagination, and the ability to make it come alive."

While she rummaged through her trunk to find fresh clothes, the decision that had taken root in her mind rapidly grew. I'm going to stay here, she silently vowed.

She had come to Grenada to find her father and, through him, to find a purpose for her life. Maybe you're gone, she thought, tears threatening once again, but your spirit lives on in the estate that you built. She scrubbed away the tears with balled fists and squared her shoulders. "I'm going to carry on with my plan," she declared. "I came here to get to know you, and get to know you I will. If I can't do it in person, I'll do it through L'Etoile."

Her chin set, she nodded at the clothes suspended in her trunk. The only uncertainty that now remained was how to address the image of her father shining pure and perfect in her mind. Absolutely everyone seemed to refer to him as Cecil. "That would be disrespectful," she decided. "I shall call you Papa."

Extremely pleased, she turned her attention to dressing. She put on a clean camisole, stepped into a pair of pantaloons, and reluctantly laced herself into her corset. She slipped a petticoat over her head, adjusting the puff that flared out over her rear, and rolled on white cotton stockings that fastened above her knees with garters. She pulled on a mutton-sleeved shirtwaist of tucked batiste, expertly fastening it from the top of its high collar all the way down her back. She hooked a pale blue linen skirt around her narrowed waist and settled its matching jacket across her shoulders. With each succeeding layer, she grew progressively hotter. After a moment's debate, she took off the jacket and stuck it back in her trunk.

As Allegra sat down on the edge of the bed to button her shoes, Oliver MacKenzie intruded in her thoughts for the second time that morning. While pledging herself to L'Etoile, she had momentarily forgotten his presence. With a start that made the button hook tear a tiny hole in her stocking, she realized that she had not only inherited her father's estate, but she had also inherited his partner. The very idea gave her goose bumps.

"I shall have to be firm with him," she informed the room at large in an unsteady voice. "I shall have to make him understand that his presumptions are unacceptable." Her voice gained resolution as she found refuge in the lessons of her youth. With what she imagined to be a dignified nod in the general direction of the white wicker night table, she said, much more determinedly, "I shall tell him that I am a well-bred person. Yes. That's it. I shall tell him that I am decent and refined; that I am unused to being treated coarsely. I shall protect myself from him with a shield of gentility."

Proud of herself for having solved her predicament, Allegra managed to ignore that such decorum was a state she had always found difficult to achieve and impossible to sustain. For the moment, however, she was pleased with herself. Standing, she tossed the button hook aside, then crossed the room. Her hand was on the doorknob when another thought struck her.

"Oh, no," she moaned, letting her hand drop in despair. "He owns half the house, too. I can't expect him to sleep outside indefinitely." Her moan deepened almost to a wail as she added, "But I can't let him sleep inside, either. It isn't proper."

Recrossing the room and reseating herself on the edge of the bed, her mind reached frantically for an answer. For an instant she considered setting up a schedule so that each alternately could have the run of the house, but discarded the idea immediately. She had no intention of spending her "off" night in a shed or a stall. Another plan, for dividing the house in two, also met with rapid rejection. That would leave one of them with a dining room but no parlor, while the other would be left with exactly the reverse. Besides, it would spoil the design her father had created.

Several more equally untenable solutions had been eliminated when inspiration struck. It was so simple. If her reputation were in peril because she was living at L'Etoile unchaperoned, then she didn't need to change L'Etoile, she needed to find a chaperon. It happened all the time in the novels that she read; usually, a plain-faced, impoverished second cousin was selected. Lacking a relative, mousy or otherwise, Allegra decided she would hire a companion, an eminently proper, preferably elderly, female companion.

Wholly satisfied with this scheme, she sailed out the door, untroubled by several obvious questions. First, where would she find such an exemplary person? More importantly, having found her, hired her, and installed her at L'Etoile, would she be able to stand her? At the moment Allegra could not be bothered by details. Besides, having missed most or all of the last four meals, what concerned her now was breakfast.

Her plan for a sweeping entrance into the dining room fizzled when she found it empty, its long mahogany table bare of any place settings. Puzzled, she searched for a breakfast nook, and, failing that, for the kitchen. Nothing fitting either description seemed to exist. Walking through three elegantly arched doorways, she found the parlor, and off at one end, an airy looking library. At the other end, she saw what was obviously the office. The room next to it was furnished with a billiard table, a grand piano, and a glass case containing brightly colored stuffed birds.

Upstairs were seven big bedrooms, one of them obviously Oliver's. Allegra stood in its doorway, looking furtively around. Her eyes skimmed over the bureau with its predictable lack of grooming aids, past the wardrobe, a mirror, and a bentwood chair, but when she saw a pair of trousers sprawled across the bed, a wave of embarrassment flushed her face. She backed out hurriedly and went downstairs.

She was standing halfway between the dining room and the gallery, wondering how her father could have forgotten to include a kitchen in his Caribbean great house, when a voice from the corner said, "Well, good morning. I was beginning to think you going to sleep clear through next week."

Allegra looked into the dining room and saw a black woman kneeling by the cabinet putting away the glasses and plates that had been used yesterday. When the woman rose, Allegra could see that she was very tall and very handsome, with velvety dark skin stretched over high cheekbones. "Good morning," she responded, shifting uncertainly from one foot to the other.

The woman smiled, a warm, easy smile that enhanced her expression of serene hospitality. "Yes, it do you good, though," she said, moving forward. She walked deliberately, the hem of her simple cotton dress swishing gracefully around sandal-shod feet. "Well, I mean to say, you looked very faded yesterday, like an old dress that is scrubbed on the rocks in the stream and left for so in the sun." Stopping a few feet in front of Allegra and examining her carefully, she concluded, "Today you woke up like a brand new frock, just bought at the store."

"I *do* feel much better, thank you," Allegra said tentatively. She wasn't exactly sure what this woman was saying, but she liked the way it sounded. Her voice was slow and husky and her words came out in lilting cadence. "I'm a little bit hungry, however," she added, wondering if this were the person she ought to ask about the mystery of the missing kitchen.

Apparently it was. "Come," the woman said, turning toward the door at the far side of the dining room. "We'll find you some provisions. Yesterday you eat only as much as a butterfly. No wonder your tummy talking to your tongue."

She led the way out the door, across a porch, down a short flight of stairs, and out onto the lawn. Stepping quickly to keep up with the woman's long-legged stride, Allegra asked, "Were you here yesterday? There were so many people and I was so tired. I'm sorry, I don't remember seeing you . . ." Her voice broke off in embarrassment.

The woman waved a forgiving hand. "I was here," she said. "I always here. I'm Elizabeth Stephen; I cook the meals for your daddy and Oliver, and I tell the girls where to clean."

"Oh," Allegra said, a little nonplussed by this display of informality. She covered her surprise by saying, "I wanted to ask you, where is the kitchen?"

"Right here," Elizabeth answered, entering a small cement building painted pale pink and white.

Allegra stepped in and stopped short. "Oh," she said again. "Oh, my." This was nothing like the utilitarian kitchen she had left behind in Connecticut, whose mammoth cast-iron stove the simpleminded Lucy Johnson had blacked twice a month. Like everything else at L'Etoile, this room was spacious, airy, and enchanting.

Elizabeth saw Allegra's expression of amazement and explained, "Your daddy, he liked the fete. Always music and dancing, sometimes for two or three days. And food. Well, I mean to say, Cecil would feed the world if I could cook so much. He want everyone to eat my food. He always tell me, 'Elizabeth, your cooking not only fill the stomach, it nourish the soul.'

"That the way Cecil was. He always want just the best that can be got. And he make everyone else want it, too." She shook her head, a fond smile on her face.

"Oliver, now," she continued, no less affectionately, "he just as happy to have his plate in here. He like to sit right by that window so he can watch the sea."

Allegra avoided the stool Elizabeth pointed to, perching instead on the one standing opposite. She could well imagine her charming, gay father hosting celebrated parties, while Oliver, blunt and boorish, lurked in the kitchen. Although, she grudgingly admitted, it was a lovely and colorful kitchen to lurk in. She liked it very much herself. And she was beginning to like Elizabeth, too. She liked her strong, calm features and her delightful way of phrasing things.

"That's it!" she exclaimed. "*You* can be my companion. It's the ideal solution. You are already at L'Etoile, and I am sure you are very respectable."

Startled, Elizabeth looked up from the fruit she was deftly cutting. "Pardon?" she asked politely.

"My companion," Allegra repeated. "I must have a companion. You see, it is quite unacceptable for me to share the house with Mr. MacKenzie if I am unchaperoned. People will talk, and my reputation will be ruined. Even though we own the estate equally, we simply cannot live in the house together. And I suspect Mr. MacKenzie will not be content to sleep in the shed very much longer."

Elizabeth gave a low, rolling giggle. "Mmm," she agreed, "I suspect the same thing, me, too." She handed Allegra a plate of beautifully arranged fruit, orange and yellow and pink and white slices.

Distracted, Allegra studied the plate raptly, then looked up at Elizabeth. "Pineapple, grapefruit, paw paw," Elizabeth enumerated, touching each one with the tip of her knife. "And this pretty little one, she is called cashew apple."

Allegra popped the radish-colored fruit in her mouth. It was crunchy and clean. She contrasted it with a bite of paw paw, melon-colored and melon-textured, but tasting much meatier and richer than any cantaloupe she had ever eaten. Elizabeth drizzled it with a few drops of juice from an odd little yellow lime. It was delicious. "Why, I'll bet that lime came from the tree outside my window," Allegra said, enchanted by the thought. It seemed incredible to have an exotic fruit growing in the front yard.

Elizabeth giggled again. "It all come from outside your window," she said, indicating the greater outdoors with a sweep of her knife. She then sliced a piece of a banana bread and placed the slice on a plate beside an array of coconut muffins and currant-studded scones. "Oliver, he got to have his scones," Elizabeth said as she set the plate on the table next to Allegra. "He give me his mother's recipe and say, 'Elizabeth, I born in Grenada and I proud of it, but I got Scotland in my blood. If you don't want me to dry up and die, you got to feed me scones.'"

"Mr. MacKenzie was born in Grenada?" Allegra asked, surprised by this fact but trying not to seem unduly interested. Without taking her eyes off Elizabeth, she broke off a chunk of banana bread and stuffed it in her mouth. It was moist and sweet and spiced with cinnamon.

Elizabeth flicked at a fly with her knife. "Oliver born in Carriacou thirty-two years ago. Same as me," she said.

"Carriacou?" Allegra asked around a corner of coconut muffin. She was avoiding the scones as she had Oliver's favorite stool, determined to keep her distance even as she found herself hopelessly fascinated by him.

"Carriacou is a little island, just up there," Elizabeth pointed out the north window with her knife, using it as a conductor would use a baton. "She is one of the islands they call the Grenadines, but she is a parish of Grenada. Oliver's daddy, Angus, he come to Carriacou from Scotland to build boats. He say the weather and the politics much sweeter here. A little while later Oliver's mother come along to marry him. And a little more while later," she added with a grin, "Oliver come, too.

"He live just nearby to me at Windward, so close I could hear his mother singing to him at night. What pretty songs." Elizabeth sighed, remembering. "She sound like the breeze in the immortelle tree. Shoooo, shooo, shooo, and the flowers come dancing down."

"I thought he lived in England," Allegra said, digging for information with more curiosity than discretion. She took a bit of the pineapple. It tasted tart after the sweet cakes. "He seemed so disdainful of England, I thought for sure he had lived there."

Elizabeth nodded, settling herself on the corner of the table. "When Oliver was ten years old, his mother die. I think she go off to sing in the Lord's choir. After that, his daddy send him to England. Oliver, he don't want to go. He was happy playing on the beach and in the boatyard, jumping into the sea. Well, I mean to say," Elizabeth said with a shake of her head. "You could hear the hollering clear to L'Esterre.

"Finally Angus, he say, 'Hear me now. It like this: If life is a bakery, England makes the cake and her little colony Grenada sweep up the crumbs. You can stay here and have crumbs, or you can go there and get the recipe for cake.'"

"So Oliver—I mean, Mr. MacKenzie—went to school in England?" Allegra probed, eyeing the scones. She couldn't resist taking a taste. The buttery flavor and crumbly texture seemed cozily familiar among the more exotic treats. "How long did he stay?"

"Well, now," Elizabeth speculated, delicately scratching her chin with the tip of her knife. "He come home for good the year my third son born. Harold is eleven years old, just now. Oliver, he come home after all that university and build boats with Angus."

Allegra did the arithmetic. Oliver had been in England for eleven years and home for as many. Her mind seized another subject. "You have three sons?" she asked, amazed.

"Four," Elizabeth answered proudly.

"Oh, dear." Allegra sighed. "I suppose that means you won't be my companion, after all. I didn't realize you had a family. I thought that you lived here on the estate alone. I didn't see any signs of children when I went through the house."

Elizabeth laughed. "Well, I mean to say, the great house, it big as a cricket field, so I don't know what it is make you worry.

You two shake around in there like seeds in a calabash. Besides, I don't have time to be a companion." Hesitating, she scratched her chin again. "I don't think I know how, either. I cook the meals and bring them to the table and tell the two girls how to sweep and wash the clothes. But then, I am finished." She cut the air decisively with the knife. "Then I go down the hill to my own house and to Septimus, my husband. He is the overseer when Oliver is away."

Allegra washed down the last bite of scone with the last section of grapefruit. "It isn't hard to be a companion," she explained earnestly. "All you really need to do is protect my reputation with your presence. And we make calls together and do bits of embroidery and shop for ribbons and lace." She hesitated, too. "At least, I think so. I've never actually had a companion before," she admitted. "But that's what they've done in all the novels I've ever read."

"Well, I don't know," Elizabeth said slowly, mystified.

"No, no," Allegra agreed. "You have your family. I need a widow or a spinster."

"Well, I don't know," Elizabeth repeated.

Allegra, however, thought that she did. Feeling tremendously refreshed by both the food and the company, she was ready to tackle her opponent head on. With what she thought was ultimate practicality, she decided to go find Oliver and apprise him of her plan. She was sure he would appreciate hearing about a resolution of their problem as soon as possible. Besides, it would give her a chance to explore a little bit, a prospect that appealed to her rejuvenated sense of adventure.

"Do you have any idea where I might find Mr. MacKenzie?" she asked Elizabeth as she stacked her dishes in the sink and looked around for the soap and the rag.

"Don't you wash them," Elizabeth admonished from her seat on the table. "That's for Ivy and Jane when they come up from Gouyave. I didn't want them clankin' and blammin' around the house this morning with you asleep, so I send them down for fresh fish." When Allegra willingly ceded the chore to the missing maids, Elizabeth continued, "Oliver? He's in the groves with everyone else. The harvest has started."

"The groves?" Allegra questioned. "What groves? What harvest?"

"The cocoa groves, that's what," Elizabeth patiently explained. "They harvesting the cocoa. That's what pay the bills."

Half an hour later, Allegra set off down the drive, garbed in summertime walking attire. Elizabeth had eyed the white gloves, beribboned bonnet, and lacy parasol somewhat dubiously, but had dutifully given direction to the harvest site. When she had warned that the groves were more than a mile away, Allegra had airily dismissed the distance. "In Connecticut I routinely walk three or four miles." Elizabeth had given a fatalistic shrug.

The great house was built on top of the highest hill on the estate, and the long, winding drive down was lined with imperial palms. Allegra sauntered leisurely, enjoying the majestic view. At the bottom of the hill, she stopped uncertainly. The road to the right, which Elizabeth had told her to follow, was nothing more than a wide path through the forest. To the left were the stables and sheds, all seemingly deserted, and the road that wandered down to Gouyave. With a fatalistic shrug of her own, Allegra adjusted her parasol and turned to the right.

It didn't take her more than a few minutes of walking to remember the peculiar characteristic of Grenadian miles of which Jamie had spoken: They were extremely long, being more vertical than horizontal. Away from the grounds surrounding the house, carefully tended by man and goat, lush vegetation took over, practically shooting out of the earth on all sides of her. It inhibited her every stride and seemed to stifle the air, blanketing the cooling trade winds that always blew on top of the hills.

On either side of her were strange, squatty trees bearing absurd looking pods, either leaf-green or maroon or yellow or red. The pods looked like small pumpkins that someone had stretched on each end until they were ovoid; they grew straight out from the trunks and hung off the branches, comical pendants in an overgrown fairy tale forest. Although Allegra was initially intrigued by their oddity, her interest was soon overpowered as branches began to tear at her pretty parasol.

Doggedly, she pressed on. As she brushed past a burst of hibiscus, the long stamen left a yellow streak on the puffed sleeve of her blouse. The blue linen hem of her skirt turned red from dragging in the dirt as she dipped and twisted along the path. Her honey-blond hair, neatly coiffed beneath her bonnet when she left the house, began popping out in haphazard curls. Her face, already flushed and damp from the heat, got even redder when she furiously slapped an annoying mosquito. To make matters worse, she took a wrong turn in the tangle of trees and would have become hopelessly lost if a small boy on a burro hadn't appeared out of nowhere and set her straight. As it was, she had to backtrack up a steep slope.

By the time Allegra arrived at the harvest site, she was completely frazzled. Oliver saw her coming and suppressed a smile. A less than luxurious night's sleep in the cocoa shed had intensified his disgust with her attitude, but the sorry sight of her softened his feelings. Her disheveled appearance was at odds with the image of delicacy she had tried to cultivate last night. Once again, despite his determination to resist her, he found himself attracted to and amused by her spirit, by the look of triumph over adversity that lit up her appealing face.

Remembering the discord of the previous evening, however, he didn't yield to this attraction. He kept his tone deliberately neutral, devoid of surprise at seeing her here, a long, hot mile from home. "Good morning, Miss Pembroke," he said civilly. "Lovely day for a walk. It seems the heat wave is still with us, though, doesn't it?"

Disappointed by Oliver's failure to compliment her, or at least comment on her fortitude, her reply was as short as her breath. "Apparently," she snapped. Her irritation at his indifference was aggravated by her envy of his cool clothing. He could afford to be nonchalant about the temperature, dressed as he was the first day she had met him in a loose cotton shirt, trousers, and his star-studded braces. Both his attitude and his attire reaffirmed the conclusion she had come to: He was an unrefined oaf.

Allegra straightened her shoulders, artfully angled her tattered parasol, and smoothed a wrinkle from her creased and stained skirt. So intent was she that she didn't notice the suspicious twitch at the corners of Oliver's mouth. "I must tell you my plan," she began finally, meaning to outline her idea for hiring a companion, but her voice trailed off when she found herself addressing his back.

"We'll take that tree down, Septimus," Oliver said to the tall, lanky black man who had come up to him. "It's got a bad case of beetles and it isn't worth keeping it until the end of the season. The gain from its yield is far outweighed by the infection it can spread to the other trees."

Septimus nodded gravely. "Finbar and Johnny can chop it down and cart it to the pit," he said, nodding toward the next hill over. "It make fine charcoal." He turned and beckoned to two young men leaning against one of the strange, squatty trees.

"You were saying, Miss Pembroke?" Oliver asked politely. Before she could gather herself again, however, he was striding down the trail between the trees, calling to a skinny boy aiming a machete at one of the elongated pumpkins. "Not that one, Frank. It's not ripe enough yet. Give it another week or so, and that purple color will become more red."

When Oliver showed no sign of returning to where she stood but instead positioned himself with arms across his chest to watch Frank select another fruit, Allegra moved toward him. "Yes, Mr. MacKenzie," she said as she drew near. "I think that, given our particular circumstances . . ."

"Here, Clarice, you've missed some," Oliver interrupted, again moving forward. He scooped one yellow and two red pods out of the grass and tossed them into the basket a sturdy black woman was balancing on her head. She gave him a grin and started off down the trail, one hand on her hip, the other lightly steadying her burden.

Oliver started after her, pausing to inspect the work of a wiry, white-haired man wielding a long bamboo pole with a mitten-shaped blade tied to the top. Expertly, the man searched among the big leaves until he found a fruit ripened to the right shade, then sliced its stubby stem with either an upward thrust of the mitten's fingertips or a downward yank of its crooked thumb. The ground around him was littered with pods. "Good job, Jonah," Oliver murmured.

Allegra caught up with him just as he was moving on. "It is imperative that we resolve this problem, Mr. MacKenzie," she said, breathing hard and jerking her parasol free of an entangling branch. "And I think I have just the notion . . . ohhh!" Her foot twisted on an uneven patch of ground, and one knee buckled, throwing her off-balance. Oliver's hand shot out and grabbed her upper arm, crushing the voluminous puff of sleeve but keeping her from falling.

"Steady, Miss Pembroke," he said calmly.

"Uh, yes, thank you, Mr. MacKenzie," Allegra answered. Unlike last night, the contact was impersonal, and as soon as she was upright again, he released her. He seemed to be paying her so little heed, Allegra vaguely wondered how he could have been aware of her precarious footing. "I really think you will find my idea completely reasonable," she said hurriedly, hoping to hold his attention. But he was already off. Annoyed, Allegra stumbled after him.

"Really, Mr. MacKenzie, I *must* have a word with you," she demanded.

Oliver halted so abruptly she nearly collided with him. "By all means, Miss Pembroke," he said, turning to face her.

Disconcerted by his sudden shift of attention to her, Allegra groped for her thoughts. "I was starting to say," she began, then stopped. They were no longer ducking under branches on a narrow trail, but were standing in a small clearing. Behind Oliver, Clarice was emptying her basket onto an enormous pile of the red and yellow pumpkins, around which sat twenty or more men and women.

As Allegra watched, fascinated by this gathering in the woods, the men proceeded to grab pods from the pile and whack them open with practiced blows of wicked-looking machetes, exposing pulpy white flesh and neat rows of large, faintly pink seeds. Tossed down on a blanket of banana leaves, these pieces of pod were next attacked by the women, who, armed with wooden spoons, deftly detached the seeds and slid them into woven vine baskets. The ravaged pods were then discarded.

"You were starting to say," Oliver prompted, refusing to let the amusement he was feeling show on his face.

"Uh, yes," Allegra muttered, reluctantly looking away from the intriguing scene and refocusing on Oliver. "I was starting to tell you my idea." Her eyes wandered back to the workers and her attention followed. "What are they doing?" she burst out, her companion completely forgotten. "Why are they chopping up those pumpkins? Elizabeth told me you were harvesting cocoa."

The time Oliver let his laugh out. "She was quite correct, as usual. We *are* harvesting cocoa."

Allegra gave him a quick, incredulous glance before refastening her gaze on the graceful ballet of swinging, sweeping, slashing, stretching arms. "That can't be cocoa," she said reproachfully, sure he was playing a crude joke on her. "It isn't the right color, and it surely isn't the right consistency. It must be one of those tropical fruits Elizabeth gave me for breakfast. So please stop teasing me, Mr. MacKenzie, and tell me why you aren't harvesting the cocoa."

Oliver laughed again and folded his arms over his chest. "I

wouldn't dare to tease you, Miss Pembroke," he said dryly. "I promise you, this *is* the cocoa harvest. Those are neither breakfast fruits nor pumpkins; they are cocoa pods, and the seeds being scraped out of them and saved are the cocoa beans."

When Allegra only gave him another suspicious glance, Oliver asked, "Did you think the cocoa harvest would be like the wheat harvest in your Midwest? That a giant combine would scythe through cocoa grasses, spewing streams of chocolaty powder into pretty tins?"

"Well," Allegra answered, hesitating. Though perhaps a trifle exaggerated, that was closer to what she'd had in mind. She certainly hadn't imagined an airless jungle whose haphazard collection of comical trees bore no resemblance to the orderly rows in William's apple orchards. "I think you are fooling with me," she decided, and stepped around him before he could reply. "Cocoa may not grow like wheat, but it can't possibly grow like this."

She bent to pluck a seed from a brimming basket set off to one side. Unmindful of the mess it made of her lace gloves, hopelessly grimy by now anyway, she held it up and sniffed. "It hasn't the least scent of cocoa," she chided him, the few freckles on her nose wriggling as she sniffed. To further prove her point, he popped the grape-sized seed into her mouth. The bits of pulp clinging to it were sweet and refreshing, and she started to nod in vindication. Then she bit into the hard seed. With distinctly unladylike vigor, she spit it out. It was vilely bitter.

A chorus of giggles and chortles from the watching workers embarrassed her further. "That was an unkind prank, Mr. MacKenzie," she accused, her mouth still puckered from the unpleasant taste.

Oliver had the grace not to grin, though he couldn't keep the amusement out of his voice. "I didn't promise you a bonbon," he said. "I told you they were cocoa beans, and that's what they are. Raw, unprocessed cocoa beans. Here, Edmund, pass me your cutlass." He caught the machete that one of the men threw him and used it to fork a split pod into his hand, then slice out a section of pulp. He offered it to Allegra on the tip of the knife. "That should wash down the flavor," he said.

When she grudgingly accepted it, he went on to explain. "They're weeks away from being edible, or drinkable. It's a long process they must go through to reach the table in a familiar form. From here they go down to the cocoa boucan for fermentation and drying and polishing and sacking. That's a good two or three weeks, right there."

"Boucan?" Allegra questioned, still mistrusting him. "What's a boucan? It sounds like a hiding place for trolls in a fable."

"Hardly," Oliver said, allowing the grin to emerge. He offered Allegra another slice of pulp, then handed the cutlass back to its owner. "The boucan is a collection of buildings in the cocoa yard where the beans are processed. It's a term that was borrowed from the French buccaneers—those barely legalized pirates who built sheds and huts along the shores to store their extra provisions and to smoke the fish they caught."

"Hmmm," Allegra said, sucking on the soothing pulp and trying to decide whether or not to believe him.

"By the time the beans leave the boucan, they smell like cocoa," Oliver continued, ignoring her indecipherable comment. "And they are ready to be sold, though there are still a number of steps they must go through in order to be ready for consumption: roasting, sorting, shelling, grinding, and then conversion into either cocoa powder or candy. That last step, of course, is done after the beans leave Grenada, mostly in England. Although," he added, "we do keep a few here for making 'cocoa tea.'"

Though she now was more convinced that he was telling her the truth, she still felt compelled to try and trip him up. "If the beans must be further cooked and so forth before they can be eaten," she said cautiously, testing her own logic, "I should think it would be simpler to do that here, *before* they leave Grenada."

Oliver raised his eyebrows in agreement. "It would be a great deal simpler," he said, his tone no longer full of humor. "And also a great deal more profitable. But, unfortunately, it is contrary to British colonial laws. They are quite specific about allowing only raw products to be exported. Finished goods are forbidden. It is one of the ways England has of ensuring our dependence."

"That's not fair!" Allegra cried, the last vestige of suspicion rousted by outrage.

"Welcome to the colonies, Miss Pembroke," Oliver replied with a hint of grimness.

Allegra understood that he was saying nothing could be done about the situation, but she still railed against such inequitable rules. "It's just not right," she said darkly. "Imagine, growing these beans all your life and never being able to sell the cocoa powder. It's incomplete. It's like cutting the cloth for a dress, then not being allowed to sew it up."

Oliver's smile came back as he watched her shaking her bedraggled parasol for emphasis. "I agree with you, Miss Pembroke," he said. "And so did your father. He was tremendously frustrated by the limitations placed on colonial cocoa planters. He was a man whose mind was continually in motion, with new ideas rising in the ashes of the old ones. That's why he went back to England to start a chocolate factory."

"He did what?" Allegra asked, her astonishment wiping out her outrage as thoroughly as her outrage had wiped out her suspicion.

"Ah, another surprise," Oliver observed. "Yes, he went back to England almost three years ago." He resumed his tour of the cocoa groves but set a more leisurely pace down the trail. Allegra had little trouble keeping up with him, pausing only occasionally to yank her hem free of fallen brush. Finally realizing that her parasol was more hazard then help among the low branches, she collapsed it and used it as a walking stick, listening intently to Oliver's explanation.

"When Cecil bought L'Etoile from Patrice Le Ciel, it was only the boucan, some cocoa trees, and a termite-ridden house," he said. "In a typical whirl of enthusiasm, your father immediately cleaned up the groves, increased the area under cultivation, and built the great house. That done, he felt he had more or less conquered the cocoa culture and was ready for a fresh challenge.

"As you noted, the next logical move is processing the raw product, and that's what Cecil wanted to do. He had seen and tasted enough of our homemade chocolate to stir his imagination —to whet his appetite, so to speak. It was to raise money for his new idea that he sold half interest in the estate to me. He was just as happy to leave the management of it in my hands, as well, because he was almost always in England. It was pure coincidence that he was here when you arrived: he had only just returned."

"And what of the factory?" Allegra asked excitedly, envisioning huge halls filled with chocolate cakes and chocolate candies and steamy cups of frothy cocoa. "What a wonderful idea. Can't you just see it? Can't you see the workers bustling about in starched white aprons, their cheeks very rosy and dimpled, smiling happily as they arrange delectable confections in beautiful boxes painted with angels and hearts and bowers of flowers like the one over the front gate?" She gulped for air, then asked eagerly, "Was it like that?"

Although amused by her description, Oliver shrugged. "As I told you, Cecil had only just arrived, so we didn't have the opportunity to discuss it," he said. "But I can take a guess."

He paused a moment before continuing carefully. "You must understand that while your father's ability to create a business was unparalleled, his aptitude for the reality of running it was a wee bit less brilliant. And he tended to be, uh, overenthusiastic, shall we say, in his approach to finances." He shrugged again. "I doubt that the factory got a proper start up."

"What a shame," Allegra said, referring as much to her father's flaws as to the delicious chocolate fantasies that were fading fast. Yet the discovery that Cecil was imperfect didn't cast a shadow on her resplendent image of him as much as it made him seem more real. And made her suddenly miss him. She felt the heavy crush of sadness for the first time as she finally mourned her father who was, after all, a man.

"I'm sure he enjoyed what he was doing," she said affectionately and half to herself. "I'm sure he was truly intrigued by cocoa, or he wouldn't have sold half of L'Etoile."

Oliver gave her a sideways glance, expecting sarcasm, but her expression was innocent, even melancholy. Bending to pull a broken branch off the path, he remarked, "Cocoa has a history of intriguing men. And of figuring strongly in their finances." When he saw that Allegra was interested in what he was saying, he went on.

"The Mayan Indians were the first people to cultivate cocoa," he told her. "Although it may have been harvested before that by the ancient South American tribes. When the Mayans were conquered by the Aztecs, they were made to pay tribute in sacks of cocoa beans and baskets of ground cocoa. It became a form of currency, and very organized, at that. Just as we have shillings and pence making pounds sterling, they had coultes and xequipiles equaling loads. And when you think that it is recorded that in Nicaragua ten beans bought a rabbit and a hundred beans could procure a 'tolerably good slave,' you can see the value cocoa was given."

"It sounds to me as if everyone was so busy peddling the

beans, they couldn't afford to drink them," Allegra interrupted. "Except perhaps the very wealthy."

Oliver grinned. "One advantage to cocoa money," he said, "is that almost anyone can mint it. An early observer called it 'Blessed money! Which exempts its possessors from avarice since it cannot be hoarded nor hidden underground.' Although," he added, "what you say is true, too. Until the eighteenth century, it was a beverage of the very wealthy, on both sides of the Atlantic.

"In early Aztec times, it was reserved for warriors and noblemen. By Montezuma's rule, his whole household imbibed it—up to two-thousand cups a day. The emperor himself drank it exclusively and had it served in goblets made of hammered gold with spoons of highly polished tortoise shell. Legend had it that he would use the goblets only once, then throw them into the lake."

As he talked, Oliver automatically scanned the trees around him, looking for trouble. When he found none, he looked back to Allegra and continued. "Cortes, in turn, conquered the Aztecs and brought cocoa beans back to Spain, as part of the tribute to *his* king. In short order, it again became the drink of royalty. For a while, the Spanish kept it a secret, but when Princess Anne married Louis the XIII in 1615, she brought him some chocolate as a wedding present. It didn't take long for the French court to adopt the drink. A few decades later, an enterprising shopkeeper carried it across the Channel and introduced it to England.

"By the end of the century, Europeans were discovering what the inhabitants of the New World already knew: that chocolate was a sublime drink. The Aztecs thought it gave a man courage in battle, wisdom in life, and, uh—" he temporized, remembering his audience's sensibilities. Then in typically frank fashion, he finished, "And vigor in making love." When Allegra met this statement with a mortified look, he grinned.

"The English tended to extol its digestive virtues," he went on in a more circumspect vein. "Samuel Pepys drank it morning and night to settle his stomach. A hundred and fifty years later, Brillat-Savarin touted it as an all around elixir. He claimed that habitual drinkers enjoyed 'the most equable and constant health.' I suppose it received its ultimate accolade when the Swedish botanist Linnaeus, in the process of classifying all known flora, gave cocoa the name of 'Theobroma,' Greek for 'Food of the Gods.'"

"Is it true?" Allegra demanded, intrigued now, herself. "Is

chocolate really an extraordinary tonic? I know that it is delicious and that it is considered very nutritious, but does it also have medicinal values?"

Again Oliver shrugged, though this time his gesture served more to stimulate than to stifle fanciful images. "You must realize that the chocolate drink, as it was first conceived, was quite different from the cocoa you drink today. Now it is served hot, with milk and sugar, but in Aztec times, and in the early Spanish days, it was served cold. Then, the beans were roasted and ground with vanilla and pepper and other strong spices, mixed with honey, and beaten to a thick froth. Sometimes this drink was mixed with fermented maize, sometimes with wine or brandy. Sometimes, the Aztecs even ground up the bones of their ancestors and added it to the brew as a cure for dysentery. I must say, though, it certainly didn't do much to improve the health of their sacrificial victims. The poor souls were given a cup of chocolate to drink before they had their hearts cut out."

"How dreadful," Allegra said, shuddering. "What a terrible fate."

Oliver reached over to a nearby tree and pulled off a cocoa pod, pecked by a bird and rotting. "It depends on your perspective," he said matter-of-factly. "It was often considered an honor to be sacrificed. It meant that your spirit would go off to heaven, a sort of companion to the gods."

"A companion!" Allegra exclaimed, stopping in her tracks. When Oliver stopped too and looked around at her, she said, "That's what I came to talk to you about."

"Oh?" Oliver replied, deadpan. "And I thought you came to have a lesson on cocoa."

"Well, yes," Allegra said, fumbling to regain her manners. "It's been extremely informative, I assure you. Very edifying, indeed."

As her voice took on a stilted tone, a look of renewed disgust crossed Oliver's face. He settled himself on braced legs and again folded his arms across his chest. "Quite so," he said shortly. "But something more urgent is on your mind." He made it a statement rather than a query.

"Well, yes," Allegra said again, suddenly unsure of how to proceed.

"You mentioned a plan," Oliver prompted. "And apparently it involves a companion."

"Yes, that's right. I thought it would be the perfect solution to our delicate situation." Once launched on her idea, Allegra quickly gained momentum. "Considering that I cannot possibly live in the house alone with you, and you, I am sure, will not move out, the ideal answer is to hire a companion. We can find some eminently respectable female whose very presence will preserve my reputation and convey an atmosphere of refinement and propriety."

Warmed up now, Allegra began to embellish. "Perhaps she will even be destitute. We will be rescuing her from a life of genteel poverty. Yes, that's it." She poked the ground with the tip of her parasol for emphasis.

"I read a novel once about an orphaned girl who was very beautiful and wealthy," she went on excitedly, "but she was miserable with loneliness. You see, she lived in this huge mansion with only her uncle who was old and crotchety and kept to his rooms. Then one day when she was in town to select ribbons for a sachet she was making, she saw a thief snatch the purse from a young woman who was quite pretty and refined-looking, despite her shabby clothes.

"The young woman looked so distraught, as if she'd lost her very last cent—which indeed she had—that the beautiful girl went over to her..."

"Wait. Let me guess," Oliver interrupted. "And the poor pretty one became the companion of the rich beautiful one, and they both married handsome dukes."

"Well, yes," Allegra said, somewhat miffed at having her story cut short. "Except they weren't dukes. One man owned a number of properties, and the other man was wealthy and devoted himself to good works."

"Good works," Oliver murmured, rolling his eyes skyward. "I suppose this is another lesson in life from Miss Lorna Lockhart?"

"No," Allegra said. "It is a novel by Mrs. Mary Waverly. But if you don't like the idea..."

"I don't like the idea." His tone was definite.

"Then my companion needn't be penniless," Allegra replied. "It was only a thought. Maybe she will have a bit of a limp, instead." She paused and reconsidered. "Nothing very serious, mind you, and of course she accepts her handicap with courage and good cheer."

"Stop," Oliver said bluntly. "I have a better plan."

"You have?" Allegra asked, emerging from her fantasy.

"Yes, I have," Oliver answered. "I propose to take you, tomorrow, to Carriacou where I shall leave you safely and, above all, respectably, in the care of my father, my stepmother, and my three sisters, none of whom are either impoverished or lame."

"What?" Allegra sputtered, clamping her hands on her hips in indignation. "You can't just cart me around at will, leaving me like a steamer trunk in the lost luggage department. I won't go."

"Nor will I continue to sleep in the boucan," Oliver retorted. "Or be plagued by hysterical accusations of 'unseemly' behavior." And by an ever deepening attraction to her. He meant to put as much distance as possible between himself and her random flashes of spirit and charm.

"But I offered you a solution," Allegra protested, still incensed.

"And I offered you a better one," Oliver said, determined to stand fast throughout the battle.

"Anyway," Allegra said, dropping her hands and taking off on another tangent, "Elizabeth didn't tell me that you had three sisters. I somehow had the impression that you were the only child."

Startled by this meteoric shift in moods, Oliver answered before he had a chance to reflect. "They are my half-sisters, actually. My father remarried while I was in school in England, and had three daughters with his new wife. They are each more delightful than the next; I am sure you will enjoy their company."

"Perhaps." Allegra was noncommittal on the latter point, but shamelessly curious on the former. "Elizabeth said you came home from England eleven years ago and built boats with your father. How did you happen to end up here?"

"Elizabeth was quite chatty this morning, wasn't she?" Oliver commented. He was not as voluble on the subject of his personal life as he was on the subject of cocoa. "Did she tell you also how pretty it is on Carriacou?"

"We had a pleasant discussion," Allegra responded, not willing to be thrown off the track. "Didn't you like boat building?" she prodded, with as little delicacy as he had shown her last night. "Or was it simply that during your years in England, willy-nilly, you had learned to bake the cake?"

"Good God!" Oliver exclaimed. "What other details of my life did Elizabeth share with you?"

"Not too many," Allegra said, shaking her head almost regretfully, but waiting for a reply.

There was silence for a moment as each stubbornly stared at the other. Finally, Oliver's innate sense of fairness won out. After all, he had been equally as indiscreet in exacting information about her life, and she did have the right to know something of her partner's background. "All right," he conceded.

"I liked building boats well enough, but I liked sailing them even better," he explained. "After only a few months with my father I saw that was the case, so we built a schooner for me. For a year I ferried freight around to Barbados and Trinidad and even Venezuela. With the profits I made, I had another one built and sent it on the northern loop, St. Vincent's and St. Lucia and up as far as Martinique, with a good captain in charge. As the years went by and my reputation grew, I kept adding schooners to the fleet until I had a dozen running from Bermuda to Brazil.

"By that time, I had acquired the warehouse and office in St. George's, and even had a manager, but still had no home of my own. I was getting a wee bit tired of sleeping in rented rooms or on the slat board berths of a schooner, never knowing where I'd left my clean shirt. And despite the lure of the sea, there is nothing like the feeling of owning land. It must be the Scottish in me.

"I knew Cecil through my friendship with Jamie, so when he approached me about buying half interest in L'Etoile, I found the offer irresistible. I liked Cecil, I liked the estate, and I liked the location, just a short distance from the pier at Gouyave. All the elements were right." He didn't add that Cecil's absence in England was also an enticing factor. Given his partner's tendency toward distraction, and his own abilities to be logical and organized, he was better off running the business himself.

At the end of his explanation, Allegra absently slung the parasol over her shoulder and used it to rub at an itch. "Considering the way each of your businesses has bloomed from the seeds of the last, more or less the way you say my father's have, I am surprised that you haven't carried them on to England, too." She made the observation thoughtfully, almost sadly, suddenly aware that she didn't really want him to do so.

"Not a chance," Oliver said shortly, cutting through her musings. "The day I left England, I vowed never to return. It's a promise I intend to keep."

"But why?" Although strangely relieved, Allegra was also

mystified. To her, England seemed a place of immeasurable sophistication and she was hard pressed to understand Oliver's obvious aversion to it. "Why on earth do you dislike it so?" she
asked, further emulating his directness. "Did you do poorly in
school?"

Oliver's expression was somewhat exasperated, but also
amused by her assumption. "No, Miss Pembroke," he said dryly.
"I did not do poorly in school. On the contrary, I was an excellent
student and a capital athlete, quite the sustaining force of the
rugby team." His tone grew harder as he added briefly, "Whatever my accomplishments, however, I remained the son of a colonial tradesman, deemed a lesser mortal, and that seemed to be
the ultimate gauge of my worth."

"Oh, I see," Allegra said, temporarily quelled by another example of injustice. Somehow, she couldn't conceive of him in a
position of inferiority. After a moment, she asked, "Don't you
think people would have a different opinion of you now, seeing
how successful you've become?"

"I doubt it," Oliver answered grimly. "In any event, they shall
never have the opportunity to judge. The only trip I intend to take
is to Carriacou, tomorrow," he said, closing the subject. "I expect
that you will find my father's house in Windward very comfortable."

His words brought the present situation back with a jolt, effectively banishing the uncomfortably tender feelings that were
building up inside her. "I am sure that it is quite nice, Mr.
MacKenzie," she said, straightening her shoulders and bringing
her parasol back down to the ground with a jab. "However, *I*
have no intention of having the opportunity to judge. I mean to
stay at L'Etoile and to hire a companion. I am not going to Carriacou."

"And I, Miss Pembroke," Oliver returned, just as adamant,
"will not have a prim and prudish female limping around my
home, telling me what I may and may not do. The solution,
therefore, is for you to go to Carriacou."

"No," Allegra said vehemently. All at once, she was tired of
being treated like a child, tired of having her wishes overridden.
"I don't want to go, and you can't force me to." She stuck out her
chin and looked him full in the eye, daring him to differ.

For a moment, Oliver glared back, realizing she was right.

There was no way he could physically compel her to go if she didn't want to. He changed his tactics.

"As you like, Miss Pembroke," he said mildly. "However, I must tell you that *I* am going to Carriacou tomorrow to consult with my father on the schooner he is currently building for me. It bothers my conscience to think of you here at L'Etoile alone." He paused a moment before delivering the coup de grace. "It isn't proper."

The angry retort Allegra was preparing dissolved in her mouth. Proper. That word again. It worked on her like the strings on a marionette, jerking her into actions at war with her instincts. Proper. Faced with such an unassailable argument, Allegra's resistance crumbled. The next morning, she went to Carriacou.

Chapter
Four

Allegra sat on the hard edge of the *Miss Lily*'s berth, her hands clasped in her lap. Sleepiness from her early rising muffled her resentment at the way in which Oliver had shanghaied her. For a good half hour, she stared blearily at a chipped mug swaying on a hook under the shelf until it occurred to her that, although slightly slanted in the water, the schooner was not bucking and plunging as it had during her previous voyage.

Heartened by this discovery, she stood up tentatively and slid open the door. When nothing calamitous happened, she stepped out on deck. Unlike the last time, today the sea was deep and calm, only a steady rhythm of waves swelling the surface. The sky was clear and cloudless, the wind blowing no more than enough to propel them at a comfortable clip. It was a wonderful day.

Coming fully awake with a deep breath of salty air, Allegra leaned her back against the cabin and watched the green, steep coast of Grenada slide by. When the wind persisted in plucking at the brim of her bonnet, she unpinned the flimsy creation and tossed it inside. She would rather stand out here, refreshed by cool sea breezes and inspired by dramatic scenery, than sit neatly and tediously in the tiny cabin.

After a while the balmy air restored not only her alertness, but also her optimism. She almost forgave Oliver his underhanded tactics and his unchivalrous manners in her enjoyment of the sail. Buoyed by this sense of benevolence, Allegra made her way aft to find him.

From his position behind the chest-high wheel, Oliver saw her come around the corner of the cabin, and he fought to control another surge of intense attraction. Her golden hair was touseled more than usual, the light gleaming on every errant curl. The morning sun and wind had whipped pink color into the creamy skin of her face and had multiplied the tiny freckles dotting her nose and scattered across her brow. Wide and bright, her eyes seemed a reflection of the deep purple sea. Despite his insistence that she was a hopelessly ordinary woman, stiff and staid, he found her utterly enticing.

"Have you come to stand your watch?" he asked lightly.

"Have I what?" Allegra answered, puzzled, looking at her feet to see what she had stepped in.

"No, no," Oliver assured her with a grin. "I merely wondered if you had come to take your turn at the wheel."

Allegra's eyes grew even wider and brighter. "Oh, yes," she said excitedly. "May I please?"

Oliver let one hand go and moved back from the helm, motioning her to take his place. She came forward quickly and grasped the big spokes, but where Oliver had seemed to steer the schooner effortlessly, the wheel docilely responding to his touch, it spun heedlessly in Allegra's hands. *Miss Lily* followed suit by turning crazily in the waves and by sounding an ominous crack as her canvas slacked, slapping emptily against the mast.

Hoots of laughter sounded on the foredeck where the crew was lounging sleepily in the shade. "Hey mahn," came a shout. "You making snake wake!" Other taunts died unspoken when three black faces peered over the cabin top then sank swiftly from view with expressions of astonishment.

Allegra might have been mortified if she hadn't felt so frantic. She gripped the wheel desperately, unable to get the schooner back in control, not even knowing, for that matter, how to attempt it. Her pounding heart suddenly leaped as Oliver's strong, tanned hands settled over hers. Slowly, deliberately, he coaxed the schooner back on course, the sails giving a satisfied huff as they refilled with wind.

He remained where he was, standing so close behind her, Allegra could feel his breath in her hair. "Like this," he said calmly, seeming not to notice her sudden confusion or her shortness of breath. "You must fall off; she's headed up into the wind. Don't let her luff or you'll broach."

Nodding because she knew a response was expected of her, Allegra had no idea of what he was saying. Even if she had understood what the words meant, her blood was racing so fast, it blocked her reasoning. All she was aware of was the wind against her hot skin and Oliver's fingers wrapped around her own. She could feel the strength in his arms as he moved the wheel one way and the other, pulling her along with him. She swallowed hard.

"Ease up," Oliver murmured in her ear. "This schooner has a weather helm; she wants to head up into the wind." He smiled into her knot of curls as she nodded again, just as tensely and just as unknowingly as before. "Look," he said. "Sailing a boat is simple. It's only a question of knowing where the wind is coming from, and in this part of the world it's always blowing from the east north east. From Africa. All you have to do is make sure the wind angles into the sails. If you are hardened up too much, steering too much to the east, the sails will go slack and you'll turn sideways in the water. Then, instead of shoving you along, the waves will smack into your side and swamp you. Understand?"

Allegra gave another nod, but, miraculously, this time his words were starting to make sense. Some of the tautness went out of her shoulders, and his touch began to feel warm and familiar.

"If you fall off too much," he continued patiently, "if you steer too much to the west, the sails will overfill with wind. In a light little boat, it can knock you down, but a schooner is built for abuse. You'll just heel way over and Thomas will holler at you from the foredeck because the crew is sliding around and the chickens have fallen overboard."

Allegra managed a weak smile, but kept her eyes fixed on the sea in front of her. In part, she was afraid to remove her gaze from the direction in which she was headed. But in larger part, she didn't dare to look directly at Oliver. The straightforward force of his dark blue eyes was more than she could cope with right now.

"Next you have to realize that the sea is a source of power, too. As it carries you up to the crest of a wave, it is making you fall off. So you harden up to compensate. There, just a little." He turned the wheel, his hand tightening over hers, just enough to keep them on an even keel. "And now down the other side of the wave. Do you feel it? Fall off a bit. Good."

He talked her through wave after wave, his voice as steady and rhythmic as the sea itself. She vaguely wondered why she had ever found his frank tone brusque; it now seemed soothing, calming, his clear logic settling her flustered nerves. Gradually he loosened his grip on her hands, gradually gave over the steering to her. Each time they turned the big wheel, she could feel it demanding more of her, feel the sea pulling inexorably against it.

Eventually Oliver released his hold entirely and stepped back. When the *Miss Lily* continued to plough placidly through the swells, he went to sit on the rail where he could watch Allegra, enjoyment wrinkling the corners of his eyes. She looked so thrilled, so pleased and proud, it was hard to remember that he wished she would return to Connecticut.

"This is splendid," she said with a happy laugh. "I see now why you prefer sailing boats to building them. It would distress me no end to labor for months on a boat then watch someone else sail away on it, knowing what a glorious time he was having."

"Of course, it's not always a glorious experience, as you may recall," Oliver responded, smiling. "There are moments when a cozy job in a shipyard seems definitely preferable."

Allegra shrugged away the bad memory. "This more than makes up for it," she said. They were silent for a few more minutes, each reveling in the peace. The only sounds were the creaking of the masts and the whoosh of waves against the hull.

"You know," Allegra mused, finally breaking the quiet, "I think I understand now why you decided to sail freight boats around the islands. And what you say about wanting to own L'Etoile makes sense, too. But what I don't understand is why, when you have no intention of ever returning to England, you chose to own a business like Star Shipping, Transatlantic Commerce." She cast a quick glance at him and saw that some of the pleasure had left his face.

"That was more to protect my current profits than to create new ones," he said tersely. When Allegra made no comment, only pressed her lips hard against each other, Oliver sighed and offered a better explanation.

"There's an estate in St. Andrew's Parish, near Grenville, on the other side of the island, called Argo. They say that its present owner won it in a card game. I suppose it's possible; when you live five thousand miles from your land, I imagine it loses its value." Oliver kicked at a coil of rope. "The new owner, Argo

Ltd., was considerably more thorough than the old one. In an attempt to expand their interests in the West Indies, you might say to *control* them, they started a shipping company called Argo Shipping.

"Most of the cocoa shipping contracts were signed, not on the estates or in solicitors' offices in St. George's, but in gentlemen's clubs in London. The owner of Argo used his social contacts to monopolize the business."

"Is that very bad?" Allegra asked, keeping her eyes straight ahead this time. Oliver sounded grim.

"That's how business is done," he admitted. "And ordinarily I would accept it. But it was soon apparent that Argo Shipping was run very much in the manner of the Argo estate, minimum care taken and maximum profit expected. Shipping fees went up, but shipping conditions degenerated. Cocoa agents and buyers were complaining about the poor quality of the beans when they arrived in England, but, by then, the previous shippers had lost interest in this route or had established other trades."

"So you enlarged Star Shipping," Allegra concluded.

"Yes."

For a while Allegra watched the lump on the horizon that was Carriacou come nearer. Then she asked, "Did you use your contacts to win contracts, too?"

A grin wiped out the grimness of Oliver's expression. "Of course," he said.

By the time they docked in Carriacou that afternoon, Allegra's conscious assessment of Oliver as rude and ill-mannered was very much in conflict with her involuntary admiration of him. She found herself drawn, against her will, to his plain-spoken, painstakingly reasonable approach. As reluctant as she was to admit it, she was finding the very attitude she professed to loathe increasingly refreshing, and her grudging but growing attraction enhanced every time she remembered the feel of his hands closed over hers.

They left the schooner tied to the pier in Hillsborough, the tiny town that boasted one meandering main street lined with shops and houses, many built from stone or mortar on the bottom with wood-shingled second stories up above. If Oliver had been greeted with respect in St. George's, here he was treated like a favorite old friend. Everyone stopped to talk to him or tease him or slap him on the shoulder. He had no trouble borrowing a well-used carriage and a lazy horse that started them over the sun-bleached island to Windward, on the other side.

Allegra continued to be enthralled by their journey. Though practically within spitting distance of Grenada, Carriacou was completely different. Not nearly as high, its gently sloping hill-sides were swept smooth and golden by sun and wind. Patches of green bordered the fields, empty except for a pile of cactus or a lone, leaning tree, its branches and leaves blown permanently toward the west. When they went over the top of the island, the sea came into view again, a stretch of turquoise, brilliant and clear, divided from the deeper navy blue water by a ribbon of frothy white surf.

"Oh, my," Allegra murmured in awe.

"Yes," Oliver agreed.

Here and there they passed a house, a couple of cows, or a group of goats. Mostly, though, there were just the dry fields, the green groves, the sea, and the heat.

It seemed even hotter here than it had been in Grenada, espe-cially after the cooling respite under sail. By the time they reached the collection of houses haphazardly gathered along a mile of beach, that was Windward, Allegra's clothes were stick-ing to her body and the bones of her corset felt like forks.

They drew up in front of a solidly built two-story house with white gingerbread trim trailing down the roof lines and hanging over the inviting front porch. "Och, look at this, will you," came a shout. "I swear, Oliver, the life of a planter is swelling your head. A carriage, no less. Next you'll be wanting doilies and finger bowls."

A man appeared over the bluff from the beach, an older, hus-kier, more weathered version of Oliver, with a carpenter's long wooden tool box balanced on his shoulder. "There was a time, laddie, when shanks' mare was good enough for you," he said, setting the box on the porch steps. "To mention nothing of the fact that I've built you twelve stout schooners. Have you gotten so used to living on land that you've forgotten how to sail the damned things? We do have a pier here, you know."

"Watch your language, Angus," Oliver said, laughing. "I've brought a lady to visit. This is Cecil's daughter. And I know you have a pier here, though a sorry affair it is."

"Well, well," Angus said, coming up to Allegra and squeezing her hand in a mighty shake. He carefully inspected her. "You have the light of your father in your eyes," he decided. "But you have more stubbornness in your chin."

"Angus," Oliver said warningly. His father was one of the few people in Grenada Cecil had failed to charm. Cecil's extravagant spending habits and lack of stick-to-itiveness were heresy to a died-in-the-wool Scotsman like Angus.

"How do you do, Mr. MacKenzie," Allegra said, completely at a loss for further comment. Just when she was getting used to the forthright ways of the son, the father unsettled her with his even more unabashed behavior. As he continued pumping her hand and studying her face, a flush of embarrassment colored her cheeks.

"I do very well, Miss Pembroke, and don't shush me, Oliver," Angus said, finally releasing her hand. "A little stubbornness is a very good thing. Besides which, I don't deny that Cecil was a bonny fellow whose eyes showed more enjoyment of life than any man I've ever met. If he did nothing else, he passed that on to his bonny daughter."

Allegra's blush deepened and she shifted from foot to foot, but neither man seemed to notice.

"He built L'Etoile, Angus," Oliver said in the weary tone of one who's made the same argument a dozen times before. "That's hardly nothing. Where everyone else saw a broken down holding in the middle of a jungle, Cecil imagined a great estate. And he made it happen."

"Aye. With a barrel of cash and your hard work," Angus muttered under his breath. "But that's not for now," he said, brightening. "At the moment I'm as parched as the desert and liable to faint if I don't have my tea. So come in and join me, Miss Pembroke, and meet Rose and my girls."

Although Allegra would rather have listened to more about her father, building on the image in her mind, Angus apparently had decided he had said enough. Nor did Oliver seem inclined to elaborate. She followed Angus up the path to meet his family. She had just reached the porch when they came bursting out the door, calling excited greetings to Oliver. The smallest, a girl around twelve years old, launched herself off the top step and into her brother's arms.

"Hello, Miss Lily," he said, holding her in a bear hug. "I have your namesake in Hillsborough Harbor, unloading lumber for the Bullens."

"Did you also bring the sheet music I wrote you about?" asked a girl of eighteen who seemed to be the oldest. "H. O. Payne's advertised new songs and dance music in last week's *Chronicle*."

"Yes, Violet, I did," Oliver said, setting Lily down but keeping an arm slung around her shoulders while she gripped his waist. He set a kiss on her beatific face before adding, "I brought you 'Monte Carlo,' 'Les Fleurs,' and 'Only Once More.' They looked to be the best of the lot."

"And my jam, Oliver?" the third sister asked. She was the plumpest of the three and about fifteen. "Did you remember my jam?"

"Raspberry, strawberry, and gooseberry," Oliver answered promptly. "And, Iris, I've also got you a tin of sweet meal biscuits."

"Shame on you, girls," an older woman reprimanded mildly from the porch. "Here you are begging your brother for presents while our guest is left standing in the sun." She turned to Allegra and said, "You come right in. Don't you mind my family. They got more jump than a puddle full of frogs, and just as much croak, too. Leave them and come have a cup of tea." She waved Allegra up the steps with the same unflappable authority she had shown her daughters, and Allegra, totally bewildered, obeyed.

"I'm Rose MacKenzie," she said, holding out her hand. "And I know you must be Cecil's daughter. You have his look in your eyes." Though her comment was the same as Angus's, it was more a compliment than a criticism.

While Allegra shook her hand, Rose added, "I used to think that Cecil's eyes were so blue because they were part of the sky, the way he seemed to see everything from one horizon to the other. And they'd get so sparkly when he looked at something pretty, I couldn't help but be pleased myself. What a pity they're closed now."

She shook her head sympathetically. "We just heard the terrible news yesterday morning. Augustine Stiel came back from Sauteurs, visiting his brother, and told us. I feel very sad for you. Come sit here while I bring the tea." She patted a rush-backed rocker. "You look like you're turned up for down."

Allegra dropped into the indicated rocker, still not having said a word, confusion completely tying her tongue. It was overwhelming enough to have these MacKenzies clamoring all around her, but what ultimately dumbfounded her was that, except for Angus and Oliver, they weren't white.

Rose MacKenzie was a striking woman who carried herself with grace and self-confidence. Allegra was as immediately impressed by Rose's composure as she was by her complexion, rich, smooth, and coffee-colored. She was what the islanders called Creole, a woman of both African and European ancestry. Her three daughters, with their flowery names, had all inherited their mother's lovely features, luminous brown eyes, and unaffected assurance.

Nothing in Allegra's experience had prepared her for a situation like this. There had been few enough black people in her small Connecticut town, and those several had kept to themselves. Even her four days in Grenada, where the majority of faces ranged from light beige to dark brown, hadn't led her to consider that all those colors could exist in one family. The discovery in no way disgusted her, though she could practically see her grandfather's face, rigid with disapproval. Still it surprised her, and, being surprised, she became awkward, as usual.

Intentionally or not, Oliver came to her rescue by monopolizing his family's attention. He pumped Angus for details of the new schooner being built for him, he copied the recipe for ginger tea cakes that Rose recited, he teased Lily, traded jokes with Iris, and answered Violet's endless questions about what was happening in St. George's. Through it all, Allegra sat silently drinking her tea and gathering her disorganized thoughts.

In the end, it was Violet who put her at ease with overtures that were half-envious, half-awed. When the Grenadian girl learned that Allegra had traveled all the way from New York, her expression was so wistful it won Allegra's heart. She knew exactly how Violet felt, yearning for excitement and glamour beyond her reach. Allegra settled more comfortably in the rocker and took a second cup of tea.

"Did you find New York very elegant?" Violet asked.

"Oh very," Allegra replied grandly. "I was born there," she added more modestly.

Violet came closer and seated herself on the railing in front of Allegra. Her brown eyes were big and expressive in a perfect heart-shaped face. Pretty black curls pulled free from the knot on top of her head and fluffed against her forehead and cheeks. Her skin was smooth and clear, the color of toasted coconut. "How wonderful to live in a big city and to be always surrounded by fascinating people and important events."

"Of course, I moved to the country when I was very tiny," Allegra hastily amended. "But my mother and I did go to New York once a year to visit Aunt Eleanor. At least we did until she died six years ago."

"And did you go to the opera and the theater?" Violet asked breathlessly. "Did you go to splendid balls?"

"Nooo," Allegra answered slowly, remembering how desperately she had longed for precisely the same thing. "We did attend the ballet once, though we sat in the upper balcony and my view was mostly blocked by the bonnet feathers of the lady in front of me. And we went often to afternoon concerts and to the Metropolitan Museum of Art. I always enjoyed that, especially the trolley ride up Fifth Avenue, past all the mansions and the carriages in Central Park."

"Please," Violet begged, "tell me all about it."

Allegra did. She told Violet about her own limited adventures, then, warming to her appreciative audience, she told her about ones she had read in novels. All during tea they discussed the splendors of New York, and they speculated on life in London. Much as Violet adored her brother, she discounted his assessment of that city, unable to accept that it could be anything less than thrilling.

After tea, when Oliver and Angus went down to the beach to inspect the skeleton of the new schooner growing out of the sand, Violet and Allegra trailed in their wake. They talked about Allegra's voyage, all alone on the *Creole Prince*, and about the ports of call in St. Lucia, St. Vincent, and Roseau, Dominica.

"You lead such an exciting life," Violet said, sighing. "Knowing how adventurous Cecil was, I shouldn't be surprised. Still, imagine just packing your bags one day and sailing off to see the world. I'd give anything to have so much courage. You're like the heroine in one of the novels you told me about."

Allegra laughed. "I wish it were true," she said. "But until two weeks ago, all my adventures took place in my head. You can't believe how ordinary my life has been, just keeping house for Grandfather: cooking him cabbage and boiled beef on Mondays, mashed potatoes and boiled beef on Tuesdays, baked beans and boiled beef on Wednesdays . . . Well, you get the idea. And even if Lucy Johnson blacked the stove and Mrs. Hubert did the laundry, there was still dusting and sweeping and marketing." She cut herself off and dismissed that dreary routine with a shrug.

"The highlight of every week was the Thursday afternoon stitching party at Millie Bowman's, and if you knew how horribly inept I am at needlework, you would realize just how dull my life was. It was the very opposite of exciting."

Violet was unconvinced. "But you've been to the ballet and to concerts, and I'll wager you've even worn silk dresses," she said, her head nodding knowingly. "I've only ever seen them in magazines. And six-month-old magazines, at that. If Oliver didn't bring me to visit my Aunt Ruby in Grenada every now and again, my entire life would take place in the twenty-two square miles of Carriacou. If you knew what *that* was like, your needlework parties would seem elegant and entertaining."

Allegra laughed again, basking in Violet's admiration. "I'm not so sure," she said. "Life here seems very agreeable." She took Violet's hand and gave it a squeeze, feeling a warm wash of affection for her new friend.

In fact, standing on the strip of white sand, the trade winds rustling the palm fronds and brushing her skin, MacKenzies in front of her and next to her and splashing in the shallow turquoise water behind her, Allegra suddenly realized that, despite the confusing twists and turns her life had taken, she was, at this moment, very happy.

Oliver saw the radiant look on her face, though he didn't know what had brought it on. While pretending to inspect the sturdy ribs of his new schooner, he watched Allegra's hands wave gracefully through the air as she described something to his sister. The late afternoon sun was at her back, turning her profusion of uncombed curls into a halo around her head.

Once again, he felt the strong pull of attraction; once again he saw the tremendous spirit and imagination he had enjoyed so much in Cecil. This time he knew it was not an aberration or a mirage as he had once thought. He understood now that her rigid behavior was the false part of her personality; it was the starched manners that were unnatural. For whatever reason she had adopted them, they hid her buoyant enthusiasm for life.

Wishing he had not had the thought, Oliver forced his attention back to the boat and to Angus's explanation of a particular curve in the stem. Allegra had been far less tempting when he had regarded his late partner's daughter as a prim and proper woman with a penchant for tripping. For the sake of a smooth business relationship, it was much safer to think of her in those terms. It seemed wiser than ever to leave her here in Carriacou until other arrangements could be made.

He told her so the next morning. Poking his head into the bedroom she had shared with Violet, he watched a minute as she bent over the bed, plumping the pillows in place. "I think it best that you remain here," he said without preamble.

Allegra started, her heart banging wildly; she hadn't heard him approach. Clutching a pillow in front of her and trying to calm her pulse, she straightened and backed away. "Oh, no," she said weakly, struggling to collect her thoughts. "I mean to go back to L'Etoile. I told you as much the other day." Her voice grew stronger. "I only agreed to come because you had to attend to some business," she reminded him. "Because you said it wouldn't be proper for me to stay on the estate alone."

"Nor would it be proper for you to stay on the estate with me," Oliver countered, hoping the same tactic would work twice.

It didn't. Although Allegra shifted awkwardly from one foot to the other, this time she didn't give any ground. "I told you my plan," she said. "I told you that I mean to hire a companion: someone who will give the situation respectability. I told you *that* is the perfect solution to a very delicate problem."

"And I told you that I don't want a lame, threadbare female taking up residence in my house, sniffing and tsking at me," Oliver returned, stepping farther into the room to emphasize his point.

Allegra took a few corresponding steps back until she bumped into the wall, setting askew a framed photo of a schooner tied to the Carenage. "We can hire someone who is physically sound, then," Allegra conceded. "She needn't have a limp. That was only an idea. And if you object so terribly, we can also require that she have an independent income. Perhaps a pension from the army for her husband who was killed heroically in the war," she mused, her imagination beginning to embellish again.

Oliver stifled another grin as he asked, "What war would that have been?"

"What?" Allegra responded, roused reluctantly from the picture she was creating in her mind. "What war? Well, I don't know." She shrugged. "There's bound to have been a war. The history books are full of wars."

Oliver shook his head. "Not recently," he said solemnly. "There hasn't been a war recent enough to leave our grieving widow much under sixty.".

"Then perhaps she has an inheritance," Allegra said, annoyed at his stubbornness. "Or perhaps she owns a bit of property and collects a rent. Perhaps . . . well, it doesn't really matter, does it?"

"No," Oliver agreed genially. "It doesn't. Because the whole idea is preposterous. A much better plan would be for you to remain here, swaddled in your prized respectability, until you decide what you want to do."

"I already know what I want to do," Allegra retorted, punching the pillow she was still clutching in front of her. "I want to return to L'Etoile."

"I thought you liked it here," Oliver said, searching for some means of convincing her. "I thought you were enjoying Violet's company. From the way you two have been talking, I thought you'd become fast friends."

"We have," Allegra answered, uncertainty starting to erode her conviction. Hugging the pillow closer, she remembered the sense of complete happiness she had felt yesterday on the beach. Maybe it wouldn't be so bad to remain among these lively people, only a few steps from the sea. "No," she said decisively, more in answer to her own proposal than to his. "I came to Grenada to be with my father. If I can't be with him, at least I can be in his home." She looked hard at Oliver and added urgently, "It's important."

She hoped he would understand what she barely grasped herself, that through some association with Cecil and L'Etoile she would find the adventure and the romance she was searching for, and that they would lead ultimately to the fulfillment of her long hidden desire to make a mark on the world. She stood up straighter, clasping her hands firmly around the pillow. "I intend to return to the estate today," she announced. "I won't be dissuaded."

Oliver shook his head in exasperation. "You may not be dissuaded," he said shortly. "But you won't be accommodated, either. The *Miss Lily* is bound for Bequia and St. Vincent's before heading back to Grenada. Unless you hire a fishing sloop, you'll never make Grenada today."

"I'll go along with you," Allegra said eagerly, taking a step forward and lowering the pillow. The thought of the cool sea breezes and the excitement of steering the schooner up and over the endless purple swells was very inviting. Then she remembered the heart-stopping sensation of Oliver's hands settling over hers on the big wheel, and, in quick succession, her vow to keep him at a distance by building a wall of propriety around herself. Standing on the aft deck, legs braced, curls flying, freckles popping out on her nose would do nothing to uphold that vow. She stepped back and raised the pillow protectively. When she also realized that the contemplated trip would mean spending several nights in the small cabin of the schooner, with just Oliver and the crew, a blush flooded her face. "Perhaps I'll wait here," she amended.

"Right," Oliver said dryly.

"But you must come back for me," Allegra said resolutely. "You must stop here on your way back to Grenada and pick me up."

"We'll see," Oliver hedged, meaning to leave her here until it was convenient.

"No, no," Allegra warned. "You *must* come back for me. Or else I *will* hire a fishing boat and go to Gouyave." Her chin took on a dangerous tilt. "You must promise."

"Right," Oliver said again, more wearily this time.

Despite her conviction that she belonged at L'Etoile, Allegra immensely enjoyed being in Carriacou. Without Oliver's presence and the tension it created, she was able to relax as she never had before. In all ways, life in the sturdy house in Windward seemed completely compatible with her instincts. No one chastised her or criticized her; on the contrary, they were extremely complimentary. She looked forward to every minute of every day, to the spontaneity, the laughter, the family warmth.

Her fourth morning in Carriacou brought weather even hotter and more sultry than the preceding days. Allegra would have been content to sit on the porch and sip limeade, playing backgammon with Iris and cutting paper dolls for Lily, but Violet had other ideas. "I think we should have a sea bath, Allegra," she said, fanning herself with last week's *Chronicle*. "After I prepare the coconut milk Mummy needs for supper, let's go down to the beach."

Lily jumped up in an instant, spilling snips of colored paper from her lap. "Let me come, too," she pleaded. "I'll help you grate the coconut, Violet, so we can go sooner. But you have to squeeze it because your hands are stronger and you can get more milk to drip out."

"That's fair," Violet agreed. "I suppose you want to come along, too, Iris?" When Iris nodded absently, her round face intent on the backgammon board, Violet hastily added, "That is, if you don't mind, Allegra."

Allegra rocked back in her chair and patted her damp forehead with a handkerchief dipped in Florida water. "I doubt that I mind," she said. "But I'm not really sure I know what it is you propose we do."

Violet looked momentarily puzzled. "A sea bath," she repeated in her lovely West Indian way. "You know, jump in the sea and swim about."

A look of longing crossed Allegra's face, but she politely declined. "I'm afraid I can't swim," she said. "So there's no use my accompanying you. But please go along without me. I don't object in the least to sitting here by myself. It's quite peaceful, and I have Mrs. Waverly's new novel that I just started reading."

Violet was stunned. "You can't swim?" she asked. Except for Ronnie MacPherson, who lost his leg when he slipped down the sluice of a sugar mill, she didn't know anyone who couldn't swim. It didn't seem possible that there was anything that Allegra didn't know; in Violet's eyes she was practically perfect. When Allegra shook her head regretfully, Violet asked, "Would you like me to teach you?"

Allegra started to demur. Then she felt the heavy heat hugging her body. She looked off the end of the porch and over the bluff at the sea, clean, calm, invitingly blue. "Yes, I would," she decided.

"That's it, then," Violet said happily. She stood up, grabbing some coconuts from the pile on the porch, ready to do her chores and be off.

With her face still pondering the backgammon board, Iris said practically, "If you are going to give Allegra a swimming lesson, we can't go down to the beach. All the boys in Windward will get word and they won't cease to tease us."

Violet looked crestfallen at the thought; Allegra looked horrified and on the verge of declining, after all. Lily saw her chances for a swim with her big sister and their guest evaporating and desperately suggested, "Let's go to Anse La Roche, instead. There's no one about there to bother us."

Violet brightened. "Yes, let's," she said. "It's the perfect spot for a sea bath."

"It's such a long walk," Iris protested, finally looking up.

"We can borrow Augustine Stiel's donkeys," Lily said quickly.

"If we've got the donkeys to ride, we might as well pack a lunch and go even farther," Violet elaborated. "We can give Allegra a good tour of Carriacou."

"We can go to Tyrell Bay," Lily offered.

"The tree oysters in the mangrove swamp there are delicious," Iris said dreamily.

"And the mosquitoes are ferocious," Violet added.

"Hillsborough Bay, then."

"No, Kendeace Point."

"The waves are too rough."

"Craigston."

"L'Esterre."

"Sabazon."

Allegra looked from one sister to the next, her head turning with each exchange, as if at a tennis match. The suggestion of Sabazon brought a sudden stillness. Everyone was in agreement.

An hour and a half later, Allegra found herself sitting sideways on a donkey, one hand clutching the guide rope, the other tightly grasping the animal's dusty mane. Although very nervous at first, Allegra relaxed a little when she realized several things. First, if she fell off, the ground was not very far away, but second, her tiny steed was even less inclined than she to race or gallop or perform other exhibitions of speed. In fact, he seemed practically asleep where he stood, his long, shaggy ears flopping somnolently on either side of his face.

Having quickly conquered her fear, Allegra became enchanted with their excursion. They rode through lime groves and alongside dry meadows; they went past mud ovens redolent of freshly baked bread, and fence posts sprouting foliage and pink flowers; they crested a hill and had a spectacular view of the sea and the sky and the green and gold land. Allegra was finding that the tropics were arousing her natural instincts from their lifelong imprisonment, making her feel immensely alive.

By the time they arrived at Sabazon, Allegra was ready for anything. Or almost anything. When the MacKenzie sisters tied their donkeys under trees, set their lunch basket on the beach, and started to strip, Allegra turned bright red. Dressed only in camisoles and pantaloons, the three girls waded eagerly into the water, leaving Allegra standing on the beach getting hotter every minute.

Allegra looked enviously at her hostesses, started to unbutton her blouse, then clasped her arms to her chest. Anxiously, she scanned the area for intruders. There were none. Except for their already dozing donkeys, some buzzing insects, and themselves, there were no other creatures in sight. There was just a long sweep of packed white sand where the sea gathered into waves and pounded ashore. Directly in front of her, though, was a pocket of water so clear and so pale blue, it scarcely seemed real. Protected by a craggy spit of land at the end of the beach, this perfect patch of sea rippled gently to shore.

Quickly, before she could change her mind, Allegra unbuttoned her blouse and flung it to the ground. The sensation of sun and breeze on her bared arms was so sublime, she hurried out of the rest of her clothes. When she unlaced her corset and let it drop to the sand, the fragrant whoosh of breath that filled her was exhilarating.

Clad in just her thin cotton underclothes, Allegra took three steps into the water, stopping when it swirled around her legs. It felt wonderful. "Come farther," Violet shouted. "It isn't deep. Watch me. I'm standing."

Allegra looked fifteen feet in front of her and saw her friend standing, drops of water shining among her black curls and along her wet arms. The sea nudged at her waist, making her sway in the sunshine. Bravely, Allegra went forward. The sea rose higher and higher, plastering her pantaloons to her legs. She stopped for a moment and looked toward the bottom. Her feet were big and blurry, wavering on the clean sand. She scooped up a handful of water and dribbled it down an arm, almost shivering with pleasure as it cooled her hot skin. With both hands cupped, she splashed some water on her face, sighing delightedly as it flowed down her neck and under her camisole. She doused herself over and over, thoroughly relishing this luscious new feeling.

"Come with me," Violet said, suddenly appearing beside her. "Let's go a little deeper. Don't be afraid."

"I'm not afraid," Allegra answered honestly, looking around the benign, baby blue corner of Caribbean Sea. "I think I like swimming very much."

"You're not swimming yet," Violet said, laughing. "So far, you are just barely wet. Watch me. Swimming is like this." She slid down and slowly stroked a few yards. "You try," she said, standing again, water streaming from her.

Willingly, Allegra copied her actions. Or attempted to. The next thing she knew, she was face down in the water, her arms and legs churning furiously, her knees bumping the bottom. Somehow she righted herself, sputtering and gasping for air, more astonished than frightened, and more thoroughly wet than she had ever been. "It looked so easy," she wailed.

Violet's moment of worry vanished when she saw that Allegra was undaunted by her dunking. "It is easy," she encouraged. "Watch me again." As before, she took a few slow strokes, but this time she was interrupted by Lily.

"It's simpler to do like this," she advised, dog-paddling in front of her sister.

"Floating is easier," Iris interrupted. "Like this." She flopped on her back between them.

Allegra tried floating and dog-paddling; she tried treading and kicking; she tried swimming sideways and frontways and backwards. She followed every shouted instruction, every graceful demonstration, and succeeded only in laughing uproariously and in swallowing great gulps of the sea.

A sudden heavy splash, thirty feet in front of them, brought an abrupt end to their frolicking. They stood stock-still, eyes fixed on the wake, waiting in apprehensive silence. From out of the dark blue, deeper water came the form of a man, swimming swiftly beneath the surface. They all stiffened in fear, looking around for an escape, but before any of them could move, Oliver emerged among them, wearing only his white trousers and spouting like a whale.

Lily recovered instantly. "Naughty you!" she cried, smacking her hands in the sea and splashing him hard. Oliver shook the water from his hair, laughed in amusement, and feinted a charge at his little sister. With a shriek, she eluded him.

"You gave us a good scare," Violet said reprovingly. "Where did you come from?"

"From Bequia," Oliver answered.

"You jumped off those rocks, didn't you?" Iris demanded, pointing at the promontory where layers of red rock were stacked haphazardly like slices of bread.

While Oliver bowed his head in mock confession, Allegra struggled to draw breath. Her heart, pounding initially in panic, refused to slow down. She couldn't keep her eyes off him. The sun gleamed on his chest and on the muscles in his arms, bare and tanned and wet. A few drops of water glistened in his long lashes, and, as he joked with his sisters, his white teeth flashed in a grin, his blue eyes creased in the corners. Handsome, strong, full of humor and life, he was undeniably appealing.

Allegra was suddenly aware of how her thin cotton underclothes were stuck to every curve of her body, of how much skin was exposed. And how much of Oliver's was, too. Mortified, her correct Connecticut upbringing clashing with feelings unleashed by the Caribbean sunshine, she turned to flee. Awkward as she always was when in a state of confusion, and still unaccustomed to the weight of the water, she lost her balance, swept over by a small swell.

Flailing frantically, she was about to sink when she felt Oliver's arm slide around her waist. Floating effortlessly beside her, he held her up. She caught a quick glimpse of his face, of the intenseness of his expression, before she shut her eyes in a vain attempt to shut out her involuntary reaction to his presence.

"Oliver, *you* must teach Allegra to swim," Violet decided, not noticing the flush on Allegra's creamy skin or the slight tightening of her brother's jaw.

Allegra's eyes flew open in horror at the proposal, but Oliver broke out in a wicked grin. "I'll do my best," he said solemnly.

"Oh, no," Allegra protested loudly and quickly. "Of course, I do appreciate your kind offer," she said, trying to regain her composure and her proper parlor manners. "I really think I have had enough sun and swimming for one day, however. I am beginning to feel a bit weak."

"Just a few more minutes," Lily begged, paddling up beside her. "You'll see, Oliver is a very good teacher. He taught me to swim when I was only four."

"I'm sure he did," Allegra said, swallowing hard and trying to edge away from him. Somehow, the sea kept pushing him closer. Refusing to look him in the face again, although they were only inches apart, she concentrated on the bedraggled bow on the neck of Lily's camisole. "I think, perhaps, I am getting hungry. Shouldn't we eat the lunch we packed?"

That idea appealed to Iris, but Violet and Lily outshouted her. Like a chorus of mermaids they quelled each of Allegra's objections. Oliver ended the argument by saying, much to his own surprise, "Be sensible, Allegra. If you are going to live on an island, you ought to know how to swim."

Allegra was too nonplussed to reply. Oliver's familiar use of her name was as disturbingly intimate as his tacit acceptance of her presence in Grenada.

He took advantage of her silence. Without giving her the chance to make any more excuses, he simply started the lesson.

Smoothly, easily, he flipped her over in the sea, holding her head out of the water and her oddly weightless body suspended. Allegra thrashed about in shock, gasping at the feel of his hands pressed against her belly, separated from her skin by just a wet bit of batiste. Unlike the last time, when his touch practically paralyzed her, now it galvanized her, making her frantic.

"Slowly, Allegra, slowly," Oliver ordered, his firm voice cutting through the frenzy of her feelings. "Kick slowly. Never mind your arms for now. Just kick slowly." He reached out and pinned her hands to her side, his fingers intertwining with hers as he held her arms still. "I won't let you go under," he promised. "Just kick slowly."

Allegra hardly heard what he said. Her heart was thudding wildly. She was aware only of being helpless in the water. And helpless in his hold. "One leg at a time. Up. Down. Slowly, Allegra. I have you. Trust me." Eventually, she did. She responded more to his strength than to his instructions, intuitively knowing he would keep her safe. Her kicking slowed.

"Good for you," Oliver approved. Strangely enough, his compliment seemed to steady her. Her breath came more regularly. "Now for your arms," he said, releasing his grip. "Pull them slowly through the water. Pull. Pull. Here, cup your hands." Once again their fingers twined together as he shaped them into a paddle, his arm resting along the length of hers. "Pull, Allegra. Pull the water toward you."

Gradually, Oliver's insistent directions penetrated. She wasn't sure when, but at some point, she ceased to focus solely on his touch and managed to make sense of his words, as well. Buoyed as much by his plain praise as by his hands still holding her up, she kicked slowly and pulled slowly until suddenly she was swimming.

Violet, Iris, and Lily cheered and sent celebratory geysers sparkling into the air. Oliver applauded. The pride Allegra felt from her accomplishment, and the pleasure she felt from the MacKenzies' rejoicing, were almost as intoxicating as the feel of Oliver's arms wrapped around her under water. Her heart, pounding in agitation only minutes before, now swelled with indescribable elation.

The euphoria carried her ashore like a wave to the beach, washing over her inhibitions, submerging the specter of her gilt-edged book of etiquette. She found herself sitting cross-legged in the sand, only a petticoat and an unbuttoned blouse covering her wet underwear, following the example of the three Grenadian girls. Black and gold curls fluffed in the breeze, damp and disheveled. Oliver lounged opposite them, his white duck trousers rolled up above brown knees.

"We look like castaways," Allegra decided, delighted with the observation. The idea of being marooned on a deserted island, far from accepted civilization, seemed vastly appealing, especially with these four companions.

"What are castaways?" Lily asked, poking around in the picnic basket. "Are they like pirates?" She found a mango and a knife and proceeded to peel away the green skin and to slice through the fibrous orange fruit.

"Pirates have more fun than castaways," Iris answered, taking possession of the hamper. "Pirates come and go as they please. They take people captive and threaten to make them walk the gangplank unless they do exactly as they are told." She found a plate full of pasties stuffed with spicy beef, took two, and passed the rest around. "They can capture a cook and make him bake fancy sweets for them every day. You see, Lily," she explained, wagging a half-eaten pasty, for emphasis, "if we were castaways, we would have to catch fish with our bare hands and eat them uncooked. Being a pirate is much better."

"When I sally forth to seek my prey, I help myself in a royal way," Oliver suddenly sang in a rich, pleasing baritone. "I sink a few more ships, it's true, Than a well-bred monarch ought to do!"

Lily, Iris, and Violet joined him on the chorus.

For I am a pirate king!
And it is, it is a glorious thing
To be a pirate king!

While Oliver sang another refrain from *The Pirates of Penzance*, Allegra sat on the beach beaming, a slice of mango in one hand, a meat pasty in the other, both exotic tastes mingling in her mouth. The flash of undiluted happiness that had filled her four days ago in the boatyard came back full force. She had the definite feeling that she had realized her dreams. Laughing, singing, and swimming, clad only in her underclothes, surrounded by a warm, humorous family who thought she was wonderful, she had escaped a stifling life in favor of adventure and excitement.

Across the stretch of tropical sand, Oliver gave her a grin. Allegra's already full heart fluttered to her throat. Today was absolutely perfect.

It wasn't until they had emptied the hamper, awakened the donkeys, and headed for home, singing snatches of Gilbert & Sullivan most of the way, that reality started to set in along with the sunburn. By evening, Allegra was extremely uncomfortable, both physically and mentally. Her flaming skin succeeded in breaking the magic spell of the beach and in making her increasingly appalled by her behavior a few hours earlier. It was almost as if the sunburn were punishment for her blithe state of undress, her unforgivable immodesty.

For the second time that day, she took off her blouse and unlaced her corset, but this time behind the closed door of the bedroom with only Violet in attendance. While she moaned in anguished embarrassment, Violet split open a fat frond of aloe and solicitously daubed the oozing cactus over Allegra's tender shoulders and back. She winced at first, but as the cool, soothing gel sank in, some of the sting disappeared.

"Is that better?" Violet asked anxiously. She was very distressed by Allegra's sudden switch in moods, and could only imagine that the sunburn was causing it.

"Mmmph," Allegra answered, slumped forward on the chair, her face buried in her hands.

"Allegra," Oliver called, knocking on the door. "I want to talk to you. May I come in?"

"No!" Allegra cried, instantly sitting upright, clutching her blouse in front of her. "No, you can't come in." Her voice held a note of near panic. She couldn't bear to face Oliver fully clothed, let alone in her half-dressed condition. His continued use of her first name served only to heighten her sense of shame. She shut her eyes for a moment. How had she let things get so out of hand? "What do you want to talk about?" she asked.

"This is ridiculous, Allegra," Oliver said. "We can't have a conversation through a wall. If you don't want me to come in, you come out."

"No!" Allegra said again, desperately pushing a handful of blouse high around her neck. "Tell me what you want, Mr. MacKenzie."

"Ahh," Oliver said in such a way, Allegra could practically see him crossing his arms in disgust. "So that's how it is, eh? Very well, Miss Pembroke, I'll tell you what I want." His voice was less friendly than before. "I want you to stay here while I return to L'Etoile tomorrow. I have five-hundred acres of cocoa to harvest, and I can't be bothered playing parlor games with you."

"I am going back to L'Etoile, too," Allegra answered quickly. "I have already told you that I have no intention of staying here indefinitely. My place is at L'Etoile, carrying on the work my father left me." A touch of drama entered her voice as her imagination started to embroider on her inheritance.

"Your father didn't leave you any work," Oliver said bluntly. "Cecil left you half an estate whose whole responsibility he had given to me. If you truly want to follow in his footsteps, you'll do the same."

Allegra wasn't sure how to dispute that remark, so she just repeated stubbornly, "I'm going back to L'Etoile. I mean to live in my father's house."

"I do, as well," Oliver said warningly. "I will not sleep in the boucan anymore. If you come back to L'Etoile, you do so at the risk of your reputation."

"But I've told you my solution," Allegra protested. "I've told you time and again that I mean to find a companion. Once I've done that, it will be perfectly acceptable for you to stay in the great house, too."

"That's enough, Allegra," Oliver snapped, his patience finally worn out from arguing through the door. "We've been over this ground any number of times. Put aside all your gothic notions and be realistic. There are no impoverished war widows or genteel spinsters available for the post."

Violet, who had been standing unhappily through this exchange looking back and forth between Allegra and the closed door, saw an opportunity to end the quarrel and seized it. "A companion?" she said ingenuously. "I can be a companion. I would love to come live at L'Etoile."

"There!" Allegra cried, rising and taking two triumphant steps toward the door. "You see? We've settled the problem." She whirled around and asked Violet, "Are you sure you want to?"

·   When Violet nodded eagerly, Allegra turned back to call through the wall, "It's the perfect answer. There is no one I can think of that I would rather have as my companion than Violet, and surely you can't object to having your own sister in the house." Once again in her enthusiasm, she overlooked a pertinent fact: an eighteen-year-old girl, and a sister to boot, was hardly a suitable chaperon for a twenty-five-year-old woman; if anything, it should be just the reverse.

Oliver's sense of logic was not nearly as befuddled, but he refrained from pointing out the flaw in Allegra's thinking. The fact was, his determination to keep her as far from temptation's path as possible was weakening all the time. Although he had seemed calm and controlled this afternoon when he had held her suspended in the sea, he had been anything but. And when she had sat opposite him in the sand, her wide blue eyes sparkling with life and her lips open with laughter and song, she had been irresistible. It didn't matter that she was now going through another spell of inflexible behavior; he was also uninterested in whether or not Violet was appropriate as a companion. He simply gave in to his desire to have Allegra near him.

"No, I don't have any objections," he said finally. As his footsteps faded down the hall, Violet and Allegra looked at each other, grinning.

Chapter Five

Though Violet may not have filled the requirements for a proper companion, she was, in fact, perfect for this particular position. Her unaffected ways combined with her unreserved admiration created the ideal atmosphere for Allegra's adjustment to her new life. Continuing the process that had started in Carriacou, she let her true spirit surface, a spirit more in tune with the radiance of the tropics than with the chilly climes of Connecticut. She never quite attained that euphoric sense of fulfillment, that absolutely uninhibited elation, that had carried her ashore at Sabazon, but each day she stripped away another dreary layer smothering her soul. She was hesitant, at first, still responding to lifelong reflexes, but she came increasingly to relish the change.

Even her attitude toward Oliver softened. Violet's heartfelt adoration of her big brother had a good deal to do with it, but mostly it was the memory of him lounging in the sand and singing, "I am a pirate king . . ." that eased her stern image of him. He had been so appealing that afternoon, it was hard to remember she had decided he was an unrepentant boor.

It was especially hard to remember how annoyingly frank he could be, because he was absent much of the time, even for meals. Although he was occasionally called away on shipping business, more frequently Oliver deliberately found things to occupy him at the far ends of the estate. His purpose in doing so was a renewed determination to put distance between Allegra and himself.

The more she unraveled her spirit, the more enchanting he

found her, and, ironically, the more impatient he grew with the remnants of her rigid propriety. Even while he was admonishing himself to keep their relationship on a business level, he was wishing he could break down the last few barriers blocking her spontaneous nature. One morning at breakfast, this desire overcame all caution, and collided head on with Allegra's still tentative identity.

"Elizabeth told me the name of a good dressmaker in Gouyave," Allegra said to Violet while dabbing tinned Danish butter on crispy cassava bread toast. "Perhaps this morning we can ride down and see her. I'm afraid the clothes I brought with me are not really meant for such heat. Even my summer linens are too heavy." She scooped a spoonful of guava jelly onto her plate and began to spread it on the toast. "I think I should have more muslins and Egyptian cottons," she decided, biting into the delectable morsel.

"Victoria lawn is always comfortable," Violet offered, thrilled to be participating in such sophisticated prattle. Around the table in Carriacou, they discussed the comparative qualities of cedar planks or salt pork, never fine fabrics and fashion.

"If you are really interested in comfort," Oliver interrupted with characteristic bluntness, "you should do away with your corset." He ignored Allegra's gasp of shock and the sound of her butter knife clattering to her plate. "It's a cruel contraption in any climate, more like a cage than a piece of clothing, but in this temperature, it is deadly. You'll do yourself an enormous favor if you discard yours."

"How could you?" Allegra asked, her face flushed, embarrassment making her stammer and washing away all the gains she had made. "How could you speak to me that way? Just because I've overlooked your forwardness in addressing me by my first name, it doesn't give you permission to become so, so... personal." Her face turned redder just saying the word. "You are taking advantage of my cordiality," she added accusingly. She pushed back her chair and stood to deliver her parting shot. "It's a scandalous breach of etiquette."

Having made her objection, she twirled away from the table with what she hoped would be haughty grandeur. Unfortunately, her swinging arm knocked over a pot of tea, and, as she tried to escape the ensuing splash, her foot caught on the leg of the chair.

The next thing she knew, she was pitching headfirst toward the floor.

Oliver caught her before she fell. He had risen as she did and was rounding the table as she twirled, somehow sensing what was going to come next. He snared her around the waist and set her upright, but didn't release her immediately. Instead, he tapped his fingers on the whalebones hugging her ribs. "This is a lethal device," he said in complete disregard of her speech. "And it's squeezing the life out of you. Your ability to breathe is not governed by etiquette."

Allegra's ability to breathe, or rather her difficulty in doing so, was governed neither by etiquette nor by her corset, but by the hands spanning her waist and by the dark blue eyes fixed intently on her own. As in the past, his touch set her heart racing and sent a disturbingly intimate tingle through all her limbs. It took a tremendous force of will to return her concentration to his offensive conduct. "Really, Mr. MacKenzie," she rebuked faintly, trying with a trembling hand to disengage herself. "This discussion is most inappropriate."

"Inappropriate?" Oliver repeated, giving her an annoyed shake. "Do you ever worry about anything besides some arbitrary standard of appropriateness? As far as I am concerned, it is much more inappropriate to faint dead away or to go into shock because your liver is squeezing your lungs."

Allegra found that graphic description extremely unsettling. It effectively banished all the pleasurable thoughts and feelings Oliver's nearness brought on and set her on course. She pulled free of his grip and took a few steps back, drawing herself up with dignity. "This has gone far enough," she said severely. "I think you are forgetting yourself."

Far from being intimidated by her tone, Oliver greeted her dramatic cliché with a shake of his head. "I very seldom forget myself," he said, a hint of amusement edging out the frustration in his voice. "However, I believe *you* are forgetting yourself. Or perhaps I would be more correct in saying you are disowning yourself. You are a lively, spirited woman who is, at the moment, living in a climate completely incompatible with the corsets, gloves, and silly bonnets so in favor in the north.

"It is another English—and by extension, American—conceit to think that the clothes you wear in winter weather are somehow more civilized than those worn by the natives of the tropics." He paused to snort contemptuously. "What they are is ridiculous. You don't see Indians and Africans parading around in the noonday sun in woolen worsteds and neckties. It positively defies nature. You would do very well not to forget *that* fact, Miss Pembroke," he said pointedly. "Try not to forget you are living on a working estate only twelve degrees north of the equator; that you are not a debutante in the Court of St. James."

"I could scarcely forget that, Mr. MacKenzie," Allegra retorted genuinely angered by his insinuations. "When I am continually confronted by your rudeness and incessant bullying. How could I fail to remember that I am at the back door of refined society? Your vulgar manners are a constant reminder."

Oliver started to reply, then changed his mind. Instead, he just shook his head and left the room. Allegra plumped her hands on her hips and glared after him, her heart now beating in wrath.

From the silence behind her came an awed sigh from Violet and a chuckle from Elizabeth. "Well, I mean to say," she said, stacking plates of empty grapefruit rinds onto a tray, "you told him plain and straight. Just the way he does."

"I've never heard anyone but Papa talk to him like that," Violet agreed.

Allegra spun around to face the audience she had forgotten was watching this scene, her anger instantly dissolving into shamefaced chagrin. One hand clapped over her mouth, initially in a gesture of embarrassment, but as her natural good humor returned it covered a giggle. "I suppose I got carried away," she admitted, without any show of remorse. "I'm afraid his attitude is contagious."

She thought she was referring only to Oliver's brusque way of speaking, but when she and Violet rode down to Gouyave later that morning, her gloves and parasol were left behind. At the time, she rationalized that her gloves would only be ruined by the reins and that the parasol was too awkward to handle from the back of a burro. However, when she stood in front of Mrs. Straker's mirror, being measured for new dresses, her corset lying crumpled on the floor, Allegra grudgingly acknowledged Oliver's influence extended further than she had first thought. Although she was much more comfortable, she remained irritated with him for being so ungraciously right. Again.

* * *

For a while, Allegra found just living at L'Etoile sufficient to satisfy herself. She enjoyed Violet's constant company and Elizabeth's occasional placid commentary. The almost daily donkey rides to Gouyave for fittings at Mrs. Straker's and for tea and sweets at Matthewlina Cameron's cafe, were enough of an adventure. Life in Grenada was growing on her.

"Ivy and Jane got titiri in Gouyave this morning," Elizabeth announced from her station behind the kitchen table one day. "But maybe you don't like them for dinner."

"I'm certain that I do," Allegra replied, setting her dishes from a lazy, late breakfast in the sink. "What are they?"

"Little fishes," Elizabeth said. "This little." She held out her knife and laid a finger across it an inch from the tip.

"They're no bigger than bits of twine," Violet added, "but when they're dipped in a batter and fried into cakes, they're delicious. Do you use orange peel for flavor, Elizabeth?"

"Sive and time," Elizabeth answered calmly.

Violet laughed at the puzzled expression on Allegra's face. "Chives and thyme," she translated. "We always use them together. They're even sold in one bunch at the Saturday market."

"It sounds very tasty," Allegra decided. "I'm willing to try anything Elizabeth cooks. Well, *almost* anything," she amended. "I can't say I'm ready for that dish you call sea eggs. Those slippery lumps of sea urchin are not at all appealing." She gave an exaggerated shudder as she sat down on a stool. Too late she realized it was Oliver's preferred perch, but after an instant she shrugged away her anxiety.

"You missing something good," Elizabeth warned, taking her usual place on the edge of the table. "Sea eggs are my favorite."

"I love them, too," Violet said, settling herself on the other stool, "but I understand if you don't want to try them. I think you are being very gracious about sampling our island foods, Allegra. After all, you like to eat boiled beef and potatoes, and we never have them here."

"Oh, no," Allegra said, waving both hands in correction of that mistaken idea. "It was Grandfather who liked them. In fact, he wouldn't accept anything else for his supper. Which was just as well, I suppose, because I am as much a menace with pots and pans as I am with a needle." Leaning back against the wall, she cheerfully confessed, "I haven't got the patience."

"I know you are being too modest," Violet said loyally. "If *I* can cook, I'm sure you can. With your imagination you must think up wonderful meals."

"I can think them up," Allegra admitted, "but what a time I have making them. I remember I decided once to cook an elaborate French meal. You see," she said, propping her feet on a stack of empty crates, "I had just read a novel in which a beautiful girl is kidnapped by a dashing French count who is determined to marry her. He takes her to his chateau where he gives her magnificent gowns and priceless jewels. When she comes down to dinner, the table is laid with crystal and silver and exquisite porcelain plates. Course after course is set before her: caviar on toast points, roast quail in pâté choux, prawn and salmon terrain . . . well, it went on and on.

"I spent our whole week's food budget and all day in the kitchen trying to duplicate even a few of the courses. I'll never forget the look on Grandfather's face when he saw what was for supper." She laughed now at the memory, although at the time she had been in tears. "He told me never, ever to be so frivolous again." With another laugh she concluded, "I can't say that I blamed him that much. It did taste dreadful."

"Prawns probably too old," Elizabeth said.

It didn't take long, though, for Allegra's newly awakened senses and her freshly alerted mind to get a little restless. The more she became her own person, the more of a person she wanted to become. She still couldn't define who she wanted to be, or how she wanted to go about the transformation, but she was more sure than ever that she wanted it to happen. She knew, also, that it was connected to Cecil.

It took a visit by Col. Horace Woodbury to set her on the right track. It was not the track that Woody, as he was called by his male cronies, would have knowingly suggested. His military life in various equatorial colonies had firmly fixed his ideas about where a woman belonged: either on a pedestal or in a brothel, but absolutely not in business, politics, or anywhere near the cocoa boucan.

While Allegra sensed his attitude and was not at all unfamiliar with it, it didn't stop her from tagging along when Oliver and Woody went off after lunch to inspect the cocoa crop. She was less intimidated by Woody's outlook now than she would have been just a few weeks ago. Besides, she was bored. Violet was upstairs in bed, sleeping off a bad batch of sea eggs (justifying

Allegra's suspicion of them), and Allegra was already tired of reading, stitching, and painting watercolors.

Although she had always cast a curious eye at the stir around the sheds as she rode by the boucan on her way down to Gouyave, she knew only vaguely what really went on. Now, as she entered the area, her interest was aroused. "This is wonderful," she exclaimed, looking about.

Five buildings built of planks, louvers, and galvanized tin roofs sat around a vast cement yard. The biggest, standing along one entire side, had eight doors and twelve batten windows, hinged at the top and propped open with sticks. Steel rails ran into the yard on raised cement cracks, and immense wooden trays on wheels ran on top of those. Donkeys and workers moved back and forth; little children raced. Everywhere there was activity. And everywhere there were cocoa beans. Millions of cocoa beans. White ones, beige ones, and chocolate-brown ones. Baskets of them, sacks of them, trays full of them.

"Think how many rabbits we can buy," Allegra said, awestruck.

Woody looked puzzled at the remark, but Oliver laughed, pleased that Allegra remembered his lesson on the ancient Indians' system of cocoa bean currency. "Lower your sights," he advised dryly. "Not all the beans belong to us. Twenty percent of the cocoa we process belongs to planters with very small holdings, five acres at the most. They bring their raw beans here to sweat and to dry, and in return they help us harvest our crop. See?" he said, kicking one of the huge wooden trays, totally covered by a carpet of purplish brown beans. "This drawer is Gabriel Mitchell's cocoa. His name is chalked on the side."

Allegra was bursting with questions. "What do you mean they bring their beans to sweat?" she demanded. "And why do you call it a drawer? Which is *our* cocoa? Is it the browner?"

Woody's look of puzzlement was replaced by one of annoyance. "I say, Miss Pembroke," he interrupted, barely concealing his dislike for her interference. "MacKenzie is a most capable chap. Suggest you leave the business to him and not bother your head with these matters."

It was Allegra's turn to look confused. Although she resented the colonel's condescending remarks, she didn't want to seem a nuisance, either. She wasn't sure whether she ought to withdraw in demure silence or continue her questioning. Once again, Oliver came to her rescue.

"It won't do to have an uninformed partner, Woody," he said easily. "It's bad advertising." When Allegra gave him a surprised but grateful glance, he gave her a grin. "Let me answer your questions in their correct order," he suggested, directing himself again to Allegra. "Come."

He led the way to a building on the other side of the yard, completely enclosed except for a door on each end. "This is the sweating house," he explained. "It's the first stop for the beans when they leave the groves." He stepped inside the building. Allegra and Woody followed. Groups of six wooden boxes, almost like small stalls, sat along the walls. The smell of fermentation that permeated the yard was particularly pungent in here.

"The fresh beans get dumped into the first bin of a group," Oliver said, stopping by a six-foot tall stall. "They are covered with banana leaves and left for three days." Allegra stood on tiptoe and peered over the edge of the planks. It was full to the brim. Oliver lifted a layer of banana leaves for her inspection, and a cloud of tiny white flies shot into the air. Startled, Allegra took a step back. But when Oliver told her that the bugs were harmless, she leaned back over the gate to look at the incredible pulpy mass of white and pale, pale pink beans.

"They start sweating almost immediately," Oliver said. "Feel them. Go ahead, stick your hand in there." Allegra gingerly laid a few fingers in the box. She withdrew them quickly, amazed at the heat. "Do you feel how hot it is?" Oliver asked. "The temperature can reach 140 degrees. It's this fermentation that dissolves the pulp covering the beans, literally sweats it away. It also sets up a chemical reaction that gradually changes the color and the flavor of the bean. You might say that the chocolate is born right here."

He let the leaves fall back into place and moved on to the next bin. "After the third day, the beans are transferred into here. We use these wooden spades so as not to damage the cocoa." He pointed to a hand-hewn mahogany shovel leaning against one wall. "They need to be stirred daily and exposed to air, or they'll turn black and be ruined. So each day we shift them to a new bin. By the end of the eighth day, they're finished sweating."

Allegra skipped the intermediate stalls and peeked into the last box. It was only a little better than half full, but the beans were clean and brown. "This must not have been a full batch," she said innocently.

Woody gave a small sigh of exasperation at such ignorance, but Oliver patiently explained. "It was full to the top eight days ago," he said, watching the colonel's unspoken criticism send a lovely pink blush over Allegra's face. "They lose almost forty percent of their mass in the fermentation process, and they're still a long way from dry. That's the next step. That's what we do in the drawers. Come, I'll show you." He gently beckoned her back in the yard, wishing that the hovering, harumphing Woody would disappear.

"First off," he said, standing in the center of a sea of brown beans spread out in the room-sized trays, "they are called drawers because they slide underneath the building like drawers in a bureau. Or, on some estates, there are just roofs that slide over them." He gave a shove with his foot, and the twelve-foot-wide tray rumbled on its steel wheels into the cement foundation of the big building. He shoved on a second, slightly narrower drawer, and it slid in under the first. A wooden hatch dropped down over them, sealing them inside.

"The beans need the sun to dry," Oliver said, going forward to retrieve the drawers. "But if it gets too strong in the middle of the day, they can get parched or shriveled. Then, in they go, until the sun wanes a wee bit."

"Mustn't get too damp, either," Woody pointed out imperiously.

"Right," Oliver said, a touch tightly. "I was just getting to that." His tone eased again as he turned to Allegra. "They are also pushed inside at sunset, or on rainy days. If they get too wet at the improper moment, they'll rot. But if all goes well, in another eight days they're dry."

"Is that what the other drawers are for?" Allegra asked, nodding her head to indicate the other fifteen drawers lying open in the yard. "Must they be moved from drawer to drawer each day, like the sweating beans?"

Oliver smiled appreciatively at her logical question, but shook his head. "It isn't necessary to transfer them, although they do need stirring," he answered. "Otherwise they'll stick or cake. It's done in the tray, with wooden hoes. Watch over there. Eleanor is turning the beans." Allegra looked toward the farthest drawer and saw a tiny woman, armed with a long-handled hoe, carefully pushing the beans from place to place, occasionally bending over to pick out a bad one.

"They're almost ready," Oliver observed, half to himself, half to Allegra, his gaze fixed on the far drawer.

"How can you tell?" Allegra demanded, doing her best to ignore another irritated snort from Colonel Woodbury.

Oliver turned his attention back to her. "Experience," he said solemnly.

"Oh," Allegra said, dropping her gaze in respect.

Oliver's heart surged at the sight of her eyelashes feathering delicately on her cheeks and of a few wild curls bumping against the freckles on her forehead. His voice remained level, however, as he elaborated. "There are a few signs to watch for," he said. When Allegra's eyes came up again, he couldn't resist. He reached his hand out, wrapping his fingers around her arm, and guided her over the rails to where Eleanor was working. "Here," he said, picking up a dark, reddish brown bean and squeezing it between his thumb and forefinger. A hard outer shell shattered, revealing a chocolate-colored kernel. "This, finally," he said, "is what makes cocoa. This is what it should look like."

Allegra tried desperately to concentrate on the bit of bean laying in the palm of his hand rather than on the involuntary tingle his touch always brought. In the end, her interest in cocoa overcame, barely, the distraction of his contact. With slightly trembling fingers, she picked up the kernel and gave it a nibble. "Well," she pondered, her face screwing up in an attempt to identify its flavor. "It doesn't taste as nasty as it did when it was raw, but it doesn't taste like chocolate, either."

"Has to be roasted, for pity's sake," Woody snapped, all out of patience.

Starting at the vehemence in the colonel's voice, Allegra looked quickly at Oliver to see if he were equally provoked. He wasn't. He gave her a slow smile. Although she again felt her heart leap, she also thought it was wiser to relieve their guest of any additional suffering. "So now they are sacked up and shipped away," she concluded hastily, turning to find her way out of the yard.

"Not quite," Oliver said, reaching out and seizing her arm again. He wasn't as concerned with Woody's comfort as she was; he was enjoying her curiosity too much. "This last is the part that will amuse you the most, Allegra."

Another wave of pink flooded her face. It was one thing for him to call her by her first name in front of Violet, but it had an entirely different connotation in front of a man like the colonel. That intimacy, combined with the renewed thrill of his hand holding onto her, left her powerless to speak. Heart thumping, she turned back to the drawer.

"When the cocoa is thoroughly cured," Oliver said, pretending to be unaware of her agitation, "it is sprinkled with water."

"I thought it wasn't supposed to get wet," Allegra protested, her fascination with the lecture once again overcoming her fascination with the lecturer. "It will rot."

"It will if it's wet down before it's been cured," Oliver agreed. "But at this stage, it's part of the polishing process. After it's been dampened, a couple of people get into the tray and polish the beans with their bare feet. They scuffle around and sometimes work up a rhythm. We call it dancing the cocoa."

"Dancing the cocoa," Allegra repeated in delight. "That's lovely." She beamed at Oliver. Even if she hadn't already found the cultivation and curing of cocoa an utterly intriguing occupation, this one phrase would have won her over. "Dancing the cocoa in the boucan," she murmured again, savoring the expression. "Truly, it sounds like a scene from *Alice in Wonderland*."

"Nonsense," Woody scoffed, vindicated in his belief that exactly such silly notions were always the result when women interfered in serious affairs. "Just a fanciful local term for polishing the beans. Must be done, you know," he added. "Spoil in three to four months if they aren't polished."

For a moment there was silence as Allegra waited for the colonel to tell her how long they would last if they *were* polished, but Woody offered no further information. She opened her mouth to ask her question, then closed it again, dreading another peeved reply.

"The cocoa will stay about a year if it's properly polished," Oliver said smoothly, anticipating her problem. "After it's danced, we leave it another day in the sun to make sure it is completely dry. And then, finally, it's sorted and put into sacks, ready for shipping. Come inside and I'll show you where the last bit of the process occurs." He motioned her up three stairs to one of the open doors.

Allegra went willingly, stepping over the threshold into an extraordinary room. The building looked even bigger on the inside than it did from without, much longer than it was wide, well over a hundred feet, with a peaked roof twenty feet high. Exposed rafters and studs and side wallboards were unpainted, providing dark, cool relief from the brightness outside. Except for blocks of sunshine on the burnished plank floor in front of the doors and propped up windows, the light was mercifully mute.

At the far end of the room sat a giant wire-mesh contraption with four chutes on the front and a huge crank on the side. It was silent at the moment, but well-muscled men were loading baskets of beans in the tops of the chutes, and a burly youth was stepping up to the crank.

"It's our sorting machine," Oliver explained, leading Allegra closer. "It sorts the beans into four size groups. The small size is mostly chaff and broken bits; the largest size is usually double beans that were sealed together during fermentation. And the two in between sizes are the bulk of the yield. Number three is superior."

As Oliver finished talking, the young man started turning the handle and an unholy noise arose. The sound of thousands of beans clattering against metal filled the air. Even when they moved away from the machine, normal speech was impossible. Allegra contented herself with looking around and absorbing the engrossing atmosphere.

In one corner, two men sat stenciling a star and the legend, COCOA L'ETOILE GRENADA BRITISH WEST INDIES 180 LBS. on each of a tall pile of burlap bags. In another corner, straining workers wrestled each full sack onto a platform scale, checking its weight. Scattered around the area, women with rapidly darting needles stitched closed the bags. Other men stacked the finished sacks against every available inch of wall. There were hundreds of bulging bags, untold tons of cocoa beans grown in rich soil, cured under the Caribbean sun, and smelling like the tropics and fermentation and burlap sacking and, ever so faintly, like chocolate. Allegra loved it all.

That evening at dinner, away from Woody's disapproving presence, Allegra asked dozens more questions. Violet was still absent, having taken some weak broth and dry biscuits on a tray in her room, and Oliver and Allegra were alone at the enormous dining table. Allegra never gave a thought to the possible impropriety of the situation, her attention fixed on the subject of cocoa.

She demanded more information, and Oliver, pleased by her interest, supplied it.

He told her that there were two types of cocoa, Forastero and Criollo; that the coarser Forastero provided the body of chocolate while the more delicate Criollo was the flavor bean. He described how the first cocoa trees were probably planted in Grenada around 1714, and how last season over eight million pounds of cocoa were exported. He explained that the cocoa grown in Grenada, along with that grown in Trinidad, was considered to be the finest in the world. "Cocoa was once nicknamed 'the golden bean,'" he concluded, "because of the fortune it's made for so many men."

Allegra listened with fascination to everything, even the most unexciting facts. She was totally capitivated. When Oliver paused for breath and a bite of fried flying fish, she blurted out, "I want to help. You must let me help with the harvest." She had no idea what role she could possibly play, but she wanted to be involved. She felt strongly that the key to fulfilling her unspoken, imprecise ambition to make something of her life lay somewhere in Cecil's cocoa.

Oliver, however, had slightly different feelings. Swallowing hastily, he answered, "We really have things worked out very well. There's no way that you could give any help." Although he found her keen curiosity refreshing and delightful, he was not anxious to have her participate in the daily activity. Not only was he still attempting, albeit with decreasing determination, to keep her at arm's length, but he was also well aware that she was Cecil's daughter. While he enjoyed the great spirit they shared, he was under no illusions about their ability to do business. The fire-bright enthusiasm, the ever spinning imagination, the unlimited sense of fantasy and adventure had no place in the repetitious tasks and the tedious tallying that built up a successful concern.

With rare diplomacy, though, he sought to moderate his unequivocal rejection. "If you really want to help with the estate," he said, "there are any number of things that require attention right here in the house. We need someone to take charge of the household, of all the details that make life so comfortable but require so much time and talent." He ignored the ominous pause in Elizabeth's step and the murderous glance she threw at him as she yanked his half full plate from under his fork. "I am quite confident you will do best applying yourself in that manner."

The eager hunch of Allegra's shoulders slumped. "I suppose so." She sighed. For all the changes she had made in the last few weeks, she was not yet certain enough of herself to overthrow ingrained attitudes. All her life she had accepted, with unspoken frustration, her grandfather's views. Listening to Oliver now, her frustration deepened, but her acceptance remained. Watching her from across the table, Oliver was surprised it was not relief he felt at her mild tone, but a strange sense of disappointment.

The next few days brought no further opportunity for Allegra to pursue her fledgling interest in cocoa. Violet recovered rapidly and reclaimed Allegra's attention with their daily trips to Gouyave and with her insatiable demand for tales of the world beyond Grenada. Though the golden beans never ceased to tickle the far corners of her mind, Allegra willingly allowed herself to be distracted. On the weekend, Jamie Forsythe arrived, having begged to be invited for some fishing, some good food, and a respite from work. In the excitement of hostessing her first house party, however small and informal, all thoughts of cocoa receded from Allegra's mind.

As she remembered from those first two confusing days in Grenada, Jamie was courteous, kind and very easygoing. Immediately comfortable with him, she was glad he had come. She was amused by his mock laziness and amazed by his ability to manipulate the indomitable Oliver. Within two hours of his arrival, he had routed Oliver from the cocoa groves and had him, racket in hand, on the tennis lawn, all the while marveling at his good fortune in falling into such a tailor-made doubles match. Allegra found herself chasing a tennis ball under the hot sun, panting and laughing and enjoying life immensely.

It was only when she descended for dinner that evening, refreshed by a long, cool bath, that she was reminded of the business of L'Etoile. Politely and unimposingly, Jamie pulled her into the library for a private chat. Although he had come to the estate to escape from work, he had nonetheless carried some with him. "I've had a cable, finally, from Cecil's London solicitors," he said, plumping up the chintz-covered cushions of a small setee and motioning her to sit. While Allegra sat down, suddenly tense, Jamie flung himself into an armchair.

"They're a tight-lipped lot," he continued, shaking his head ruefully. "I can just see them hovering over my querying cable, trying to determine how they can answer it and still divulge as little information as possible. They're guarding Cecil's will as if it were state secrets."

"You're going to tell me that I haven't inherited L'Etoile after all, aren't you?" Allegra blurted out fearfully. A melodramatic scenario instantly sprouted in her mind, replete with a clandestine lover and destitute children and even a faithful valet all claiming first place in Cecil's affections.

"No, no, no," Jamie reassured her, erasing the image before an ancient but wonderfully wise nanny could be added to the list of legatees. "You are your father's sole heir. They did commit themselves to that, but they said that all other details would follow by post. My guess is, however," he added, tapping the arm of the chair with the tip of his forefinger, "that there aren't any other details of substance. Only the tedious, technical items that solicitors invent to keep themselves in business."

When Allegra gave a tremulous smile, weak with relief, Jamie said, "I may not have drawn up the will, but Cecil discussed it with me at one time. Despite his irregular approach to being a parent, I know that you were dear to him and that he meant for you to inherit everything he had."

A tear suddenly rolled down Allegra's cheek. A fresh wave of sorrow swept over her, grief at having lost this gallant man before she could know him. She was moved by his decision to leave the results of his life's dreams and endeavors in her hands. I won't betray your trust, she silently promised the ghost of her father. And I won't let your vision be lost. I'll work hard to make sure L'Etoile carries on as you created it.

No sooner had she made that solemn vow than another thought struck. This was what she had been looking for, the direction she had been seeking. Here was her chance to do something and to become someone important. By assuming Cecil's role at L'Etoile, she could also assume his luster and purpose.

I knew it, she thought, still addressing her father's spirit. I knew that you and your cocoa would help me. I knew it from my first days in Grenada. In fact, I knew it from the moment I read your letters to Mother. That's why I came here, and oh, Papa, I'm so glad I did.

Her heart grew full as she contemplated Cecil's magnificent gift. By passing on his dreams, he was fulfilling hers. *Thank you*, she thought fervently. You won't regret this. I won't let you down.

"I'll make my father proud of me," she said out loud.

Jamie looked at her, dressed for dinner in lilac silk with rows of ruffles around her shoulders and her lovely neck. Her curls for once were behaving, brushed until they gleamed like old gold. Her wide eyes were lit with inspiration and resolve. "I'm sure you will," he answered softly, thinking how pleased Cecil would have been with the picture she presented. His blue eyes would have lit up, as they so often did. Cecil had admired, above everything, great beauty and spirit. "I'm sure you already have."

Allegra had no chance to implement her decision that evening, but this time it didn't disappear. It remained fixed in her mind all through dinner. With only half an ear, she listened as Violet and Oliver alternately pumped a genial Jamie for the social and business gossip of St. George's.

In answer to Violet's questions, Jamie told her about the pomp and ceremony and seventeen-gun salute to greet the arrival of Sir Charles Bruce, the new governor of the Windward Islands. He told her that Lady Bruce had announced she would receive visitors on Wednesdays from 4:30 until 6:00 P.M. Ignoring Oliver's exclamation of disgust with these royal trappings, he went on to tell Violet that the plans had been laid for Royston Ross's annual New Year's Eve ball at his enormous house overlooking St. George's.

Finally acceding to Oliver's demands for more serious news, he told him that the new governor was well thought of and that he had done his time in the tropics, having served in Mauritius, Ceylon, and British Guyana. He told Oliver that reports of the cocoa crop seemed favorable, though it was still very early; some estates had just barely begun picking. In a grimmer tone, he also reported an increase in cocoa raids around the island.

"The bandits are doing their deed in the middle of the night," he lamented. "When all good folks are asleep, they come tippy-toeing in to steal the fruits of another man's labor." He shook his head in dismay at such immorality. "There are even those who are hiding cocoa in coffins, relying on superstition to keep the suspicious from prying. It's a disgrace."

"It's even more of a disgrace that nothing is done about it," Oliver amended harshly. "Those rogues are too busy wasting ammunition saluting the new governor to do something that might actually help the citizens of Grenada. While the large landholder might be only discommoded by a theft of cocoa, the small grower can be devastated. As always, though, the official policy of the colonial government seems to be indifference to the planters' plight."

"It's not simply government indifference that is devastating the planter," Jamie corrected, only half defending the Crown. "It is also the greed and dishonesty of some agents and shippers."

"You are, no doubt, referring to Argo," Oliver said. It was more a cold statement than a question. When Jamie nodded briefly, Oliver went on. "I heard in St. Vincent's that Argo is applying pressure. Barely veiled threats. That sort of thing."

Jamie nodded again, a bit more sadly. "I suppose this is as good a time as any to tell you that Star Shipping has lost another account to Argo."

Oliver waved a hand in dismissal. "That would be the Mt. Pleasant Estate, am I right? They're in St. Andrew's Parish, too near Argo Estate to do otherwise. I expected them to switch long before this."

The conversation was interrupted by Elizabeth, bearing a platter of bananas flambé. "Figs on fire," she announced matter-of-factly, calling the fruit by its local name. The somber mood was broken, and Jamie gladly changed the subject.

"Enough of this gloom and doom," he decided. "I came here to be entertained. Oliver, stop grinding your jaw and play us a few tunes after the sweet. Some of your beloved Gilbert and Sullivan would set the world right again."

Oliver broke into an obliging grin, but Allegra, whose full attention had been restored by the discussion of cocoa theft, demanded, "What do you mean, 'Play us a few tunes?'" She turned to Oliver. "Is it *you* who plays the piano?" Somehow she had assumed that the grand piano in the billiard room belonged to her father.

"It's always a surprise to discover our friend has a few refinements, isn't it?" Jamie answered in Oliver's place. "Just when we are thinking there is no hope for him, that he is the despair of civilized living, he'll pull some pretty trick out of his tattered sleeve and we all think the world of him again!"

"Yes," Allegra agreed, "it's true." She remembered how her opinion of him had changed that day at Sabazon, softened by his singing and by his gentleness with his sisters. Then realizing what she had said, she turned bright red and stared at her plate.

Although a smile pulled at the corners of Oliver's mouth,

Jamie seemed not to notice her embarrassment. "Truthfully, Allegra," he said sympathetically. (He had started calling her by her given name in the middle of the tennis match, following the example of the MacKenzies.) "I don't know how you have stood him all this time. I half-expected to arrive here and find you raving mad or in a puddle of tears. Instead, you seem to have bloomed since I last saw you. Either you are blind and deaf, or life at L'Etoile agrees with you exceedingly." While Oliver grinned devilishly, Allegra mumbled a reply.

She regained her composure by the next day's fishing expedition, sitting in the sixteen-foot sailing dory Angus had built for exactly such a purpose. It was another brilliantly sunny day, making the refreshing breeze on the water welcome. A basket of food sat at their feet, from which everyone pulled out pieces of fried chicken or cucumber and mint sandwiches as the mood struck. Allegra contentedly cast her line over the side and occasionally hauled in small jackfish. More often than not, however, she ignored the tentative nibbles on the end of her hook, willingly allowing her bait to be stolen while she gloried in the day.

"Why do we only catch jackfish?" she asked idly, watching a flying fish sail out of the water ten yards away, glitter briefly in the sun, and disappear beneath the navy blue swells. "Why don't we catch flying fish? Don't they eat the same bait?"

"Flying fish don't eat anything but the wind," Oliver answered seriously. "That's what makes them fly."

Allegra turned toward him quickly, an incredulous expression on her face. She was about to voice her disbelief when she saw the crinkles of humor around his eyes and heard Violet's giggle. With a sheepish smile, she turned her attention to lunch, rummaging around in the hamper until she found a slice of baked breadfruit pie and a bottle of limeade. Jamie eyed her plate and reached into the basket in search of another piece of pie. A satisfied sigh accompanied his discovery.

"There is no one who can cook like Elizabeth," he said, savoring the custardy mix of onions and seasonings and mashed breadfruit. He took another huge bite, chewed it slowly, stretched his legs out in front of him, and adjusted the panama hat shading his fair face. He sighed again, his pleasure evident.

"If I were in your shoes, Allegra," he mused, "I'd buy the most comfortable hammock I could find, string it between some trees, and only stir from it for meals and fishing trips. Och, what a life."

"I, on the other hand, intend to take part in the work of the estate," she announced with such determination Oliver's jaw tightened and Jamie's jaw dropped.

"Work?" he cried, aghast. "Whatever for? There's Oliver to do the cocoa, with Septimus Stephen to take over when he's away. There's Elizabeth to do the cooking, and Jane and Ivy to do the house. Mrs. Straker can do all your sewing, and you have me to take care of anything else. Why would you want to work?" The very idea was unimaginable to him. "Besides, what is there left to do?"

"I mean to work with the cocoa," Allegra answered airily. "I mean to become involved in every aspect of the business, from growing to shipping." She could practically see her father up in heaven, smiling his approval. The image filled her with pleasure.

Again Jamie tried to dissuade her, tactfully pointing out how unnecessary it was. When his delicately stated points made no impression, Oliver cut in. "It's a ridiculous notion," he said bluntly. "What could you possibly do?" Although his question was essentially the same as Jamie's, his tone was entirely different. It gave Allegra pause, her happy image fading.

"Well, I'm not precisely sure," she said. "But there's bound to be something." She had been so taken by the general idea, she hadn't concentrated on the specifics.

"There isn't," Oliver replied. "There's nothing that you can do. By your own admission, you know nothing about growing cocoa. Until a few weeks ago, you thought it grew in a tin, wanting only milk and sugar to make a finished product. The best help you can give is to leave the cocoa to me."

As accustomed as Allegra had become to Oliver's outspokenness, her confidence was not yet strong enough to withstand this unvarnished attack. The absolute authority in his tone created a reflexive ripple of self-doubt, and with the uncertainty came clumsiness. At a loss for an immediate reply, she started to tidy up the lunch things, awkwardly shoving cups and plates into the basket.

"There must be something I can do," she started to insist when her inept packing dislodged a linen napkin. Freed from its biscuit-tin anchor, the embroidered bit of cloth blew over the side. Hastily rising to seize it, Allegra followed suit.

This time no strong arm broke her fall, no steadying hand set her safely upright. Her cry of distress was cut off by a choking mouthful of water. She plunged deeper into the sea, her frantic gulps for breath stifled by salt water searing her lungs, her kicking legs helplessly tangled in her skirt and petticoat, the soaked mass of mutton sleeves weighing down her arms. She kept sinking, terrified.

Just when she thought her limbs would break in utter exhaustion, when her body would burst for want of breath, she was grabbed around the waist and carried upward. She broke the surface, coughing and sputtering, greedily gasping for air. Still overwhelmed by the ocean, still overcome by panic, she kicked weakly, struggling, too frightened to notice the look of relief on Oliver's face at having fished her out alive.

"I've got you, Allegra," he said urgently. "I've got you and I won't let you go under again. Stop fighting. You're safe now." His own heart was beating rapidly, catching up with his reaction to seeing her fall overboard. Knowing that her one brief swimming lesson would never be sufficient to keep her afloat in this situation, he had tossed the main sheet to Jamie and had dived in after her, fear lending power to his muscles as he stroked swiftly toward the spot where she had disappeared. He held her now, stunned by the ferocity of his emotional response. "I've got you, Allegra," he repeated more tenderly.

He pushed off her shoes and skinnied her skirt up around her waist. "That should make it easier," he said. "Just kick slowly, like I taught you at Sabazon. As if you were taking a stroll." He ran his hand down her leg to regulate the rhythm, calming her faint flailing, settling her frenzied nerves.

Allegra shivered, then gulped, then gripped Oliver's arms. As his steady strength and cool commands placated her terror, she yielded to his protection. She wholeheartedly accepted his reassurances and obeyed his instructions. She clung to him with absolute faith.

Oliver was so moved by the trust in her wide, violet-blue eyes, so stirred by the sight of her lovely face straining toward him, he couldn't resist the temptation. Slowly, still treading water, he pulled her closer, held her tighter, touched his lips to hers. When she didn't resist but seemed, imperceptibly, to relax in his hold, he kissed her again, longer, more fully, rolling his wet cheek against hers.

This time, Allegra was not in the thrall of some drummed-in sense of decorum; the bleakness of Connecticut winters and her grandfather's parlor remained thousands of miles away. This time, she responded only to the vast Caribbean Sea carrying her up and down swells, to the bright sun blazing over her head, and to the powerful man embracing her. She responded to the sanctuary of his arms and to the salty taste of his mouth pressed against hers. This time, she responded to Oliver.

For a moment, they were all alone in the ocean, their bodies tugged apart and bumped together by the waves. For a moment, Allegra felt her whole being almost ache with uninhibited desire, fed by Oliver's kiss, by the feel of his lips on her skin. For a moment, she abandoned herself to the vibrant sensations rippling over her as relentlessly as the sea.

Then the little sloop was sailing alongside them, Jamie's and Violet's faces peering anxiously over the rail, their arms outstretched to help. The moment was gone. They straggled back to port and carried their strings of fish up to L'Etoile.

Allegra was unusually subdued that evening, shocked more by her own willing reaction to Oliver's kiss than by her near drowning. She hardly noticed Violet's solicitous hoverings or Jamie's attempts at lighthearted humor, and she particularly avoided Oliver's intent stares. As soon as politely possible, she made her excuses and went up to her room, hoping to find refuge from her roiled emotions in sleep.

Chapter
Six

Sleep did not come. Despite her desperate wish for oblivion, Allegra rolled one way and another for hours, alternately flustered, frustrated, and thrilled. She kept seeing Oliver's face bobbing in the swells of deep blue ocean, and feeling his lips, wet and salty, on her own. She didn't know what to do about the way she felt, how to reconcile her professed horror at Oliver's conduct with the intense pleasure she took from it. Nothing in her life, not even her innermost dreams, had prepared her for the moment she had surrendered, willingly and joyfully, to her senses.

Unable to bear the confines of her bed any longer, she batted aside the mosquito curtain and lunged to her feet. For a few minutes she prowled around her room, bright in the light of the full moon, restlessly picking up and putting down framed photographs and collected sea shells. Finally seeking relief for her fevered state in the cool night breeze, she slipped through the French door of her room to the veranda.

It was hard to believe that only three weeks before she had stood in her room swathed up to her chin and down to her toes, too embarrassed to step outside in her nightwear. Now she perched on the veranda railing, unselfconscious in a thin sleeveless shift, yet consumed by the same thoughts that had troubled her then. She was absorbed, as she had been that morning, by the disturbing memory of Oliver's kiss.

Allegra stared out into the night, watching the paw paw trees and imperial palms cast giant shadows across the brilliantly lit bit of estate road that she could see from where she sat. Smaller shadows wove in and out, making a velvet pattern at the bottom of the hill. She gazed out absently for a full five minutes, barely aware of what she was seeing before it registered that the smaller shapes were not the shadows of breeze-tossed bushes, but moving people.

Startled, she stood up and stared harder, this time concentrating on the scene below. The moving people were men carrying heavy sacks. Sacks of cocoa. They were silently transporting cocoa away from the boucan down the road and into the night. Cocoa raiders!

Allegra clapped one hand to her mouth to stifle a gasp and the other to her heart to still its sudden, wild beating. She whirled and raced into her room, seizing the first clothes that she found. She had her skirt over her head and fastened at the waist before she flew through the door. As she sped down the stairs, she poked her arms into a blouse, closing it haphazardly with two misaligned buttons. By that time, she was across the front lawn and running down the road.

It vaguely occurred to her that the best course of action was to awaken Oliver or Jamie and let them handle the situation. That faint notion, however, was swamped by stronger forces. In part, her newly unleashed sense of adventure propelled her, but in larger part she was genuinely outraged. It angered her greatly that the cocoa was being stolen. Cecil's cocoa. *Her* cocoa.

For the first time, she felt a real sense of proprietorship, a sense that she belonged here, that this was her home. And now her home was being invaded, her property was being plundered. A fierce desire welled up in her, pounding into her conscience with the rhythm of her heels pounding the packed dirt. Her desire was to protect L'Etoile from the raiders, to fend off this contemptible attack. Just how she, a half-clad, barefoot, lone woman proposed to do it, was unclear. As usual, she allowed her ungovernable impulsiveness to guide her.

It was only when she reached the bottom of the hill that uncertainty set in. No longer viewed from an elevated distance, the scene took on a different tenor. The stealthy figures ceased to be part of a shadowy pattern and became, instead, big, menacing men. A large number of them. Moonlight gleamed on the hard muscles of their bare arms and chests; it caught the cold, wicked steel of the cutlasses tucked in their belts.

The spontaneous anger changed instantly to fear, making her

heart race once again. Quickly Allegra stepped off the road and behind a stout breadfruit tree, devoutly wishing that her blouse was not quite so white, her scattered curls not quite so blond, and her skin not quite so pale. She tried to smother her labored breathing in her sleeve, but every rasp for air sounded like an entire chorus to her straining ears. She was paralyzed in place, afraid to go forward, afraid to retreat up the open road to safety.

The rustle of a footstep in the brush behind her sent her heart suddenly leaping to her throat in terror. Forgetting the danger of the well-lit road, Allegra lunged toward it, but she wasn't fast enough. An iron hand clamped over her mouth and a strong arm dragged her back into the shadow, pinning her tightly against an unyielding body. Her attempts to struggle free were thwarted by a merciless grip. Out of the corner of her eye, she could see a dark head bending over hers, could feel lips moving closer. Fear choked the breath out of her; it turned her mouth to dust.

"Be still, Allegra," came Oliver's low voice. "Don't make a sound."

She went limp in utter relief. Drained of tension, her muscles became shaky; the once ominous arm that imprisoned her was now familiar, supporting her sagging body. The hand over her mouth loosened its hard grip, and, when she weakly nodded her head to acknowledge his command, it slid away completely. Although Oliver still held her close to him, Allegra was too stunned to either savor or suffer the sensation. She felt only gratitude for the strength that braced her while her breath came back and her racing heart slowed.

Nor was Oliver affected by their intimate position. His attention was occupied more by the scene in front of him than by the woman in his arms: He held her only to keep her motionless while he grimly studied the thieves in the cocoa yard. When there was a slight lull in their movement, he bent again and said into Allegra's ear, "I want you to stay here. *Exactly* here." His voice was soft but his tone was hard. "Don't make any noise; don't shift an inch. Do you understand me?"

When Allegra didn't answer, only rolled her eyes up toward him, he gave her a brisk shake and demanded more sharply, "Do you understand me, Allegra?" She finally nodded again, slightly frightened by his fierceness, and he relented a little. "I can take care of this," he said. "I won't let them get away, but I don't want you in the middle of it. You *must* stay out of sight."

His terse explanation reassured her somewhat. "I will," she promised quietly. "I'll stay right here."

Because it was dark, Allegra couldn't see the doubtful expression on Oliver's face; because she was still very shaken and only too willing to remain hidden in the shadows, she didn't realize how reluctantly he released her. She only knew that suddenly the powerful arms that secured her were gone, and, the next instant, so was Oliver. Her heart jumped again, this time more in anxiety than panic. Though she was hardly aware of it, her concern was as much for Oliver's welfare as for her own. She wished the thieves would disappear and the night would return to normal. An adventure was one thing, but these sinister looking men were quite another.

Obeying Oliver's orders explicitly, Allegra remained frozen in place. For what seemed like an eternity, she stood behind the breadfruit tree, waiting. Her legs grew stiff from the tension of being absolutely still, her throat grew sore from scarcely swallowing. She didn't dare make the smallest noise or the faintest movement for fear of being detected.

Yet there was only so long she could sustain both her position and her acute apprehension, especially since the raiders were somewhat removed. After a while, the burly figures gliding by in front of her became more familiar, and with familiarity came a diminished sense of alarm. She sidestepped a few times to ease the ache in her legs and gulped a few times for her throat. After a little more watching and waiting, her concern began to outdistance her fear. Once again, she worried about the vast quantities of cocoa vanishing down the dark road.

Just when her pulse began beating normally and impatience was eroding the earnest promise she had made Oliver, the eerie silence of the night was shattered by a single piercing war cry that made Allegra's blood run cold. While her heart stopped, then started racing again, her eyes opened wide in shock. The rhythmic routine of the cocoa raiders was suddenly disrupted by the charge of fifteen men swinging machetes, clubs, and rock-hard fists. The raiders leaped to meet them, and the moonlit yard became the site of a wild melee.

Allegra immediately recognized Oliver at the head of the attackers, and as her shock abated, her worry increased. In the jumble of emotions spinning through her, she felt relief that the cocoa thieves had been thwarted, that L'Etoile's honor and stolen cocoa were being avenged. At the same time, she was terrified that Oliver would be hurt. She didn't stop to think where this feeling came from or why it gripped her so strongly; she was too consumed by it to analyze it.

Allegra watched the fierce battle, transfixed, her eyes hardly leaving Oliver's twisting, turning body. For every punch he threw, she unconsciously jabbed out with her own clenched fist. For every punch that landed on him, she flinched. And when the fighting took him out of sight, her view blocked off by a branch, she jumped out in the open, unconsciously inching closer to the arena.

She wasn't even aware of moving, until suddenly she was at the edge of the cement yard, a split and spilled sack of cocoa only a few feet in front of her. She looked at it in horror, the realization of her exposed position suddenly coming to her. At the exact same moment, Oliver caught sight of her, gleaming brightly in the moonlight.

"Get back, you damned fool!" he yelled, his fear for her safety lending ferocity to his tone. His attention was momentarily distracted.

A six-foot tall raider, his muscles bulging, took good advantage of that moment. He let loose a backhand swipe that knocked the breath out of Oliver and sent him crashing to his knees. With a vicious kick of his bare foot, the big thief toppled him on his back, then advanced with his cutlass raised.

As if in a dream, Allegra saw Oliver's face contorting as he shouted at her. She saw the raider land his devastating blows, and she saw Oliver crumple to the ground. For a fraction of an instant, she watched the sweat glistening on the raider's naked chest; she watched the malevolent expression baring his teeth in a grin. Then, as his arm swung up, she moved.

She launched herself across the cocoa yard, propelled by pure emotion. There was no sign of clumsiness or uncertainty as she raced forward. There was no sign of awkwardness as she bent to scoop up the spilled sack of cocoa without breaking stride. There was only fluid grace as she bowled the burlap bag directly at the raider's legs.

Had the sack been full, it might have inflicted some serious damage. Instead, the beans flew out of the bag as it skidded toward its target. The dead hit served only to distract, not to disable. With a howl, the big man turned his outraged attention on the object of his new attack.

Utterly weaponless and finally starting to realize what she had done, Allegra backed away, dodging and darting as the raider toyed with her. His slashing machete came down, again and again, within a hair of her, each time sending Allegra's heart to her throat. When her foot jammed against the raised rail of a cocoa drawer, the cutlass sliced through her sleeve and etched a warm, stinging line down her arm. Blood instantly soaked through the cloth, a black blotch in the cool light of the moon.

The sight of the bloody sleeve, almost more than the pain, made Allegra cry out in sheer terror. Taking her eyes off her foe, she turned to run, but her bare foot slipped on the cocoa beans scattered along the cement. With another cry, her arms waving wildly for balance, Allegra fell down. Knowing escape was impossible, now, all she could do was instinctively cover her head with her hands and wait for the final stroke to descend.

When the raider's anguished oath came instead of his blade, Allegra peeped out between her fingers. Recovered from his blow, Oliver had hurled himself at the thief, taking the big man to the ground. Still on all fours, Allegra quickly crawled out of the way, wedging herself into a corner of the yard, her back to a set of stone stairs. Her knees drawn up almost to her chin, she watched Oliver fight with the raider.

It was rather one-sided. Although the man had the advantage of fifty pounds on Oliver, Oliver had the advantage of six years of boxing lessons in England. He also had the advantage of violent rage. Although he usually kept his temper, settling his arguments with logic rather than with force, he was now provoked beyond reason.

With uncharacteristic savagery, he pummeled his opponent, exacting revenge, not for the attack on himself, but for the one on Allegra. As the image of her pale, frightened face remained fixed in his head, as the thought of her falling helplessly to the cement under the threat of a machete flashed through his mind, his fists smashed harder. Within moments, the man was whipped and limp. Oliver leaped up, his blood racing, ready to take on another raider.

There were none. The yard was quiet again. Four of the thieves had fled into the night; nine more lay bloody and battered, Septimus Stephen and the rest of the L'Etoile crew standing vigilantly over them. Up the road from Gouyave came five donkey carts heaped high with stolen cocoa. A simultaneous attack at the thieves loading point, half a mile away, had surprised the two men left on lookout, and they had been easily overcome. The raid was over.

Oliver took several deep breaths to regain his control. Though his nerves continued to tremble, his voice was calm as he said, "Well done. Now, let's clean up this mess." While the men grinned proudly and strutted about flush with victory, Oliver issued crisp orders.

"Reggie, fetch the baling twine and the first aid kit from inside. You, Tom, tie the hands of everyone who isn't bleeding. Bring the wounded to me and I'll bandage them up. Dennis, you and Johnny throw some tarps over those carts, then put the donkeys in the pen. We'll unload the cocoa in the morning. Septimus, take five men and march this two-legged fish bait and his cronies down to Gouyave. Wake up the police magistrate and have him lock them in jail. Tell him I'll be down to see him tomorrow. Everyone else go home and go to bed. You'll feel this night's work in the morning, I'll wager."

Hunched in her corner, Allegra watched as Oliver wound gauze around wounds, and as Tom wound baling twine around the raiders' wrists. She watched as the donkey carts were lined up in the yard and the donkeys led away. She watched as the thieves were shoved and goaded down the road by their triumphant guards, and as the rest of the men drifted into the night, laughing away black eyes and swapping boasts. She watched as Oliver stood, hands on his hips, surveying the suddenly silent yard, assessing the amount of cocoa spilled on the ground. She watched it all, completely bewildered.

Now that it was over and the yard was empty again, she couldn't believe it had happened. She couldn't believe the violence she had witnessed or the deadly peril she had been in. The emotions she had felt seemed unreal: her stark terror, her frantic concern, her fierce defense of Oliver. Most of all, she couldn't understand why Oliver was ignoring her.

He seemed unaffected by the night's events, giving commands and creating order as he always did, his voice level, his back straight. It was incomprehensible and deeply disappointing that after the danger they had shared, he could completely disregard her. A few minutes before, they had risked their lives for each other, and now it was as if she didn't even exist. Dazed, Allegra rose unsteadily to her feet, hoping to slip away while Oliver's attention was occupied with the damage. She had taken three steps when his voice rang out.

"Hold on one moment, Allegra," he said. "I have a few things to say to you."

She froze in midstep, unsettled by his harsh tone of voice.

"Just what the devil did you think you were doing?" he demanded. "What bird-brained, feather-headed idea inspired you to come charging down the road, all alone, in the middle of the night? Did you think it was some grand adventure? Did you think it was one of those heroic fantasies in the novels you seem to favor? Did you think it was romantic? Glamorous?"

Allegra had no way of knowing that the intensity of his attack was a reflection of the depth of his feeling for her. She retreated before its force without answering.

"In the second place," he continued to storm, not caring that she hadn't replied. "What stupid, thoughtless notion ever possessed you to come out from behind that breadfruit tree? I told you not to move an inch. Not to blink. Not to twitch. Not even to breathe. You *promised* you would stay put. And yet you came strolling out to watch what was going on as if you were attending the Derby at Ascot. For God's sake, Allegra, are you so completely daffy you didn't know how dangerous it was? Did you think those cutlasses were for show? Didn't you know they can *kill*?"

Allegra's face flooded with shame. Under the circumstances she could hardly tell him that she'd been possessed by her tremendous concern for him. Instead, she answered faintly, "I knew that. I only meant to help."

"Help?" Oliver roared back. "I've had a surfeit of your blundering help. It's gone far enough. I don't care how much of the estate you inherited; I won't tolerate your 'help' any longer. Your damned, half-witted help nearly cost me my life tonight!"

Her blush of embarrassment turned to a flush of anger at the injustice of his last remark. "That's the most ungrateful comment I've ever heard," she shouted, her own overwrought emotions now seeking an outlet, too. "If you could stop being so nasty for a moment, you might remember that I *saved* your life tonight. I threw that bag of cocoa at the raider, and it would have knocked him down if the beans hadn't spilled out. As it was, I distracted his attention while you recovered your wind. But instead of thanking me for it, all you can do is call me horrible names and make cruel accusations."

"Thank you?" Oliver echoed furiously. "You expect me to *thank* you for what you did? If I hadn't been frightened half to death that you would be hurt, I would have had my mind on what I was doing and that thug would never have gotten the best of me."

Allegra gave a gasp at his words, not because they continued to be brutal, but because they contained, however ungracious, an admission of affection. It was more than her raw nerves could take. She burst into tears.

For another incensed moment, Oliver watched her, her hands over her face, her body wracked with sobs. The sight of her in such distress, coupled with the awareness of the feelings fresh out of his mouth, were enough to evaporate his anger. He moved forward to comfort her. Then he saw the blood on her sleeve.

"Good Christ!" he exclaimed, crossing the distance between them in a few swift strides, fear once again filling his heart. He lifted her, unprotesting, into his arms and carried her up the three steps to the boucan. Inside, the big building was fragrant and dark, except where a block of light slanted in from the open door. Oliver kicked a bundle of burlap bags into the light and set Allegra down gently on top of them.

Despite her feeble attempts to shrug him away, Oliver unbuttoned her blouse and slid it off her shoulders. "Let me see," he commanded, taking her bare arm in his hands. Relief poured through him when he saw the wound was only superficial and that it had already stopped bleeding. "Just a scratch," he murmured, wadding up her shredded blouse and wiping the wound clean.

Allegra tried to reply, tried to gather her social graces, but tears still choked her. "Don't talk," he advised her. "Just rest." He tossed away the ruined shirt and sat down on the floor beside her, his back against a stack of cocoa sacks. "Come here," he said, pulling her tenderly into his arms. "Just rest," he repeated, pressing his lips against her silky curls.

Allegra gulped in another attempt to get hold of herself. For a moment, she remained rigid in his arms. Then a shiver ran through her and fresh sobs broke out as she succumbed to the desperately needed comfort he offered. All the sorrow and fear, all the confusion that had been dealt to her since her arrival in Grenada welled up and overflowed. She cried for her loneliness in the world, without mother or grandfather, without the father she would never know. She cried for the strange turns her life had taken, for the realization that she would never be able to return to her old one and that she wasn't yet firmly set in her new one.

Pushing closer to Oliver, she sought solace from the rock-solid strength he possessed, from the great warmth and kindness she now knew were as much a part of him as his bluntness. She soaked up the soothing strokes of his fingers as they brushed over her shoulder and down her arm. She let his confession that he cared for her seep through her, balming her emotional bruises. Eventually, she stopped crying.

"I've made your shirt all damp," she said apologetically but without raising her head from his chest.

"It will dry," Oliver answered. Then he hooked his thumb under her chin and turned her face toward his. Softly, lightly, he laid a kiss first on one wet cheek, and then the other.

Allegra felt another shiver go through her, not of grief this time, but of anticipation. She shivered again as he wiped the tears from her face with the tips of his fingers, letting them trail slowly across her cheeks and disappear into her hair. His lips followed the course of his fingers, lingering, caressing, swelling the sensation inside her. She was suddenly very aware of him, aware of his scent of salt and spices, aware of the passion in his touch.

Turning her head slightly, her mouth met his, and she responded. She responded to the exotic atmosphere of the tropics and to the extraordinary tension of the night. She responded to the emotions unleashed in her and to the potent feelings that were stirred. As she had an eon ago, only that afternoon, she responded to Oliver.

She let herself be lowered onto a rough bed of burlap bags, let Oliver slip off her skirt and ease her shift over her head. She heard his breath come faster, saw his deep blue eyes grow brighter as he looked at her, naked and marble-white in the moonlight. Then he drew his hand up the side of her thigh and slid it across the soft curve of her belly. Her own breath came harder and her skin grew hot. Excitement spread, pounding through her limbs.

She threaded her hands underneath his shirt, gasping in shock when her fingers brushed his flesh. Hurriedly she helped him shrug out of his clothes, eager now to run her hands the length of his long, strong frame. Her pulse raced when he sank down next to her on the sacks. When their bare bodies pressed together, she felt as if her heart would burst. His legs twined around hers; she wrapped her arms around his back; their mouths found each other's in a kiss. It wasn't tender and soothing as it had been before, but long, urgent, and fierce.

Never had she felt like this, oblivious to everything but the craving of her senses. She was incapable of reason; she could only react, wildly returning Oliver's kisses and caresses, wildly matching his rhythm and thrust. Never had she been so consumed by the need to feel pleasure, never so completely controlled by the demands of desire. And never had she been so exquisitely content as when that need was sated, when her desire was satisfied, and when she lay peaceful and protected in Oliver's arms.

Chapter
Seven

It was afternoon when Allegra finally woke, groggy in the midday heat. As soon as she moved, her body reminded her of yesterday's incredible events. Her arm throbbed, every muscle ached, she felt generally stiff and sore. The involuntary groan that came forth, however, was more an expression of despair than of discomfort. "Oh, no," she said out loud, sitting up slowly. "What have I done?"

A few hours later, Allegra tracked Oliver down in the office where he was catching up on the paper work for his various enterprises. Favoring ample twinges and bruises of his own, he had chosen this sedentary chore over anything more active. He had already ridden down to Gouyave to give the magistrate a full report on the raid and to see off Jamie, much miffed at having slept soundly through the excitement. Despite his horse's easy gait, the short trip had not been pleasant, and Oliver had gratefully settled into his well-cushioned chair.

When Allegra entered, he looked up, his welcoming smile turning to a resigned sigh as he saw the determined thrust of her chin and the rigid way she sat on the edge of the chair opposite him. He knew her well enough by now to recognize an impending argument. Warily, he waited to hear what scheme she had up her pink-and-white striped sleeve.

Taking a page from Oliver's book, Allegra didn't keep him in the dark for long. She came right to the point. "I intend to act as an equal partner in L'Etoile," she said firmly. "I mean to accept an equal share of the responsibilities involved in running the estate."

Oliver sighed again. "Allegra . . ." he started to say.

"I won't be fobbed off," she interrupted, anticipating his objections. "And I won't be told I'm needed to arrange the cut flowers or to count the bed linens. I want to work with the cocoa." Her voice took on a more dramatic timbre. "It was my father's ambition to build a great cocoa estate; it was his wish that I should inherit it. I can do no less than honor his memory and the trust he blindly put in me by continuing his work and fulfilling his ambition."

Swallowing the snort that was rising in him, Oliver forced himself, with remarkable willpower, to answer blandly, "No doubt Cecil did want L'Etoile to be a great estate. He always wanted the best in life. But he was quite content to give over the job of achieving it to me. And," he added, rocking back in his chair and steepling his fingers under his chin, "if you'll permit me a moment of immodesty, I must confess I have been rather successful. L'Etoile is one of the most productive estates in Grenada."

He set his chair back down with a thud. "If you really mean to carry on in Cecil's footsteps, you'll leave the cocoa to me, as he did. Especially," he concluded with emphasis, "since you know far less about its production than he did."

Allegra shifted uneasily in her chair but maintained her ramrod straight posture. She had to concede his last point, but she wasn't going to surrender completely. "I'll admit that you have a valid concern," she said, but so reluctantly Oliver had to hide a smile. "However, I am very willing to learn. I think you'll find I am a ready pupil. Grandfather always said that when I was interested in a subject I would go right to the top of the class." Pausing, she remembered but refrained from adding how he had also said that when she wasn't interested in a subject, she could be as dense as a stick of wood. "I'm *very* interested," she assured him.

"I don't deny your enthusiasm," Oliver granted gallantly. "And I would be happy to answer any of your questions, but . . ."

"I don't insist on assuming any authority immediately," Allegra interrupted again. "I understand that you have far greater experience, and I am glad to let you assign me tasks while I learn. However, my participation in the estate's affairs is not open to debate. I *must* take part in running L'Etoile."

There was such a note of desperation in her last remark, Oliver studied her more seriously before replying. "Actually, Allegra," he finally said, very slowly, "after last night, the type of partnership I was thinking about is marriage."

Allegra gulped and looked down in her lap, her lashes delicate against suddenly flushed cheeks. She started to speak, but no sound came out. Clearing her throat, she tried again. "I think not," she said, barely above a whisper.

Her answer startled Oliver. Thinking she hadn't understood him, he said, more sharply, "I'm asking you to marry me, Allegra."

She nodded her head without looking up. "Yes, I know," she said. It was the most unromantic, left-handed proposal she had ever received or read about, but she recognized it for what it was.

"And you are refusing." It was more a flat statement than a question.

Again Allegra nodded.

"Why?" Oliver asked, clearly astonished. He leaned back, trying to find some reason. "Last night was certainly unusual," he said, groping for an explanation as he went along. "Our emotions were highly charged by the raid. Danger will do that. Undoubtedly, that agitation contributed to, to—" he paused, looking for a discreet way of phrasing it, "to what happened," he concluded.

Then he sat forward, more sure of what he was saying. "There was nothing false about the way we felt, though," he told her. "Our reaction may have been extraordinary, even immoderate if you will, but our feelings, our desires, were very real."

Allegra still didn't speak or lift up her eyes. Although her mouth worked a little, as if trying to form a thought, no words issued forth.

More hurt than he could admit by her continued silence and rejection, Oliver grew sarcastic. "I would have thought that after last night's affair," he observed, "marriage would be the *only* acceptable avenue for a woman with your keenly developed sense of *proper* behavior."

The word had its usual effect on Allegra, turning her face red and creating an air of awkwardness about her even as she sat. Her chin sank lower, and she still couldn't meet Oliver's gaze. However, it did not, as Oliver had hoped, serve to embarrass her into accepting his offer. Rather, it added to the confusion that caused her to refuse him.

He was quite right when he said that the heightened emotion created by the cocoa raid had precipitated their passion. Coming on the heels of her near drowning that afternoon, the terror of the night had left her vulnerable and defenseless. Her wrenching tears had washed away all barriers, leaving her open and desperate for Oliver's comfort and contact. In the bright light of today, however, that "extraordinary" reaction was incredible. It was so far removed from anything she had ever experienced or imagined, it seemed unreal. The sensuous responses that had been natural in the moonlight were inconceivable in the sunshine, even in the brilliant, tropical sunshine. The feelings that Oliver insisted were genuine remained obscured by this suspension of belief. And by the aches in her body.

In the wake of last night, it became more important than ever for her to take part in running L'Etoile. It was the only thing left. Having cast herself off from her old life in Connecticut, she was now severing a conventional solution to her new circumstances. Through all of this change, the only thing that stayed constant was her desire to accomplish, to achieve, to become someone. By following her father, whose traits she had inherited along with his estate, by taking up the reins he had dropped, she was sure she would fulfill this ambition.

She didn't accept this realization grimly; actually, she greeted it with excitement. Standing out from last night's turbulent emotions was the sense of fierce possession that had filled her when she saw the raiders making off with their cocoa. She remembered feeling affronted, outraged because L'Etoile was being invaded, its golden beans stolen. For the first time in her life, she felt really at home. After the confusion of last night, this straightforward feeling was very welcome.

But being unable to unravel these jumbled thoughts and impressions for her own understanding, she could scarcely explain them to Oliver. Instead she simply stammered, "I can't accept your proposal. I don't think . . . That is, it wouldn't . . ." For a brief instant she looked up at him, but not finding an answer or even encouragement in his expression, she looked back at her lap. "I can't accept your proposal," she repeated.

Perhaps if he had come over to her, had twisted his fingers through her curls, perhaps if he had cupped her chin in his hand, had tilted up her face and kissed her, perhaps then she would have capitulated. Perhaps then those feelings hidden by emotional turmoil would have asserted themselves.

He hadn't, though. Bruised inside now, as well as outside, he sat in his cushioned chair, his desk between them. When she reiterated her intention of involving herself in the workings of the estate, he didn't argue any further. "Very well," he said in a cold, humorless tone, snapping shut the ledger he was examining. "You apparently know what you want. Work on the cocoa starts at seven in the morning. If you are serious about participating in the business, I'll see you then." Rising stiffly, he stalked out.

Allegra felt curiously deflated. She had imagined that she would be jubilant at this moment, triumphant at having finally convinced Oliver to let her help. Instead, she was disappointed, her enthusiasm dampened by his tight-lipped withdrawal.

It occurred to her then that part of the tremendous appeal of L'Etoile, part of the magic pull of cocoa was Oliver. She saw him in the groves, skillfully slashing pods with a machete, and in the cocoa yard, expertly assessing beans as they cured. She heard him patiently explaining the export figures for 1893 and reciting the ancient Aztec recipe for frothy chocolate. Allegra stamped her feet in annoyance to dispel this disturbing image. It was just like him, she decided, to spoil her sense of success. "There. You see. I was right to refuse him," she said to herself. "We are better off keeping our relationship on a strictly business level."

Despite their individual preoccupations with injured pride, and despite their opposing but equally stubborn stances on Allegra's involvement with the cocoa, it didn't take more than a few hours the next morning for their chilliness to thaw. For Allegra's part, she enjoyed every aspect of the cultivation and curing so much, she was so thrilled by the feeling that she was doing something important, she forgot to act aloof.

For Oliver's part, he simply couldn't resist her. He found her excitement refreshing, her enthusiasm contagious. It was impossible for him to remain angry with her when she presented such a captivating picture.

Not for the first time, he found himself comparing her to her father. He couldn't believe he had ever thought her a pale imitation; now he found her far more engaging. She had all the qualities that were so attractive in Cecil—his spontaneity, his curiosity, his optimism. In Cecil, however, they had been compromised by his inherent weakness; in Allegra they were high-lighted by her honesty and innocence. Oliver shook his head in amazement. Although he had neglected to mention it when he asked her to marry him, he was very much in love with her.

For the present, though, he bided his time, enjoying their working relationship. As the weeks went by and Allegra maintained both her attendance and her interest, his pleasure in watching her increased. More often than he wanted to acknowledge, he would surprise himself just staring at her, a delighted smile turning up his mouth.

She attacked all tasks with equal eagerness: whacking open cocoa pods with such blithe swings of the machete Oliver feared for her fingers; shoveling fermenting beans from one bin to the other until her blouse stuck to her back from the exertion; cranking the sorter with so much energy the men filling the hopper grumbled about keeping up with her pace. Their complaints were only for show, though. Allegra easily won over everyone on the estate. As much as they had liked Cecil, they liked his daughter even better.

The more Allegra learned, the more she wanted to know; and the more information she took in, the more suggestions she put out. "Oliver," she would say thoughtfully, pushing an errant curl back into place, "I have an idea."

"Yes, Allegra?" Oliver would answer in a mixture of amusement and dread. He always wondered how she chose one curl out of dozens to discipline.

"What if we start a competition?" she offered one day. "We could divide all the workers into teams, with one person to cut the pods from the trees and one person to gather them from the ground and one person to break them open and two more people to scoop out the beans. Then, at the end of the week, whichever team had gathered the most would win a prize. Say a case of tinned milk or a sack of rice."

"This isn't a game, Allegra," Oliver told her. "This isn't recess at school."

"Nooo," Allegra admitted. "But you said yourself only the day before yesterday that the sweathouse and the drawers could handle more than they do, even with the cocoa we process from the small holdings. If people thought they were going to win a prize, they might work harder and faster; we could increase our harvest at the same time we make work more enjoyable. A contest is always fun."

"We aren't in business to make sure our employees have fun," Oliver said mechanically. He was weakening already.

"It needn't be all gloom and nose-to-the-grindstone, either," Allegra replied, in direct opposition to everything her grandfather had taught her. "Couldn't we try it just for one week? Please?"

Oliver gave in, as he did to all but her most outlandish suggestions. He was even forced to admit, with a certain amount of chagrin, that some of her ideas were excellent. The competition, for example, worked very well. There were fewer empty sweating bins and fewer ripe cocoa pods left to fall off the trees and rot for want of a picker. A similar series of incentives for the boys who searched out and destroyed the larvae of longicorn beetles from under the bark of the trees had equally good results.

He also liked her idea of expanding the nursery, their home-grown source of replacement plants. Cocoa trees started bearing at four or five years, reached their prime age at twelve, and were finished at thirty. Along the way, they could fall victim to the cocoa beetles or to a ruinous parasite called witches'-broom. They could suffer and sicken from not enough sun, or from too much. Mature cocoa needed the shade of trees like the lofty immortelle, which dropped bright orange or red flowers to the ground every spring to feed the soil; immature plants needed "cocoa mothers," low-growing vegetation like pimento or cassava or banana. Often, the only practical solution when a tree was too far gone was to pull it out and plant a new one. Having an abundant supply of healthy young trees made perfect sense.

Other of her schemes were frankly foolish, and she was the first one to see their folly and abandon them. She never brooded about her failures, though. In fact, hardly anything punctured her buoyancy these days. She was happier than she had ever been in her life, exercising both her body and her boundless imagination, thinking, working, creating. Instead of being chastised for her unladylike energy, as she always had been, she was actually being admired. It gave her a world of satisfaction to feel that she was finally doing something worthwhile.

Although she still told herself it was her father's lead she was following, it was Oliver's approval she subconsciously sought, his appreciation which added immeasurably to her sense of accomplishment. Although she still told herself that she wanted to keep their relationship on a strictly business level, whenever she entered the cocoa boucan, often several times a day, a warm rush of desire rippled through her. She remembered Oliver lying next to her, naked in the moonlight, remembered the feel of his lips sliding over her skin. Then, she would hurry through whatever task had brought her into the building and leave it quickly, hoping to leave behind the memory that complicated her clearcut state of contentment.

The only person not completely pleased with Allegra's new role as a cocoa grower was Violet. While not averse to an occasional hike across the estate, she had little real interest in its daily functions. The hustle of towns and cities fascinated her more, as did Allegra's fanciful descriptions of city life. Nowadays, however, it was only when her brother was away on one of his infrequent business trips that she was able to coax Allegra away from her beloved cocoa.

A month went by before Violet made an allusion to her restlessness. At dinner one night she said, "The next time you have a schooner going to St. George's, Oliver, would it be all right if I went along and spent a few days with Aunt Ruby? She wrote recently that the merchants are starting to receive their Christmas stores. It would be a good opportunity for me to do my shopping while you and Allegra are occupied here."

Oliver gave his sister a thoughtful look. For the first time he realized how bored she must be. At least in Carriacou she had Lily and Iris, not to mention a score of friends and neighbors within hailing distance. Regretfully, he told her, "The *Pride of Windward* is going tomorrow morning, but I am going on her as well. I've got to meet someone in town, and it won't do to leave Allegra here alone. Maybe next week you can both go off on a spree."

Violet was content knowing that she would have Allegra's company in Oliver's absence. Allegra, however, feeling guilty about her abandonment of Violet, didn't let it pass so easily. "You needn't stay here on my account," she said in another complete reversal of the attitude with which she had arrived in Grenada. "I have plenty to keep me busy until you come home, especially if Oliver is away."

"Yes," Oliver agreed seriously, "someone has to be in charge. I intend to be home tomorrow evening, if I can find Frederick

Smart and do my business fast enough. But it relieves my mind to know I am leaving things in capable hands."

Allegra knew that he was teasing and that Septimus was more than able to oversee the harvest, but she still felt a flush of pleasure at his praise. A month ago, he wouldn't have made such a statement, even in jest. "Don't feel obliged to rush," she told him airily. "I can manage perfectly well without you."

Grinning, Oliver didn't offer an immediate reply. It was Violet who continued the conversation by innocently asking, as she reached for the bottle of hot sauce, "Frederick Smart? Isn't he the cocoa agent?"

Oliver nodded. "Usually I have the contract for the year's crop at this point in the season, but for some reason, Smart hasn't been around to see me yet. I suspect he's getting too fat and lazy to make the trip. I want to sign an agreement before the market gets overloaded and the price drops." Too late, Oliver saw Allegra come to attention, her chin thrust out, her eyes flashing. He stabbed his fork into the stuffed jackfish on his plate, annoyed with himself for speaking so unguardedly.

"Why didn't you tell me there was a problem with the cocoa contract?" Allegra demanded. "And why didn't you tell me that was the purpose of your trip? I want to go along with you. It's an important aspect of the business, and I mean to be present."

With a sigh, Oliver explained as patiently as he could, "I grant you it's an important aspect of the business, but it's not the sort of thing that requires two people. Essentially, we negotiate a price based on the quality of our product. We have an excellent reputation, so it generally isn't too difficult to obtain the top price possible. I assure you I will represent L'Etoile in the best possible way. There is really very little you can do to help, and, in fact, knowing the type of man Frederick Smart is, your presence might only make things unpleasant."

While not so long ago this last argument would have made Allegra hesitate and eventually submit, she viewed things differently now. Her determination to be involved in the cocoa trade had done wonders for her self-confidence. "Mr. Smart's feelings about me are unfortunate," she said adamantly, "but unavoidable. I must remind you, and him, too, that I am half owner of L'Etoile and of the cocoa he is buying. I have every right to be in attendance when he buys it, and I intend to exercise my rights."

Oliver sighed again. It was not her rights that he questioned, but her ability to cut a deal. Although she had acquired a knowledge of cocoa cultivation and processing with an enthusiasm and a thoroughness that surpassed even Cecil, she was still her father's daughter when it came to figures. Too impetuous to bargain shrewdly, too impatient to sort through accounts, Allegra was hardly a model businesswoman. He put it to her more mildly.

"You've gained a lot of expertise in a very short time," he said honestly. "But you still lack experience in financial matters. This time around, I think you would do better to leave it to me."

"I think differently," Allegra retorted. She frowned, unseeing, at the cup of mango fool Elizabeth was setting by her plate. "And I also think you used the same argument, lack of experience, to prevent me from taking part in the work of the estate. It was proven to be a misguided argument then, and it is equally as ill-taken now. The only way I can gain experience is by practice. I am going with you tomorrow."

With very little expectation of success, Oliver tried one last tack. "It's a rather critical stage of the harvest. Don't you think that one of us ought to be here to make sure everything moves smoothly?"

Allegra didn't even deign a spoken reply. She just waved her spoon in dismissal of that absurd idea, then dipped it into the delicious custard in front of her. "What time do we leave in the morning?" she asked.

"Eight," Oliver answered resignedly. He took a few bites of his dessert, too apprehensive to notice the sweet, fresh flavor. "I want you to promise me you will just watch and listen," he added more darkly. "No interruptions or questions or opinions until the contract is signed."

"I promise," Allegra agreed grandly.

When they set off the next morning, Violet, who had inadvertently precipitated the whole excursion with her request for a trip to St. George's, was the only one left behind. Partly as penance for her friend's woebegone face, Allegra remained in the cabin of the *Pride of Windward* the whole sail. She didn't want to enjoy herself while Violet had to stay home. Partly, too, she was resolved to make a professional impression. Remembering her trip to Carriacou at the helm of the *Miss Lily*, she didn't want to give Oliver the opportunity to get his arms around her, or to set her heart pounding with distinctly unbusinesslike feelings. Nor did she want to appear before the unknown Mr. Smart, windblown and sunburned, looking like a country mouse in the city.

As soon as they entered Frederick Smart's office, a cluttered corner of Hubbard's Feed Store on the Carenage, Allegra knew she needn't have bothered on the latter score. Smart was a man as ill-suited to his name as to his trade. More cunning than smart, he was immensely fat, making what should have been routine rounds of inspection to groves and sheds almost impossible. He had numerous chins dripping over his collar and numerous rolls of stomach dripping over his belt. So much weight was a burden in any climate, but it was an especially heavy load in the tropical heat. His round face was constantly wet with perspiration, and his breath came in gasps.

Allegra wasn't sure whether it was his wheezing or the way his washed-out brown eyes darted nervously above his fleshy cheeks that made her instantly uneasy. For a moment, she almost wished she had yielded to Oliver and remained home with Violet. Reluctantly, she admitted that he was right; her presence at this meeting was going to be more hindrance than help. Taking a deep breath, Allegra sat sedately in the chair that Oliver held out for her, attempting to maintain her dignity and ignore Frederick Smart's leer.

Both efforts dissolved as soon as he spoke. "Well, well, well," he said, twining chubby fingers over the lump of his stomach like a malevolent Tweedledee. "Nice of you to drop by with the pretty lady, MacKenzie. She certainly does dress up the place, eh? She's a welcome change from the bales of jute bags and the sacks of oats I get to look at all day long."

"*Miss* Pembroke and I are here to sell L'Etoile's cocoa," Oliver interrupted brusquely. "You know it's of the highest quality. We always deliver the best."

"Yes, the best," Smart said slowly, his eyes moving up and down Allegra until she wanted to squirm. "So this is Pembroke's gal, eh? I heard she was living at L'Etoile. She's got her dad's looks, no gainsaying it. The same coloring, same eyes. He always was a pretty one, too."

"The cocoa, Smart," Oliver reminded him, steely jawed.

"Too bad about his accident, eh?" the agent continued conversationally, ignoring both Oliver's pointed prompting and Allegra's distress, getting obvious enjoyment from the power he wielded. "Cut down in the prime of life. So much left undone.

Always had a dozen irons in the fire, that one did. I never saw the match for him when it came to schemes."

"We're here to sell you the estate's cocoa," Oliver cut in harshly. "We've come to draw up a contract for this year's crop."

"A contract?" Frederick Smart said, arching his sparse eyebrows in surprise. Seeming to comprehend the purpose of their visit for the first time, he finally brought his gaze around to Oliver. "You want to sell me L'Etoile's cocoa? Well, well, well." He paused to give a humorless laugh, which sounded more like a strangulated gurgle. "I would say you were a good deal too late for that. Your cocoa was contracted *and* paid for some three months ago. Yes, indeed, Mr. Cecil Pembroke signed the papers and collected an advance in London on the ninth of September."

Allegra felt herself freeze in shock, then her blood started racing. Bouncing up in her chair, she opened her mouth in denial of such a vicious lie, but Oliver's voice cut her off. In a deadly cold tone he said, "I want to see both the signed contract and a signed receipt of payment."

"Of course you do," Frederick Smart said with false heartiness. "You're nobody's fool, MacKenzie. I just happen to have them here." He leaned over his desk with difficulty and pulled a folder off the top of a pile, tossing it toward Oliver. "I even have the endorsed check for you to inspect," he added, giving a conspiratorial wink. "I had a sneaking feeling your partner 'forgot' to inform you that he had sold the crop. He was a right charmer, but a bit dodgy, eh? I'll wager this isn't the first time you've caught him with his fingers in the biscuit tin."

"How dare you?" Allegra burst out. She was outraged at the way her father's bright image was being filthied in this obese man's mouth. "How dare you make such slanderous accusations? You've no notion at all of what happened, yet you jump to conclusions, making horrible attacks on a man who isn't here to defend himself." Having no idea of what had happened herself, Allegra nonetheless jumped to a few conclusions of her own.

"It was all a misunderstanding," she said hotly, sitting at the edge of her chair, her body rigid with anger. "It was a problem of correspondence, I'm sure. I feel certain that he wrote to explain, but the mail is unreliable. Who knows where his letter ended up?" Leaning forward as if she could physically convince the cocoa agent of her father's innocence, she said, "If he were here today, he would tell you exactly that; I know he would. He was an honest man and he loved L'Etoile. He would never have done anything to cheat it. The pity is he died before this could be straightened out."

"*Lucky* for him he died before he was *found* out," Smart retorted nastily. He was unused to being scolded by a woman and he didn't like it one bit. "That's what comes of females who meddle in men's affairs," he rasped, addressing the room at large. "A load of hysterical babble. They can't see beyond a handsome mug. Give them a gay smile . . ."

"That's enough!" Oliver thundered, rising and pounding his clenched fist on the desk so hard piles of papers jumped. Had the agent been any lighter, he might have jumped, as well. As it was, he attempted to shrink back in his chair, cowering from Oliver, poised menacingly above him.

"Miss Pembroke has every right to concern herself with the affairs of L'Etoile," he said in a cold, controlled voice. "She is half owner of the estate and a knowledgeable, working partner. I strongly advise you to remember that fact and to treat her with the respect she deserves."

"Of course, of course," Smart wheezed, thoroughly frightened by Oliver.

"Moreover, the actions of Miss Pembroke's father, my late partner, are not open for speculation and assumption. If, in fact, the documents you show were genuinely authorized by him, we will honor them without hesitation."

Frederick Smart held up his fat hands in a gesture of wholehearted agreement. "No harm intended," he said with forced cheerfulness. "I was just repeating the idle gossip, but I'm satisfied if you are satisfied. I'm sure you'll find all the papers in order." He gave the folder a tiny shove across the desk with the tip of his finger.

With a last grim look at the agent, Oliver picked up the folder and sat back down in his chair. For a few moments there was only the muffled sound of business being transacted on the other side of the big feed store while he read over the contract and studied the signature on the canceled check. Peering anxiously at the papers, Allegra barely resisted the urge to snatch them away and rip them to shreds. Smart fidgeted.

Oliver finally looked up, throwing the folder back on the desk. "You paid 48 s. per hundred weight," he said flatly. When Smart only nodded nervously, Oliver added in a more ominous tone, "You are paying 56 s. for the poorest grade cocoa now, and you know that L'Etoile produces a superior product. It's worth half again as much as you paid. It was worth more back in September, too."

"Well, we had to carry it over," the agent blustered. "It was practically a loan, wasn't it? Getting paid in September for goods shipped in January or February. We're entitled to some interest."

"Fifty percent isn't interest," Oliver said. "It's usury."

"That's the price agreed to, and that's the price he was paid," Smart said sulkily. "He was happy enough to get his hands on some cash."

Oliver didn't argue any further. "I told you we would stand by the contract," he said, rising to his feet again. "And we will. But you'll never buy another bean from L'Etoile. It was a short-sighted bargain that you made, Smart. You did your company a disservice." He offered his arm to Allegra, who stood shakily and accepted it. Without further comment, they turned and walked out.

They didn't look at each other or say a word, just walked arm-in-arm, eyes looking straight ahead along the Carenage. When people called out greetings to Oliver, he solemnly nodded his head in acknowledgment, but didn't reply. Allegra never glanced around. It took every ounce of willpower she possessed to contain herself, to present a facade of poise to the public. The last thing she wanted was to make a scene that would be reported back to the grotesque Frederick Smart. That was one satisfaction he would not have. She was determined that the Pembrokes, pere et fille, would provide no more fodder for his idle gossip.

The *Pride of Windward* was tied a hundred feet away, opposite Oliver's office. A chain of bare-chested, hard-muscled men unloaded cocoa from the ship's hold, lugging the heavy sacks into the warehouse. Bales of flattened bags, two Bentwood rockers, and crates of tinned meats, milk, and cooking oil sat on the dock waiting to be loaded in their turn. Oliver handed Allegra on board, then followed her as she made her way around to the back side of the cabin and collapsed on an upended keg of nails. Seating himself on the rail opposite her, Oliver waited for her to speak. He didn't have long to wait.

"I know he meant no harm," she said immediately, almost pleading with him to agree. "It was a mistake; it was unintentional." When Oliver's face remained noncommittal, she reached more wildly for excuses. "Perhaps he misunderstood the procedure. Perhaps he thought you meant for him to make the sale in England. The money is sitting safely in the bank, probably, ready for you to spend."

"It's not in the bank, Allegra," Oliver said wearily.

"Then there's a good reason," she declared recklessly. "Maybe he was very sick and he needed to pay his medical bills. Or perhaps he knew someone who was destitute. You said he was always generous, impulsively helping others. Maybe he gave the money to some orphan children, or to an apprenticed boy who was being beaten, or to . . ."

"This isn't a Charles Dickens novel, for God's sake," Oliver interrupted impatiently. "And the only orphan involved was Cecil."

"I know he meant no harm," Allegra repeated more weakly, as much to reassure herself as to convince Oliver. She couldn't bear to think of her father in any but the most exemplary way. She had created a shining image of Cecil, had set him up as her guiding light. All her achievements of the past weeks, all the strides she had made and the confidence she had gained, she attributed to him. She was carrying on the legacy she had inherited, developing the personality he had passed on to her. The discovery that her father was dishonest, his character flawed, was devastating.

"He was a good man," she insisted less certainly. "He was loyal and honorable," she said, reciting the qualities she wanted him to possess. "He never would have taken the money for his own gain. He wasn't selfish. He couldn't possibly . . . he couldn't . . . he wouldn't . . ." She floundered, unable to utter the incriminating word.

Oliver did it for her. "Embezzle," he said shortly. "I believe that's the term you're looking for."

Allegra's shoulders slumped in defeat, but she managed a last feeble protest. "He didn't realize what he was doing," she mumbled.

"Yes he did, Allegra," Oliver said bluntly. "He knew exactly what he was doing. He was, as the eminently quotable Mr. Smart said, 'getting his hands on some cash.'"

Although Oliver had refused to allow the cocoa agent to cast aspersions on Cecil, there was no doubt in his mind that Cecil had embezzled the money. His doing so was not a surprise. It was entirely in keeping with his usual pattern of fiscal irresponsibility, with his history of spending more than his income. Oliver remembered his suspicion of Cecil's motives when he had shown up unannounced from England. This latest incident was exasperating and expensive, but it wasn't extraordinary. What infuriated Oliver more than the way Cecil had cheated him was the way Frederick Smart had cheated Cecil.

Nonetheless, Oliver wasn't in the mood to listen to Allegra's idealized description of him. "Perhaps now you'll accept Cecil for who he was," he said. "And perhaps now you'll have a more realistic picture of your father's contributions to running the estate. He was only a man, a dashing and delightful man in his way, but an all-too-human one."

He was about to go on, to paint an accurate portrait of Cecil, but he stopped. Allegra looked so crushed that Oliver's heart wrenched, his annoyance evaporating. Cecil's deceit no longer mattered as much as his daughter's despondency. He wanted to pull her into his arms and comfort her, as he had done that night in the boucan; he wanted to tell her not to worry, that he would always take care of her. He wanted to tell her he loved her.

They were in wide open view of the harbor, however. Dories and sloops and schooners sailed back and forth, bumboats plied their wares, water taxis ferried passengers, and a steamer sat at anchor across the horseshoe-shaped harbor. Oliver knew this was not the time or the place for that particular declaration.

Instead he forced himself to say, "No doubt you're right, though; he didn't mean to be dishonest. I'm sure he meant to pay the estate back." He realized that unlikely as it was to ever have happened, it was probably just how Cecil had rationalized it. More easily, he added, "Your father was always very naive about financial matters. He had a simple concept of money. Chances are, he regarded the transaction as a harmless loan."

Oliver was rewarded for his effort by a visible rise in Allegra's spirits. With an expression of renewed hope, she grabbed onto his explanation. "Of course that's what happened," she said excitedly. "I knew it all along. He never meant to steal the money; it was just a loan, like you said. He died before he could repay it, but Oliver, I *promise* you I will pay it back."

A smile touched the corners of Oliver's mouth. "No one holds you responsible," he said. "You had nothing to do with it."

"No, no," Allegra returned adamantly. "Just as I assumed possession of my father's estate, I'll assume possession of his debts.

It's not fair to accept the one without the other. Besides, I don't want ill will to cloud his memory. I won't take a penny of profit until your share is paid back. Not a penny." Her forehead wrinkled in thought. "Or is it a pence?" she asked.

Oliver let the lurking smile spread over his face. He didn't want her money, but he couldn't refuse her, either. It was a point of intense pride, he could see, her sole means of redeeming Cecil's tarnished honor. "It's a penny," he said. Then he added more softly, "But really, having you here is payment enough."

He didn't give her time to respond, but stood and lightly touched her cheek with his fingertips before going off to check on the cargo. Allegra was left sitting on the barrel, her face hot and tingling from his touch, her heart pounding furiously at his words. The feelings she had been resisting for more than a month rose perilously close to the surface.

Chapter
Eight

Although Oliver's unexpected tenderness had momentarily threatened to topple the barrier Allegra had built around her feelings, by the time they returned to L'Etoile that night she had succeeded in resurrecting it. Part of the mortar she used to close up the cracks was a renewed concern for the cocoa harvest. It now seemed more important than ever to take her part in reaping L'Etoile's crop. She wanted desperately for it to be an outstanding one.

She had jumped eagerly at Oliver's suggestion that her father had innocently considered the money a loan, but on further reflection, unwelcome doubts were sidling in. Refusing to recognize or identify them, refusing to allow her perfect image of Cecil to be diminished, Allegra couldn't ignore the uncomfortable feeling settling in the back of her mind. Without really calling it by name, she decided that the best way to banish that uneasiness was with cocoa. She intended to bury her doubts under tons of cocoa, her father's golden beans.

Although Allegra wouldn't analyze or even admit to the problem, it preoccupied her. Not since her first days in Grenada had she been so subdued. To the disappointment of both Oliver and Violet, the exuberant and seemingly endless stream of ingenious ideas and enchanting anecdotes slowed down to a mere trickle. All her attention was focused on the aromatic burlap bags bulging with cocoa beans accumulating in the boucan and being carted off to St. George's. It was almost as if she were mentally calculating how many sacks it would take before the "loan" was paid off and her father's honor was restored.

Oliver silently accepted her distraction. Though it hurt him to see her so somber, he was certain that her spirit would eventually triumph over the thoughts that were troubling her. Violet, on the other hand, sought to speed up the process. After a week of watching her friend brood, she took action.

She intercepted Allegra early one morning, just after rising. Allegra was splashing Pears soap suds off her face with cool water when Violet came into her bedroom and sat down on the bed. "Good morning," she called. Still bent over the basin, Allegra waved a wet hand.

Violet waited until she had finished washing and was buried in a towel before speaking again. "Oliver told me he has a schooner going to St. George's on Thursday," she said nonchalantly, brushing a wrinkle out of the sheet. "Wouldn't that be a good time to go on our shopping trip?"

"What shopping trip is that?" Allegra asked, placing the towel on the rack and coming into the bedroom. Her skin was pink and glowing. Already wearing a chemise and bloomers, she searched through her wardrobe for a skirt and shirt. Several layers of clothing had been eliminated from her dress in the past six weeks.

"The one you promised we would take when you went to town with Oliver last week," Violet reminded her, turning her attention away from the rumpled bed and focusing it on Allegra. "Remember? First Oliver promised to make it up to me because I had to stay home; he said we would have a spree when you returned. Then you agreed."

Allegra's face was full of guilt as she pulled her shirt over her head. "Oh, Violet, I'm sorry," she apologized. "I'd forgotten all about it." She fastened the skirt around her waist and stuck her arms through the sleeves of her shirt. "I don't know how I can keep that promise," she said regretfully. "The harvest is at its peak right now. I really must stay here and work. Couldn't we postpone it? In another month it will be nearly over, and then we can take a nice long time in St. George's. Maybe even a week or ten days. I promise. And this time I won't go back on my word." She finished buttoning her shirt and pawed through her drawer for a pair of stockings.

"In another month Christmas will be long gone," Violet said

lightly, her hands folded in her lap. "So will New Year's Eve, for that matter, and Royston Ross's ball. We won't have shopped for any Christmas gifts, nor picked pretty goods for our ball gowns."

"Christmas?" Allegra asked incredulously. She came over to the bed and sat down slowly, a single stocking dangling from her fingers. "It can't be Christmas," she said, more to herself than to Violet. Christmas meant cold weather, even snow. It meant holly wreaths and steaming bowls of egg nog, fur-collared carolers and candles flickering behind frosty windowpanes. Christmas meant Connecticut with her mother and her grandfather, who, full of holiday spirit, were more indulgent of her excesses than usual. "It can't be Christmas," she repeated.

"But it is," Violet insisted gently. "In ten days' time it will be Christmas."

"How do you have Christmas in Grenada?" Allegra asked, bewildered. There wasn't even a blue spruce to serve as a tree.

"In Carriacou we have weeks and weeks of singing and a Maypole dance," Violet answered. "On Christmas day we have a big dinner of roast turkey and potatoes and plum pudding." After a pause, she added more thoughtfully, "I don't really care for the pudding, but Father insists on it."

Allegra nodded knowingly. "We had plum pudding, too. At least we did when Mother was alive. She remembered to make it in advance and soak it down frequently with brandy. The one time I tried to make it, I forgot all about it and it had turned rancid by Christmas dinner. After that we had Mrs. Hubert's mincemeat pies." She giggled a little and her gaze grew distant as memories overwhelmed her. For the first time, she felt a melancholy twinge of homesickness.

"Tell me what else you did," Violet begged, always eager for a glimpse of sophisticated living. "Did you have parties? Did you wear beautiful dresses?"

Allegra nodded again. Under Violet's prodding, she recounted the caroling parties and the gay dances; she described the houses, festively trimmed with garlands of pine tied in red velvet bows and with bunches of mistletoe hanging by ornate gold ribbons. She talked about their tall tree, draped in dainty decorations, about their roast goose, deliciously accompanied by oyster dressing and cranberry jelly, about cheerful fires in the hearth and stockings suspended from the mantel, about St. Nicholas and sleigh rides and gingerbread men. Christmas was the one time of year when their drab daily routine gave way to enjoyment.

Not only did she completely captivate Violet, but in short order, Allegra talked herself out of her serious mood. With the enthusiasm Violet had grown to know and expect, Allegra resolved to create a splendid Christmas here at L'Etoile. Violet was delighted; her plan had succeeded even better than she had hoped. After that, it was easy to convince Allegra to leave the estate.

By midday on Thursday, they were climbing up and down the steep streets of St. George's, entering all the shops, inspecting, selecting, and checking items off their lengthy lists. It was the first time Allegra had really explored the small city. It was one of the prettiest in the West Indies, with pastel painted buildings and spectacular views over red fish-scale roofs. Allegra thoroughly enjoyed herself, very glad that she had come.

They spent the night with Violet's Aunt Ruby and her large noisy family. After a breakfast of hot Johnny Bake, a baking soda bread made with wheat flour and coconut, tinned kippers, and coffee, they set out again for the shops. At the Market Square they went separate ways in search of the other's gift, agreeing to meet at Jamie's law office at half-past ten. With characteristic quickness, Allegra purchased a mother-of-pearl comb, brush, and mirror set, had it wrapped, labeled, and sent to the schooner. She arrived at Jamie's office very early.

He was surprised to see her, although accepted without hesitation her invitation to spend Christmas at the estate. His heat-reddened face lit up at the pleasurable prospect of several days of loafing and feasting. "I can see why you've neglected us in town," he said teasingly. "Our poor charms can't hope to compete with the comfort of L'Etoile—or with Elizabeth's cooking."

Allegra waved a hand in denial. "That's not the reason," she said. "We've just been so busy with the cocoa. I wouldn't even have come now if Violet hadn't reminded me that Christmas is almost on us."

"Oh?" Jamie's nearly invisible eyebrows rose in astonishment. "Did you make good your threat? Did you ignore your solicitor's advice to plump yourself down in a hammock?"

"As soon as you left," Allegra answered with a smile. "I've become very involved in the production of cocoa."

"And Oliver has allowed it?" Jamie asked, his amazement overcoming his usual tact.

The smile faded from Allegra's face and her chin thrust out dangerously. "It is not for him to allow or disallow," she said darkly. "I am an equal owner of the estate. You said so yourself."

"Yes, yes, of course," Jamie corrected hastily. "I didn't mean to suggest any differently. It's only that Oliver is so—well, let's say he is very *definite* about what he wants. And the way he wants it done."

"That's true," Allegra admitted, losing some of her bristle. "But *I* am very definite about wanting this, too."

"So I see," Jamie responded wryly. "Though I confess I still don't understand why you would want to pass by a heaven-sent opportunity to sit in the shade sipping limeade in favor of, of . . ." He paused and looked at her intently. "Just what is it that you do instead?" he asked curiously. "How do you help with the production?"

"Oh, I do a little of everything," Allegra said airily. "Cutting, breaking, gathering, working in the sweathouse, raking the drawers. Everything."

"You work in the groves?" Jamie was appalled. "And in the boucan? God in heaven, Allegra, I didn't think you meant *that* kind of work. That's hard labor."

"It's the only way to learn the business," Allegra replied practically. "Besides," she added, more in keeping with her usual spirit, "it's a lot of fun."

Jamie looked unconvinced but didn't press the point. "Well, then," he said, sitting back in his chair and projecting a heartiness that was a bit forced. "They say it's going to be a banner year for cocoa. Are you finding that true at L'Etoile?"

Sitting forward in her seat, Allegra launched into a detailed response. She was too fascinated by the subject to recognize that he was only politely humoring her. "We're already ahead of last year's tally, and we still have a good month of harvesting ahead," she said enthusiastically. "Part of it, of course, is simply due to the unusual yield, but two hundred new acres that my father planted are starting to bear significantly. They'll probably only bring one and a half to two pounds of beans to a tree this year because they're still very young, but it will be a sizable bonus."

Though Jamie looked a bit stunned by this barrage of information, he managed to ask, "And the three hundred acres that were already cultivated? Are they yielding well?"

Allegra nodded. "The trees continue to bear all year long, although we harvest the bulk of the pods right now, but I should say we'll average three and a half or four pounds of cured cocoa per tree, over all."

"That's quite good," Jamie said, now more engrossed in the conversation. After all, L'Etoile was one of his clients, and cocoa was its business.

"Some trees will give us seven pounds or better," Allegra said happily. "But those afflicted with beetles or witches'-broom bring the average down. We've started a serious program of replacing poor trees and upgrading the acreage in general. Oliver is quite vigilant about improving the groves. Would you believe that some acres averaged fewer than two hundred trees?"

Without waiting for an answer to her question, she plunged on. "Even the worst land should support two hundred and twenty-five trees, and the best should have three hundred or more. We intend to bring the estate up to full potential. As we replant, we're going to use only the Criollo variety. The estates started in Portuguese Africa are rapidly becoming a major source of competition, but they seem to be growing the Forastero cocoa. If we convert to the more delicately flavored bean, we'll still have a secure market in years to come. Perhaps even a premium one."

When Allegra paused for breath, Jamie broke in. "You truly have been learning the business, haven't you?" he commented, much impressed. "Your father would have been tickled silly to see how you've taken L'Etoile to heart. He would have been proud of how well you've done."

Allegra beamed in pleasure at his remark. As the memory of her visit with Mr. Smart intruded, however, her joy subsided. "It won't be quite as rewarding a harvest, financially, as it might have been," she said carefully. "Apparently Mr. Smart, the cocoa agent, advanced my father some money in London, against the cocoa, and he died before it could be repaid." Ebullient and animated only a minute before, Allegra now sat quietly with her hands in her lap, unable to look Jamie in the eye.

"I heard about the money," Jamie said ruefully. That brought Allegra's face up in surprise. "It's all over town," he added. "Frederick Smart can't resist telling the story to everyone he meets. He has a loose mouth and a mean soul."

Allegra looked down again, her cheeks bright with embarrassment. It was hard enough to endure her father's deceit in the privacy of her own thoughts, but to have it bandied about the whole island of Grenada was unbearable. She could rationalize Cecil's actions to herself, earnestly explain them to Oliver and Jamie, but she couldn't hope to defend them to fifty thousand people. His damaged reputation badly affected her own sense of worth.

"Now, now," Jamie soothed. She looked so stricken he wanted to console her. "You mustn't let the talk get you down. It's the way of the island, you know. People here gossip more naturally than they breathe. For a few days the tale will be on everyone's tongue, then something more exciting will come along, and it will all be forgotten. In fact, there is already another rumor taking people's interest." Realizing what he had said, he stopped. "I mean, there are always rumors floating about," he amended, rather lamely for a lawyer.

Despite her dejection, his fumbling caught her attention. "What other rumor?" she asked, her eyes meeting his again.

"Nothing," he said, waving it off. It was his turn to look away.

"Tell me, Jamie," she demanded, suspicious of his refusal to meet her gaze. "Tell me or I'll go out in the street and stop every person I see until I get the story."

Jamie didn't believe she would really carry out her threat, but he gave in, anyway. "Only some foolish nonsense going around," he said lightly, hoping she would take it in the same vein. "Cyril Joseph, the overseer at Argo estate, is making ominous noises about the rash of cocoa raids this season. He's dropped a few hints that L'Etoile is behind them. He's even gotten some poor lying sod with a sore leg to say he was wounded fending off an attack by one of L'Etoile's workers." At Allegra's gasp of outrage, he hastily added, "No one really believes him though, and you mustn't take him seriously, either."

"Not take him seriously?" Allegra stormed, standing and starting to pace the wooden floorboards. "It's an out and out lie. It's shameless slander. It's, it's, it's . . ." She was so angry she was practically spitting. "It's unfair!" She stopped to glare at Jamie as if he were the source of this wicked rumor. "What about the fact that *we* were raided?" she asked fiercely. "How can he explain that? If we are behind all the robberies, how does it happen that our cocoa was stolen, too?"

"It was all recovered, though," Jamie said warily. He didn't want to incite her any further, but he didn't know how to stop her outrage. "Joseph is using that fact as proof that Oliver staged the raid himself to confuse the authorities."

"That's preposterous!" Allegra shouted. "Men went to jail for that raid. Does he think they would be fools enough to go to jail for the sake of appearance? To protect our dishonesty?"

"No," Jamie replied coolly. "But he does think they would go to jail for the sake of a few pounds in their pockets. There are any number of men who would do that, many who would prefer jail to the wretched living conditions they endure on some of the estates. You are only familiar with L'Etoile, which has a history, going back before Cecil's ownership, of treating its workers humanely and fairly. But some of the estates are a disgrace. Argo, for an example."

That unsettling information slowed Allegra's pacing, but did not entirely calm her anger. "That may be so," she snapped. "But it does not apply to this particular case. That was a very real raid, with very real bloodshed. Even if men were willing to go to jail for a sum of money, they wouldn't gash themselves with cutlasses and risk being killed for it."

Jamie could have disputed her on that point but refrained from doing so. He regretted having let slip his disgust with certain social conditions; he preferred, professionally and personally, to remain neutral on such issues. "The idea is absurd," he agreed. "Joseph hasn't a leg to stand on. No one is swallowing it. They all know about the feud between Oliver and Argo, and they're assuming this is one more episode in it."

Allegra stopped short. "What feud?" she asked. "Do you mean the competition between the shipping concerns?"

"Uh, yes," Jamie answered blandly. "People are saying it's all part of the business rivalry, Star and Argo vying with each other for shipping contracts."

Setting her hands on her hips, Allegra studied Jamie intently for a moment. "Jamie Forsythe," she said slowly, "now I think that *you* are lying. There is something more to the story than that, isn't there?"

Jamie had the grace to blush. "Yes, there is," he admitted. "But since it seems that Oliver hasn't told you, perhaps I shouldn't be the one to do so."

"How is it that everyone in Grenada may know about this feud, but I may not?" Allegra retorted.

"They don't all know why," Jamie started to say, then sighed. He was beginning to recognize the stubborn set of Allegra's chin and to realize the futility of arguing with her. She could be as bad as Oliver. "Very well," he acquiesced. "But don't you dare tell Oliver you heard it from me," he warned.

"I won't," Allegra promised, sitting down in her chair again.

Jamie rested his elbow on the arm of his chair. "It goes back to England," he said. "To Oliver's days in public school. One of his classmates was the son of a Lord Fenwick, a wealthy and important man. It was a natural contest, right from the start. Both lads were handsome and bright, both were able athletes, both were born leaders. But Oliver was always a wee bit better." Jamie smiled affectionately at the thought of his youthful friend.

"You know Oliver," Jamie continued, not seeing Allegra look quickly away. "He took it all in stride. He never gloated or boasted when his marks were higher or when he won sporting events, but the future Lord Fenwick was terribly affronted. He resented taking second place to anyone, let alone the son of a colonial tradesman, and he never lost an opportunity to remind poor Oliver of his inferior social status."

"That's why he's so contemptuous of English society," Allegra interrupted, finally understanding Oliver's disdain.

Nodding, Jamie went on. "The climax came years later, at university, when a pretty young lady took a capricious fancy to Oliver. It seems our jealous young noble had taken a fancy to *her*. It was the proverbial last straw. He got roaring drunk and vowed to everyone he staggered into that he would have his revenge on Oliver, that he would prove once and for all time that a colonial upstart was no match for a nobleman."

He gave a shrug. "Of course, no one paid him much mind. He was in his cups and an arrogant sort to begin with. Oliver came home for good shortly after that, and the feud seemed over. Until four years ago when the Argo estate changed hands." He paused ominously. "Lord Fenwick won it with three jacks and a pair of sixes."

"Ahh," Allegra breathed, suddenly remembering Oliver sitting on the rail of the *Miss Lily*, explaining how he had come to be in the transatlantic shipping business. How admirable of him that his description had been so brief and impersonal.

"Left to his own devices, I rather think Lord Fenwick would have sold off his new property, or tossed it into the lap of a solicitor as his predecessor had done, but his son had other ideas. Although he has never appeared in Grenada, he has used that estate in every way possible to humiliate and bedevil Oliver. The schoolboy rivalry has come of age."

"How petty!" Allegra exclaimed, incensed anew, though on Oliver's behalf this time. "Doesn't he have any honest ways to expend his energy?"

Jamie shrugged again. "Apparently not," he said. "From all reports, he is a spoiled cub who lavishes money on clothes and entertainment, and who has not worked a day in his life. With so much free time, it's no wonder he's come up with these plaguey schemes." He shook his head despairingly. "And now he has Cyril Joseph spreading unpleasant rumors and Frederick Smart pretending to believe them. Who knows how much he paid Smart to piously proclaim he won't do business with thieves and that he intends to ship all his contracted cocoa with Argo instead of Star?"

"He's going to do what?" Allegra cried, on her feet again. "He's taking all those accounts away from Oliver? My God," she stopped, momentarily stunned as another thought struck her. "If he is going to ship *all* his contracted cocoa, that means L'Etoile's, too!"

She clutched her face in both hands, her eyes enormous in horror. "Jamie," she said, removing a hand to point her finger accusingly, "you told me there was nothing to worry about, that it would all pass in a few days' time. This is more than wretched gossip. This is terrible. It's a disaster!" Both hands clenched in front of her, she started pacing again, practically bursting with emotion. She was furious at the unfair accusations that had been made and guilty at her father's unwitting role in this wicked charade. Mostly, she was overwhelmed by concern for Oliver. It hurt her to think how unjustly he was being treated and how that foppish young lord in England was manipulating his future.

"There has got to be something I can do," she muttered.

Jamie rose too and started following her up and down. "There really isn't anything," he said. He was about to add that Oliver could handle it, as he had handled Fenwick and Argo all his life, but the door to his office opened and Basil Cunningham walked in. Cunningham, a starch-collared civil servant, took off his hat to Allegra and shook hands with Jamie.

While he was explaining the purpose of his visit and politely suggesting that he could come back at a more convenient hour, Allegra grabbed her reticule and fled out the door. She headed straight for Hubbard's Feed Store, intending to confront the fat cocoa agent. When she arrived, her heart thumping from anger and exertion, his corner office was empty, the earlier clutter on his desk reduced to last week's issue of *The St. George's Chronicle and Grenada Gazette*.

"Are you looking for Mr. Smart, Miss?" a feed clerk inquired. When Allegra nodded, still too breathless to speak, he said, "He's gone for the week to St. Andrew's Parish. He's buying cocoa there."

"Where?" Allegra asked.

"Near Grenville," the clerk responded. "At Argo estate."

Allegra's heart leaped at the name. "Argo," she echoed.

"Yes, Miss," the clerk said politely.

"How can I get there?" Allegra demanded. "What's the best way to go?"

"By schooner," the clerk said decidedly. "Or by government steamer. There's one on Tuesday morning."

"No," Allegra said wildly. "Now. I must go right away. I can't wait until Tuesday."

The clerk took half a step back in the face of her vehemence. "Well, Miss," he said hesitantly. "You could go by horse or by cart over Grand Etang, but it's a very long ride."

"That's what I'll do," Allegra decided instantly. "Where can I hire a carriage?"

"In Market Square," the clerk said, edging away. "Or on the Esplanade."

Allegra was immediately out the door and laboriously climbing up the steep pitch of Young Street. In Market Square she found a likely looking carriage and finally, with an exorbitant sum of money, convinced the driver to take her where she wanted to go. Settling herself on the seat, she was off to St. Andrew's Parish, propelled by her usual impulsiveness.

She didn't stop to think things over. Instead, she charged into the fray as she had charged down the hill the night of the raid, determined to protect both the estate and Oliver. Especially Oliver.

Inordinately upset, she scarcely realized how she ached at the thought of his being injured in any way. Nor did she connect that tearing pain to other more tender feelings, feelings that she had been blocking out of her heart since the night in the boucan. In the satisfaction of working the estate, she had been able to push away the confusing memory of lying next to him on a bed of burlap, of the strange and powerful emotions it had aroused. Now, unfettered by rage and an unbearable concern for Oliver's well-being, those feelings sent her racing across the island.

It wasn't until they reached the brown Grand Etang Lake in the volcanic crater at the center of Grenada that Allegra began to feel doubts about the sagacity of this trip. It was already afternoon, and they were only halfway there. Granted the remaining half was all downhill, but the horses were lagging and the driver looked unwilling to continue. For the first time, she wondered exactly what it was she meant to say to Frederick Smart and Cyril Joseph, how she intended to get them to recant their malicious lies.

With a shake of her head she decided to pursue her impetuous course. She didn't allow her uncertainty to linger, but impatiently brushed it aside. She would think of something to say, she decided, rekindling her ire. Somehow she would make their attackers withdraw. Perhaps, she thought, rubbing her back, stiff from the hours of jouncing, they would be so impressed by her courage they would retreat in shame.

Standing before them in the office at Argo much later that afternoon, Allegra realized the error of her thinking. Smart, with his wheezing breath and damp face, was no less repulsive than he had been in St. George's. Cyril Joseph, as whip thin as Frederick Smart was fat, seemed equally malevolent. A tall Creole man whose face was disfigured by a livid scar, he regarded Allegra with the unpleasant expression a cat would reserve for a wounded mouse. She was instantly uneasy.

"Well, well, well," Smart said, leaning back in a sturdy chair and folding his fat fingers over his stomach. "*Miss* Pembroke. I must say, this is a surprise. Yes, indeed, a surprise." His darting eyes looked her up and down. "Tell me, *Miss* Pembroke," he continued in an offensively intimate tone. "How does it happen that your 'partner' permitted you to come here? Or perhaps he sent you?"

"He knows nothing about this," Allegra hotly denied. "I'm

here on my own." She regretted the words as soon as they came out of her mouth. The smirk on the cocoa agent's face made her feel suddenly vulnerable and helpless. Nonetheless, she took a deep breath and plunged forward, gathering momentum from her still simmering sense of injustice.

"I've come because of the dreadful talk I've heard," she said. "I've come to tell you I think it is mean-spirited and shameful of you to spread those wicked lies."

"And what lies are these?" Smart asked, sitting more erect in his chair, his tone getting nastier. He disliked being crossed by anyone but especially by a woman. "I'm not aware of any lies."

"You," she said, turning to face Cyril Joseph, lounging like a coiled snake on the corner of the desk, "are telling people that L'Etoile is behind the recent cocoa raids. And you," she said, turning back to Frederick Smart, "are pretending to believe it and to use it as an excuse not to ship your cocoa with Star Shipping. You know there's no truth behind those rumors. You're behaving not only dishonestly but dishonorably."

"Is that so?" Smart sneered. "And who says there is no truth to the story? I've heard it from the lips of an eyewitness, a bloke who saw every minute of the raid and who identified three or more hands from L'Etoile among the thieves."

"I say it's true," Cyril Joseph broke in. He had a rasping voice, like a saw biting through wood. "I say that Oliver Mac-Kenzie is the ringleader of a gang of robbers. He's got everybody fooled, but I say he's been stealing for years. How else did he get where he is so fast? It wasn't so long ago that he was building boats with his father, and now he's living like a bloody king. How else did he fill his pocket with that much silver?"

Allegra gasped in sheer outrage. "How can you say such a thing?" she demanded. "He's worked hard and made wise investments. He's earned every penny he has. Everyone knows he's scrupulously honest." Her defense of Oliver was impassioned and effusive. "He has the best of reputations throughout the West Indies. People know they can trust him. They know that when he gives his word, they can count on it forever. It would never cross his mind to steal something. If he can't get it honestly, he's not interested in having it." She gulped and vehemently concluded, "It's a *vicious* act to try and ruin his good name."

Cyril Joseph spat to express his scorn, but Smart said smarmily, "My, my, you are a loyal little supporter, aren't you?

Things must be quite cozy over at L'Etoile. Yes, indeed, you 'partners' really stick together." He gave a gurgly laugh at his own uncouth joke. "Stick together." He laughed again, joined this time by a few hard coughs of humor from the overseer.

Allegra turned not red, but very pale. For the first time she realized these men were not merely unpleasant and misguided, not naughty children in need of a good scolding. They were ruthless and immoral, utterly indifferent to her righteous demands for justice. She realized she was in a very dangerous situation. "That's despicable," she said quietly, rallying her disintegrating courage.

"Don't you call me names, Miss High and Mighty!" Smart screamed at her, his face turning maroon from the effort. "I've had enough of your snooty airs, telling me I'm lying or I don't understand. I know what I see, and I see plain as day that you and your dear daddy and your golden boy partner are a band of thieves and cheats, hiding behind your society manners. You can't fool me with your la-di-da ways, talking to me like I was the carpet under your dainty slippers. I know you for what you are: a cheap, little tart. So don't come here saying I can't ship my cocoa any way I please. You just make sure you deliver what I already paid your rogue pa for."

Allegra felt weak from his attack, drained by his explosion of venom. "You have no right to speak to me that way," she said faintly.

"Right?" Cyril Joseph asked ominously, uncoiling himself from the corner of the desk. "You are an odd one to talk about rights. You come slamming in here without being asked, and you tell us about your rights." He advanced menacingly toward her. "This is private property," he rasped. "On Argo *I* make the rights."

The uneasiness Allegra had felt suddenly became stark fear. Cyril Joseph was no more than a few feet from her and coming closer. There wasn't a bit of gentleness about him, not in his lean, sinewy body, not in his grating voice, not in his feral face. Especially not in his face. There was no mistaking his expression, calculating and crude. She took an automatic step backward, seeking escape, then another and another as panic set in. Too late she tried to turn and organize her flight. Her heel caught in the hem of her skirt, and her knees buckled, sending her toppling toward the floor.

A strong arm caught her before she landed and set her upright again. Indescribable relief flooded through her. It was Oliver. She recognized his touch, the spicy scent of his skin. She knew, by some unfathomable instinct, it was he.

But in the next instant when she saw his face and heard him speak, she scarcely recognized him. His voice was not dry and humorously blunt, but so icy cold and quiet that an involuntary shiver ran down Allegra's spine. "If you ever lay so much as one unwelcome finger on Miss Pembroke," he said to Joseph, drawing his words out slowly and carefully, "I'll rip it from your hand."

Without a single overt gesture of threat he conveyed such a powerful message of force it was Joseph's turn to back away, his feline eyes shifting uncomfortably. Oliver stared at him until he was satisfied with the overseer's submission. He flicked his glance from him in disdainful dismissal, and focused it on Frederick Smart.

"Miss Pembroke and I have some business to discuss with you," he told the sweating agent. "It concerns the shipment of our cocoa."

"Now see here, MacKenzie," Smart blustered, wiping his sleeve across his greasy forehead. "I'll tell you the same thing I told her. That cocoa is bought and paid for, and I'll ship it whichever way I like." His tone, however, was a great deal less certain than it had been with Allegra.

"Get out the contract, the receipt, and the canceled check," Oliver said in the same slow, deadly cold voice he had used with Cyril Joseph.

Smart nervously patted his face again. "But you've already seen them," he said weakly.

"Get them out!" Oliver roared, closing the distance between himself and the desk in two strides. Smart leaned hastily over the desk, shuffling through piles of papers, his breath coming in noisy gasps. He finally found the incriminating documents and reluctantly held them aloft. Oliver stretched out his hand. Even more reluctantly, but without a peep of protest, the agent laid the papers in it.

Oliver gave them a brief examination to make sure they were the same ones he had seen before. Then he pulled a check from his pocket, set it in the folder where the papers had been, and tossed it across the desk to Smart. "I'm refunding the money you advanced against the purchase of this year's cocoa," he said. "L'Etoile's cocoa no longer belongs to you."

"You can't do that," the agent cried, making a feeble motion to grab the precious papers. He tried to rise out of his chair, but his bulk held him prisoner.

"I am doing it," Oliver replied briefly. He took a match from the box on the desk, ignited it with his thumbnail, and held it under the documents. In seconds they were ashes, curling on the floor.

"I advise you not to invent any stories concerning this 'meeting'," he said to Smart in a dangerously calm tone. "If anyone asks, which they might well do after all the bragging you've done, simply tell them our agreement has been terminated. If either Miss Pembroke or I hear any whisper to the contrary, we will put about our own account of what went on here today. And we will not feel any obligation to tell the truth." He let his deliberate words sink in before he added, "I leave it to you to decide whose version the public will find most credible."

Smart didn't offer a response, but he didn't look Oliver in the face, either. Oliver didn't press the fat man any further; he had made his point. He turned to Cyril Joseph, standing sulkily by the window, and said, "You'd do well to follow the same advice. Your reputation won't stand much more damage before decent people will cross the street when they see you coming. I'm tired of hearing rumors about my role as the leader of a gang of thieves."

For a mutinous moment, Joseph met Oliver's gaze. "I don't care," he growled.

Oliver fixed his hard blue eyes on the overseer until the man looked away in defeat. "You will," Oliver promised softly. Turning, he took Allegra's arm. In dignified silence they made their exit.

Aware that the windows of the office overlooked the drive, they didn't speak while walking toward the carriages. Oliver paid off the hack she had hired in St. George's, politely handed her into the buggy he had driven from L'Etoile, and slapped the reins on his tired team. They moved slowly down the road. Oliver and Allegra sat stiff and erect. They could practically feel the eyes boring into their backs. Despite their sedate pose, though, they were both bursting to talk.

As soon as they turned a bend in the road, putting the buildings of Argo out of sight, Allegra got out the first words. "What sort of rumors are we going to start?" she asked with evident relish. "I think that's a splendid idea. A dose of their own medicine, as Grandfather would say. They deserve the bitterest elixir we can brew after the unforgivable way they behaved. I wish I had thought of doing it."

"Thank God you didn't," Oliver said fervently. He was a bit startled by her question. He had been prepared for either a tearful collapse or a dramatic defense of her actions, but once again, she had surprised him. It momentarily threw him off-balance and diverted him from the unvarnished upbraiding he had been rehearsing during his frantic drive from L'Etoile. He had meant to tell her immediately that her expedition to Argo was half-witted folly, that it exceeded by far her most brainless schemes, but instead he found himself saying, half wishfully, half warningly, "You'd best forget the idea, too. I won't be embroiled in any mad story you are apt to concoct. It will accomplish nothing but to give those two snakes license for further mischief. Things have gone far enough."

"Then why did you say that we were going to start nasty gossip about them?" Allegra asked indignantly. She was very disappointed by his restraint. Still extremely wrought up by the day's events, she longed for the pure satisfaction of revenge.

"Because they are bullies," Oliver answered. "And all bullies are basically cowards. They'll push a situation as long as they feel they have the upper hand, but as soon as someone stands up to them and makes a few threats, they'll slink away."

"*I* stood up to them," Allegra protested, hurt by his implication that she hadn't. After all, she had undertaken this uncomfortable journey just to confront the agent and the overseer about their treacherous deeds. She was insulted that Oliver was overlooking her efforts. "I told them they were behaving badly," she said. "I told them they were spreading wicked lies."

For the first time since Jamie's telephone message that morning, for the first time since Elizabeth had come running to tell him of Allegra's perilous mission, Oliver felt a smile forming. "Fierce words," he murmured dryly. "Unfortunately, men like Joseph and Smart aren't impressed with Sunday School sermons. And even standing up to them on tiptoe, you are not tall enough or tough enough for them to be scared. They only understand hard words and hard muscles. Don't look at me like that," he added, referring to the glare she was giving him. "I didn't make the rules."

"It's not fair," Allegra muttered.

"That's the way it is," Oliver said practically. "I wish you would realize that instead of tilting at windmills. Which brings me to another point," he said darkly, trying to summon his wrath, which had somehow been diffused.

Allegra sighed elaborately and looked away. She knew a lecture was coming, just as she had always known when her mother or her grandfather were about to deliver themselves on the subject of her unseemly behavior. Where once she had accepted the absolute wisdom of that rhetoric, she now resented having to quiver like a child in anticipation of a reprimand.

"Just what the devil possessed you to go traipsing over the mountain in search of those two disreputable characters?" Oliver demanded, ignoring her pointed sigh. "It was an idiotic escapade at best, an extremely dangerous caper, at worst. Any number of tragedies might have happened. What made you do it?"

Allegra shrugged, still examining the scenery by the side of the road, her mouth working to frame a reply that wasn't there. She could have said that she did it to defend L'Etoile or to assuage her guilt at Cecil's role in this affair, which were true enough. The real reason, though, was because of Oliver. In retrospect, she was shocked at the intensity of her desire to strike out at the men who had so spitefully wronged him, but she was afraid to say that to Oliver because then she would have to admit it to herself.

She would have to admit to the passion she had experienced the night of the cocoa raid, and to the deep pleasure she felt now, just sitting next to him, all alone on a country road. She would have to admit to the feelings she had been covering up with a frenzy of interest in cocoa. For all the liberation of her spirit, for all the vitality of her soul, the depth and magnificence of those emotions was more than she could comprehend by herself. Despite the novels she had read and the romances she had imagined, she still wasn't prepared for the intensity of the real thing. She shrugged again.

Exasperated by her silence, Oliver pressed harder. "Didn't it occur to you that I knew how to handle those two?" he asked. "Why didn't you listen to Jamie when he told you there was nothing to worry about? Did you really think I was going to allow L'Etoile's cocoa to be shipped by Argo? There was an easy solution; one that didn't involve any high tension and drama. All I had to do was pay him off. Didn't you see that?"

Allegra turned back to him, picking up the one point she finally felt sure about. "I'll pay you back," she said earnestly. "You know, I have money in the bank in Connecticut, proceeds from the sale of Grandfather's house and his school. It will more than cover the check you gave Frederick Smart. I'll send for it immediately and reimburse you as soon as it arrives."

"I don't care about the money, Allegra," Oliver said, with less than his usual patience. "It's not important. I'll trade you the money for an explanation of your actions."

"Oh, yes, it's very important," Allegra said, hastily returning to a safe subject. "It was bad enough that this loan jeopardized your share of the annual profits, but now that you have had to repay it out of your own pocket, it's clearly my responsibility. I accepted my father's assets, and it's only right that I accept his liabilities, as well. I can't have this debt hanging over the business or clouding my father's good name. It's my name, too, after all. I'll write to my bank as soon as we get to Grenville and mail the letter this evening."

It was Oliver's turn to sigh. He could have continued the argument, telling her once again that he didn't hold her responsible for her father's financial indiscretions. Or he could have told her that he would willingly change her name. But he didn't. He recognized the mulish tilt to her jaw, the stubbornness that Angus insisted set her apart from Cecil. She wasn't about to be persuaded on either score.

Although Allegra was sincere in wishing to eliminate her father's debt and the shadow it cast on the Pembroke reputation, she was also using the issue to divert Oliver's attention from his probing questions. She was suddenly very tired. The strenuous drive and the emotional stress had completely worn her out. To her great relief, they completed the rest of the short drive to Grenville in silence.

It was far too late for them to consider returning to L'Etoile that evening. They found accommodations at Grenville's lone boardinghouse, rooms that were neither overly clean nor comfortable. Continuing her attempt to keep Oliver distracted, Allegra made an obvious show of buying a sheet of paper and an envelope, of writing to her banker, and of posting the note. Then, genuinely exhausted, she retired to her bed.

Nor was she feeling tremendously refreshed when they set out the next morning. The bed had been lumpy and the sheets had smelled sour. From the tight-lipped expression on Oliver's face, she could tell he hadn't slept any better. For hours they drove steadily without saying anything, mostly uphill and mostly in the hot sun. They had gone over the top and were starting down the other side of the mountain, tired, sticky, and grumpy, when Oliver muttered, "To hell with it!" and pulled the horse off the road onto an overgrown track. Too sunken in the doldrums to ask what was happening, Allegra sullenly pushed branches away from her face and waited to see where they were going.

Twenty minutes later, her wait was rewarded. They emerged from the clutch of bushes into a clearing where the air was cooled by a small waterfall pouring noisily into a clean, fresh stream. The stream bed was strewn with boulders around which the water gently eddied and swirled. The far bank was high and hung with rhododendron leaves the size of elephant ears, but in front of them a patch of purple windflowers and wild watercress spilled over the edge of the stream, low, lush, and inviting. "How heavenly!" Allegra cried, the memory of the grimy boardinghouse banished, her crossness expunged.

She jumped from the carriage almost before it stopped moving and hopped, first on one foot and then the other, pulling off her shoes and stockings and letting them lay where they landed, leaving a trail behind her as she ran to the stream. "Ahh," she breathed ecstatically, stepping up to her ankles in running water, her skirt hitched up in her fists. She just stood there, reveling in the cool water rushing by her toes and staring wistfully at the waterfall.

Behind her, Oliver tethered the horses, looked across at her, and smiled. "Don't just tease yourself," he called. "Get a good dousing. I intend to."

Allegra glanced casually over her shoulder, then turned quickly forward, blushing bright red. The next instant, Oliver waded past her, white from his waist to his knees, his clothes left in a clump by the carriage. Allegra watched him step easily from one rock to the next, zigzagging his way to the waterfall, his muscles bunching beneath his pale skin. She watched as he stood under the cascade, his rugged face turned up toward the sky, his eyes closed, his lips apart. She watched as the water crashed over his head, plastering his long, lovely eyelashes to his cheeks, then splashing away, refracting in a thousand rainbows as a shaft of sunshine pierced through the vines.

She almost forgot to breathe. She let her hem fall unnoticed in the stream. She was utterly transfixed, paralyzed with admiration, with awe, with powerful desire. It flooded through her, filled her limbs, sent her blood rushing warmly through her body. She was unaware of anything else. Her mind was empty except for the image of Oliver, tall, strong, and naked, washed clean and pure in the sun-speckled falls.

He turned toward her, his eyes open and dark blue. "Allegra," he said, his voice mixing with the roar of the water. "Come here, Allegra."

She gulped, embarrassment jolting away the mesmerizing trance. "No," she said, but didn't move. Oliver came toward her, lightly crossing the stones. "No," she said again, suddenly panic-stricken. She turned to flee, afraid of the passion still pounding through her, afraid of the suppressed emotions crowding uncontrollably into her heart. "No," she repeated, scrambling up the bank of cress.

"Yes," Oliver said, catching her around the waist and hauling her close to him. The wetness of his bare skin soaked through the thin batiste of her blouse, sending shocks rippling across her back. His chilled cheek pressed against the skin of her neck, his cool lips hovered over her curls. "Yes," he whispered into her ear.

When she didn't answer, didn't move, only slightly hunched her shoulders, he slowly, deliberately, turned her around toward him. He cupped her face with both his hands and traced her cheekbones with his thumbs, wiping away drops of water that had fallen from his hair. Looking directly into her wide open, violet blue eyes, he said again, very definitely, "Yes. I love you, Allegra."

The last splinter of her barricade broke, the last brick fell away. The glorious feeling, the sublime force she had been holding back, refusing to acknowledge, came bursting through. "Oliver," she said gladly, "I love you, too."

When he kissed her now, she didn't resist, rather she met his mouth willingly and clasped her arms around his smooth back. Their lips lingered, taking slow pleasure from the taste, from the sensation of the other. Finally Oliver leaned back a little, though he kept her close, one arm crooked around her neck. Brushing the curls from her face and smiling tenderly, he said, "I've made your shirt all damp."

It was what she had said to him that night in the cocoa boucan when she had sobbed brokenly in his embrace. Remembering and acknowledging, she returned his smile. "Not to fret," she said and answered as he had then. "It will dry."

"I hope so." Oliver's smile deepened. "Perhaps we should remove it just to make sure." His fingers were already at work on the mother-of-pearl buttons.

"Perhaps we should," Allegra agreed, again not resisting, but leaning forward to place a kiss on his chest. His skin was still wet and cool. Luxuriating in its smoothness, she rolled her cheek against it. She could hear his heart beating, steady and strong. Her own heart beat harder in response.

She stayed as she was until she felt him undo the last button and tug the shirt free from her skirt. She straightened; he pulled the sleeves off her arms. Then, suddenly impatient, he yanked her camisole over her head, pushed her skirt and bloomers to the ground. It was his turn to lean forward, to place a kiss on her chest, to roll his cheek against the soft, warm skin of her breast. Despite the heat of the sun, Allegra felt a wonderful shiver run through her.

Together they sank into the patch of wild cress and wind-flowers where, misted by the waterfall, they made love. It was slow and leisurely, as had been their kisses and their easy conversation, not hurried by the midnight violence that had driven them before. Today there was only the delicious ache of pleasure as their bodies pressed together, as they savored the satisfaction of their desire.

In the mellow aftermath, cradled in Oliver's arms, the crush of cress beneath her, the cloudless blue sky above, Allegra felt none of the confusion that had followed their night in the cocoa boucan. This time, as she leaned across to kiss the burnished skin of his chest, to run her lips over the tips of his fingers and the palms of his hands, this time she felt absolutely sure. Finally she had put the wintry scenes of Connecticut completely behind her; finally she was fully absorbed into the fragrant and overblown atmosphere of her tropical home. She was blissfully happy, a magnification of the elation she had felt on the beach at Sabazon. This time she was in love.

Chapter
Nine

It was almost sunset when they arrived at L'Etoile, tired, very hungry, and wonderfully happy. Their euphoria, however, didn't make it across the front veranda. Elizabeth met them at the gate, in the bower of bougainvillaea. "You got callers," she announced grimly, the serenity of her handsome face unusually disturbed.

Surprised, Oliver glanced back in the drive for a horse or a buggy he might have overlooked. Allegra chose a more direct method of identifying the unexpected guests. "Who are they?" she asked.

"Call themselves Pembrokes," Elizabeth answered disgustedly. "Well, I mean to say, maybe it's true. The young one, he look like Cecil, but they don't act like him, neither one."

"Pembrokes?" Allegra interrupted excitedly. "Relatives of mine? Who do you mean?"

"Your uncle and your cousin, that's who I mean," Elizabeth said, annoyed. "From England." She jerked her head in the direction of the house. "They in the parlor."

Oliver took a cue from Elizabeth and was filled with instant foreboding. Allegra was thrilled to find she had a family, after all. As she rushed toward the parlor, dozens of delightful images flitted through her mind, from gala gatherings at Christmas and on birthdays to heartwarming reunions at ancestral homes. Within seconds of entering the room, however, the cozy scenes she had envisioned completely disappeared.

Two men sat there in silence, gentlemen from the cut and the cloth of their linen jackets and the refinement of their features.

Half-empty glasses of punch stood on the tables beside them, palm frond fans moved languidly in their milky white hands. They rose automatically as soon as she burst through the door, the older gentleman stepping forward to meet her.

"May I assume you are Miss Allegra Pembroke?" he asked in a tone as cold and uncaring as if he were inquiring about the kitchen cat.

Allegra stopped short, disillusionment deflating her. "Yes, I am," she answered quietly.

"I am Sir Gerald Pembroke," the gentleman continued with a barely perceptible nod of his head in acknowledgment. "I am your father's elder brother. As such, I am also our father's heir."

"How do you do," Allegra murmured, not finding his introduction at all avuncular. In fact, nothing about Sir Gerald Pembroke suggested familial warmth. He was of only average height and build, but the hauteur of his expression gave him the appearance of being much bigger. His hair was graying, his features angular, his eyes cheerless, brown, and assessing. His was a face completely devoid of humor and nuance, its pale skin etched with the lines of fifty-five years of privileged English country living. Elizabeth was right; there was no resemblance to Cecil.

"My son, Mr. Bartholomew Pembroke," Sir Gerald said tersely, indicating the other gentleman as if the time and politeness it took to perform this social nicety were ill-spent.

Allegra perfunctorily murmured, "How do you do," in the direction of her cousin. To her surprise, he answered, "Very well, thank you," and held out his hand. As she shook it, she looked at him more carefully. For a fraction of an instant, her heart skipped. Elizabeth was right again. He looked very much like her father.

Bartholomew Pembroke was tall and fair with Cecil's classically handsome features and arrestingly blue eyes. At first glance, though, he seemed much more his father's son than Cecil's nephew. He had a seriousness of demeanor that could very easily be mistaken for Sir Gerald's imperiousness. Closer inspection revealed a certain gentleness in his touch, a kindness in his tone, that hinted at a more sensitive nature behind his somber exterior.

Allegra was instantly and instinctively drawn to her cousin. Perhaps it was his physical likeness to her father that she found appealing, or perhaps the fact that he seemed to be close to her own age. Perhaps, she felt that Bartholomew, despite his solemn air, was the more accessible. Whatever the attraction, Sir Gerald didn't give it a chance to develop. His next words made it clear that he hadn't come to pay a social call on his niece.

"I received word of my brother's demise two months ago," he said in his unfeeling, upper-class way. "It seemed the appropriate time to set past accounts straight."

Allegra's mouth fell open at such callousness, and Oliver, who had come in behind her, looked uncommonly stern. Sir Gerald deigned no notice.

"I suspect you are not aware," he continued, "that Cecil purchased this estate in 1888 using, in major part, a loan from our father. A loan, I might add, that was never repaid. As the heir to our father's entire estate, I inherited all properties and assets, including my frivolous little brother's outstanding loan. I spoke to Cecil about it at our father's funeral, and reluctantly agreed to extend his term of repayment. Now that he has passed on, however, with no fluid capital and no mention of this debt in his will, I can see no point in delaying the proceedings any further. I've come to foreclose on L'Etoile."

For a long moment Allegra couldn't even grasp the scope of what he had said. As it gradually sank in, she felt herself turning cold with shock, her breath congealing painfully in her chest. Not only was L'Etoile in grave danger, but so was her father's good name, the name she had just redeemed with pledges of her maternal inheritance, the name on which rested her own sense of self-worth. The news was so devastating she didn't know how to respond.

Oliver, however, had no trouble either finding his voice or collecting his wits. "If that is the sole purpose of your journey, you've wasted your passage," he said bluntly. "L'Etoile carries no foreclosable mortgage."

"I beg your pardon," Sir Gerald said, raising his eyebrows. "My business is with Miss Pembroke." He gave Oliver a glance that would have withered lesser mortals, a glance that flicked contemptuously from Oliver's scruffy canvas tennis shoes to his collarless, faded shirt.

It was a look Oliver was very used to, however, one that had driven him from England and had given him such disdain for the English. He was more than equal to it. "If your business concerns L'Etoile," he said coolly, his gaze unflinching, "you'll speak to me, as well. My name is Oliver MacKenzie, and I am half owner of this estate."

Sir Gerald's eyebrows went up again at being addressed so brazenly. "MacKenzie?" He said the name as if it left a foul taste on his tongue. "Ah, yes, I believe your name has come up in connection with the property."

"As well it ought," Oliver returned, entirely unintimidated. "It is on the deed."

"A document I have not yet read," Sir Gerald said with increasing haughtiness. "As they do insist on keeping such papers here rather than in the Home Office in London."

"How disobliging," Oliver said sarcastically. "When you do read it, you will learn that the deed to L'Etoile was issued to Cecil Pembroke, alone and without encumbrance, in April 1888. In September of 1890, it was redrawn to record me as an equal owner. Again, there was no mention of liens, loans, or prior claims. Now that Cecil has died, the deed will be re-registered to bear the name of his only heir, Miss Allegra Pembroke. In view of the straightforward nature of all transactions, I would say any pretensions you may have about ownership are baseless."

Rather than attempt to argue against such evidence, Sir Gerald tried again to stare Oliver into withdrawal. He was as unsuccessful as he had been before, and in the end it was he who looked away. He inflicted his gaze instead on Allegra, who was a more rewarding victim. He misjudged her mettle, however, when, after watching her shift her feet nervously, he said, "My brother's will, of course, has yet to be probated. I believe there was some question about his involvement with that American woman. Naturally, our solicitors are making enquiries to determine the legitimacy of all claims. As I recall, at the time she cajoled my foolish brother into a union there was some fuss with her father. No doubt he was most distressed to find Cecil cut off without a farthing. I suspect my father's wise move put a crimp in their plans."

Allegra's head shot up, and her feet fixed firmly on the floor. Eyes wide and snapping, she said, "The American woman you refer to was my mother, and her 'union' with my father was a marriage certified by Grace Church and the State of New York, on August 4, 1867." Although Allegra's good image of her father and his family was rapidly eroding with disastrous consequences to her own sense of identity, there was one thing about which she was crystal clear: the irrefutable respectability of her mother and her grandfather.

"The only 'plan' she had was to love my father forever and to live a long happy life. The only 'fuss' my grandfather made was in regard to their happiness. Any other suggestion is insulting. Their morals were impeccable, their gentility unquestionable."

Sir Gerald raised his eyebrows once more and gave her the same scathing scrutiny he had given Oliver. His cold eyes took in her crumpled and grass-stained dress, her uncontrollable curls, the unfashionable freckles on her sunburnt nose. Satisfied by her blush, though, he refrained from making further comments about the American half of her family.

He contented himself with saying, "Nonetheless, I intend to settle this long overdue account. Our father was far too indulgent of Cecil's extravagances. He allowed his pursestrings to be opened over and over in support of one ridiculous scheme after another, without any substantial repayment. I, however, am not so sentimental, nor so forgiving. I mean to collect this debt."

"Not with L'Etoile, you won't," Oliver said before Allegra could answer. "You can call in your loan from some other source, if, indeed, there was a loan at all. Since you raised the question of legitimacy of claims, let us ask you to present yours. We have yet to see any proof of your preposterous demand."

"Among gentlemen, one's word is considered more valid than a mere scrap of paper," Sir Gerald said icily. "My father, and I after him, always assumed we were dealing with a gentleman."

"Now you may assume you are dealing with business people," Oliver responded grimly.

"Perhaps we should postpone any further discussion until after we've given the matter more thought," Bartholomew interjected diplomatically. He had been standing a few feet away from them, listening gravely to all sides of the argument. It was impossible to tell, by his sober expression, whose part he took. Like Solomon, he seemed to sympathize with everyone. "It has been a long journey for us and jolting news for you. I am sure all our views will benefit from rest and calm consideration. No doubt there is an equitable solution to the problem if we just approach it rationally."

Oliver regarded the younger man thoughtfully. He was drawn to Bartholomew, as was Allegra, because of Bartholomew's resemblance to Cecil and because he sensed something appealing

behind his staid facade. Oliver approved of Bartholomew's request for reason and logic, though he was quite convinced that
nothing could change his mind. He nodded his grudging consent.

"Will you stay here?" Allegra asked, half question, half invitation. She felt suddenly dislocated, as if this weren't really her
home, as if she had no place asking her uncle and her cousin to
accept L'Etoile's hospitality. Wearily, she rubbed her face. An
hour ago, she had been on top of the world; now she didn't know
which way it was spinning.

Though Sir Gerald cast a patronizing glance around the open,
airy room, Bartholomew said, "Thank you very much. It would
be our pleasure. Under the circumstances, it is an exceedingly
kind offer."

Dinner that evening was, to say the least, a strained affair.
Elizabeth stalked around the table, jabbing platters of food at Sir
Gerald and mumbling under her breath. Sir Gerald looked
through her as if she didn't exist. He included the poor quality of
servants on his list of complaints about the colonies. Confronted
by the attitude he despised most, Oliver remained forbiddingly
silent, knowing that even one word would precipitate an unpleasant argument. It was left to Bartholomew to make innocuous
comments, while Allegra made stuttering replies. Her head was
throbbing by the time the sweet and savory arrived. She barely
managed to down a few mouthfuls before excusing herself and
stumbling off to her room.

Allegra closed the door behind her with a sense of enormous
relief. She felt completely unraveled, unable to summon up the
slightest amount of energy. The afternoon's elation seemed a million miles away in a distant dream, or in someone else's life. The
strong, sure love she had felt was now lost. It belonged to the
moment in time before she realized her father, her romantic, adventurous, golden-haired father, whose charmed life was his legacy, was no more than a cheat. There was no rationalizing his act
as financial naiveté, no calling it a misunderstanding. Cecil had
quite simply been selfish and irresponsible.

The realization left her father's image considerably tattered,
and quite effectively pulled the rug out from under her newly
blooming self-confidence. The life she had built, using him as
her foundation, lay in shambles. Everything connected to that life
seemed similarly shattered. Grenada. L'Etoile. Oliver. They were

all gone, and she didn't know how to regain them, didn't know where to go. She felt empty and useless.

Despite a haunted night's sleep, Allegra stayed in bed late. In part, she wished to avoid breakfast with her uncle and her cousin, but in larger part, apathy kept her pressed against the pillows. She had no reason to rise. The all-consuming love and loyalty that had sent her racing to Grenville in defense of Oliver and L'Etoile no longer seemed real. The cocoa was no longer important. It wasn't hers. It never had been. It was just another of Cecil's magic lantern tricks. She had been fooling herself these past two months, wasting her time.

It was after ten when she finally came down, looking pale and tired and acting unusually reserved. She went instinctively into the office, hardly expecting to find Oliver, but somehow hoping he would be there. She felt herself falling, not physically, but in spirit. She wanted him to catch her, to set her upright, to restore her balance as he had done so often in the past. She needed his no-nonsense strength, his humorous common sense. There was no one in the office.

"Gone to town," Elizabeth told her when Allegra tracked her down in the kitchen. She was still looking less than serene.

"To Gouyave?" Allegra asked.

Elizabeth shook her head, vigorously grating some cassava root. "To St. George's," she said. "Arnold Baptiste telephone him this morning about some mess in the warehouse. Oliver said he just as soon go unwrinkle it himself, that way he knows for sure it is straight." She scooped the grated cassava into a square of muslin, caught up all four corners, and began squeezing the bundle. A small stream of starchy liquid squirted into a bowl. "He also said he might as well go talk to Jamie about this deed stuff. Said he pays him for legal advice, about time he got his money's worth."

She opened the cloth and began rubbing the wrung out cassava between her fingers, sprinkling in a little salt as it got mealy and dry. "He'll bring Violet home with him when he comes this evening. Told me they'd be here by dinner." She carried the cassava mixture over to the stove and began heaping it on the hot griddle, flattening each lump with the back of her fork. "Are you going to eat your breakfast in here, or in there with them?" She jerked her head in the direction of the great house, as she had done last night.

"Haven't they eaten yet?" Allegra wailed, her heart sinking even farther. She hadn't managed to avoid her unwelcome relatives, after all.

"Nope," Elizabeth answered, flipping the wafers. "They're sitting in the dining room, waiting for me to feed them, like this was Buckin'ham Palace." She piled the crunchy cassava toasts into a basket, pulled a tray of fish cakes out of the oven where they had been keeping hot, and headed for the house. "You coming?" she asked over her shoulder. Reluctantly, Allegra followed.

"Good morning," she said, with as much cheerfulness as she could muster. Both men rose when she entered the dining room, but only Bartholomew answered. "Good morning," he said, coming around the table to hold out a chair for her. "It seems to be an exquisite day. Is the sun always this brilliant?"

"Almost always, yes," Allegra answered. She didn't have the energy to explain about the dramatic cloud covers or the fierce monsoons as she might ordinarily have.

"Too hot," Sir Gerald said crankily, heaping his plate from the platters Elizabeth plunked on the table. "It takes away one's appetite."

"Hmmph," Elizabeth commented, filling their cups from a china pot.

"What's this?" Sir Gerald asked, eyeing the fragrant brown liquid suspiciously. "I wanted tea."

"It's called cocoa tea," Allegra said. "It's quite good."

"It's chocolate," Bartholomew said, taking a sip. "No it isn't exactly chocolate, either. Fascinating. How is it made?"

"From the local cocoa," Allegra answered briefly, sure that would suffice.

"Just cocoa?" Bartholomew asked, obviously not satisfied with her response. "It's a different consistency than our breakfast cocoa. I seem to detect other flavors, also. Vanilla, perhaps?"

"It's not vanilla, it's tonka bean," Allegra found herself explaining. "The taste is similar to vanilla, but it's another plant entirely, a tree, actually, rather than a vine. The tonka beans are put into a cauldron with roasted cocoa, sapote seeds, cinnamon bark, and bay leaves, then pounded into a paste. The paste is formed into balls, which, after hardening, are grated, melted in boiling water, then mixed with milk and sugar."

"Fascinating," Bartholomew murmured again, taking another sip.

"It's rather greasy," Sir Gerald griped. "It's just not breakfast without a good cup of English tea. Fortnum and Mason makes the blend I like. Oh, heavens," he interrupted himself. "The toast is deadly dry."

"It's supposed to be dry," Allegra said edgily, fingering her own portion. She had little appetite herself, though it wasn't due to the heat. "It's made on the griddle. From cassava root."

"Cassava?" Bartholomew asked, helping himself to a piece. "Isn't cassava extremely poisonous unless it's boiled first? I thought I read that the Arawak Indians dipped their arrows into a concoction they made with unboiled cassava."

"That would be the bitter variety," Allegra said, ashamed of the pleasure she took in watching Sir Gerald hastily set his toast aside and take a gulp of cocoa tea. "That's what tapioca is made from. This is the sweet variety, however. It's safe to eat raw, as well as cooked."

"I haven't had a decent roll since we left England," Sir Gerald lamented, taking a bite of the fish cake. He promptly turned purple and nearly choked. "Good God!" he exclaimed, half a cup of cocoa tea later. "It's positively laced with red pepper. How is one expected to survive this meal?"

"There is really nothing extraordinary about eating highly spiced food in a hot climate," Bartholomew answered pedantically. "Around the globe, one finds the cuisine of tropical cultures dependent on a variety of peppers and sharp spices. India is the perfect example, with her curries and her potent chutneys. In Siam, a paste made of red chilies and curry powder is a favorite seasoning. Mexico is another country that consumes an inordinate amount of chili peppers.

"It is only as one travels north, to more temperate climes, that regional dishes become blander. By the time one reaches the frozens lands of the Yukon or Siberia, the food is almost entirely devoid of flavoring. Naturally, one can make the argument that the strong spices don't grow in the colder areas, but there is also physiological evidence to support the efficacy of eating fiery foods in the heat. They seem to thin the blood and to regulate the body temperature to levels more compatible with the climate."

Allegra was a little stunned by this dissertation, but she was grateful for her cousin's interference. Not only was he defending, albeit in a roundabout way, Elizabeth's fine cooking, but he was also effectively silencing his father with a barrage of esoteric information. It was becoming apparent that information was Bartholomew's hobby; he was a walking encyclopedia, a compendium of facts on a multitude of subjects.

Allegra looked at him with new respect, her instinctive attraction finding a more specific basis. It was obvious that Bartholomew possessed the keen Pembroke sense of curiosity. Where in Allegra, it was realized more in experiences and adventures, in Bartholomew, it manifested itself as an insatiable appetite for tangible details. He was undiscriminating about their nature; he seemed to welcome, equally, all topics.

"I should really enjoy a tour of the estate," he said, pouring himself a second cup of cocoa tea. "I've never seen cocoa raised."

"Cocoa is *grown*, not raised," Allegra corrected automatically. With a stab of nostalgia, she remembered how Oliver had set her straight on that same point her second day in Grenada. Her life had changed enormously since that evening on the veranda railing.

"Just so," Bartholomew said, accepting her correction. "My knowledge on the subject is sorely lacking. It would benefit greatly by authoritative instruction. Perhaps when Mr. MacKenzie returns I can persuade him to take me around." He paused, then added very fairly, "Although I should certainly understand his reluctance to do so."

"I'll take you around," Allegra volunteered, as much to her surprise as to Bartholomew's. While it hadn't occurred to Bartholomew that his lovely cousin would be familiar with the workings of the estate, it hadn't occurred to Allegra that she would want to act as a guide. It seemed vaguely like giving a thief the key to the vault, but she shrugged off the thought. She didn't know what else to do with her relatives all day; sitting with them in the parlor would be torture.

Although the expedition started out dismally enough, with Sir Gerald complaining about the heat and the steepness of the hills and the overgrown paths, it was, ultimately, very satisfying for both Allegra and Bartholomew. Bartholomew was intrigued not only by the whole process of growing and curing cocoa, but also by his cousin. He found her knowledge of the golden beans remarkably comprehensive and her enthusiasm contagious. Since he wasn't given to making snap judgments of people, it would be a mistake to say he had misjudged her, but he was astonished to realize how much he enjoyed being with her.

For Allegra the tour was a tonic. The more questions Bartholomew put to her, the more she found her spirits rising. It was a balm to her injured sense of self-esteem to hear how easily she answered him. "These beans need another day in the sun," she told her audience, running her hand through the cocoa in one of the drawers. She automatically picked out a bad bean and tossed it beyond the cement yard. "We had a rainy afternoon last week and the drawers remained shut," she explained. "It delayed the drying."

"Yes, yes," Sir Gerald said. "Obviously you will have to keep them in the sun an additional afternoon to compensate for the rainy one."

"Actually," Allegra said, standing up straight and looking directly at her uncle, "they will have to remain out for more than one extra afternoon. Not only must they make up for the sunshine they missed, but they must lose the extra moisture caused by the rain."

"In other words," Bartholomew said, "there is no precise formula for determining when the beans are cured. It is essentially a matter of individual discretion."

"No," Allegra answered, turning her steady gaze to her cousin. "It isn't a matter of individual discretion. It's a matter of experience."

"Quite so," Bartholomew murmured, much impressed.

Quite so, Allegra thought. Experience. Oliver had said it first, on that day when her fascination with cocoa had begun, but she had gained it herself. She looked back across the yard, the open drawers making an immense patchwork of cocoa, cocoa she had helped harvest. She brought her hands up, ostensibly to shade her eyes from the sun, but really to hide the tears of pride filling them. Experience, she thought again, liking very much the way it felt. It was one thing she hadn't inherited from her father. Nor could her uncle take it away.

She realized then just how much the estate had come to mean to her. It was more than eight-hundred acres of land with some cocoa groves and a comfortable house. It was inextricably tied to the most intensely lived weeks of her life, weeks that had changed its entire course. Here she had gone from a state of fearful dependence to one of happy self-confidence. Here she had healed her disappointment and sorrow with satisfying fulfillment. And here she had replaced her loneliness with love. In her heart, L'Etoile was inseparable from Oliver.

I'm not going to give up that easily, she thought as she led her uncle and cousin through the boucan. I am not going to meekly turn over L'Etoile to Sir Gerald. And I'm certainly not going to go back to the way I used to live.

"This is where the beans are sorted, sacked, and made ready for shipping," she shouted above the clatter of the sorting machine, no longer paying any attention to the tour. She was preoccupied, renewing previously made pledges.

I promised once before that I wouldn't let you down, Papa, she silently informed the heroic man in her mind. And I'll promise you again. A little of the luster had dimmed from her father's bright image since the last time she had made that vow, but she wasn't dismayed. With rejuvenated optimism, Allegra decided that if she couldn't ride on Cecil's coattails to the rewarding future she wanted, Cecil could ride along on hers.

First I'll have to settle those careless debts he's accumulated, she thought. Once the money is paid back, it should be simple enough to repair the damage to his reputation.

When they returned to the house for coconut cakes and real English tea, Allegra started her campaign. "Could you tell me please, the amount my father borrowed to buy L'Etoile?" she asked her uncle in the most businesslike tone she could muster. Ruefully remembering her dash down the hill the night of the cocoa raid, and her equally impetuous dash to Argo the other day, she resolved to be painstakingly professional this time. "As I wasn't aware the loan existed, I don't know the exact figure in question."

Sir Gerald flared his nostrils to indicate his disdain of discussing finances with a woman. Nonetheless, his miserliness overcame his distaste. "Three thousand pounds," he answered succinctly, dabbing his lips with a lace napkin.

It was Allegra's turn to raise her eyebrows. "Three thousand pounds?" she said, hope lending excitement to her voice. "That's not much, is it? Three thousand pounds is only, uh, is um, four threes are twelve plus, um . . ."

"Fourteen thousand six hundred and ten American dollars," Bartholomew supplied punctiliously.

"I have that much money," Allegra exclaimed, astonished at

how easily the problem was being solved. "Between the sale of my grandfather's properties in Connecticut and the funds he put aside for me over the years, I have that amount. Even allowing for. . ." she stopped short of blurting out, "the money I promised to repay Oliver," not wanting to let her uncle know about her father's light-fingered financing. She had no wish to give him any more ammunition for his attack on Cecil. Doing some further calculating, her fingers scribbling on her skirt and her lips murmuring sums, she concluded that she could pay back all the money Cecil owed and still have one hundred and four dollars to spare.

Bartholomew watched her do her laborious computation, aching to be able to aid her, but too polite to ask what she was figuring. It hurt him to see how she struggled with her sets of numbers when, for him, numbers fell in line so easily. He was very relieved when his cousin seemed to conquer her accounts and announced again, triumphantly, "Yes, I can pay you the three thousand pounds, and that will cancel any claim you have on L'Etoile."

"Generally speaking," Sir Gerald said with a coldness that shriveled Allegra's momentary sense of victory. "One expects interest paid on a loan of this nature. It has been outstanding now for six years. Had it been invested in the most conservative manner, it would have yielded in excess of three hundred pounds."

Allegra's heart sank. Even without converting that amount to more familiar currency, she knew she didn't have it. She had come so close to setting everything right, so close to saving L'Etoile, but not close enough. "I haven't got that much," she said softly.

Bartholomew looked from Allegra's forlorn face to his father's, unconsciously holding his breath. Normally, he acquiesced to his father's decisions, cultivating an abstract, academic air to distance himself from the less palatable ones. He took his role as Sir Gerald's heir very seriously. Duty was duty. Up until now. For the first time, he found himself being swayed by sentiment. He found himself hoping against hope, against proper procedure and objective business sense, that his delightful American cousin would not be defeated.

Miraculously, his silent wish was rewarded. "I suppose we might waive the interest payment," Sir Gerald conceded grudgingly, "considering that it is a loan within the family." Unlike his son, Sir Gerald's generosity was not motivated by the transparent emotion in Allegra's expression, but rather by pure expediency and concern for his own comfort. He believed that his niece was telling the truth, that she didn't have any more money. His only recourse was to attach the estate, and he was no longer interested in doing that. He had started their tour this morning mentally estimating how much profit could be wrung from L'Etoile, but now he was just as glad to cut his losses and leave.

He hated Grenada, hated everything about it. The brilliant colors clashed with his bleak spirit, the hot, soaking sun irritated his cold soul. He found the lyrical West Indian accent annoying, the leisurely pace intolerable. The food was abominable, the amenities execrable, and the people, well, the less he had to do with these people the better. His disheveled niece was too like his foolish brother to suit him. As for the uncouth Mr. MacKenzie, his lower-class intransigence could present a problem. All things considered, he decided, this was the best possible plan.

"We'll go to St. George's tomorrow," he announced with what passed for pleasantness. "We'll see your bankers first to settle this out, then we'll make arrangements for our immediate departure."

Allegra, whose spirits had soared and plummeted and soared again with each new utterance from her uncle, felt another tremor of despair. "I'm afraid we can't quite conclude our business tomorrow," she began hesitantly, dreading one of Sir Gerald's icy attacks.

It came at once. "And what impediment have you unearthed now?" he asked, setting his teacup in its saucer, his meager good humor evaporating.

"The money," she said miserably. "I don't have it."

"What's that?" Sir Gerald's eyebrows shot up with his voice. "You little minx! You led me to believe you possessed an inheritance, and that you were ready to repay your father's debt. I made you a handsome concession on this basis, waiving six years of interest, and now you tell me you haven't the capital, after all."

"Oh, no, no, no," Allegra hastily retracted. "I do *have* the money, it's just that I don't have it *here*. It's still in Connecticut, in my bank there. But I've already written to Mr. Barker to send it to me," she added desperately. "I know he will act as soon as he receives my letter, but it might take some time."

"Of course it will take some time," Sir Gerald snapped, severely vexed. "And in the meanwhile, I must bear the brunt of this irresponsible delay, forced to endure this beastly backwater."

"It's a perfectly understandable situation," Bartholomew put in. "Cousin Allegra has only recently arrived in Grenada, herself. It is to be expected that her bank has not yet transferred accounts." Although his tone was mild, Bartholomew was inwardly astonished. He had never rebuked his father before, never interfered with Sir Gerald's fulminations, but somehow he had felt the need to defend his cousin. He glanced at her, trying to understand what had precipitated this phenomenal reaction and was instantly warmed by the look of gratitude she gave him.

Sir Gerald, on the other hand, glared angrily at his son. Bartholomew had never crossed him before, and he definitely didn't like it. He sought a way to punish him for his disloyalty, along with Allegra, for discommoding him. "Since neither of you find any objection to this atrocious inconvenience," he said tightly, "I shall make the conclusion of this transaction your responsibility.

"From you," he said, indicating Allegra with a nod of his head, "I expect a note stating your intention of repaying this obligation in full, citing the cocoa estate as collateral. Your partner seems to place a great deal of importance on written documents, so I intend to present him with an unbreachable contract. Once the note is drawn I can have my trunk packed," he said, turning his chilly gaze on his only child. "Bartholomew shall await the arrival of funds and the subsequent termination of this matter while I return to England." He picked up another coconut cake and settled back, well pleased at having accomplished all his objectives.

Understanding the reprimand, Bartholomew only nodded, but he felt curiously undismayed at the thought of having to stay an indefinite time in Grenada. Allegra bounded out of her chair, eager to put an end both to discussion of the debt and to Sir Gerald's visit. "Let's go into the library," she suggested. "There are pens and paper at the desk."

She had just signed her name with a flourish, when Oliver entered the room, a wide-eyed Violet hard on his heels. "What's going on?" he asked without preamble, immediately zeroing in on the paper Sir Gerald was tucking into his breast pocket.

"Miss Pembroke and I have been attending to family business," Sir Gerald said superciliously, patting his lapel back into place. "And now I intend to take a rest in my room before dinner." With no further indication that they existed, Sir Gerald left the library.

"I think Miss Pembroke and I have some business to attend to now," Oliver said with deadly softness. "In the office." The look on his face and the tone in his voice allowed no room for protest. With a sigh, Allegra rose and followed him into the office.

"What the devil have you done now?" Oliver demanded, slamming the door behind them. "What mutton-headed mess have you made this time?"

Allegra's face turned red at his harsh tone, partly in embarrassment as she remembered her previous business blunders, but mostly in anger. "How dare you say that?" she retorted. "You don't even know what transpired, and yet you assume the worst."

Sitting down on the edge of the desk, Oliver crossed his arms over his chest. "It's obvious that you signed some paper," he said. "Unless it was an agreement whereby your uncle renounced all past and present claims to L'Etoile, a circumstance I seriously doubt, I can assume nothing but the worst to have transpired. What was it?"

"It was between my uncle and me," Allegra told him, annoyed by his low opinion of her abilities. "As he said, 'family business.'"

"Allegra," Oliver said warningly.

She sucked her tongue against her teeth in an unconsciously West Indian gesture of disgust. "It was a promissory note," she said with irritation. "I discovered that I have enough money to honor my father's debts. *All* of them," she added pointedly. "I want to wipe the slate clean."

"A promissory note," Oliver repeated quietly, the calm before the storm. "Using L'Etoile as collateral?"

Allegra lost a little of her steam. "Well, yes," she admitted.

"What in the hell were you thinking of?" Oliver exploded, coming to his feet. "Whatever induced you to do such an idiotic thing? You created an obligation where none existed; you volunteered to pay a debt you don't owe, possibly with the estate. There is absolutely no proof that this 'loan' was ever made to begin with. Or how much it was. Or what it was for. Or that it wasn't repaid years ago. All you have is the word of that tight-fisted, arrogant uncle of yours. He walks around with his nose in the air and his hand in your pocket, and you as much as say 'thank you'. There was no call for you to sign a note, none whatsoever. And there is no reason for you to throw your money away, either."

"Of course there is a reason," Allegra retorted, hurt by his bitter attack. "The reason is the three thousand pounds my father borrowed to buy L'Etoile."

"But you don't know that!" Oliver shouted in frustration. "You have no proof that loan ever existed."

"Really, Oliver," Allegra fumed, frustrated, herself. "I was only following all the advice you've ever given me. You told me to be more realistic about my father, to start realizing his faults, his carelessness with money. We both know that my uncle didn't make up that debt, and we both know it was never repaid. And you've always said, 'Get everything in writing,' which is exactly what I did. I think I put the whole transaction on a professional level."

For a minute, Oliver towered over her, glowering, then he sank back down on the desk, his fury fading to forbearance. He rubbed his face wearily with the palm of his hand. How could he argue with such convoluted logic? She was so earnest, so convinced of the soundness of her reasoning. He made one last attempt to set her straight. "Gerald inherited a bloody fortune," he said. "Cecil got nothing. And now the bastard has come dunning you for a few thousand pounds he'll never even spend. It's pure greed and spite that makes him do it. Even assuming your father borrowed the money and never repaid it, the sheer inequity of the situation requires that you ignore the debt. Under the circumstances, it was completely unnecessary for you to commit yourself to repay it. Or to forfeit L'Etoile."

Allegra lifted her head proudly. "Certainly it was necessary," she said, her voice as quiet as his. "It's not for me to judge the way my Grandfather Pembroke chose to dispose of his estate, or to demand an inheritance he declined to give me. If my father owed him money, I won't sneak out of repaying it. I won't have his past debts or obligations clouding the title to L'Etoile. Nor will I have people whispering about us or laughing at us or even feeling sorry for us. I want no suspicion cast on our honesty and integrity."

Oliver sighed. Although he didn't agree with her methods, he sympathized with her motives. "I may question your sanity," he said with affectionate resignation, "but never your integrity."

The familiar humor in his voice loosened Allegra. Waving her hand airily, she concluded, "Besides, there is no risk that I'll forfeit L'Etoile. I made sure of that. I can retire this debt as soon as my bank account is transferred from Connecticut. Then L'Etoile will truly be mine."

"Half yours," Oliver corrected with a smile.

"Half mine," Allegra agreed, returning his smile.

Chapter
Ten

"Uh, apparently it has been left for us to introduce ourselves," Bartholomew stammered. "I am, uh, Bartholomew Pembroke." He was mesmerized by the sight of Violet, by the silky luster of her toasted coconut skin, by the exquisitely wrought perfection of her heart-shaped face, by the tiny black curls escaping from her upswept bun. He was enchanted by her lovely brown eyes, spell-bound by her poise and beauty. Unceremoniously abandoned with her in the library, he found himself flushing with desire, utterly captivated.

"I am very pleased to meet you," Violet replied, unaware of his stuttering. "I'm Violet MacKenzie." He was different from any man she had ever encountered; he was like the magical prince of her dreams. Not only did he look like the illustration for a fairy tale hero: tall and straight and handsome, with shiny blond hair, and, china blue eyes, but he acted like one, as well. There was a grace about him, an air of refinement totally missing from the young men she knew in Carriacou and Grenada. Even her beloved brother lacked the innate gentleness and gentility she immediately sensed in Bartholomew.

"We've just finished tea," Bartholomew said, unable to stop from staring at her. "But perhaps I could ring for a fresh pot for you?"

Violet was thrilled by how grand that sounded, but declined his offer; there was no bell system at L'Etoile. "I had a cup of tea onboard the schooner as we sailed from St. George's," she said, thinking with horror of the chipped mug that had been filled from a kettle simmering in a coal pot on the foredeck. At the time it had tasted good, hot and sweetened with condensed milk, but now it seemed so inelegant.

"I see," Bartholomew said, at a loss for further words. All he wanted to do was gaze at her. Seeing her walk through the library door a few minutes ago had been the stunning finale to the two most extraordinary days in all his twenty-four years of life.

He had been raised in an orderly world, one where there were few surprises in either people or events, and certainly not in traditions. As was expected, he had passed from the nursery at the family manor to boarding school to Oxford and back to his father's estate. Along the way, he had socialized with other young people of his own class, attending hunt parties and debutante balls. He had assumed that someday soon, one among the flock of blue-blooded females with an upbringing identical to his would become his wife, that eventually he would inherit Pembroke Hall, and that the whole timeless process would be repeated.

Having a genial disposition, he had not resisted this predetermined, if pampered existence. At least not until he debarked in Grenada. He had responded with extreme astonishment and pleasure to his first view of the tropical island. Everything amazed him, the colors, the climate, the accents, the scenery; this island aroused reactions he hadn't known he was capable of.

The biggest surprise, however, had been the people. He liked the slow-moving, independent Grenadians, even the muttering Elizabeth, but he was really impressed by his beautiful cousin and her plain-spoken partner. Unlike Sir Gerald, who thought that Oliver was an unwashed, unlettered colonial, and that Allegra was a fortune-hunting fraud, Bartholomew was aware of Oliver's education and sophistication and of Allegra's good breeding. What struck him most was the way they seemed almost to flout those attributes, living life intensely and unconventionally, with as much brilliance as the noonday sun. He felt admiration and even envy.

And then Violet had entered the room. After one look at her, the faces of the inevitable English debutantes were eclipsed forever. In Violet he saw a delicate essence of this exotic island, the vivid beauty, the unaffected feeling, the unrestrained life.

Silence followed his inane remark. They both stood as if planted in the center of the library, made suddenly shy by their mutual attraction. They no longer stared at each other but studied opposite corners of the room, glancing forward, then examining the floor. It was Bartholomew who gained control of himself first, innocuous conversation being a staple of his education.

"The air is delightful at this time of day," he said. "Shall we sit on the veranda?" He hated how empty his words sounded when there was so much of importance that he wanted to say, but good manners forbade it.

"Yes, that would be pleasant," Violet responded, cringing at how silly she seemed.

They walked through the open double doors of the library and carefully arranged themselves on chintz-cushioned chairs on the veranda. The lowering sun sent a shaft of light through the gingerbread fretwork, making a long, lacy shadow at their feet. Bartholomew made a show of taking a deep breath. "Splendid," he murmured perfunctorily. "The flowers always seem more fragrant in late afternoon, have you noticed?"

Violet sniffed the air, too, her hands folded neatly in her lap. "Yes, indeed," she said. "It's the jasmine, I believe, by the cistern. It's just come into bloom again."

"Ah, yes, jasminium grandiflora. One of the many treasures we have received over the centuries from Persia. It makes such a charming addition to any garden, don't you find?"

"It's one of my very favorites."

"That one is a particularly handsome specimen. I was admiring it this morning when I took a stroll, before breakfast, around the lawn. Indeed, all the plantings are extraordinary. The bed of lilies by the drive is simply glorious. I counted no fewer than eighteen different species."

"Your uncle designed the original landscaping, but Oliver has added to it. He retains a gardener just to keep everything trimmed. It grows so fast, you know."

"I can imagine. In this rich soil and hot sun, plants positively leap out of the ground."

"You are being so kind and courteous!" Violet suddenly cried, clutching the arms of her chair as if to keep from leaping up herself. "This must be truly dull for you." Raised on the forthright attitudes of Angus and Oliver, she could no longer prattle about flowers and shrubs when she wanted to tell him how much she admired him.

"I am sure you are accustomed to far more elegant surroundings, and to a much more exciting life. But how very gallant of you to take an interest in the poor amusements we have to offer when I'm sure you are thinking of all the operas and balls and important people you have left behind in London."

Bartholomew was thinking no such thing, but the notion that *she* was thinking so brought a flush of embarrassed pleasure to his pale, chiseled cheeks. He was startled not only by her ingenuous honesty, but also by her flattering assessment of him. While he knew that he was physically appealing, he knew also that he was considered to be a tiny bit boring.

Until two days ago his life had been anything but exciting: It had been as comfortably predictable as the London fog. Now Violet had burst into it, a shot of tropical sunshine, and he instantly knew things would never be the same again. His supply of smooth small talk deserted him. "Not at all," he mumbled.

Violet didn't notice the lapse in his polished politeness as another thought struck her. She wondered if she weren't being disloyal by being so drawn to a man who really was the enemy. After all, Bartholomew and his father had come here to take L'Etoile away from Allegra and to disrupt the life that Oliver loved. The realization made her sick, but the sense of balance she had inherited from her mother didn't allow her to brood. After only ten minutes in Bartholomew's company, she knew that she was utterly incapable of relinquishing her attraction to him. Instead, she decided to make Bartholomew give up his original goal.

"I do hope you won't find things so intolerable here at L'Etoile that you will be indifferent to its fate." She folded her hands in her lap again but remained on the edge of her seat, fervently pleading her case. "It would be a terrible tragedy if Allegra lost L'Etoile. She would be heartbroken. She loves this estate more than I can tell you; she loves the cocoa. And the cocoa seems to respond to her devotion. Even Oliver has said she is good for the estate, that she has suggested some sound improvements. If only you knew her better I'm sure you would realize all her remarkable qualities and that she deserves to keep L'Etoile."

"I assure you, Miss MacKenzie, it is not my wish to evict my cousin," Bartholomew answered immediately. Even if he had found Allegra to be an unbearable shrew, he would not have been able to resist Violet's appeal. As it was, he had already taken

Allegra's side, increasingly aware of the remarkable qualities Violet referred to. Violet's heartfelt tribute to her friend merely solidified the decision that had been floating vaguely across the surface of his mind.

"I shall do everything in my power to help her retain her home," he said sincerely. "At the moment, she has willingly agreed to repay the debt her father incurred with funds that are to arrive from the States. Should that scheme fail, in whole or in part, or should it become possible to persuade my father to forgive that debt, I give you my word that I shall not neglect my cousin's cause. Even in the short period of our acquaintance, I have been able to determine that your admirable championship is not unwarranted. Cousin Allegra is an exceptional woman."

"I knew it!" Violet cried triumphantly, clapping her hands together. "I knew you could not possibly be heartless. I knew you would undo this dreadful injustice. Mama always says that you can see a person's character in his eyes, and I can see in your eyes that you are a true gentleman, a fair and honorable man. Oh, Mr. Pembroke," she said, relief illuminating her face. "Thank you very much. You won't regret this decision, I know you won't."

Unnerved by this outpouring of gratitude, Bartholomew manged to again mutter, "Not at all." He was unsure of the proper response. No one he knew even admitted to having strong emotions, much less expressed them. Although Violet's stirring display touched a hidden chord in him, it was too unfamiliar for him to know how to react.

He was spared the need for further comment by the appearance of his father in the library. "Bartholomew!" Sir Gerald called irritably. "Where have you gone to?"

Both Bartholomew and Violet rose hastily and reentered the room. "Here, Father," Bartholomew replied, more assured in his role as the dutiful son. "Miss MacKenzie and I have just been enjoying the air."

"It's too heavy," Sir Gerald complained. "And there is a sickly sweet scent that is cloying."

"It's the jasmine growing over the cistern," Violet repeated, eager to please the man who was Bartholomew's father, despite her initial bad impression and her brother's poor opinion of him.

Sir Gerald ignored her. "I knew I should have brought Henderson with me," he said to his son. "It would have been worth

the price of his passage to have a decent valet attend to my needs
I was just now setting out my dinner clothes when I discovere
the presence of a repulsive reptilian creature in the wardrobe
only inches from my jacket. Really, this place is shockingly prim
itive. And the servants make no attempt to control the situation.'

"I think, perhaps, it is quite difficult to keep the outdoor
where it belongs when the house is so open," Bartholomew tem
porized.

"It's only a gecko," Violet offered with less spirit. "They ar
quite harmless."

"Regardless," Sir Gerald said frigidly, turning to her for th
first time. "I don't wish the beast to tread on my clothes." Hi
cold eyes assessed her briefly, assumed she was a maid, an
looked away. "Remove it," he commanded in dismissal.

The silky skin on Violet's throat and cheeks darkened at Si
Gerald's peremptory tone. For a few seconds, she remaine
where she was, her pretty lips pressed tightly together. The
slowly, with dignity, she moved across the room. She would de
tach the gummy footed gecko from the wall of Sir Gerald's ward
robe, not because he had ordered her to, but because he was
guest in her brother's home, a visitor in her country, and commo
courtesy demanded that she make him comfortable.

Sir Gerald's remark had an even more devastating effect o
Bartholomew. He was about to correct his father's assumptio
that she was a servant when he realized what had prompted it: he
skin. The toasted coconut-colored skin he found so bewitchingl
beautiful. An icy shock shot through him as he saw Violet for th
first time, not as an exquisite flower in an exotic land, but in th
context of reality. She was a dark-skinned woman in his ver
white world.

An enormous sense of loss filled him as he accepted th
impossibility of a relationship between them. There was an un
breachable barrier preventing it. He could rationalize he
uninhibited displays of emotion as naive enthusiasm; he coul
call her unorthodox background charming. He could easily ignor
her working-class origins, her simple education, her unsophisti
cated manner. He could excuse all those lively, lovely qualitie
that set her apart from the cool, constrained debutantes of h
circle. But he could not overcome the color of her skin.

In the flash of time that he acknowledged this insuperab
obstacle, a small, smothered voice inside him protested. A de

erate wish was formed, a completely preposterous, illogical
hope took hold that somehow, in some miraculous way, the color
of her skin would no longer matter. He longed for the first blissfully oblivious minutes of their meeting, before he had realized
there was any difference between them.

It was this unarticulated desire that made him call out apologetically to her departing back. "Please, Miss MacKenzie, there's
no need for you to bother yourself on our behalf. I'll go attend to
the creature myself. Please stay here and take the evening air."

Violet turned slowly, but did not retrace her steps. Her luminous brown eyes looked wounded, the fragile skin around them
stretched tight. "I don't mind," she said quietly. "I find lizards
quite inoffensive." She turned again and left the room, preferring
the company of a gulping gecko to that of Sir Gerald. Innocent
and trusting though she might be, she did not misunderstand his
intolerance. Nor had she failed to notice the withdrawal in Bartholomew's expression at his father's condescending command.
That hurt the most. As she made her way toward the stairs, she
felt more miserable than she ever had in her life.

Violet's obvious anguish struck raw feelings in Bartholomew,
feelings that, like many others he had discovered these past two
days, had astonishing effects on his usually complacent disposition. His guilt and frustration were vented on his father. "That
was Miss Violet MacKenzie you were so rude to," he angrily told
Sir Gerald. "She is the sister of our host, Mr. Oliver MacKenzie."

Sir Gerald's eyebrows rose, responding both to his son's unprecedented behavior and to the news he was imparting. "His
sister? What extremely careless breeding habits they have here in
the colonies," he said scornfully. Pointedly turning his back on
Bartholomew, he strolled away.

Bartholomew was left standing alone in the center of the library, feeling alternately furious and sad. He found himself wishing that his cousin's funds might never arrive from her American
bank, that he would have an excuse to remain here indefinitely,
unsupervised by his father and unencumbered by the rigid social
codes he represented. It seemed like the only solution, the only
way he could keep seeing Violet. He finally left the library, going
wearily to his room to change for dinner, glad only that his father
was leaving soon.

Sir Gerald's departure couldn't come too rapidly for any per-

son present at L'Etoile, especially Sir Gerald himself. It was
tremendous disappointment for everyone to learn the next morn
ing that there were no Britain-bound ships until after the New
Year, still two weeks away. "I telephoned the agent," Oliver an
nounced at breakfast. He had already eaten, but he put in an
appearance to relate his grim news. "The Royal Mail Packe
leaves for Barbados on January second. There is a connectin
steamer for Southampton on the following Thursday."

Elizabeth's exaggerated sigh was drowned out by Sir Gerald
pronouncement of annoyance. "How dreadfully inconvenient,
he fretted. "I shall be forced to pass Christmas with strangers, in
this alien climate. I am sure I shall be in wretched health by th
time I make my escape. This heat plays havoc with my liver."

Ignoring both Sir Gerald's liver and the obvious question o
why he had come to Grenada in this season if he wanted to pass
Christmas at home, Oliver turned to Allegro. "The *Solent* arrive
from Trinidad three days ago with a load of ice and malt," h
said. "If I understood Arnold Baptiste correctly, the *Miss Lil*
came into Gouyave with ice last night."

Bartholomew found this news only moderately interesting
barely enough to distract him from his chagrin at his father
continued presence in Grenada. While he smoothed butter an
honey on hot cornbread, he worried that, having waited two extr
weeks, his father might decide to wait a little longer and collec
Allegra's debt himself. Or even worse, he thought, nearly chok
ing on a crumbly bite, his cousin's money might arrive befor
January second, and he would be forced to depart with his father

"How splendid!" Allegra's exclamation interrupted his mus
ing. Looking over at her, he was amazed to see her face aligh
with excitement.

"Indeed?" he said politely, forcing his attention back to th
discussion at hand. "Have you run short of ice?"

"Oh, we are forever running short of ice." Allegra dismisse
that statement with a toss of her hand. "We have two cork-line
boxes in the kitchen, but no one remembers to cart them down t
Gouyave to be refilled. Whenever an ice boat comes in, though
Matthewlina Cameron makes soursop sorbet for her boarder
with a little left over for the cafe. You can't imagine how deli
cious it is, especially if she has a tin of lemon wafers to spoon i
up with. If we go down after lunch, I'll wager we can convinc
her to let us have some."

She looked around brightly to see who shared her enthusiasm. Bartholomew stared at her blankly; Violet toyed with the food on her plate; Sir Gerald was completely indifferent. Only Oliver greeted the idea with the hint of a grin. "Well, *I'm* going," Allegra said decisively. "Who is going to accompany me? Oliver?"

The grin emerged a little more, but Oliver shook his head. "I have some things to attend to," he said. "But perhaps your cousin will go in my stead."

Allegra turned toward Bartholomew who blinked several times but valiantly accepted. "Yes, of course," he said. "I'd be honored to escort you." He glanced longingly at Violet, hoping she would offer to join them, but she didn't seem to hear the conversation.

To his relief, Allegra announced firmly, "Violet, you must come, too. You've been moping since last evening. An outing is just what you need to chase away the dismals."

Finally raising her head, Violet nodded reluctantly. It made Bartholomew's heart ache to see how sad she seemed, knowing his father's thoughtless remark was the cause of it. She looked so small and lost, he longed to fold her into his arms and kiss away her unhappiness.

The idea dumbfounded him. He didn't know how it had come into his head. He had never folded a woman into his arms; never kissed one either tenderly or in passion. The fact was, there had never been a woman who affected him as Violet did, stirring up feelings he knew were immoderate, arousing desires he suspected were impermissible. Every minute that he spent in her presence made leaving her seem more impossible.

For this afternoon, at least, he didn't have to think about his inevitable return to England. For this afternoon, he was very much in Grenada. Allegra led the way down to the stables and had donkeys saddled for Violet and herself. "We have some very handsome horses," she told her cousin, "and you may certainly have your pick. I never learned to ride, so I prefer to journey by burro. That way, if I'm thrown, I don't have far to fall. Violet is kind enough to keep me company, although she is perfectly capable of managing any horse here."

That being the case, Bartholomew felt compelled to say, "You must allow me to keep you company, as well. I've never ridden an ass, but I feel sure my West Indian experience would be greatly diminished if I neglected to do so."

He was rewarded for his gallantry when, a short time later, mounted on a donkey, his long legs dangling almost to the red earth, Allegra gave him a nod of approval and Violet's face lit up with a ghost of humor. Bartholomew beamed back, not at all upset that she was probably amused by the ludicrous spectacle he made. He shook his head in disbelief. Three days ago he would have sworn it impossible for him to be involved in such an undignified escapade, but right now his dignity seemed an insignificant sacrifice for Violet's smile.

He was considerably more tentative when they arrived at the Back Door Boarding House and Restaurant and encountered the proprietress. Matthewlina Cameron was an intimidatingly tall, heavyset black woman wearing a bright indigo turban and six inches of silver bracelets on each arm. Her large size and fierce scowl seemed at odds with the sweet, delicate desserts for which she was famous.

"We've come for your world-renowned soursop sorbet Matthewlina," Allegra announced.

Unmoved by the flattery, Matthewlina remained in her chair by the door. "Finished," she said, hardly giving them a glance.

"No, it can't be!" Allegra cried. "We've ridden for days in the searing heat to reach your cafe. We've endured hailstones and spiders and poisonous snakes." She fell to her knees, clutching her throat. "We haven't had a morsel to eat nor a drop to drink," she whispered hoarsely. "Only your sorbet can revive us. Have mercy. Please."

In the silence that followed Allegra's performance, Bartholomew stood rigid in astonishment while Violet stopped a giggle with her fist. Finally Matthewlina gave an elaborate sigh, heaved herself up, and clumped off to her kitchen, shaking her head. Looking extremely pleased, Allegra got to her feet and dusted off her dress.

A few minutes later Matthewlina reappeared, bearing three frosty bowls heaped with soursop sorbet. Although her movements seemed ungraceful and her manners ungracious, she managed to arrange a lovely display on the small table, perfectly positioned to catch every bit of the breeze and to provide an unparalleled view of the purple sea.

The sorbet was cool and creamy, tasting vaguely like peaches and vaguely like bananas and altogether like quintessential summer fruit. "This is ambrosial," Bartholomew murmured, letting it slide slowly down his throat. He didn't know whether it was the soothing sorbet or the inspired setting or the delightful company he was keeping, but he felt thoroughly refreshed, in body and soul. Relaxed as never before, Bartholomew rested both elbows on the table and leaned slightly forward, as if to physically absorb the laughter and liveliness of his companions.

"You see," Allegra said triumphantly. "I knew this was the ideal outing. We all needed to get away from the estate. Things were getting entirely too grim. You look one hundred times happier than you did at breakfast, Violet. Really, I was becoming quite concerned. I thought perhaps you had eaten another bad batch of sea eggs while you were in St. George's, but you've recovered admirably from whatever ailed you. And Cousin Bartholomew, even you look substantially revived."

Violet only smiled, not wanting to admit that the real remedy was the way Bartholomew reverently gazed at her. "I *feel* substantially revived," Bartholomew responded. "This was a brilliant notion, Cousin Allegra. I would never have imagined I could enjoy myself so much."

The sight of Violet's face, rekindled with life, was more restorative than any other cure. Hardly able to tear his eyes from her, he studied every enchanting detail about her. He watched the way her pretty plum-colored lips moved, the way her large, lovely eyes glanced around the room and at him, the way her soft, dusky skin flushed a shade deeper under his admiring stare.

So mesmerized was he by her beauty and grace, and forthright innocence, that he hardly noticed when Allegra went into the kitchen in search of Matthewlina. Conscious only of the sudden stillness, sensing vaguely that they were all alone, Bartholomew stretched his arm across the small table and brushed a silky black curl from Violet's face. His hand swept over her smooth forehead, lightly grazing the fluff of her dark hair. He did it instinctively without thinking, a gesture of intimacy already rooted in his heart if not yet fixed in his head.

As welcome as it was, it startled them both. Violet's eyes shot wide open though she did not draw away. Barely breathing, her blood racing, she just stared, waiting. For a moment, Bartholomew stared back, shocked by his bold action, but riveted in place by the feel of her face beneath his fingers. The apology that rose to his lips remained unuttered. Succumbing again to her spell, he

let his hand drop, carefully covering hers. It was small and warm;
it fit perfectly against his palm.

Violet looked down at his hand, resting tenderly on top of
hers. Her pulse pounded furiously, her heart swelled; she hardly
believed how much happiness filled her. When she raised her
eyes again, meeting Bartholomew's, she saw no sign of the im-
placable retreat that had devastated her last evening. She saw no
judgment, no frozen resignation. His clear blue eyes were steady,
his face was lit with unequivocal devotion and love.

Violet's already full heart gave another leap, and her happiness overflowed. Yet even as she surrendered her spirit to him,
even as she silently pledged him her soul, she realized that he
was unaware of the emotion so obvious in his expression. It had
poured out from hidden places he hadn't known existed; it had
overwhelmed the direction and discipline he'd spent a lifetime
acquiring; it had defied his birth and his breeding. More moved
than she thought possible, Violet resolved to make him aware of
his feeling. She turned her hand over in his and gently grasped
his fingers.

In almost the next instant, both hands went scurrying into their
respective laps as Allegra emerged from the kitchen. "I've got a
packet of tea cakes to deliver to Matthewlina's daughter on the
way home," she began, then stopped. She looked from Bartholomew to Violet, first surprised then suspicious of the high color in
their cheeks and the unusual brightness of their eyes.

"Is she nearby?" Bartholomew asked, seeking to divert his
cousin's speculation. "Is she here in Gouyave?"

"She lives halfway between here and L'Etoile," Allegra answered slowly, still studying their faces.

"Is she the one with the twins named Remo and Romulous?"
Violet asked, taking her cue from Bartholomew.

"Mmmm," Allegra said, rubbing her chin between her thumb
and forefinger.

"Remo and Romulous?" Bartholomew asked, genuinely astonished. "The Roman twins who were suckled by a wolf? I must
say, I am most impressed with the imagination and the literary
allusion that goes into naming children in Grenada. We are quite
boring, in comparison, with our Johns and Marys and Edwards.
Oh, yes, and speaking of names," he added, having succeeded in
distracting himself, at any rate, "you must satisfy my curiosity on
another point. Why is it that all the maps and documents refer to

this delightful hamlet as Charlotte Town, but everyone persists in calling it Gouyave?"

"Gouyave is the original French name," Allegra answered, finally shrugging away her qualms. Her serious academic cousin couldn't possibly be guilty of the passion she thought she saw. She must have been mistaken. "The French were the first European settlers," she explained. "They came in the mid 1600s, conquering the Carib Indians in short order. The last forty or so Indians leaped into the sea from a ledge at Sauteurs, which is how that town came by its name.

"One hundred years later, the French were routed themselves. This time by the British, at the conclusion of the Seven Years War. You must know the dates, Violet. I'm sure you studied this in school. In fact, you should be giving this lesson, as I must be making a muddle of it."

"No, no," Violet assured her, "you have it right. The French recaptured Grenada in 1779, but only managed to hold onto it for four years. In 1783, it was ceded permanently to Britain, despite a bitter uprising at the end of the eighteenth century. When the English took possession, they changed a lot of the French names. Port Louis became St. George's, for example, and Gouyave became Charlotte Town. For some reason, though, St. George's stuck, but Charlotte Town didn't."

"Popular opinion has it, I might add, that the Spaniards gave the island its name," Bartholomew interjected. "Although the intrepid Christopher Colombus, sailing for King Ferdinand, discovered Grenada on his third voyage to the Americas in 1498, he called it Concepcion. Later Spanish adventurers, reminded of their lovely city in Spain, renamed it Grenada."

"I might have known!" Allegra exclaimed in mock disgust. "Here we are, telling you the island's history, and you probably have more information about Grenada than both of us put together."

"I did do a spot of research before embarking on this voyage," Bartholomew admitted. "I find it enhances any experience if one can prepare oneself with background information."

"I suppose so," Allegra said, a note of doubt in her voice. It was not the way she usually went about things. "Sometimes, though, that approach can dampen the joy of discovery. Sometimes it's more rewarding just to jump right in."

Bartholomew didn't answer, but his cousin's remark made an

impact. He looked from her to Violet, reflecting that no amount of reading could have prepared him for her, no amount of research could have magnified the way he felt. It would be impossible to describe the essence of Violet in an exercise book, impossible to reduce her sweet vitality to dry words. She saw him studying her again and smiled. His heart gave another lurch and he knew Allegra was right. Discovering Violet, and her wondrous effect on him, was a joy.

They started for home shortly after that, riding through Gouyave to see the few sights. Allegra led the way past the Roman Catholic Chapel and the Anglican Church, down dusty back lanes alive with chickens and children and postage-stamp size gardens, and out to the beach. The smooth, round rocks on the south side of town turned to hard white sand on the north side. Little boxes of houses on wobbly legs were jammed haphazardly between palm trees and brightly painted fishing boats. Salted flying fish hung everywhere to dry, suspended from poles like so many socks on a line. Bartholomew found it all fascinating, the sounds, the smells, the sun-bleached sights. Although he felt a little self-conscious astride his donkey, after Allegra made him shed his jacket and loosen his tie, he didn't feel quite so conspicuous.

They wound their way back to the road and up into the hills, moving lazily in the heat. About halfway to L'Etoile, a well-trodden path twisted off to the right, through a thicket of paw paw and calabash trees. "There's no need for us all to go deliver Matthewlina's package," Allegra said. "You two wait here in the shade. I'll just be a minute." She guided her donkey down the track, playfully batting at a round, green calabash dangling by a long stem.

Bartholomew watched her intently until she was out of sight. After she disappeared and the muffled clop of hooves died away, the only sound was the buzzing of bees as they harvested pollen from a patch of bright orange wildflowers on the opposite side of the red dirt road. Bartholomew turned his attention to them, feeling awkward. Now that he was alone with Violet, he was unsure of what to say, of how to recapture the spell that had held them in the restaurant. That moment had been completely unplanned. And completely out of character. As much as he wanted to, he didn't know how to go about duplicating it.

"Lovely flowers," he finally commented, in much the same

way he had talked about the jasmine and the lilies last evening.

"Yes, they are," Violet agreed, wondering how she could coax the light of love back into his eyes.

In the end, she realized it never really had left. All Bartholomew needed was a push, and he supplied it himself. Yielding to an impulse, he dismounted, looped his reins around a branch, and quickly crossed the road to snatch a few flowers into a bouquet. "For you," he said simply, presenting them to Violet as she sat sidesaddle on her donkey. He held them out to her, his unspoken sentiments obvious in his face.

Violet reached for the scraggly bouquet, her fingers touching his as she took it. A thrill shot through her body, and her heart pounded in her chest. "Thank you," she said softly, holding the flowers close to her. "They're beautiful."

"Not as beautiful as you," Bartholomew said sincerely, letting his heady impulse carry him on. "I've never seen anyone as beautiful as you."

Violet caught her breath in a gulp. Even though she had wished for just such words, now that they were spoken she didn't know what to say in return. Instead, she yielded to an impulse of her own. She leaned forward, slipped her arm around his neck, and pressed her lips against his.

It was a quick kiss, an inexpert caress, but there was no mistaking its message, no ignoring its undercurrent of desire. Again, it startled them both and for a moment, they just stared at each other, stunned by the intensity of their feelings. Had they had just a few additional seconds so close together, they might have expressed those glorious emotions in words.

The sound of donkey hooves on the path interrupted them, and Allegra's call drew them apart. As Violet's arm slid away, as her hand passed his cheek, Bartholomew turned his head sideways and brushed his lips along her palm. It was the only response that he had time to make, and he did it without thinking. He knew he had to answer her message, that he couldn't let things die because of decorum.

"Wait until you see what Emmaline gave me," Allegra said excitedly, holding aloft a parcel wrapped in a banana leaf. "She'd just made tamarind balls, and she insisted I take some for my trouble. That's a more than fair exchange, I'd say."

This time she didn't notice the flush on Violet's and Bartholomew's faces or the bright light in their eyes as she chatted about the candies she had been given. She didn't notice that Bartholomew's questions on the subject were more polite than curious, or that Violet wasn't eagerly demanding a sample. The rest of the way back to L'Etoile, she held forth on the tamarind: how the tree grew, how its fruit was really a seed pod, how its syrupy extract was used to flavor everything from curries to cakes. She gave recipes and examples and explained that the tamarind balls were made by kneading the pulp and black pepper with baking soda and sugar. Her listeners were only half attentive, involved in more momentous thoughts of their own, but she didn't notice that, either.

Both Allegra's oblivion and Bartholomew and Violet's introspection came to an abrupt halt on their return to the estate.

"I've had a beastly time of it," Sir Gerald bitterly complained. "This place is uncivilized. The servants are intolerably ignorant. My tea was so weak, it was undrinkable. And as if that weren't outrageous enough, the clumsy girl dropped my cup, managing to spill tea on both my jacket and my trousers. No doubt they will never get the stains out, and the entire suit shall have to be discarded. It's quite my newest suit, too. I had it made only last month."

Having felt enough of Sir Gerald's venom the previous night, Violet didn't comment, but Allegra said, "Perhaps it won't stain, after all, since the tea was so weak."

Her uncle fixed her a harsh stare, sure she was mocking him. "Were it only unadulterated water," he said in high irritation, "I am convinced that the ham-handed peasants you employ would nonetheless manage to leave the suit in ruins."

While angry color rose up his cousin's neck, Bartholomew interceded. "Surely the suit is salvageable," he said with more diplomacy of tone than of spirit. For once, he had little patience for his father's needs. He wanted to remain immersed in the intoxicating glow Violet's kiss had created. "I feel certain you are underestimating the skills of the estate's laundress. From all appearances, she does a sufficient job."

"Then you shall deal with her," Sir Gerald said pettishly. "And with all the other hopeless ninnies, as well. It is too much for my nerves to cope with these simpletons in this devastating heat."

"Very well," Bartholomew sighed, feeling the glow drift away.

"And you must not desert me as you did this afternoon," Sir

Gerald added selfishly. "While I am held captive in this wretched outpost, I shall depend on you for decent companionship."

With compliance developed over a lifetime, Bartholomew sat down in the chair opposite Sir Gerald. The glow was gone. "Yes, Father," he said.

Day followed day, each monopolized by Sir Gerald's acute discomfort. Bartholomew rarely left his station by his father's side except to send Ivy or Jane on an errand, or to humbly request something special from Elizabeth. He seldom saw Violet except across the dining table, and never once spent a minute alone with her. Gradually, as time passed in his father's oppressive company, the memory of the afternoon excursion to Gouyave dimmed. He became resigned once more to the futility of his extraordinary feeling for Violet. He gazed at her during meals, and was filled with longing and regret. He didn't know that Violet, gazing back, saw only the remoteness clouding his blue eyes and was filled with despair.

The Christmas season came and went, bringing an appearance of festivity to L'Etoile, but it didn't affect Bartholomew. Despite the Norfolk Island Pine Allegra insisted on installing in the parlor, despite the strings of shells she and Violet draped from its boughs, he didn't recognize it as Christmas. The cobalt blue sky and the balmy breezes swaying the palms were nothing like the frosty air and white snow he associated with the holiday. The roast goose had a mango dressing instead of a chestnut one, the baked potatoes were yams, and Sir Gerald nearly choked when he discovered that the delicious "tatou" they were eating was actually an armadillo.

Left on his own, Bartholomew undoubtedly would have greeted these new encounters with his customary curiosity, but dragged down by his father's daily criticisms, he only endured them. Left on his own, he would have enjoyed meeting the parade of Christmas visitors at L'Etoile, but sensitive to his father's censuring tongue, he did his best to disassociate himself from the company.

Sir Gerald caustically assumed that professional incompetence and substandard intellect were the reasons for the genial Jamie's self-exile to the colonies. He condemned the kind-hearted Mrs. Potter as a twittering fool, scorned the Reverend Smythe as a prattling parson and his harmless wife as a church mouse. Only Colonel Woodbury got his grudging approval. Thomas Henry de-Gale he ignored altogether.

Thomas's father had been born a slave, but Thomas, ambitious and shrewd, had overcome his very humble heritage. He had bought the River Antoine Rum Distillery, then had acquired several run-down sugar estates. He now fed the cane he grew into the giant crushers he owned and produced some of the finest rum in Grenada. Despite being successful and engaging, Thomas wasn't white. Bartholomew uneasily noted his father's pointed snub.

Through the sets of tennis and the tournaments of croquet during the day long excursion to watch the small boat regatta from Sauteurs Bay to London Bridge Island and back, Bartholomew sat with his father in the shade of the veranda. He sat in the cool breeze, endlessly reading or listening to Sir Gerald, forfeiting an elegant luncheon at Lt. Col. Duncan's estate higher up in the hills, and bowing out of a cricket match in an open field in Gouyave. It all became less real as the days went on, a bizarre aberration of the life he usually led.

As he listened to Oliver playing Christmas carols on the piano during a steamy tropical downpour, or as he smelled the turtle steaks Elizabeth was barbecuing behind the kitchen, Bartholomew became increasingly numb. He was in neither England nor Grenada, but in a tiny world of his own, bounded by a gingerbread railing on one side and a double door on the other. Only when Violet passed through his limited field of vision did he come out of his trance. The sight of her would fill him with very real yearning and pain, but then she would disappear and he would slide back into his dazed state.

As New Year's approached, so did his cousin. "You must accompany us to Royston Ross's ball," she said in the same tone she had used to persuade Violet to come with them to Gouyave. "He has sent a note expressly inviting you to attend; he would be terribly disappointed if you didn't."

Although she had addressed herself to Bartholomew, Sir Gerald answered. "No doubt our presence would lend cachet to his party, but I cannot be responsible for the feelings of every aspiring socialite in the colonies," he said callously. "In all probability, we should be treated to another display of cloddish behavior and undisciplined servants. I have no need to stress myself thusly in this extreme heat. We shall remain here, a case of the known misery being preferable to the unknown one."

Allegra flushed at her uncle's very obvious insinuations, but bravely persisted. "The Rosses have a luxurious home. I'd venture to say it's almost the size of the Governor's Mansion, and it sits on a bluff above St. George's that has a spectacular view and a very good breeze. I'm sure you would find it as comfortable as any place in Grenada."

Sir Gerald arched his eyebrows. "As comfortable as that?" he asked sarcastically. "No, we must decline the invitation," he added without regret. "I intend to remain here until my departure for England."

Allegra played her ace card. "The mail packet leaves for Barbados on Tuesday noon, which means that you'll have to go down to St. George's the day before. Except that the day before is New Year's Day and there will be no steamers or schooners sailing on the holiday. The *Miss Lily* is going on Sunday morning, which will be your last opportunity to get to St. George's without risk of missing the packet. As long as you'll be in town on New Year's Eve, you may as well attend the ball."

"Very neatly schemed," Sir Gerald said bitterly. "We seem to be at the mercy of this provincial place, once again. And you have successfully manipulated our misfortune to your advantage. May I presume you have also thought to provide us with lodgings?"

"Yes, you may," Allegra answered blandly, although another flush betrayed her anger at his accusation. "Mr. Forsythe has very kindly offered you the use of his house. He and Oliver will stay in his office so that you may have complete privacy."

"We seem to have no other recourse," Sir Gerald ungraciously conceded.

"Tell me something, Cousin Allegra," Bartholomew said. He had been silent during this entire exchange, looking from one strong-willed person to the other, barely caring who won the battle. Now, curiosity overcame lethargy. "You can hardly be impressed by our manners or find pleasure in our company," he said with unusual candor. "Why are you so anxious to have us attend this affair under your patronage?"

"It's simple," Allegra replied practically and with equal candor. "If you don't go then I must stay here with you. It would create gossip for me to abandon my visiting uncle on his last day in Grenada. If I don't go, then there is no way that Oliver can be persuaded to leave L'Etoile either. And if he doesn't go, then Violet would have to stay home, too, and she would be heartbroken. She has looked forward to this ball for two months and has the most lovely gown, made especially for the occasion." She stopped, thought a minute, then added, "I have had a rather pretty dress made as well. It would be a shame not to wear it."

"I see," Bartholomew murmured, more affected than the explanation would seem to demand. He was suddenly quite glad that it was his invincible cousin who had won this round, and that they would be going to the Rosses'. Although balls of far greater magnitude were standard fare for him, he found himself anticipating this one eagerly and almost against his will.

Despite telling himself repeatedly that there could be no future with Violet, the thought of sliding his hand around her small waist and leading her waltzing around the dance floor was utterly irresistible. He imagined her dressed in a beautiful gown, her eyes lit with ingenuous enjoyment of the gaiety and finery. The vision stirred him and lifted the gloom weighing down his soul.

He carried the vision of Violet with him for the next few days, using it almost like a life ring. He placed it between himself and his father so he no longer heard Sir Gerald's peevish complaints. He called on it to restore his patience as he shepherded Sir Gerald from L'Etoile's veranda to Jamie's small house. And he conjured it up to fill the suddenly empty feeling when he realized that Violet, lodged with Allegra at her Aunt Ruby's, was no longer under the same roof as he, that this was a prelude to the rest of his life without her.

It was an unutterable relief to see the vision finally realized, and much more of a thrill than he had imagined. Violet's pale peach gown was cut low and ruffled at the neck, revealing the soft, smooth skin of her shoulders and breast. The silk clung sensuously to her curves. Tiny bows on her cap sleeves emphasized the slenderness of her arms. A spray of flowers showed off the daintiness of her waist. "You are very beautiful," he told her again when he met her in the foyer.

Although pleasure at his compliment brought on warm color, this time Violet wasn't at a loss for a response. Standing before her, he seemed taller and fairer than ever in his finely fitted black evening coat. His silk bow tie and crisp shirt were impeccably white beneath his perfectly sculpted face. The words came naturally, without thought. "You are very beautiful, too," she breathed.

Bartholomew's pale cheeks turned red at her remark. Her art-

ess admiration flustered him. "No one has ever told me that
before," he mumbled.

"No?" Violet asked, astonished. "How is that possible? Are
all your friends blind?"

Bartholomew's blush deepened as he tried to extract himself,
unused to such fervent praise. "Of course not," he answered
clumsily. "It's just that 'beautiful' is not an adjective used frequently in reference to men. In general, one is more apt to describe a man as 'well turned out' or 'particularly fit.' On
occasion, even 'handsome.'"

"You are always handsome," Violet said, defending her
choice of words and her assessment of him. "Tonight, however,
you are beautiful. It's not only your clothes, although they are
quite splendid. It's the light in your face, true and clear, like the
sky at dawn. Tonight you have that light, and tonight you are
beautiful."

"If that is so," Bartholomew answered, considerably humbled,
it is because I am standing in your reflection." He took her arm
and escorted her into the ballroom, fulfilling the rest of his vision
when he led her in a dance. Although it wasn't a waltz but a
lively quadrille, he was enthralled by her gracefulness and
thrilled whenever their hands touched. It made him forget he had
decided their relationship was unsuitable; it made him forget
about England and Sir Gerald and the right and proper life he was
expected to lead. For now, there was only this moment, only
music wafting on a balmy breeze and Violet smiling up at him.

Etiquette prevented him from claiming her for more than two
dances, though he might have the honor of taking her down to
supper and attending to her needs. After the first set, he reluctantly relinquished her, presenting himself to his cousin.
Throughout the evening, whether he danced obligingly with local
ladies or stood on the side alone or with Oliver, his attention was
never far from Violet. He swelled with pride when he saw how
she and Allegra easily outshone all the other women present. He
felt a surprising stab of jealousy when he caught other men cast-
ing covetous glances her way.

The new year, 1894, was almost one hour old when he was
allowed to exercise his privilege as her partner. He brought her
into the supper room and filled her plate with lobster wafers and
pâté choux and a slightly melted champagne jelly. She picked
politely at the treats, impressed by their English elegance, but not

by their bland taste. "It's too warm to have much appetite," s
apologized. "And I am a wee bit out of breath from so mu
dancing."

Bartholomew immediately relieved her of her plate. After tw
weeks of Elizabeth's island cooking, he found the fare rath
flavorless himself. "Perhaps you would like to rest," he su
gested solicitously. "I noticed a number of settees on the fro
veranda. A few quiet moments in the air would refresh you i
measurably, I feel sure."

"Yes, that would feel good," Violet agreed. She gave a ruef
laugh. "I never thought I should say so," she confessed, "bu
would welcome a small respite from the festivity. It's exceeding
enjoyable, but more tiring than I ever imagined."

The veranda was filled with other people seeking the sar
relief they were so Bartholomew pulled Violet's arm through h
and led her down the stairs and into the carefully tended garde
The night was soft and black, illuminated only by the stars and
a sliver of moon. They strolled slowly among the poincianas a
the palms, each exhilarated by the other's presence, each untro
bled by the doubts that discouraged them in the daylight.

"The sky is so vast and deep," Bartholomew observed.
seems to hang very low overhead." All his senses were heigl
ened. Where once he would have methodically enumerated t
constellations that were visible, tonight he was only struck
their brilliance. "At home in England, the sky seems smaller a
more distant; even on the clearest summer night it doesn't see
as close."

"I should like to see the sky in England," Violet said wistful
"I should like to see *all* of England," she corrected. "I should li
to see yachts on the river Thames and carriages pulling up
front of Harrods. I should like to see the white cliffs of Dover a
the Royal Pavilion at Brighton. But do you know what I shou
like to see most of all?" she asked so intently she stopped a
stood still by an oleander tree.

"No, I don't," answered Bartholomew, enchanted by her
manticized images of England. "Tell me."

"I should like to see snow," she said, sighing. "Heaps of it
the ground and more coming out of the clouds in great big la
flakes, like the ones Lily cuts with folded paper and shears
should like to see ladies in fur coats and gentlemen in cashm

ufflers and horses with bells on their harnesses and their breath
*ming in white puffs as they pull sleighs."

"And I should like more than anything to show it to you,"
artholomew said fervently. He reached for the hand resting
ghtly on his arm and took her small fingers in his.

Violet grew suddenly shy. "Oliver says it's a horrid country,"
e said softly, looking down at her feet. "But I think he must be
istaken," she added more strongly, raising her eyes again, as if
eading with him to agree. "I think it must be wonderful."

Bartholomew thought a moment before he answered. "You are
oth correct," he said slowly, realizing for the first time it was
ue. "In many respects it is a horrid country. In other ways it can
e wonderful." A bit of breeze sent a few pink petals fluttering
rough the air. They landed in Violet's hair. "For example," he
id, tenderly untwining them from her curls, "in the spring when
e cherry trees blossom, the English countryside looks like a
agical kingdom."

"It must be lovely," Violet said, barely above a whisper. The
ngers brushing through her hair made her heart beat faster.

"It is," Bartholomew said simply. "And so are you." He
aned forward and kissed her.

As before, it was not the kiss of an expert lover; it was too
ger and inexperienced, crushing Violet's lips beneath his, as he
aught her clumsily and drew her close to him. But she returned
e kiss with equal ardor, pressing hard against him and savoring
e sensation of his body, his face, next to hers.

And as before, their awkward embrace was interrupted by an
truder. It wasn't Allegra, this time, but a stranger. They broke
art hurriedly as the shadowy figure passed within a few paces
them. "Happy New Year," he said without pausing. "Happy
ew Year," they responded, flustered. They went back to the
ll, and a short while later Sir Gerald commandeered Bartholo-
ew and demanded to go home.

The Royal Mail Packet pulled slowly away from the pier, Sir
erald braced firmly against the first-class railing. Bartholomew
ood respectfully on the dock, watching his father grow gradu-
ly smaller, occasionally raising his hand in restrained salute.
cross the Carenage, in front of Oliver's warehouse, the *Miss
ly* waited ready for the return trip to Gouyave. When the mail
at finally turned in the big harbor, taking his father from sight,

Bartholomew's soul gave a celebratory leap. He was free!

His residency at L'Etoile took on a completely different ton.
Instead of staying trapped on the veranda, he threw himself in
life on the estate. The more interest and enthusiasm he showe
the more people responded. Elizabeth stopped muttering whe
she set his spinachy green callaloo soup in front of him; Oliv
ceased growling whenever Bartholomew asked him a questio
Merely aroused before, Bartholomew's senses and spirit no
were permanently alert.

He was reveling in this extraordinary mood several evenin;
after their return when Oliver announced, "I really ought to go
Carriacou to check with Angus on the new schooner. I haver
been there in over two months. The *Pride of Windward* is bour
tomorrow morning. Care to go home for a few days, Violet?"

Violet's heart leaped in alarm. She barely managed to refra
from glancing at Bartholomew. "Oh, no," she said quickly.
couldn't leave Allegra by herself."

Allegra seemed startled, as if she had forgotten the origin
purpose of Violet's presence. Oliver looked amused. "Well then
he said, "perhaps Allegra can be persuaded to spend a few da:
in Carriacou, as well. It seems about time for another swimmii
lesson. What do you say, Miss Pembroke?"

While Bartholomew watched, mystified and apprehensive, h
cousin turned bright red. To his immense relief, she waved h
hand airily and said, "If you are going to be away for sever
days, I should remain at the estate. The harvest is far from ove
One of us ought to be here in the event something goes awry."

Oliver folded his arms across his chest and murmured, "Ind
bitably." To Bartholomew's horror, Oliver turned next to him a:
said, "I stand rebuffed by the ladies, but perhaps I can intere
you in a trip to Carriacou, Mr. Pembroke."

"I certainly appreciate your generous invitation," Barthol
mew demurred. "But I am most comfortably ensconced
L'Etoile. While in St. George's, I obtained an edition of the cat
log of birds Mr. John G. Wells prepared for the Smithsoni;
Institution. I was hoping to devote my days to identifying tl
species."

"A fascinating occupation," Oliver said dryly.

"Quite so," Bartholomew agreed seriously. "I find it affor
me the opportunity to observe surrounding environs in great
detail than I might normally. I need only be directed to appr

priate locations. Cousin Allegra, I can see that you are going to be occupied with the cocoa, so I won't burden you with my trivial demands. But perhaps I might impose on your kindness, Miss MacKenzie? Would it be asking too much for you to point me toward a glen or a copse particularly suitable for birding?"

"Not at all," Violet replied with more steadiness of voice than of pulse. "If Allegra is going to be busy at the boucan, my days are quite free. I would be glad to show you some pretty spots, Mr. Pembroke."

"Try the lily pond, Violet," Oliver suggested idly. Bartholomew's request had been couched in such formal English tourist tones, he didn't give a second thought to sending his young sister off with him alone. The proposed expedition seemed completely safe and proper, if not a little dull.

And so Bartholomew meant it to be. He had the utmost respect for Violet and didn't intend to cast a single shadow on her reputation. Just being in her company was pleasure enough. In the brilliant light of day, he ought to be able to resist the seductive impulses of the velvety night.

Violet wasn't so sure. Mounted on a nimble-footed donkey, he led the way over a few hills, through a thicket of wild cotton trees strewing bright yellow blossoms in their path, and out into a small, hidden meadow. Arrow straight bamboo interspersed among flamboyant trees with feathery foliage and long, pendulous seed pods stood guard around the edge of the little field. On the far side, at the lowest point, was a pond about as big as a good-sized puddle and clogged with Thumbellina pads and enormous, vivid water lilies.

"Exquisite!" Bartholomew exclaimed, tethering the donkeys in the shade of a tree. Violet only smiled. As they started toward the pond through the tall grass of the meadow, she reached over and took Bartholomew's hand in hers. An iridescent blue butterfly fluttered away from a wildflower in front of them. A tiny green hummingbird followed behind.

"There's a bird now," Violet said, pointing with her free hand. It's called 'colibri vert.'"

It was Bartholomew's turn to simply smile. The binoculars around his neck hung unused, the guidebook remained in his pocket. He was concerned only with the little hand resting warmly in his, with the way his heart seemed to swell with happiness. His fingers curled securely around hers.

They stopped by the edge of the pond. Bartholomew reluctantly let go of her hand so he could remove his linen jacket and spread it on the ground for her to sit on. "Oh, no," Violet protested. "It will be ruined. I couldn't possibly sit on such a fine garment."

"Were it woven of golden threads and tailored by the Queen, it wouldn't be too fine for you," Bartholomew answered gallantly, his usual courtesy embellished a thousandfold by the exotic atmosphere and emotions catching him in a magical spell.

Violet was unable to resist such an eloquent compliment. Sitting carefully on one corner of the jacket, she patted the space next to her. "You must sit, too," she insisted. With a nod of his fine, fair head, Bartholomew acquiesced.

For a few minutes, they sat stiffly, shoulder to shoulder, staring at the brilliant lilies in the pond. They were both acutely aware of the excitement and tension between them; both were barely able to contain the rapid pounding of their pulses. Yet they were innocents, unsure of what to do next.

A hawk suddenly wheeled out of the sky so close to their heads they could hear its feathers beating on the breeze. It snatched a small lizard from a rock, not ten feet away, and soared back into the air. The action was so quick and so violent, it startled Violet from her self-conscious position. With a cry, she instinctively leaned away from the menacing bird. Just as instinctively, Bartholomew reached out his arms and pulled her into a protective hug.

In an instant the hawk was gone, but Violet remained in Bartholomew's arms. She looked up, her face only inches from his. A lock of shiny blond hair lay across his smooth forehead, his blue eyes were wondrously clear. "I love you, Bartholomew," she said very distinctly, speaking from her heart.

A sense of awe filled him, a feeling of incredible good fortune. He brought one hand up to touch her face, to trail over her luscious skin, to trace the pretty mouth that had uttered those miraculous words. He bent forward and brushed his own lips against hers, softly, almost tentatively, as if ascertaining that they were real. Her lips were warm and moist, her hair smelled like flowers. He moved back a little until he could look into her lovely brown eyes. "And I love you, Violet," he said, rejoicing as he heard himself speak.

This time there was no one to interrupt, no reminders of proper manners and correct behavior. This time there was only the hot sun buzzing through their private meadow, sparkling on the water lilies. This time, on a bed of crumpled, cast off clothes, surrounded by hummingbirds and butterflies, they made love.

Chapter
Eleven

Relieved and grateful, Allegra watched Violet and Bartholomew walk down the hill toward the stable. She felt relieved to be
left on her own at last, and grateful to Violet for uncomplainingly
keeping her cousin entertained. Although Bartholomew was becoming more endearing every day, his continued presence interrupted her routine. She longed to return to her active life as a
planter. In the past few weeks she had spent too many hours
decorously sitting and thinking about her situation.

She had been extremely surprised to discover that though she
still loved Oliver every bit as intensely as she had that afternoon
at the waterfall, love alone was not enough. Her heart still surged
at the sight of him; it beat wildly at his touch. Whenever he was
in the room, he absorbed her attention entirely; when he was
gone, she missed him. But she missed her work with the cocoa
as well, missed the daily rewards that came with stretching both
her body and her mind. Without the satisfaction of her own accomplishments, loving Oliver didn't seem as fulfilling.

That can't be right, Allegra had said to herself, as she sat on
the veranda with her uncle and cousin, untangling the threads of
her embroidery. I'm sure that was never mentioned in any novel I
ever read. The heroine was always in raptures at the end. She
wanted nothing more than the eternal love of the hero.

Allegra had suddenly thrown down the knotted needlework
and had risen abruptly from her seat. Ignoring Bartholomew's
startled expression, she had stalked to the far end of the porch.
What empty-headed ninnies those girls must have been, she

thought, slapping her palm on the rail. Not one of them ever yearned to do something significant. Of course, they all wanted to be duchesses and have grand lives. She had dismissed that once esteemed goal with a toss of her head. It never occurred to them to create those grand lives for themselves.

Settled on the banister, she had looked out at her estate, remembering the rich sense of pride she had felt when she had shown it off to Sir Gerald and Bartholomew. I can't wait for my money to arrive, she had thought. I can't wait to pay off Papa's debts, to clear away all the shadows cast on his reputation. And mine. Then, when L'Etoile is set to rights again, we shall be truly equal partners, Oliver and I.

Now she was finally free to stop ruminating about the future and to get busy making it happen. Allegra was so pleased to see Bartholomew and Violet go off birding, she didn't even mind that Oliver was also absent, probably halfway to Carriacou by now. She hurried into her oldest clothes and went down the hill to the boucan.

"Well," Septimus greeted her. "I think you forget all about us. Veda Chandoo win the Christmas prize and we hear not one little peep from you."

"I've been occupied," Allegra apologized. "I'll go find Veda later, but right now I want to get down to business." Hands on her hips, she cast a knowing eye across the drawers. She inhaled deeply, filling her senses with the well-remembered aroma of curing cocoa. "Is this the lot from Wild Pig Valley?" she asked, pointing to the freshest looking beans. It felt wonderful to be back at work.

"They all done and sacked," Septimus answered. "They even gone. I send them down to St. George's with a big load on Thursday."

"I was anxious to see them," Allegra said regretfully. "Those trees were particularly hard hit with witches'-broom, and I was afraid the beans were going to be stunted."

"They small," Septimus admitted, nodding his head.

"How did they tally?"

"About four hundred pounds an acre."

It was Allegra's turn to nod, the information agreeing with her assessment. For the next half hour, Septimus stayed by her side as she walked around the yard asking questions, running her hand through piles of dried beans, lifting the banana leaf covers on the sweating ones, reading the logbook to check on their progress. She grew happier and happier the more caught up in cocoa she got. This is infinitely more appealing than embroidering butterflies on tea towels, she thought. Or cooking boiled beef and cabbage.

She stopped by one of the drawers where Agnes Samuel was dancing the cocoa, humming a tune to which her feet kept pace. Yielding suddenly to the energy built up inside her, Allegra yanked off her shoes and stockings, hitched up her skirt, and jumped into the drawer with Agnes. The rail-thin septuagenarian looked at her with surprise. Although Allegra had participated in virtually every other phase of cocoa production, she had never yet attempted to polish the beans with her bare feet.

Up until now, Allegra had been too embarrassed to expose her white ankles and feet to the world. But today those last remnants of New England modesty gave way before her need for release. Under Agnes's giggling guidance, Allegra learned how to keep the beans rolling and chaffing to a rhythm. It was just what she needed. It seemed the epitome of life at L'Etoile. There was grace and music and a hot sun and an exotic scent. It was, paradoxically, purposeful abandon, a state of being that suited her from the tops of her loose curls to the tips of her grubby brown toes.

She was so involved in the cocoa song enveloping her whole body, it was several minutes before she became aware of the silence that had fallen on the yard. Of the thirty-odd people raking, picking, dancing, dumping, and shoveling, no one was making a sound. Vaguely curious, Allegra glanced up. A shock ran through her as she did a double take, the easy cadence in her head disappearing. Her feet faltered, her heel coming down hard on a bean. She flinched in pain, but stared in astonishment. Not ten feet in front of her stood William Browne. Solid, stolid, attorney and apple farmer, William Browne.

"Hello, Miss Pembroke," he said fastidiously, mindful of the other ears present.

"Hello William," she managed to mutter, utterly oblivious to her audience. Awkwardly kicking aside the offending bean, she was conscious instead of her unkempt condition. She was dirty and sweaty, her indecently shortened dress clinging damply to her back. Two and a half months ago, she would have hurriedly unhitched her skirt and frantically smoothed her hair. Today, however, she felt only resentment.

She stared at William, noting his average height and average build, his grave face and his carefully groomed moustache. The sun glinted off his gold-rimmed spectacles and blanked out the gray eyes behind them. Just the sight of William Browne upset her. It evoked a time and a mentality only two months and twenty-five hundred miles away, though it seemed at least a lifetime ago. The memories that she had gleefully bid farewell not half an hour before came flooding back. Along with her silly sewing circle and the flavorless boiled dinners came images of the somber Connecticut town and of the disapproving expression etched permanently on her grandfather's face.

Out of the past came the familiar feeling that she was hopelessly inadequate and out of step with the rest of society. That she imagined too much and thought things through too little, that her spirit needed restraining as much as her curls. Allegra wriggled her shoulders to rid herself of that old feeling. Today, particularly, it was unwelcome.

"I can imagine you are somewhat surprised to see me," William said without a trace of irony.

"Yes," Allegra answered succinctly. "What are you doing here?"

William seemed as taken aback by her abruptness as he was by her appearance and her unusual employment. This was not the Allegra Pembroke who had left Connecticut only a few months ago. "I think, perhaps, we should adjourn to your parlor," he said rather ponderously. With Allegra still standing in the drawer, he was forced to look up at her, putting him at a further disadvantage. "My news would best be discussed in a more private setting."

"I'm in the middle of something," Allegra replied peevishly. She had only just escaped from her parlor. She had no wish to return for what promised to be yet another session of stifling behavior. The hint of remonstration in his speech increased her irritation. "I haven't a lot of time to spare," she said ungraciously. She gave the beans beneath her feet a shuffle or two to indicate how occupied she was. "Tell me why you are here."

"Really, Miss Pembroke," William protested primly. "This is hardly the appropriate location for a discussion of matters both private and personal." He glanced around him, uncomfortably aware of the workers whose expressions were alert with barely masked curiosity.

As was always the case with William, the more he insisted on a certain point, the less inclined Allegra was to agree. Unlike past times when she had repressed her opposition, today she expressed it. "I've a tremendous amount of work to do, William," she reiterated. "If you have something urgent to tell me, I suggest you disregard the surroundings and say what is on your mind."

It was William's turn to shift awkwardly, stepping from one foot to the other and pushing his spectacles higher up his nose. His ordinary face was slippery with perspiration. Indeed, he looked half-boiled in the three-piece, navy blue gabardine suit he wore all summer. He was completely nonplussed by Allegra's unusual defiance. He had never known her to be so brusque. He decided finally that it must be the tropical sun beating on her uncovered head. The best course of action, probably, was to humor her and hope she came to her senses before very long.

"I am bringing you fond greetings from all our friends," he said with forced heartiness. "Millie Bowman said to tell you that she has finished petit-pointing the covers for her front foyer divan. If you remember, it depicts a delightful scene of Baily's Pond in winter. And Miriam Lockley is learning to play the harp."

If William thought to disarm Allegra with references to the homey life she had left behind, he couldn't have been more mistaken. She felt another surge of suffocation. "Surely you didn't come all this way to give me a report on Millie Bowman's needlework," she snapped. "I wish you would tell me why you're here."

William cleared his throat nervously. He was beginning to realize that this new, obstinate Allegra was going to stand on that seed-strewn platform looking cross until she got an answer to her question. Even so, he proceeded cautiously, as was his nature.

"If I recall correctly," he began, "you were never a dedicated reader of the newspaper. You might not, therefore, be aware of the forces shaping our current state of affairs. Are you familiar with the Bland Allison Act?"

"What?" Allegra asked, clearly mystified by this turn in the conversation.

William settled himself and pushed his spectacles up his nose again. "The Bland Allison Act was passed by Congress in 1878," he informed her. "Essentially it required the Secretary of Treasury to buy two to four million dollars worth of silver each month, at the market price, and to convert that silver into dollars. This was the first in a series of woefully misguided attempts to return to the silver standard we abandoned in 1873 and to shore up the sagging mining interests in the western states. You see, major new ore deposits had been, coincidentally, discovered in Nevada, Colorado, and Utah, and the mine owners, prospectors, and citizens of those states were anxious lest their profits be diminished.

"This wholly ineffective legislation was followed in July of 1890 by the Sherman Silver Purchase Act, a law tilted even more toward the silver lobbyists. This act mandated the U.S. Treasury to purchase four and a half million ounces of silver each month, which was the current production rate. Further, the act specified that the purchase must be paid for in gold-backed, legal tender treasury notes. Needless to say, this resulted in the weakening of the gold reserves and the simultaneous, irresponsible increase of circulating paper money."

"William," Allegra interrupted, stunned by his dissertation. "*What* are you talking about?" She had expected the private mission he spoke of so importantly to be a lecture on the inappropriateness of her conduct, or a sermon on how her natural place was in Connecticut, or perhaps a stilted plea to marry him, but never this astonishing lesson in American politics.

Allegra's interruption made William lose his momentum. He shifted again from foot to foot in the blazing sun and blotted his damp forehead with his neatly folded handkerchief. "I am talking about the economy, Miss Pembroke," he answered with a touch of heat-inspired impatience. Regaining his lawyerly equanimity as well as his train of thought, he went on.

"You may also be unaware," he said doggedly, "of three other events that have a bearing on our present situation." Without waiting to see if Allegra knew them or not, he launched into an explanation. "The first was the failure, in 1890, of the British banking house of Baring Brothers. It caused British investors to immediately divest themselves of their American securities, which in turn caused a drain on the gold reserves.

"The second event also took place in 1890 and was yet another ill-formed act of Congress. This was the McKinley Tariff

Act which imposed punishing tariffs, leading to a decrease in U.S. revenues."

"William," Allegra said again, worn out by this onslaught of information. She had no idea what he was talking about, why he was telling it to her.

William didn't appear to hear her. "The third event," he continued, putting his feet together and clasping his hands behind his back in his best professorial manner, "is the ongoing depletion of government reserves by the G.A.R. pensions, for which President Harrison has crusaded."

"William," Allegra said, more strongly this time. "Will you kindly tell me what on earth any of this has to do with me or with you or with your most unexpected, and unannounced, appearance in Grenada?"

William paused, frowning studiously as he framed a reply. He kept one hand behind his back, but with the other he smoothed his moustache. "I realize that this must seem overwhelming," he granted magnanimously. "After all, there has never been any need for you to involve yourself with such matters." Not noticing that Allegra stood a little more stiffly in the cocoa drawer after that comment, or that her chin was thrust out, he went on. "What I am doing is attempting to explain how these circumstances have had an adverse effect on the gold reserves, on the stock market, and, ultimately, on the economy. The Stock Exchange crashed in June," he added more gravely. "And the Philadelphia and Reading Railroad failed at around the same time."

He was suddenly at a loss for further words. He glanced up at Allegra, hoping that somehow his message had been comprehended, that she had understood his meaning. Barely listening to his monotonous lecture, Allegra had instead grown increasingly exasperated. She curled her bare toes around a pair of beans and crankily flung them aside. She still hadn't a single idea why William had traveled so many miles to give her six-month-old news. And even though she had no intention of marrying him, she perversely wanted him to ask her.

"This is all very informative," she said shortly, placing her hands on her hips. "But will you please get to the point."

William cleared his throat again, less certain of how to proceed. "Did you know," he asked reluctantly, "that in the past year, almost five-hundred banks and fifteen-thousand commercial institutions have failed because of this depression?"

As a flash of foreboding filled her, Allegra ceased her restless fidgeting. All petulant thoughts of marriage fled from her head. "Get to the point, William," she repeated in a considerably flatter tone.

William took a deep breath and looked around the yard again at the gaping workers. "The United Merchants Bank, where you had your accounts," he said quietly, "was one of the five hundred that failed. Your money was lost."

For a few seconds there was no change in Allegra. Then her hands slid from her hips and the intense expression faded from her face. As the impact of this calamity sank in, she felt herself turning cold in the bright heat. A shiver went down her spine and her breath froze in her chest. All her money was lost. She had nothing but the few bills in her purse, the remnants of her travel funds.

She had no way to pay off her debts, to redeem her father's name, to establish her own credibility. She had lost her money. And she had lost L'Etoile. What was worse, in her effort to save the estate for Oliver, she had unwittingly made things worse. Though he wouldn't be budged from his half ownership, she had saddled him with a new, highly disagreeable partner.

Numb, she finally stepped out of the cocoa drawer. She hunched down and mechanically buttoned on her shoes. William hovered nearby, more confident now that he no longer had to look up at her. Although he wasn't insensitive to her shock, he secretly hoped it meant a return of the tractable woman he had known in Connecticut.

With the practiced solicitude of an attorney, he sympathized with her plight and told her stories of other people with similar losses. Allegra hardly heard. Words like "bankruptcy" and "credit failure" buzzed hollowly through her head. The details were immaterial. It only mattered that all her money was lost.

While William was in midsentence, she rose and started up the hill for the house. After a moment's hesitation, William fell in next to her, continuing his ponderous discourse, oblivious of her disinterest. "I might have foreseen that the United Merchants Bank would be one to fail," he said. "I always thought that Edward Barker lacked a certain ability. As you may recall, I repeatedly advised you not to do your banking with him. I recommended the National Trust Company across the street, where I myself keep my accounts. Wendel Braithwait has done an admirable job of steering his institution through this fiscal crisis with virtually no damage."

"His breath always smells like peppermints and his hands are damp," Allegra responded dully. "I never liked going into his bank."

"Those are not sensible criteria for selecting a bank," William chided indulgently. "But you should not have to trouble yourself with these complex assessments. You should have heeded my advice, offered, I might add, not only in my capacity as administrator of your grandfather's estate, but also out of personal concern for your well-being. You should have trusted me to properly read Barker's character."

"There is nothing wrong with Mr. Barker's character," Allegra said sullenly. Through the fog of her deep discouragement she was offended by William's insinuation that she wasn't capable of judging a man's merit. "He is a serious and dignified businessman." As they walked through the bower of bougainvillaea and up the path to the great house, William was clearly overcome by the colorful architecture. Allegra collapsed into the first chair she came to, an oversized wicker rocker with plump cushions. She wearily waved her hand toward a nearby chair. "Sit," she said unceremoniously.

William sat. Temporarily unbalanced by the breezy atmosphere on the veranda and by Allegra, again defying him, he sought to regain his advantage. "I think, perhaps, you were misled by Barker's pleasing countenance," he told her. "A common feminine mistake. If you could have seen him as I last saw him, only the day before my departure, you would realize my apprehension was not unfounded. When I finally searched him out, he was quite undone: ill-groomed and babbling wildly. I even detected strong spirits on his breath, though it was not yet noon. He is a ruined man. I must admit, however," he conceded, "it is to his credit that he is more distraught about the losses of his depositors than about his own difficulties. When he learned of my proposed journey, he begged me to convey to you his profound apologies. He was near to sobbing."

"What did you say?" Allegra asked abruptly, a spark flicking in her dazed mind.

"I beg your pardon?" William asked.

"What did you say?" Allegra repeated, coming to the edge of her seat as a thought seized her.

"Well, now, uh, I," William mumbled, again derailed by her aggression. "I was, uh, speaking of Barker. Of his ravaged condition. I was, uh, saying, it is lack of backbone . . ."

"No, no," Allegra interrupted impatiently. "Before that. When did you say you saw him?"

"Why, the day before I left," William answered, truly bewildered. "I don't see what difference . . ."

"The day before you left," Allegra interrupted again, pouncing triumphantly. "You had to search him out and question him about my accounts the day before your departure for Grenada. Correct?"

"Yes, that's correct," William admitted, beginning to guess at her purpose.

"So you didn't come here to tell me my bank had failed," Allegra concluded with the zeal of a lawyer cross-examining a criminal witness. "You already had planned your trip for other reasons. The bank failure was only coincidental. It was already your intention to come here. I want you to tell me why."

"Very well," William said, a trifle severely. In the privacy of her veranda, goaded by his chagrin at having been outmaneuvered, he told her exactly why he had come, without camouflaging it in economics lessons.

"It is my intention to act as your escort home," he told her stiffly. "I never wholly condoned this madcap journey. Nor did I trust your phantom father, a man who abandoned everything familiar to grow chocolate in the tropics. I reluctantly allowed you to make this voyage because you had the money to indulge your whims. But enough is enough, Allegra. I gave your grandfather my solemn word that I would protect you, and I cannot, in clear conscience, approve your continued stay here.

"Through inquiries made by Sir Gerald Pembroke's attorneys in London, and *not*, I might add, through any missive from you, I learned of your father's unfortunate demise." He paused a moment, then sonorously inserted, "Please accept my condolences for your loss. However," he added, returning to his more matter-of-fact tone, "knowing of your orphaned state, now compounded by utter destitution, I came at once, meaning to take you home."

"I *am* home, William," Allegra snapped. His speech put the starch back in her spine. Though her mind was still devastated by her catastrophic shift in fortune, now she had something specific she could combat. She didn't know what to do or think about the

great void created by her financial ruin, but it was some solace to
be angry with William for behaving in such a patronizing manner. It didn't occur to her that not so very long ago she would
have been completely accepting of his attitude. She might even
have imagined him gallant for coming so far to find her.

"I am a fully grown woman," she said passionately. "I don't
need to be led around by the hand or humored or coddled. Ther
is no question of you 'allowing' me to make a journey or 'ap
proving' of my stay in a particular place. I shall make thos
decisions for myself. And as far as your responsibility for m
goes, the way I see it, it vanished with my money. Grandfathe
appointed you look after my inheritance. Since it no longe
exists, you are freed of all obligation."

"I have no wish to be freed," William responded instantly. "
accept that obligation gladly. In fact," he said, gulping slightl
and shoving his spectacles back up his nose, "I would like t
accept that obligation forever. I am sorry if I sounded overbear
ing, Allegra, but it is only out of concern for you. It was not m
intent to offend you, but rather to make you understand my anxi
ety on your behalf. Now that you are all alone and helpless," h
said, pausing to take a deep breath, "I was hoping you migh
reconsider my proposal of marriage. It would be my great hono
to offer you sanctuary as my wife."

Where once she had demurred shyly, refusing his hand with
hesitant blush, flattered by his interest, Allegra now leaped to he
feet, her face flushed with fury. "I'll have you know, Williar
Browne," she stormed, "that I may be poor, but I am definitel
not helpless. Nor am I so desperate for a refuge that I woul
change my mind about becoming your wife. I have no intentio
of marrying simply for the sake of security. It would be a joyles
union and a barren life. I am not willing to sentence myself t
such an existence."

She started for the door, but turned around after a few step
and said with grudging courtesy, "You are welcome to remain a
a guest at L'Etoile until you can make arrangements for you
return passage. I'll ask Elizabeth to show you to a room." He
voice grew harder as she added, "However, you will be returnin
to Connecticut alone. My home is here." With as much dignity a
she could muster in her grimy condition, she turned again an
swept into the house.

Sitting in her bathtub a short while later, delayed tears stream ing into the cool water, Allegra felt considerably less confident. While she was still very definite about not wanting to marry William, she wasn't at all sure of anything else. She had no idea of where to turn next, no notion of how to solve her problems. The last time she had sat in this room wondering what to do, the day after her father's funeral, there had been a number of options. It had just been a matter of recognizing them and selecting one. Now, her choices were nil. Now, all she had was her desire for fulfillment and a debt that suddenly seemed monumental.

She laid a soaking wet face cloth over her swollen eyes and leaned back against the porcelain tub. Groaning out loud, she thought of the grand pronouncements she had made to William. Right now they seemed like empty boasts. She was no longer convinced she wasn't helpless. She felt completely powerless. And as much as she wanted it to be so, L'Etoile was no longer her home. Half of it belonged to Oliver, and the other half belonged to her uncle.

Somehow she got through dinner, and somehow she managed to sleep. She even appeared at breakfast, though Violet had to ask her three times if she preferred tea or cocoa before she realized she was being addressed. Even then, she didn't acknowledge the question, saying instead, "Cousin Bartholomew, could I speak to you privately later today?" She didn't see Bartholomew and Violet exchange alarmed looks, and she only nodded when he finally replied, "Of course, Cousin, at your convenience." Leaving William to his own devices, she wandered outside.

She was in the library when Bartholomew found her that afternoon, absently leafing through a book. When he came in, she consciously took hold of herself, setting aside the unread volume and sitting up straighter on the settee. It took great resolve to get the words out. They officially severed her from L'Etoile. "I've had very bad news," she blurted out without preamble. "My bank has failed and all my money has been lost. I have no way of paying my father's debt."

Allegra turned away after her confession, unable to look her cousin in the eye. She stared through the French door to the veranda, waiting for the axe to fall, waiting to hear Bartholomew dispassionately discuss the steps he would take to foreclose on the estate. She turned back, astounded, when instead he exclaimed, "How terrible!" His fine forehead was furrowed in consternation, his clear blue eyes reflected genuine distress.

"Are you absolutely sure?" he asked her anxiously. "Coul‹ there not have been an error made? Or perhaps a conclusio‹ drawn too quickly? Possibly even a flaw in communications?"

"No, there's no error," Allegra answered slowly, trying to un derstand his unexpected reaction. "William brought me the news and he doesn't make mistakes in matters such as these. I've los‹ everything." She caught her breath sharply and looked down a‹ her lap, once more overwhelmed by the hopelessness of her situa tion. When a few minutes of silence followed her statement, sh‹ looked up again, puzzled by the sight of her cousin chewing o‹ the knuckles of one hand while the other was clenched behind hi‹ back. "Aren't you going to tell me that we have to go to St George's so I can sign the deed over to you?" she asked tenta‹ tively.

Lowering his hand, Bartholomew looked at her somewhat dis‹ tractedly. "Let us not act with undo haste," he said. "This ha‹ come about rather suddenly, and though things may seem desper ate at the moment, I am positive that with consideration an ac ceptable solution can be found. While nothing come‹ immediately to mind, we will just hold fast until the answe‹ presents itself."

Openmouthed with amazement, Allegra watched as Bartholo‹ mew reached over to pat her arm reassuringly before bolting ou‹ the door. As he had done frequently these past few weeks, h‹ surprised her by displaying another appealing dimension of hi‹ personality. Although he had no specific recommendations fo‹ solving her dilemma, she found his concern touching and hi‹ confidence more hopeful than anything else she had heard sinc‹ William's arrival. She felt a surge of warmth for the cousin sh‹ had once considered to be stodgy and distant.

Her meeting with Oliver the next evening after dinner took o‹ a much different tenor. They were closeted again in the office the site of several previous confrontations. Oliver sat with his fee‹ on the desk, his hands clasped behind his head. Allegra paced th‹ floor in front of him.

"Well?" Oliver asked. "What's the problem this time? N‹ doubt that fellow Browne has come to claim you, but surely yo‹ can't give him a second thought. I can well understand why yo‹ ran away from Connecticut, if he's the best it has to offer."

"William is a decent man," Allegra replied automatically an‹

without enthusiasm, continuing her pacing and steeling herself to deliver the devastating news.

Oliver's eyes narrowed slightly. "More than likely he is extremely decent," he conceded shortly. "But he is also, to use your own description, very dull. I can't imagine what attraction he holds for a woman like you. You barely acknowledged him during dinner." His feet suddenly hit the floor with a thud and his hands slammed the top of the desk. "Will you please stand still and tell me what is wrong?" he demanded.

Allegra sat down abruptly in the chair opposite him, her hands wedged between her knees. "My bank failed," she said briefly. "My money is gone."

"Oh my God," Oliver said softly, for a second stunned into immobility. He came around the desk and sat on the arm of her chair, kneading her slumped shoulders. "Poor darling," he said, burying a kiss in her curls.

Allegra shut her eyes, absorbing the luxurious comfort she knew she didn't deserve. It had been such a long time since she had been this close to Oliver she almost gave in to the temptation of his touch. "I've lost everything," she whispered, her eyes still closed, just barely resisting the sensation of his fingers rubbing her skin. She wanted to press herself against him, feel his arms encompass her, blocking out all disaster. Instead, she forced herself to open her eyes and say, "I've lost L'Etoile, too."

"Rubbish," Oliver responded, giving her a gentle shake. "It's nowhere nearly lost. I'll admit that damned note you wrote has made the situation a wee bit stickier, but that's why law courts were created. We'll fight the thing, say that your uncle made you sign the note under duress. You were in shock at the time."

"But that's not true," Allegra protested, sitting up a little straighter and pulling away from him slightly. She turned in her chair to look up at him. "You know that isn't the case. You know that I willingly signed the note because I wanted to erase my father's debts and clear his name. I still do. I couldn't bear to have this dragged through a public trial, to have people saying that my father and I are trying to get something we haven't paid for. Besides," she added, shrugging in defeat, "I can't afford a legal battle."

"I can," Oliver said, shaking his head fondly at her stubbornness. Her magnificent eyes seemed nearly purple in this light. He ran his thumbs over the tender skin beneath them.

"I can't take any more of your money," Allegra replied, flinching away from his caress. "I already owe you fifteen hundred pounds that I have no way of repaying. I can't compound the debt by borrowing more."

"There's one very easy way to solve that problem and a number of others, as well," Oliver said, crossing his arms on his chest and leaning his shoulder against the back of the chair. "We'll get married."

"Oh, no," Allegra answered quickly, rising from the chair so rapidly it tipped under Oliver's weight. He caught his balance before he fell, but he stood now, too.

"Why not?" he demanded. It was hardly the response he had expected. He took a step toward her.

"Because," she said, taking a step backward. Although this proposal was as unromantic as the one he had made the morning after the cocoa raid, it made her heart leap. Unlike the last time, she now freely admitted that she loved him, but she refused him all the same.

"I won't get married simply for the sake of safety," she said. "I won't get married just to be protected and financially secure, to have my problems solved. I want to solve them myself. I *must*," she added desperately.

Oliver should have recognized her pride trying to assert itself, but his own was somewhat bruised by her rebuff. "There is more reason for us to get married than simple expediency," he said brusquely. "And you know it perfectly well."

His hurt feelings offered her a convenient refuge from her conflicting emotions. "You needn't feel an obligation to marry me," she said righteously, "just because of, of . . ." her face turned bright red as she fumbled for a way of phrasing it. "Just because of what happened by the waterfall," she finished, swallowing hard.

"I don't feel an *obligation*," Oliver said in exasperation, advancing toward her again. "I feel a *desire*. I *want* to marry you. And I feel sure that you want to marry me. The resolution of your problems would be just an incidental benefit."

Shaking her head, Allegra escaped from his contact by rounding the desk so that they now stood exactly opposite where they had when the discussion began. "My father's debts and his reputation are not incidental," she retorted. "They reflect directly on me. I must set them right before I can do anything else."

Oliver took a deep breath and leaned his palms on the desk. He tried to get a grip on himself, to curb his unusual agitation. "Very well," he said evenly. "It would seem then that the first order of business is to raise the funds to repay your uncle, however unnecessary that might be. Suppose I loan you the money, which you could then pay back to me, year by year, with your share of the profits."

Sensing that he was trying to humor her, Allegra resented it as much as she had resented William's patronizing attitude. "I've already told you that I can't accept any more of your money," she snapped.

"Then *I* will pay off Cecil's debt," Oliver said, his patience depleted. "I will buy your share of the estate from your uncle, record your name on the deed, and that will be an end to that."

"Oh no it won't be," Allegra practically shouted. "If you ever do that I shall leave Grenada on the spot. I don't care if I have to beg a ride on a fishing boat or work for my passage scrubbing decks, I will leave. I won't be bribed and I won't be bought. And I won't be treated like a child or a pet. I want to be taken seriously. I want my desire to restore my father's reputation to be regarded with respect."

"As you wish," Oliver replied, somewhat mockingly. "Although perhaps you will tell me how you intend to achieve your goal when you have no money, you've voluntarily signed away your share of the estate, and you're obstinately refusing any help."

"I don't know yet," Allegra admitted in a more moderate tone. Gathering herself together, she added firmly, "But I'll find a way."

Oliver sat down on the edge of the desk and watched her sail out of the room. His annoyance drained away as he conceded ruefully that she very likely would.

Chapter
Twelve

Despite the brave boasts she had made to both William and Oliver, the fact was, Allegra's mind came up absolutely blank every time she tried to envision a way out of her dilemma. She went over and over the entire situation, but nothing seemed to change. If anything, things looked worse. It was no longer just a question of not being able to meet her loans, no longer only the awful realization that L'Etoile didn't belong to her anymore. Now she was beginning to understand what that meant on a more basic level. She had no home, no income, no way to pay for food and shelter. She had nothing. Absolutely nothing.

Of course there were some options, she acknowledged as she walked aimlessly through already harvested cocoa groves, kicking aside discarded husks and overripe pods. She could take a post somewhere as a governess, receiving room and board and a small stipend. That idea didn't appeal to her sense of romance as it might have six months ago. She didn't imagine herself the heroine of a melodrama, mending and remending her plain, practical frock and being rewarded in the end by falling in love with the handsome son of her wealthy employer. She was quite sure she would make a terrible governess. Besides, she was already in love.

That brought her to her other option: marriage. Allegra sank down under a cocoa tree, first examining it for blight, then leaning her back against the trunk. She picked up a stick and idly twitched it at the fallen fruit. She could marry William and move back to Connecticut, pretending that her tropical experience had never happened, giving up L'Etoile entirely. Or she could marry Oliver and remain on the estate, giving up her role as an equal partner and her goal of being someone on her own.

She let the stick drop and rested her head against the tree in discouragement. Either way, she lost. If she married William, she would have to relinquish love. If she married Oliver, she would have to relinquish the dreams of a lifetime just when she was able to define them. Frustrated, Allegra banged a clenched fist on her upturned knees. Oliver wasn't helping the situation, either. He was devoting all his attention to William.

She shook her head at the thought of the two rivals for her affection. Although they were being extremely civil to one another, they gave the impression of two dogs circling for a fight. Their remarks to Allegra were less for her benefit than as veiled challenges to the other. They loaded their speech with references to her, each insinuating a special knowledge of her needs. While Oliver's measure of her was far more accurate than William's, Allegra found both her suitors provoking. She felt like a shuttlecock in a game of emotional badminton.

After three days in the middle of this maddening atmosphere, she could stand it no more. Rising early on Friday morning, she dressed in her new Liberty lawn and tiptoed down the stairs, hoping not to wake anyone. She was halfway across the foyer when Oliver's voice behind her brought her to a halt.

"You're up at an unusual hour," he said from the library entrance.

She reluctantly turned to answer him, but before she could say a word, William descended the stairs. "Good morning," he said, nodding toward Oliver but keeping his eyes on Allegra. "You look especially lovely today," he told her.

As Allegra opened her mouth to acknowledge the compliment, Oliver cut her off. "Yes," he said, his eyes squinting speculatively. "Isn't that the dress you usually save for town? Are you planning something special?"

Allegra put her hands on her hips, annoyed at this double ambush. "I'm going to St. George's," she said shortly. "I want to talk to Jamie about my father's will." It was a plausible excuse and probably a sensible idea, although her real reason for taking this trip was just to distance herself from the tension at L'Etoile. Not even Violet or Bartholomew seemed able to relieve it as they were never around these days.

"I'll come with you," Oliver said instantly, but not as fast as William said, "I'd be delighted to act as your escort."

"No!" Allegra cried, backing toward the door. "No, I don't need an escort. Or an entourage. I shall be perfectly safe on the *Miss Lily* and walking one block to Jamie's office. I am going alone. I'll be back this evening." She turned quickly and fled before they could wear her down with further arguments and entreaties.

Walking up Scott Street several hours later, Allegra was glad she had come. Although she was no nearer to solving her problem, just being able to escape it for a while was restorative. She had sat on the rail of the schooner for the whole sail, letting the sea breeze cool the turmoil in her brain. A school of porpoises had appeared to entertain her, leaping and splashing joyfully not twenty-five feet in front of her. Now, surrounded by the colors and sounds of St. George's, she felt relaxed for the first time in days.

Feeling a flash of nostalgia for her first visit, Allegra climbed the steps to Jamie's office and peered in the door. Could it have been less than three months ago? Like that first time, Jamie sat at his desk in his shirt-sleeves, chatting with another man. It wasn't Oliver this time but an older planter Allegra vaguely remembered having been introduced to at Royston Ross's ball.

"Allegra," Jamie said in surprise, catching sight of her. "I didn't expect to see you today. Are you shopping again with Violet?" Both men rose.

"No," Allegra replied, stepping just inside the door. "I came to talk to you, but I can see that you're busy. I'll do some errands and come back later."

She turned to go, but stopped again when the older man said, "It is I who shall return later, Miss Pembroke. I'm afraid I've been intruding on Mr. Forsythe's time and patience with idle gossip and complaints about my arthritis. I am quite sure he would much prefer to talk with a beautiful young woman. Please come and sit down." He held out the chair he had just vacated. Allegra crossed the room and sat, demurely murmuring her thanks and wishing she could remember the man's name.

When he had gone, Jamie sat down across from her. "Is it very bad at the estate?" he asked, his voice warm with concern.

It was Allegra's turn to be caught by surprise. "Do you know what happened?" she asked.

Jamie nodded. "Oliver wrote me a note two days ago," he said. "It was as much to warn me as to inform me. I suppose he is worried that your cousin might attempt some legal action while your guard is down."

"Bartholomew?" Allegra said incredulously, remembering his unexpected distress when she had told him of the bank failure. She shook her head. "He wouldn't," she said positively. "He is on my side."

"Who isn't, then?" Jamie asked shrewdly. "Is Oliver misbehaving?"

"No, not exactly," Allegra answered slowly, running her finger along the edge of the desk. "He's not in a rage, if that's what you mean." She didn't look directly at Jamie. "He's just being silly."

"Silly?" Jamie repeated in astonishment. Of all the unflattering adjectives ever used for his friend, that one seemed the most farfetched. He looked at Allegra more closely. There was only one time when sober, otherwise sensible men became silly: when they were in love. Seeing the way her eyelashes feathered against her flushed cheeks, the way her head cocked ingenuously to one side, Jamie realized that was precisely the problem. Oliver was in love.

"But I've really come to ask you about my father's will," Allegra said, switching the subject with forced brightness of tone. She looked up again, meeting his eyes.

Jamie graciously allowed his attention to be distracted. He wheeled his chair over to an open file cabinet and pulled out a folder. "The will actually arrived several days ago," he said, wheeling back to the desk and laying the document out in front of him. "Ordinarily I would have brought it up to L'Etoile right away, but Oliver's note arrived almost simultaneously. In view of the situation, I thought I'd let the dust settle first. Besides which, it contains nothing new or startling. It just spells out the facts we were already aware of."

"What does it say?" Allegra asked, leaning over the desk to touch the will. She felt an odd sensation, a mixture of sadness and anticipation, knowing this was a message from her father to her, the only one Cecil had ever sent.

"Well, then, let's see," Jamie answered, scanning the first page. "There is some legal prattle in the beginning. Then it says, ah yes, here we go. It says that you are his sole heir; he leaves his entire estate to you. This includes his personal possessions, which are mostly clothes and books. I understand there is a fairish painting by Caravaggio, worth a modest sum, and a signet ring, as well.

"You also inherit his liquid assets." Jamie paused to leaf through the folder for another paper. Reading it, he gave a sympathetic shrug and said, "Cecil had three bank accounts in London and Grenada, but I'm afraid the grand total of the lot is twenty-two pounds six." He set the page back on the desk and picked up the will again. "And lastly, he leaves you his properties: L'Etoile and the little chocolate manufacturing concern he was attempting to start up, Stellar Confections."

As Jamie flipped through the pages again, trying to find some small item they had overlooked, Allegra sat totally still and quiet. Her very silence finally caused him to look up sharply, afraid she was suddenly overcome by the hopelessness of her situation. Instead of seeing her face pale with despair, he saw her lovely features lit up with excitement, her violet eyes wide and animated.

"Stellar Confections," she muttered, trying it out on her tongue. "I had forgotten all about it. Actually, I never even knew it by name." In fact, she hadn't really thought about it as a business, but only as a hazy excuse for her father's financial improprieties, another in the endless stream of schemes that had fascinated him. When Oliver had first mentioned it to her that day in the cocoa grove, the idea of a chocolate factory had briefly intrigued her. As she had become more involved in the workings of L'Etoile, the factory in England had seemed far away. If it had crossed her mind at all, it was only to assume that somehow it had dissolved or disappeared at Cecil's death.

She didn't know if it were because the factory now had a name, or because she was grabbing desperately at any solution, but Stellar Confections suddenly seemed very real. It also seemed the answer to all her problems. "That's it," she said to Jamie, an exuberant smile covering her face. "Stellar Confections." She repeated it several times, happily rehearsing different inflections. "Stellar Confections."

Jamie, not nearly as familiar with the impulsive turnings of Allegra's mind as Oliver, was a little bewildered by her reaction. "From what I understand, it is not at all a profitable venture," he said gently, hating to disillusion her. "And the building is only leased, not owned outright. Still," he said, scratching his pink cheek thoughtfully, "the machinery is bound to be worth something. You should have the English solicitors sell up everything," he advised, devising a plan as he went along.

"Whatever cash you gain, you can use as a down payment on your debts. I am certain there is no need to worry about Oliver; he'll wait forever for the money you owe him. And if your uncle receives some earnest money now and the promise of other payments at the sale of your cocoa every year, I'm sure he will be satisfied." Jamie slipped the will back into the folder, well pleased with the soundness of his strategy. If Allegra were determined to honor her father's debts rather than fight them in court as Oliver had said in his note, this was the best way.

"I have a much better idea," Allegra said, her tongue practically tripping over itself in her hurry to describe her thoughts. "Instead of selling off everything, and being left with no means of making any more money, I'll go to England and take over Stellar Confections. I'll use the *profits* from the business to pay my debts, rather than the assets."

"But there *are* no profits, Allegra," Jamie said, aghast at the idea. "It's a fledgling little venture that never got in the air. Really, the most merciful thing you could do for it would be to sell it up. The only thing it has to recommend it are its assets."

"Wrong," Allegra said, not at all dissuaded. "What it has to recommend it is my father's imagination. It's his creation, just as L'Etoile was his creation. Except in the case of the factory, he died before he could realize his dream. It was part of a grand plan, I'm sure," she continued, bouncing to the edge of her seat, her voice growing more excited as she talked. "It was the last link in a cocoa chain from bean to bonbon, so to speak. First he built up L'Etoile, then he channeled funds from the estate into the final project: Stellar Confections. He even chose the name to fit in with the whole celestial theme. Don't you see, Jamie," she said, waving her arm wide to indicate the empire she was envisioning. "The estate was meant to be the foundation for the factory, just as cocoa is the foundation for chocolate. One evolves from the other, and each is dependent on the other. If his death hadn't interrupted the balance, I *know* my father would have made a huge success. He would have paid back all the money he borrowed and proven that his ideas were sound. He would have become a chocolate king."

Leaning over the desk again, she took hold of the folder containing the will as if she were accepting a scepter of office. "*I shall realize my father's dreams,*" she vowed dramatically. "I shall make a success of Stellar Confections, and I shall pay back the money he owes. His name and reputation will be restored, even enhanced."

"I fear you are not being realistic, Allegra," Jamie said worriedly. "I fear you will be dreadfully hurt."

Nothing Jamie said made any impression on Allegra. To her the plan was perfect, almost better than if she had inherited L'Etoile free and clear. The estate was already developed, an idea that needed only maintenance and, possibly, expansion. Stellar Confections, however, needed shaping. It was a way of truly making her mark, of doing something important, of finally making full use of the traits and talents that were Cecil's ultimate legacy. By restoring her father's credibility, she would be firmly establishing her own.

Nor would the satisfaction of her ambition be the only benefit. Stellar Confections also offered her an option other than marriage. In her relief, Allegra glossed over the memory of making love to Oliver in the cool bed of cress. She overlooked the utter enjoyment she got from listening to his straightforward and usually improper views on life. She dismissed the way he seemed to catch her whenever she fell, to always be nearby. Instead, she remembered only the extreme discomfort of recent times and was delighted to find a way out.

All other advantages aside, the very idea of running Stellar Confections was appealing. Since she'd begun working with the cocoa and smelling the piles of polished beans, Allegra had caught chocolate fever. She well understood what motivated the Aztecs to make it the property of royalty and their European conquerors to call it the "food of the gods." It was special, addicting. In her present mood, it was easy to romanticize, imagining herself tying satin ribbons around velvet boxes filled with plump chocolate-covered cherries far into the night, each delectable treat chipping a penny away from her enormous debt. So pleased was she with the whole idea, she hardly needed the schooner to sail back to Gouyave.

She slid into her place at the dinner table straight from the boat, her traveling dress crumpled, her curls blown askew. Her face was glowing with suntan and excitement, and she attacked her bowl of breadfruit vichyssoise with more appetite than she'd shown in weeks. "I have splendid news," she proclaimed between bites, for once oblivious to the tense atmosphere of the room as well as to the impact her animation was making.

"Did your lawyer have some useful advice?" William asked, trying to sink the chopped chives on top of his soup with the back of his spoon. He wasn't at all sure about this tropical fare. He liked his potatoes to be potatoes, not breadfruit, and he liked them mashed with gravy, not chilled and pureed with consommé.

"His advice wasn't terribly useful," Allegra said, dismissing it with a wave of her spoon. "But his information was invaluable. I had completely forgotten that my father had started a manufacturing company in England! I was so worried about paying back his debts that I didn't even think about why they had been incurred. I forgot that he had borrowed the money for a specific purpose: to start Stellar Confections."

"Ahh," William said, giving up his battle with the chives and setting his spoon aside. "So you have decided to liquidate the assets of this chocolate concern and to settle his debts with those funds."

"No," Allegra answered, scooping up the last of her vichyssoise, "I've decided to go to England and run the business, using the eventual profits to settle his debts. One of Star Shipping's freighters is leaving for England on Tuesday morning and I've booked passage."

Several seconds of absolute silence greeted her announcement. Then Violet wailed, "You can't go to England. You belong at L'Etoile. We need you here. We would miss you if you left."

Allegra's brow furrowed at her friend's words. Everything had happened so fast, she hadn't given that reality much thought. Elizabeth compounded her guilt by giving a disappointed "tch" as she cleared away the soup bowls and set out a tureen of conch stew. Allegra was trying to think of an appropriate reply when William spoke up.

"Really, Allegra," he said, smoothing his moustache with the edge of his napkin. "It hardly seems an appropriate expedition for a woman alone. To travel by yourself so far from home is dangerous. I cannot, in good conscience, condone such a scheme."

Allegra's guilt vanished. "I am going to England, William," she said, "not to deepest Africa. It's quite a modern and civilized country. I shall be in no more danger than I am right here."

"I'm not so sure," Oliver said at last. He had waited patiently while the others had their say, an icy feeling grabbing his stomach when he imagined life at L'Etoile without Allegra. Her news hit him severely. More than anyone else present, he knew it was useless to try to change her mind; it was a grave mistake to intimate that she couldn't accomplish what she claimed she could. Yet in his desperation, that was exactly what he tried to do.

"You've given this idea scanty thought," he said gruffly. A lifetime of speaking and acting directly had ill prepared him for making pretty pleas and subtle suggestions. "You've barely enough money left to pay for your passage, to say nothing of your lodging when you arrive. Before you use up the last of your funds, you should have Jamie write and find out some facts about this factory. In all probability, it is on the brink of bankruptcy, and it will only drain you emotionally and financially, leaving you stranded in a strange country. You'll find out then just how dangerous England can be." He was upset with himself for sounding so grumpy, especially when he saw her chin taking on its mulish tilt.

"You don't know that the factory is near failure," she said darkly. "You are just assuming that because my father had to borrow money for it. It's a new business, it needs time to grow. And it needs guidance. My father died before he could get it established, but I will get it on its feet and make it a thriving concern."

"Be sensible," Oliver retorted. "Just how do you intend to do that? You know you make a hopeless muddle of the account books and you do dismally at figures. Moreover, you don't know the first thing about making chocolate."

"That's what you told me about growing cocoa," Allegra flared back. "You told me I could never be an equal partner in L'Etoile because I didn't know a thing about cocoa. But I learned, didn't I? You know I've become a good planter, you have to admit it."

"I admit it," Oliver said, refraining from repeating that she was still inept at numbers. "But you were a good pupil in large part because you had a good teacher. You're a good planter because you have a good estate. And a good partner. Who do you know who can give you similar assistance with your factory?

Who do you know who has any knowledge of making chocolate
—or of Stellar Confections?"

"Well," Allegra said, chewing her lip and trying to think of a
pungent reply to what she suddenly realized was an all too valid
point.

"I do," Bartholomew said quietly. He was the only one who
hadn't yet spoken. "I know a great deal about Stellar Confections, from the state of its finances, which, as you suggest, Mr.
MacKenzie, are a trifle shaky, to the amount of chocolate it
molded last year, which was a great deal more than I think you
are estimating. I am also familiar with the process of making
chocolate. At my father's request, I researched the subject quite
exhaustively."

An incredulous silence followed his subdued remarks, broken
finally by Violet who said in wonder, "You did?"

Bartholomew nodded, embarrassed color creeping up his
cheeks as everyone continued to stare at him. "Manufacturing
chocolate is not all that complicated an operation, but it is an
exact one. It requires strict adherence to formulas and tempera-
tures, wherein lies the secret of its excellence."

When still no one acknowledged his comments, Bartholomew
went a bit further. "Actually, it is not unlike the process used in
making your cocoa tea, although the equipment employed is
more sophisticated and the methods are more scientific." As he
warmed to his subject, his natural affinity for information took
over, and he offered a more detailed explanation.

"When the beans from L'Etoile and similar plantations arrive
at the chocolate factories," he said, "the first step is to sort them.
Stones and sticks and spoiled beans are sieved out, and the varieties are carefully noted. Next they are loaded into a giant roaster
and roasted in precise accordance with a closely guarded recipe
created by the master chef, or the chocolatier, as he is known.
While the mixture of beans and the length of time they are
roasted are, as I've said, highly confidential, it is common
knowledge that longer roasting periods produce a darker, more
bitter and, to some palates, richer chocolate flavor. It is also true,
as I am sure you are already aware, that the Criollo variety yields
a more delicate taste than the Forastero variety, and that the
former is used to flavor the chocolate.

"After roasting, the beans are 'broken down'. That is to say,
they are first fed through a machine which gently cracks the thin

shell, and then fed through a winnowing machine which affects the separation of the shell and the inner kernel, known in the industry as the cocoa nib. I might add as a parenthetical comment that the discarded husks are used in Ireland for a light but savory beverage known by the appellation of 'miserables.'"

No one remarked on any facet of Bartholomew's discourse. Halting his academic assault long enough to note the stunned expressions of his audience, Bartholomew took a nervous gulp, and, too far along to retreat, plunged forward. "The next stage is milling," he said. "For this, the roasted nibs are fed into a hopper from which they are passed between granite millstones where they are crushed. Although the nibs may seem dry and brittle when they enter the hopper, after a few minutes of grinding sufficient heat is generated to liquefy the fatty content contained within the nib, and it freely flows from the stones. Although fluid or perhaps pasty at this point, immediately upon cooling it solidifies into an extremely hard cake. This cake, then, is known as chocolate liquor, and it is the basis for all future forms of eating and drinking chocolate. Its only other use in this pure state is for baking.

"When the chocolate liquor is further pressed, the fat, an amber-colored liquid called cocoa butter, is extracted. The residual mass is a dry, powdery substance: the cocoa essence sold in familiar boxes and tins for our breakfast drink. Although the Dutch prefer to subject the cocoa to an alkalizing procedure known appropriately as 'dutching' and invented, in 1828, by Conrad Van Houten, the English consume their cocoa as is.

"The cocoa butter that has been extracted is now added to chocolate liquor. These basic ingredients are melted to an exact temperature and kneaded together with sugar and possibly vanilla. After it has been properly combined, this mixture is refined, and finally it is cooled, to a constant 85 degrees. Thus the chocolate is finally ready to be variously molded, poured, or elsewise made into the confections that captivate our gastronomical fancies."

"Fascinating!" Allegra cried when he had concluded. "I should have known that if anyone had the information I needed it would be you, Cousin Bartholomew. Do you see, Oliver?" She turned toward him triumphantly. "Do you see how much Cousin Bartholomew knows about making chocolate?"

"A fine lesson," Oliver said grimly. "But does Cousin Bartholomew know how this applies to Stellar Confections? Does he know what to do when the millstones break or how to recognize overroasted beans?"

Allegra looked quickly back to Bartholomew for an answer, now completely convinced that he had one. Her cousin had continually surprised her over the past few weeks with his unending store of knowledge and his unexpected kindness. She had found herself liking and trusting him more and more, despite his association with her unpleasant uncle. At this moment, she absolutely adored him.

"I don't have a positive response for either query," Bartholomew said carefully. Allegra's heart dropped and Oliver's lifted, though the next instant it was all reversed. "However, as it applies to Stellar Confections, both problems are irrelevant since the factory does not roast or mill its own beans. As is the situation with most small manufacturers of eating chocolate, Stellar Confections purchases its chocolate liquor from a larger concern, such as Cadbury's or Fry's, concentrating instead on production of candy.

"If I am not mistaken, there is an arrangement whereby the beans are roasted according to the instructions of the chocolatier, in this case, a Mr. Bruno Pavese. He is an Italian gentleman in his upper fifties, I would guess, nearly crippled with arthritis and made quite cantankerous by it. He does, albeit, have a reputation for extremely high standards and exquisite taste. All questions of quality and flavor fall under his guidance.

"I take your point about faulty machinery, however, Mr. MacKenzie," Bartholomew added with a nod toward Oliver who was slouched, glowering in his chair. "There is a manager in charge of the overall operation of the business; presumably he has an acquaintance with the technical and mechanical aspects of the factory. His name is Albert Baker and little else is known about him. He appears to be of middle age, rather small, and possessing a slightly nervous disposition."

"There!" Allegra pounced, less concerned with the details right now than with knowing that her cousin had considered them. "You can't deny that Cousin Bartholomew has thought of everything, Oliver. Surely he has met all your objections. His knowledge is formidable."

"Yes," Oliver said with deceptive calm. "But is he willing to use that knowledge to help you?"

Allegra started to scoff, "Of course he is," but stopped before the words came out. She looked at her cousin, so grave and serious, a sudden doubt disturbing her. After all, he was Sir Gerald's son, and his specific task was to collect her debt or foreclose on L'Etoile. Anxiously, she asked, "Will you help me?"

Bartholomew steepled his long, slender fingers and rested his chin on their tips. He glanced briefly at Violet, who was holding her breath across the table, then answered his cousin's question more succinctly than he had ever answered anything in his life. "Yes," he said.

Her elation restored, Allegra let out a whoop. "This is going to be a tremendous success," she cried. "I just know it is."

"I must caution you against overvaluing my knowledge," Bartholomew warned. "It is, after all, theoretical, not practical."

Allegra waved aside his disclaimer with a theatrical flourish. "You are too modest, I'm sure," she said happily. To her ears, Bartholomew sounded like an unimpeachable authority. Besides, she had great confidence in his sobriety and propriety, attributes that seemed to be much respected in the business world. "Stellar Confections is going to be a tremendous success."

Her sense of excitement and triumph was diluted by Oliver's severe expression—and by his absence from the breakfast table the next morning. No matter how much they had disagreed in the past, Oliver had ultimately favored her insistence on certain points with an amused if exasperated look. Indeed, she realized now, she had quite come to depend on that approval.

It put a different complexion on her desire to escape from the emotional tension he was creating, although her original reasons for wanting to run Stellar Confections had been reinforced by Bartholomew's description. Still, she knew she could not leave L'Etoile with Oliver feeling as he did. She spent the entire day searching the estate for him.

By the time Septimus informed her that he'd gone down to Gouyave with a load of cocoa for the *Pride of Windward*, her hunt had become almost obsessive. Allegra slammed her hands on her hips, annoyed that he had eluded her again. She strode down to the stables, saddled her favorite donkey, and went off, determined to pin him down even if she had to go to Carriacou to do it. She finally found him on the pier in Gouyave, barechested and hoisting bags of cocoa into the hold of his schooner, his expression not at all improved.

Their tête-à-tête did not get off to a good start. Allegra, already frustrated by her day-long chase, grew increasingly agitated as Oliver left her standing in the hot sun while he deliberately finished loading the cargo. She was beginning to boil by the time he snatched his shirt off the boom and came over to her, sticking his arms through his sleeves as he walked. Without saying a word, he led the way along the edge of a bluff to a little beach lined with smooth rocks and shaded by a pair of palm trees. Oliver sank down on one end of a washed up log. Allegra sat gingerly on the other end.

"Are you still resolved to leave L'Etoile?" he asked in a low voice, struggling to control both his sense of betrayal and his intense love.

For a moment, Allegra didn't speak but just rubbed her finger over a knot in the log. The only sound was the clatter of stones rolling against each other in the gently breaking waves. The sweet salty breeze fluttered her curls and cooled her sunburned cheeks. The nearness of Oliver with his shirt open, his sleeves rolled up, his hot, tanned skin smelling faintly of cocoa, almost made Allegra break down and relent. Then she shook her head. "I don't want to leave L'Etoile," she finally answered, looking over at him. "But I do want to go to England and run Stellar Confections."

"You can't have both, Allegra," Oliver said. "You have to make a choice."

"I know," Allegra conceded miserably, looking down again.

"Stay here," Oliver urged with sudden softness, moved by the dejected sight of her. "Stay here with me. That chocolate factory is a hopeless scheme; it's a Pandora's box, a disaster. It will devour you. Stay here and let me help you solve your problems."

"No, wait! I have an idea," Allegra cried, sitting bolt upright. A happy thought popped into her head and almost simultaneously rolled off her tongue. "Why don't you come with me?" she asked, stretching her hands toward him in invitation. "Instead of sitting here warning me of all the terrible things that might happen, why don't you come along? You say you want to help me; that would be the perfect way to do so. You know about all those mechanical things like broken millstones, and figures don't fluster you in the least. It could be splendid, Oliver," she added pleadingly. "We could work together, just as we've done at L'Etoile."

"No," Oliver answered without pause for reflection. "I vowed never to set foot in England again, and I mean it." The memory of his bitter boyhood rivalry with the young Lord Fenwick and the abuse he suffered because of it was vivid in his mind, overwhelming all else. "England is a land of snobs and hypocrites who use starchy morality as a substitute for genuine feeling," he said stringently. "I've had enough of that rubbish to last me a lifetime."

Deeply disappointed, Allegra let her hands fall. "You needn't pay that attitude any more heed in England than you do in Grenada," she said. "You could ignore it."

"No," Oliver said again, shaking his head stubbornly. He wasn't seeing Allegra's hurt expression or remembering how her remarkable spirit enlivened his life. He was feeling, again, the painful sting of rebuff as, over and over, an innocent, open youth from the colonies was made to understand his social inferiority. In the West Indies, he was respected for his accomplishments and his strength of character. In England, he was judged solely by his birth. It was a point of pride for him never to return to the scene of so much personal humiliation.

And yet Allegra had a sense of pride, too, and it was injured by his rejection of her eager proposal. She vented her embarrassment in anger. "It's just as well," she said sharply. "I don't need your help. Or William's or Jamie's. I can make Stellar Confections succeed by myself."

"You don't mind accepting, even recruiting, the aid of your long-winded cousin," Oliver returned, instantly responding to her fury.

"He's part of my family," Allegra answered hotly. "He's a Pembroke. I'll show you that the Pembroke name is not to be ridiculed or patronized. You think we are only amusing, a light-minded divertissement, but I'll show you that we are to be taken seriously."

"How do you expect to be taken seriously when you pursue such an idiotic course?" Oliver asked irately, rising to his feet.

"It is *not* idiotic," Allegra shouted, jumping up also. "Just because it was my father's idea, you are convinced that it is doomed to failure. You think that because he was charming and witty and full of imagination—instead of boring, with his nose in an account book—that his business hasn't a chance."

"You should know me better than that," Oliver roared back.

"That's not the way I think at all. But Stellar Confections is debt-ridden and struggling, and you have no capital to put into it. *That* is why I think it hasn't a chance."

"Well, you're wrong! And I'll prove it to you!"

"Unlikely!"

"Shush, mahn!" An annoyed voice interrupted their argument. With a start, they both looked toward a nearby house where a woman with cornrows in her hair and a frown on her face was standing in the open doorway. "Shush," she repeated. "My baby sleeping inside."

Swallowing their remaining anger and muttering apologies to the woman, they left the beach. At the pier, Oliver made an excuse to stay on at the schooner, saying he would probably miss dinner. Fighting back tears of temper and anguish, Allegra only nodded, gathering the reins of her donkey and walking away. This meeting, this last-ditch attempt to satisfy both their individual needs and their love for each other had ended in acrimony.

Allegra spent the next day packing. Oliver passed it in the highest hills of the estate, in a thick, untouched forest, chopping down trees for charcoal. They didn't see each other until Monday afternoon when they were again on the pier in Gouyave, this time as part of a miserable group come to say good-bye.

Violet's face was raw from weeping and her words were incoherent. Elizabeth looked grim. William, pushing his spectacles higher on his nose, was perturbed. Standing next to Allegra, Bartholomew seemed uncommonly upset. They stood on the wharf, shifting from foot to foot, avoiding the final move that would take them away. When the sails were set and only the spring line held in Oliver's hand kept the schooner close, they could delay no longer. Bartholomew boarded the boat first, then reached back to hand Allegra on.

Although Oliver was standing so near Allegra could feel the heat from his body, he offered no assistance. It was only after she was on board and he had tossed the line back onto the boat that he looked at her. His eyes, deep dark blue, fastened steadily on her face, now drifting ever farther away. "Good luck," he said briefly. Allegra nodded across the widening gulf, again unable to speak. Her enthusiasm for Stellar Confections considerably dampened, her heart cold in her chest, she left L'Etoile for England.

Chapter
Thirteen

Bartholomew watched as the figures on the pier became smaller, as Violet's lovely face faded away. He could scarcely breathe. Horror crushed the air from his lungs; dread wrenched the life from his soul. In a sudden, desperate gesture, he reached out his hand to grab onto the scene slipping farther away from him. It was no use. Violet disappeared from his view. His hand dropped.

How did this happen, he wondered dully. Only five days before he had been bursting with happiness, transfixed by the passion awakened in him at the lily pond. It had overpowered everything else around him. His existence in England had receded into the hazy past and the hazier future. His only concern had been the glorious present, centered around the woman he adored. He had been vaguely aware of how subdued Allegra was at dinner, of the grim light in her usually lively eyes, but he'd been too bewitched by Violet to give it a second thought. Not even the unexpected presence of William Browne, a man whose very air of propriety ought to have brought him back down to earth, had made any impact on Bartholomew's state of uninhibited happiness.

Only when Allegra asked to see him alone did he feel his first twinge of alarm. He was so consumed by the rapture of making love to Violet, he didn't consider that any other subject could be on Allegra's mind. He was sure that she meant to take him to task for his improper conduct. He didn't even wonder how his cousin had come to find out. He spent the rest of the morning composing eloquent mental arguments, declaring the purity of his love for Violet so ardently and so often he was even more enthralled than before.

When he finally found Allegra in the library later in the day, he was completely absorbed in his emotions, totally involved in his life at L'Etoile. Allegra's blurted out words came out of nowhere and hit him like a bludgeon. "I've had very bad news," she said, her face drawn and tense. "My bank has failed and all my money has been lost. I have no way of paying my father's debt."

For a few awful seconds he was stunned into silence. His most immediate thought was that the wonderful world he had discovered was about to be spoiled. L'Etoile, lyrical, lovely L'Etoile where all his senses had come alive was going to be destroyed. "How terrible!" he exclaimed. "Are you absolutely sure? Could there not have been an error made? Or perhaps a conclusion drawn too quickly? Possibly even a flaw in communications?"

When Allegra looked at him in astonishment and answered his anxious questions in a puzzled tone, it dawned on him that the spoilers, the destroyers of this idyll, were none other than his father and himself. His horror deepened when he further realized that instead of standing there wishing it wouldn't happen, it was his mission to make sure that it did. He clenched one fist behind his back and chewed the knuckles of the other while he tried to figure a way out of this dreadful dilemma.

A sense of doom gradually descended on him, wholly deflating yesterday's euphoria, dampening the unreasonable hope that he could somehow extend his extraordinary stay in Grenada, that he could continue loving Violet always. Suddenly England no longer seemed so very remote. Its restraints and routines again became part of his consciousness. He managed to mutter a few distracted phrases of encouragement, even to pat his cousin's arm before escaping outdoors to brood by himself.

Bartholomew slumped down on a wrought-iron bench, ideally situated for viewing the deep purple sea between the blossoms of an oleander bush and the branches of a paw paw tree. He stared unseeing at the dramatic light, ironically remembering his wish that Allegra's money would never arrive from Connecticut. He gave a short, bitter laugh. He hadn't wanted the money to be lost; he had simply wanted the wait for it to go on indefinitely. He hadn't wanted his visit to end. But now it was over. He no longer had any reason to stay. All the reasons for his life were in England. All, that is, except Violet.

He lurched off the bench, suddenly desperate to see her, needing to reassure himself that she hadn't disappeared, as well. A feeling of panic seized him as he raced across the lawn, his breath constricted. His frenzy increased as he looked in one place and then another. Failing to find her, he grew irrationally afraid that she had gone without saying good-bye, that she had vanished like Allegra's money, that he would never see her again. "Not yet!" he wanted to shout.

Enormous relief filled him when he finally caught sight of her bent over some plants in the kitchen garden. Her innocent smile of welcome eased his fears immediately. He slowed his pace as he crossed the plot, letting his pounding pulse settle back to normal. "I've looked everywhere for you," he said, trying to keep the anxiety out of his voice.

Violet stood up straight, resting a basket on her hip. "Elizabeth went to Gouyave to visit her mother-in-law," she explained. "The neighbor's goat was stung on the nose by a bee and went mad and kicked Mrs. Stephen in the leg. The poor woman has been unable to walk for two days. Her left knee is swollen to the size of a bolly."

"A what?" Bartholomew asked, startled from his introspection by the story of this bizarre accident.

"A bolly," Violet said, smiling. "It's a calabash." Again she bent over the bush and pulled a green pod from among the branches, tossing it into the basket. "Anyway," she said, "I told Elizabeth not to worry about coming back in time for dinner tonight, that I would cook instead."

"You?" Bartholomew asked, even more startled.

Straightening again, another pod in her hand, Violet looked a bit baffled by his surprise. "Yes," she said. "I am going to make coco pois and salt fish souse, which I make very often in Carriacou. In fact, everyone in Carriacou makes them frequently."

"Let me help you," Bartholomew volunteered, taking the basket out of her hand. "I don't know what you've said, or what you are doing, but I want to help you." He didn't care what it entailed, as long as he could be with her.

This time Violet laughed at his obvious confusion. "I'm picking pigeon peas to make coco pois," she told him, throwing the lumpy pod she was holding into the basket and reaching for another one. "You'll see. We have to boil the peas in coconut milk until they burst, then add cornmeal and let it cook together." She paused a minute, then added apologetically, "It doesn't sound very tasty, I suppose, and it doesn't look very elegant, but it really is quite good."

"If you cook it, I am sure it will be delicious," Bartholomew said reverently, yanking a pod free from the leaves. "I shall savor every morsel."

"Not that one," Violet said, reaching over to stay his hand. "That one isn't ready yet. See? It's too flat." Her small brown fingers curled around his and gave a soft squeeze. Bartholomew immediately forgot the peas as he returned the clasp, the warmth of her touch chasing away the chilly fear of losing her.

They filled the basket with peas and walked back to the kitchen. Violet dragged a stool into the corner between a table and an open window. "You sit here," she instructed, patting the seat. When Bartholomew obligingly sat, she set a bowl in his lap and an empty basket by his feet. She dumped the pigeon peas in a pile on the table, then showed him how to shell them, splitting open a pod with her thumb, flicking the fat peas into the bowl and dropping the husk in the basket. She watched a minute while he shucked several pods, carefully following her directions. Nodding her approval and giving him a smile of encouragement, she tied an apron around her waist and pinned its bib to her blouse. Then she moved off to prepare the rest of the meal.

After the first few peas, Bartholomew's prowess improved. He soon fell into an easy pattern of reaching, splitting, flicking, and dropping. It was a soothing rhythm that didn't require his attention, and he let his thoughts wander as he watched Violet grate a coconut to make coconut milk. He was mildly astonished to find himself in this position. He never set foot in the kitchen at Pembroke Manor.

Since his mother had died in his infancy, all culinary decisions had been the province of Mrs. Griswold, the housekeeper. Indeed, all household needs were efficiently handled by that formidable and unapproachable matron. Although Bartholomew occasionally made a request for fresh raspberries and cream, or for extra towels after a swim in the lake, he usually just accepted the regular flow of life.

He took for granted the appearance of meals on the baronial table. He took for granted the suits his valet pressed and the crisp bed linen the maid changed daily. He took for granted the warming winter fires the houseboy laid in the hearth and the crystal snifters of brandy the butler set silently at his elbow. Endlessly curious on a vast variety of subjects, Bartholomew spent his days filling his head with esoteric information while remaining completely ignorant and unquestioning about the basic tasks of living.

He had never been so aware of his inability to manage the details of everyday life—until now. He watched Violet soak the grated coconut in water, then strain it through a muslin square, squeezing every drop of essence from the sweet, milky fruit. Setting the bowls aside, she turned her attention to the souse and removed a pot of salt fish from the stove where it had been simmering. She drained the water and set the fish on a plate, picking away flakes of it with a fork. Her movements about the kitchen were assured. She radiated self-sufficiency.

Bartholomew sighed and reached for another pea. Although perfectly comfortable having people wait on her, Violet was equally as capable of taking care of herself. She could keep herself dressed and pressed, could keep flavorful food on her plate. Although he had never seen Oliver and Allegra working in the kitchen, Bartholomew instinctively knew they possessed the same capabilities. Only *he* was helpless, dependent on servants and a bottomless bank account to pay them, for the comfort of his existence.

Wrenching open a pod with enough force to send its peas skidding across the kitchen floor, Bartholomew bitterly acknowledged that he wasn't even able to keep that bank account filled. His exclusive, expensive schooling had prepared him to parse sentences in several languages, to quote eruditely from Shakespeare and Sophocles, to debate differing philosophical viewpoints, and to unravel the medieval history of England. In short, he'd been groomed to be a gentleman. His education hadn't prepared him to enter a profession or a trade, to run a business or manage an estate. Sir Gerald jealously guarded the proceedings at Pembroke Hall, reluctant to let anyone else have access to his affairs. Up until today, Bartholomew had been content with life as it was, but now came the awful realization that without his father's prodigious purse, he was like a turtle on its back.

He didn't waste even one minute hoping the purse would not be withdrawn if he chose to remain in Grenada. Or, even worse, if he brought Violet to England. Any man who could pursue a dead brother's debt so ruthlessly, ignoring the plight of his orphaned American niece, would not lightly accept his only son's marriage to a woman with African, Scottish, and French blood in her veins. Quite unequivocally, if Violet were to be part of Bartholomew's life, Sir Gerald's money would not be.

He finished shelling the peas and set the bowl on the table, leaning back against the wall to let the breeze from the open window blow across him. The sun was slipping away, turning the sky deep rose and sooty purple and making the light in the kitchen muted and magical. Violet's black curls caught an occasional gleam of the fading sun and her creamy beige skin seemed even softer.

She combined the flaked fish with chopped onions and chilies, drizzled it with olive oil, and placed it on a bed of lettuce. Intent on her creation, she arranged paper-thin shards of green pepper for a garnish, wiped her hands on her apron, and stood back to admire the salt fish souse. She looked over at Bartholomew and smiled.

The sweetness and trust on her face went right through him. Her exquisite beauty made him ache. In that instant, he became sure of two things. He would never stop loving her, longing for her, but he had to leave her. There was no more wishing for indefinite delays and impossible scenarios. He simply couldn't have her. He loved her too much to destroy her with his inadequacy.

Since he had been in Grenada, more than one person had remarked on his similarity to Cecil. He realized that without exception they were referring to his looks, for no one could confuse the sedate, slightly boring nephew with the charming, gay uncle. But Bartholomew now detected some other traits they shared, ones that most observers overlooked. Surely his enchantment with the tropics came from Cecil, rather than from his conservative father. And just as surely his head-in-the-clouds approach to life was another legacy of his uncle's.

Although his head might be in academic clouds, while Cecil's had been in adventurous ones, the result was the same. He was dependent, as his uncle had been before him, on his father's wealth to shepherd him from one cloud to the next. When Cecil had fallen in love and married against his father's wish and without his quarterly stipends, the marriage had ended in devastating poverty and despair. Bartholomew could not bear to repeat this mistake by marrying Violet. He could not will Amelia's fate on her.

"What is troubling you, Bartholomew?" Violet asked softly when her smile brought only a faint response. "Is it Allegra? Did she scold you? Did she warn you to behave properly toward me?"

Bartholomew leaned his elbows on his knees and covered his face with his hands. "No," he said wearily, massaging his temples with his fingers. "She didn't speak of us at all. Her mind was occupied with other matters."

Violet crossed the kitchen and came to stand in front of him. For a moment she didn't say anything, only gazed sadly at his hidden face. Then she reached out and brushed a single blond strand from his forehead. "What is it then?" she asked gently. "What is making you so unhappy?"

Her feathery touch unleashed the anguish building up inside him. With a groan, he lowered his hands from his face, wrapped them around her waist, and dragged her into his lap. He held her warm body tightly against him, burying his nose in her hair, absorbing the clean kitchen scents clinging to her. She was so alive, so vital, she filled the cool recesses of his soul. He needed her as much as he needed his heart to beat. He held her closer.

Her face turned toward his, her delicate brows quirked inquiringly. Instead of answering her, he kissed her, letting his lips linger over hers, letting them slide over the smooth skin of her cheeks to tenderly caress her closed eyes. His kiss trailed off into her curls as he pulled her tighter into his arms, finally whispering in her ear, his voice hoarse and broken with emotion, "I love you so much, Violet. I love you so much, my wonderful flower. And I don't know what to do about it."

Reacting to the misery in his voice, Violet felt a shiver run through her. An intuitive fear chilled her, despite the warmth of his embrace. She eased herself back so she could look into his eyes, so she could cradle his cheek in her hand and trace her thumb across his lips. "What's wrong?" she asked again, more urgently this time. "What has happened?"

Bartholomew took a deep, shuddery breath, then turned his head so he could press a kiss against her palm. "My cousin's American bank has failed," he said tonelessly. "All her money was lost. She has no way of paying the note she signed to my father." He stopped and took another gulp of air. His eyes closed briefly as he leaned into her hand, gathering courage from the feel of her small fingers against his skin. "Which means I no longer have any reason to remain in Grenada."

"Oh dear God," Violet said quietly, another shiver going through her. He didn't have to explain any further. Her head sank back against his shoulder.

They remained as they were, twined around each other until after the sun had set and the kitchen filled with shadows. The only light came from the stove, a tiny glow in the velvety gloom. At last it was Violet who reluctantly rose, stirred by the practical need to tend to dinner. She walked across the kitchen and lifted the lid on the coco pois, hardly seeing what was in the pot.

"Let it go," Bartholomew pleaded. "Let it go and come back to me. I can't imagine that anyone cares about eating this evening. No one has an appetite."

"My mother always says that you must feed a shock," Violet answered, absently sticking a wooden spoon in the cornmeal mush. "She says the best cure for bad news is a good meal."

Bartholomew didn't argue, or even move from his stool, but his eyes followed her every movement, hungrily watching, collecting images he could draw on in the cold, empty future.

Over the next few days he was never far from her side, again storing memories against the inevitable moment of his departure. The events around him made little impression on his attention, only Violet mattered.

He was dimly aware of Oliver's return, of the increase in tension his presence seemed to generate, but he didn't ponder the cause. Other people's problems paled next to his. He managed to summon enough concentration to be vaguely ashamed of his indifference to his cousin's imminent destitution, but in the back of his mind he knew that somehow she would survive. He had confidence in her ability to overcome these obstacles, to come out best in life's battles. It was his own fate he wondered about.

Even though Bartholomew had concluded that it was impossible for him either to stay in Grenada or to bring Violet to England, he questioned the alternatives. The predictable, comfortable life he had always complacently accepted now seemed utterly foreign. Returning to it was as out of the question as marriage to Violet. So he floated along in limbo, waiting for something to happen and staying as close as he could to the woman he loved. Every minute that he spent with Violet was one minute less of his life that he had to spend alone.

When Allegra returned from her day trip to St. George's and startled everyone by announcing her immediate departure for London, Bartholomew felt his heart stop. This was what he had been waiting for. If his cousin left, there was not a single reason for him to remain. The time had come for him to return to England.

It was only after Allegra and Oliver had been arguing for some time over her ability to run the chocolate factory that their words filtered through the numbness in his mind. Better than anyone there, better than Allegra herself, he recognized her scheme for what it was: an attempt to take care of herself, to be self-sufficient. Out of admiration for her ambition, and out of some unarticulated wish that her ability would be transferred to him, he aligned himself with his cousin. He attached himself to her attempt at independence, the way a drowning man grabs at a log.

"Who do you know who has any knowledge of making chocolate or of Stellar Confections?" Oliver was demanding, obviously hoping to dissuade Allegra from carrying out her improbable plan.

"I do," Bartholomew said, committing himself for better or for worse, once and for all. He glanced over at Violet, directing his subsequent explanation to her, silently begging her to understand. "At my father's request, I researched the subject quite exhaustively," he concluded.

He deliberately didn't mention that when his father had first learned of Cecil's death, he'd had Bartholomew investigate both Stellar Confections and L'Etoile to see which was the more profitable enterprise to claim. Although Sir Gerald would have preferred to take over the chocolate factory, as it was only hours from home, Bartholomew's report was so bleak he took aim at the cocoa estate instead. Now Bartholomew overlooked the disastrous condition of Stellar Confections and made light of it in his aside to Oliver. He needed Allegra to go to London as much as she did. What life he had left was irrevocably linked to her ability to survive.

Having something to return to didn't make it any easier to leave. The night before their departure, Bartholomew could barely drag himself out of the parlor after dinner. He couldn't stand to let Violet out of his view. He lay in bed unable to sleep, agonizing over the time he was wasting, his last hours in Grenada passed alone in the dark. Pent-up passion finally drove him to his feet and set him pacing the veranda, peering over the tops of paw paws and palms in the light of the half moon.

Fearing he would waken Oliver whose open windows and door also gave onto the veranda, he went back into his room and sat tensely on the edge of his bed. His stomach was churning, his head pounding. Hot flashes baked his skin and icy emotions froze his heart. Thinking a glass of brandy might help calm his nerves, he crept downstairs barefoot and made his way into the library. He lit a small, shaded lamp in one corner of the room, then went over to the cabinet containing an array of cut-crystal decanters. He lifted each stopper and sniffed, but none contained brandy. In the end, he poured out a tumbler of golden-colored rum.

"Bartholomew," said a small voice behind him as he set the decanter back on the shelf. He whirled around, the rum forgotten, his heart leaping with joy. Violet stood in the doorway dressed only in a sleeveless white shift, her loosened black curls floating like a cloud around her face and shoulders, her bare arms slim and satiny in the dim light.

Without stopping to think he crossed the room in a few strides and scooped her tightly into his arms. "My love," he murmured.

Through the thin fabric of their nightclothes he could feel the warmth of her skin, the tantalizing softness of her body as she pressed against him. His fingers disappeared in her billowing hair as he pulled her head toward his, covering her mouth with desperate kisses. Driven by a passion more potent than he'd ever imagined, he carried her to the divan, stripped off their scant clothes, and made love to her. Violet responded with all her heart.

Sometime before dawn they slipped back into their night dress and sat huddled together on the edge of the divan. Almost fearfully, Violet finally asked, "Why can't you stay here, Bartholomew? Or why can't you take me with you? Don't you love me enough?"

"No, Violet, no," Bartholomew protested softly, holding her to him and rubbing her bare shoulder. "It's because I love you too much." He sat silent a minute, then told her the truth. "My father would never approve of our marriage," he said, hugging her close to counteract the cruel fact. "He would completely disown me. I would be a pauper, condemned to an impoverished existence."

"Couldn't you find work?" Violet asked, even more timidly.

"You are so knowledgeable, I should think you could have you choice of jobs. Though perhaps you aren't willing."

Bartholomew shook his head sadly, then rested it on hers. ' would gladly labor day and night to provide you with a suitabl home," he told her. "But I am unfit for employment. I know little about many things, but not a lot about one thing. The best could hope for would be a post at a mediocre boarding schoo The living situation would be stifling and the pay would be pittance. As much as I might wish it otherwise, I am trained onl to be my father's son."

Only to himself did he add that he couldn't bear to see hi tropical blossom beaten down. He refused to be the cause of he degradation.

Her face hidden in the comforting crook of his shoulder an neck, Violet nodded miserably, not pressing the point any furthe She understood what he was saying and accepted his explanatior She couldn't bear to see her fairy tale prince cut off from hi castle. She refused to be the cause of his degradation.

Chapter
Fourteen

Taking tea in the drawing room at Pembroke Hall, Allegra wondered, not for the first time in the last several weeks, whatever had possessed her to leave the sunshine and human warmth of Grenada. Their voyage had been miserable, plagued by fierce storms and winter weather. Bartholomew, usually full of interesting information, had been extremely subdued. His inexplicable withdrawal had left Allegra with little to do but sit in the ship's tiny salon, sliding from one end of the leather settee to the other, thinking of Oliver. And missing him terribly.

Nor had their arrival done much to boost her flagging spirits. Although she had been excited to see the huge mortar and stone house within a manicured park where her father had grown up, she had been considerably less delighted with Sir Gerald's reception. Insufferable as he had been as a guest in her home with the promise of payment only weeks away, he was even more intolerable on his own grounds knowing she was next to destitute.

"Careless," her uncle said for the umpteenth time. "You have inherited your father's exceedingly careless attitude toward money. To have let your entire inheritance dissolve into dust is a profligate waste. Cecil had identical habits."

"But I didn't know the bank was going to fail," Allegra protested wearily, breaking the tip off a sugar-powdered ladyfinger and taking an uninterested nibble. "It's been there all my life. It seemed the safest place in the world."

"You should have been more alert to the ominous economic conditions," Sir Gerald returned severely. "Had you taken the matter at all seriously, you would have investigated the bank before entrusting your entire fortune to its care. A careful depositor would have questioned the bank's investments and studied their soundness. As a further precaution, you ought to have spread your funds among several institutions with differing endowments."

Thinking of William's earnest recommendation of the National Trust Company and her irrational rejection of it, Allegra didn't respond. She took another sip of the tea Sir Gerald had specially mixed at Fortnum & Mason and sullenly pushed aside the rest of her ladyfinger.

"And now you expect me to rescue you," Sir Gerald continued bitterly. "Just as your foolish father did. He was always so convinced his ridiculous schemes were going to yield enormous profits. How he would laugh at me when I voiced sensible and practical objections. He called me unimaginative and conservative. He accused me of lacking the nerve to take risks. Somehow he always managed to charm our father into giving him the capital he required, making grandiose promises that he was invariably unable to fulfill. And when his ventures failed, just as I predicted, he would be back without any sign of remorse, begging for another grant. I can see he has passed his improvident and irresponsible ways on to you."

Although Allegra longed to shout that her father was right, that Sir Gerald was unimaginative and dull and, moreover, jealous and stingy, she restrained her tongue. "I am only asking for a little extra time," she said. "I should think you would prefer to have the money than to have a property you dislike. With a little extra time, I can raise the money from Stellar Confections."

"Don't you dare to presume what I should prefer," Sir Gerald said in a voice as cold and harsh as an Arctic blizzard. "And don't think to manipulate me in the manner of your father. I cannot be gulled into believing that precarious bonbon business will ever accrue any profits. It was an absurd idea that was poorly executed from the start."

"It has a certain potential," Bartholomew intervened before Allegra could sputter a hasty reply. "Although it will require assiduousness and diligence, I believe Stellar Confections can be made to operate gainfully."

"Perhaps," Sir Gerald responded austerely. "But how can I be assured such sterling qualities will be applied toward that end"

Certainly there is no family history of such industry."

"I think you may have underestimated my cousin's determination," Bartholomew said even more mildly. "In any event, I have promised to give her my assistance and to work with her toward achieving her objective. Surely you don't doubt my seriousness."

"I don't doubt it," Sir Gerald said suspiciously. "But I do wonder at it in this instance."

Bartholomew shrugged with as much nonchalance as he could muster. It would never do to show his father how much interest he took in either Allegra or Stellar Confections. That would be an open invitation to have him thwart it. "It will be a challenge," he said simply.

Sir Gerald regarded his son reproachfully for a moment. "I don't know why you have chosen to involve yourself in this matter," he finally said. "But as long as it amuses you to dabble in this chocolate concern, I suppose I can suspend immediate collection of the debt. However," he added, lest his generosity be misinterpreted, "do not imagine that I intend to forgive or forget this loan. Nor will I extend the repayment period indefinitely. I retain the right to call in this note at my discretion. Do you understand?"

Swallowing hard to hold in her annoyance, Allegra could only mutter, "Perfectly. Thank you."

Two days later, she wondered how much of a victory she had actually won. The hack deposited them in front of a grimy brick building on the other side of the Thames. Its unwelcoming appearance was made worse by the fog, heavy with the soot of coal-burning chimneys. Taking a deep breath and her cousin's arm, Allegra walked through the peeling, painted door of Stellar Confections. She was immediately assaulted by the confusion of moving gears and belts, the cacophony of steam machinery, and the overriding smell of chocolate.

That familiar scent, magnified a hundredfold over the cocoa aroma of L'Etoile's boucan, was the only reassuring note in an otherwise bleak scene. The huge, long room was virtually windowless. Meager gray light sifted through soot-encrusted skylights. Groups of workers with gloomy faces and grubby smocks manned their various stations, hardly looking up at the entrance of strangers. Allegra had the uneasy impression that the dimness was almost a blessing, that it hid untold evidence of neglect. For a desperate moment, she yearned for the brilliant sun and clean, sweet air of the tropics. Grasping her arm a little tighter, his fine jaw clenched, Bartholomew seemed to be signaling his agreement.

"May I help you?" a small man with dark hair and a dark waxed moustache shouted at them over the noise. He had nervous brown eyes in a pointed face, and ears that were almost perpendicular to his head.

It was Allegra's instinct to shake her head and flee, but Bartholomew answered with practiced poise. "May I present Miss Allegra Pembroke," he said, "the present owner of this establishment. I am her cousin, Mr. Bartholomew Pembroke. You may remember that I was here briefly, several months ago."

A panic-stricken expression filled the small man's face as he rubbed his hands together, then down the sides of his ill-fitting suit. "Yes, yes," he said quickly. "I was told you had inherited the business. But I thought you were in America."

"Apparently not," Bartholomew again answered, with the icy irony of the British upper class. "And you are Mr. Baker?"

"Yes, yes," he repeated even more rapidly, nodding his head this time. "I'm Albert Baker, the manager of Stellar Confections."

Introductions over, they stood staring at each other, uncertain of the next move. "Is there an office?" Bartholomew finally asked, raising his voice to be heard. "Someplace slightly quieter?"

"Yes, yes," Albert Baker replied again. "Come right this way."

He led them through a door not far from the entrance. The room, though definitely quieter, was tiny. When all three were inside and the door was closed, there was scarcely room to turn around without bumping into each other or into the furniture which comprised a desk, two chairs, and a filing cabinet. In such close quarters, the odor of Mr. Baker's hair oil was overpowering.

"May we be shown the operation?" Allegra asked, curious about the factory and eager to be back in the larger room.

"Well," Mr. Baker waffled, not looking directly at either of them. "We're not in the habit of giving tours. It's all very confidential, you understand."

"I can think of no one more rightfully privy to the secrets of this business than its owner," Bartholomew responded. "I seri ously suggest you comply with Miss Pembroke's request."

"Yes, yes, of course," Mr. Baker said, even more nervously. "I didn't mean to imply to the contrary."

Again he led the way and they followed into the heart of the noise. "This here is where the chocolate liquor is melted down and stirred," he shouted, stopping before an enormous shell-shaped trough filled with gallons of dark liquid chocolate. Attached by a maze of drive shafts, cog wheels, and wide rubber belts to a steam engine in the cellar, great rollers churned slowly in the trough, making thick, brown waves in the shiny, smooth surface.

Albert Baker was ready to move on, but Bartholomew remained where he was. "This process is called conching," he told Allegra, who couldn't take her eyes off the rich chocolate sea. "As essential as it is in ensuring the smooth consistency of the candy, it is, surprisingly, a recent invention. Rudolph Lindt, a German Swiss, developed the process in 1879 when he discovered that the continual kneading of softened chocolate, with the addition of cocoa butter, produced a far more agreeable texture and a superior taste. Previous to this invention, the chocolate liquor was melted and mixed with sugar and flavorings in a machine called a melangeur. There are many manufacturers who still favor that method, but I daresay they will all become convinced of the virtues of conching eventually."

Allegra nodded. Yielding to an overwhelming temptation, she was leaning forward to scoop some of the enticing mixture onto her finger when she heard Bartholomew's warning. "Careful, Cousin Allegra! It's hot." As she jerked back her hand, he explained, "At this stage, the chocolate is kept at about 130 degrees, though the temperature can vary from 110 to 200 depending on the individual preference of the chocolatier. Similarly, the length of time the chocolate is conched, anywhere from three hours to two days, is the province of the chocolatier. It is generally acknowledged, however, that the longer it is conched, the smoother it becomes."

"After it's conched, is it ready to be made into candy?" Allegra asked, still wistfully eyeing the churning chocolate. "Surely, it's too hot to work with."

"It is," Bartholomew answered in Mr. Baker's stead. "Although this mixture now contains all the necessary ingredients, chocolate liquor, cocoa butter, sugar, and possibly vanilla, it needs tempering."

"That takes place over here," Mr. Baker interrupted, not to be outdone. "Come along with me."

Once again they followed the little man as he moved along the path of a chocolate-lined duct which split off in three separate directions, each one emptying into a giant cauldron. Another network of steam-driven belts and gears kept a large paddle turning the chocolate slowly in each kettle. "We keep the temperature at exactly 86 degrees now," Mr. Baker announced, taking his cue from Bartholomew and trying to sound scientific.

Bartholomew was not the least impressed. "The chocolate ought to be turned every four or five hours while it's waiting to be molded," he explained to Allegra as she peered into a vat. "Crystals form during the conching process, which could make the chocolate taste grainy. Also the butterfat tends to become glued together, resulting in a sticky texture. The combination of exact temperature and steady stirring keeps the fondant at the proper consistency and produces a fine, silky tasting chocolate with a desirably glossy appearance."

"Now is it ready?" Allegra asked again, trying not to notice the accumulation of dried chocolate that had dripped over the edge of the kettle and spotted the floor.

"That's what they're doing," Albert Baker said, jerking his thumb at the groups of workers gathered around each tempering tank.

They watched as the gray-faced workers, showing none of the salubrious effects of chocolate that Brillat-Savarin had written about, clamped together sheets of metal stamped with bunnies, hearts, and the trademark stars. They filled the molds from a spigot at the side of each tank, and stacked the filled molds onto trays. The workers next carried the trays to a shaking machine, where the machine vibrated the molds until all the air bubbles were eliminated. The molds were then loaded onto a trolley and wheeled into a cooling room so the chocolate could harden.

The tour moved down the line, stopping at a long bench where more drab-looking workers unmolded the candy. The chocolate fell carelessly into heaps on tin trays, which were transferred to still another bench. Here, a row of girls and young women whose white aprons and fingernails could have benefited by more contact with soap and water packed the confections into cardboard boxes of various sizes and designs. None resembled the satin and velvet packages Allegra had romanticized about.

In fact, none of the factory was as she had imagined it. She ruefully remembered her very first vision of her father's venture, conjured up in the cocoa groves her third morning in Grenada. When Oliver had mentioned that Cecil had gone to England to make chocolate, ornate halls full of candies and cakes and smiling, rosy-cheeked workers had filled her mind. Later, in Jamie's office when he had read her Cecil's will, Stellar Confections had become a chocolate stepping stone to a business empire.

In reality, though, on this gray February morning in 1894, her father's chocolate factory was neither. It was dirty, dark, and gloomy, and its most dominant feature was the incessant screech and moan of ungreased machinery. The employees were sullen and sloppy, taking no pride in their product. The molds and boxes, though showing an attempt at creativity, were poorly constructed and improperly stored. All in all, it was a dreary picture.

Mr. Baker seemed unaware of his audience's fading interest as he continued the tour. He showed them the warehousing room where great slabs of chocolate liquor sat side by side with stacks of packaged confections waiting to be loaded onto wagons and delivered to shops around London and the rest of the country. A salesman togged out in a glaring houndstooth check suit gaped openly at them as they took a cursory look around. Made uncomfortable by his stare, Allegra and Bartholomew backed hastily out of the room, bumping squarely into a man coming up behind them.

"This is Mr. Bruno Pavese," Mr. Baker said in a not overly fond tone. "He's the chocolatier."

At first glance, the Italian seemed more the embodiment of his reputation for irascibility than a renowned talent for making chocolate. He was tall though the arthritis that gripped his body bent him into a crabbed position. His face was strong and fierce, his nose like an eagle's beak. Deep-set brown eyes shone brightly, but belligerently. He nodded his head, barely acknowledging the introduction.

"For you, signorina," he said in an Italian-accented voice that sounded like boots shuffling through gravel. He pressed an octagonal blue box decorated with yellow stars into her hand.

"Oh," Allegra said, startled. "Thank you very much," she added as he disappeared behind a rack of empty molds. "And thank you very much, too, Mr. Baker," she said, edging toward the entrance, Bartholomew by her side. "You've been most generous with your time, especially as we arrived without an appointment."

Propelled by an intense desire to be away from this depressing scene, she didn't stop to think how incongruous that sounded. I hadn't yet registered that she was not an incidental visitor but tha she owned this dismal place and that Albert Baker was in he employ.

"I think your solicitor may have made a wise suggestion afte all, Cousin Allegra," Bartholomew said as they crossed Londor Bridge in a hack, heading for the lodgings he had helped he locate. "Perhaps it is best that you sell up and use the capital as a down payment against your debt. I promise you, I will speak or your behalf to my father. Undoubtedly he can be persuaded to le you repay the balance in annual installments." Giving a sligh shrug and raising his eyebrows in response to some inner com ment, he added, "I imagine it's possible that he will add some amount of interest to the outstanding figure. However, I shoul be honored if you would allow me to make you a gift of th interest."

Allegra didn't answer. She leaned against the side of the cal and stared out the window, her fingers drumming on the box o chocolates in her lap.

"I should be less than honest if I didn't tell you that the factor has deteriorated considerably since I investigated it in No vember," Bartholomew said more earnestly. "Although," h added thoughtfully, "I suppose it's possible that my memory wa embellished by wishful thinking."

That brought Allegra's attention away from the window. "Yo wanted it to be better?" she asked him, again surprised by hi interest in her business.

"Yes, I did," Bartholomew answered truthfully. Aside fron the promise he had made Violet to help Allegra out of her diffi culty, he now had more selfish motives for wanting Stellar Con fections to be a promising prospect. He needed the factory an Allegra's restoration of it to provide a reason for his life. Bu turning that filthy operation into a profitable business suddenl seemed a daunting task. The courage Allegra had inspired in hir was outweighed by the enormity of the situation.

"I did, too," Allegra said, turning her head back to the window.

"Perhaps then you would be best advised to discontinue it. Surely, there can be nothing more disheartening than to pursue a misapprehended goal."

Again, Allegra didn't respond, her fingers tapping the box once more. She didn't agree with Bartholomew, but she didn't exactly disagree with him either. They arrived at her lodging house and went into the parlor, winding their way through a labyrinth of chairs, tables, plant stands and horsehair settees. At this hour of the day, they were the only occupants of the room.

Allegra slumped down on a sofa, tossing the box of candy she was still clutching onto a small, petticoated table at her side. Bartholomew sat more correctly on a cane-seated chair opposite her. Neither said anything. Each was wrapped up in thought. Dim light, filtering through thick lace under curtains and around heavy chintz drapes, barely illuminated their glum expressions.

Depressed though she was, one thought continued to make its way through Allegra's disappointment. Somehow the grim scene at the factory just didn't tally with the portrait she had composed of her father. Maybe I exaggerated his abilities, she reluctantly decided to herself. Oliver had told her often enough that she should be more realistic where Cecil was concerned.

The next instant she changed her mind again. No, she thought, Papa might have been a little bit irresponsible about money matters, but no one has ever accused him of having low standards or poor taste. Certainly not Oliver. Not even Angus. If Stellar Confections were truly a product of Papa's imagination, it would be clean and lovely and filled with dazzling flourishes. No, she thought again. Somewhere, something is wrong.

Sighing, she reached her hand over to finger the tassled edge of the tablecloth, absently rubbing the soft fringe as she brooded. Trying to equate what she knew to be true about her father with the dingy factory she had seen today, her fingers inched across the table and pried open the octagonal blue box. Without thinking, she plucked out a five-pointed chocolate star and stuffed it in her mouth. It melted on her tongue, smooth and rich and laced with tiny, crunchy bits of mint. Still puzzling out her problem, her attention only vaguely piqued by the dark, delicious chocolate sliding silkily down her throat, she popped in another. It tasted equally elegant.

Allegra straightened up slowly on the settee, her eyes fastening on the table beside her, comprehension dawning. That was the answer, right there in that half-opened cardboard box. Oh Papa, she thought, I didn't exaggerate your abilities at all. If anything, I underestimated you. You knew that what the factory looks like is unimportant. What matters more is how the chocolate tastes. So you saved up all your dazzling flourishes and hired Bruno Pavese. It was your crowning achievement. That crusty Italian makes ambrosial chocolate!

The discovery left Allegra simultaneously excited and relieved. Relieved because her faith in her father was restored. He hadn't been a fool, as she had been beginning to fear. For once, he had acted shrewdly. She felt her heart beating with pride at his outstanding business maneuver. It made his death before he had a chance to get production well under way that much more tragic. But I'll do it for you, she silently promised.

Allegra grabbed the box off the side table and shoved it in front of her cousin's surprised face. "Have a chocolate," she said.

Bartholomew's brow furrowed faintly. "Thank you, but not at the moment," he politely declined.

Allegra insisted, pushing the box almost under his nose. "*Have* a chocolate."

Bartholomew looked at her more carefully, afraid her senses had snapped under the strain. "Splendid idea, thank you," he murmured, fastidiously selecting a star and taking a well-bred bite.

"Well?" Allegra asked eagerly.

"Well, uh . . ." Bartholomew said, struggling to return his mind to the present instead of wondering what Violet was doing at this moment. He had no idea of what Allegra wanted. "Well, do you find your rooms satisfactory?" he asked.

"Never mind the rooms," Allegra answered impatiently. "What about the chocolate?" Thinking he hadn't had a proper taste, she shoved the box at him again. "Here, have another."

"What? No, I still have a piece," Bartholomew protested, more and more confused.

"Well, then? What do you think?"

"Think?"

"Is it *good*?"

"Ah," he said, finally understanding her request. "Yes, of course. It's quite nice."

"Don't you see?" Allegra demanded. "That's it!"

"What's it?" Bartholomew asked, genuinely bewildered again. "What should I be seeing?"

"The chocolate," Allegra explained excitedly. "It's superb! It's the key to Stellar Confections. Ultimately, it's what really matters. All the rest, the shabby building, the dirty conditions, all that is not important, it is incidental. After all, we are selling chocolate, not tours of the factory, and the chocolate is marvelous. Don't you see?" she asked again. "We were looking at the business from the wrong end."

"Ummm," Bartholomew answered slowly. "I understand what you're saying and I applaud your optimism, but I am still a touch skeptical. I am not wholly convinced that Stellar Confections can be retrieved from its abysmal decline. Despite what you say about selling chocolate, there is more to running a successful business than merely manufacturing a product, no matter how superior it might be."

Allegra was undismayed. "On the other hand," she said persuasively, "if you *don't* have a product, preferably a superior one, it is impossible to run a business, no matter how clean and tidy the factory is. Now, I realize that Stellar Confections has a chance to succeed, and I think it's a good one. I'm more sure than ever that the factory can be made to prosper. Oh, Cousin Bartholomew," she pleaded, "say that you think so, too. Say that you'll help me."

While he still had his doubts about the factory's odds for survival, his faith in his cousin's chances was renewed. Her enthusiasm was contagious. "Yes, certainly I'll help you, Cousin Allegra," he said.

Their return the next day took almost everyone in the factory by surprise. After yesterday's visit, the consensus was that Stellar Confections either would die a lingering death or would be sold up for a pittance. No one expected the lovely blond heiress or her handsome cousin would bother coming back. Only Bruno Pavese seemed unamazed by their presence.

Nonetheless, Allegra and Bartholomew spent the day standing around, uncertain how to proceed, each waiting for the other to take the lead. Allegra expected Bartholomew, with his sobriety and knowledge, to know what to do, while Bartholomew was counting on Allegra's zeal to forge the way. Both were too polite to question Albert Baker's methods, or to pry into the specifics of the business. Having accomplished very little by late afternoon, they went out to tea.

"Really, Cousin Allegra, you've every right to know the minutest detail of the operation," Bartholomew told her while convincing himself as well. He dabbed clotted cream and wild strawberry jam on a scone and continued, his orderly mind warming up to the subject. "Most especially, you ought to acquaint yourself with those details which are not visible: the finances. You ought to be aware of your assets and liabilities, your capital, your deficits, your accounts payable and receivable. You ought to know what it costs to produce, for example, a pound of chocolate stars, including boxing and delivery, as opposed to the price for which you sell it. A graph ought to be drawn for each type of candy, showing its production-to-profit ratio, as well as its anticipated volume according to the area of consumption and time of the year."

"Oh, dear," Allegra said when he paused to take a bite of the delicious treat he had built. "I suppose that's all very important, isn't it?"

His mouth full, Bartholomew only nodded.

"I'm not awfully adept at figures," Allegra admitted in a low voice, toying with a slice of date and nut loaf. She could practically see Oliver's face grinning with agreement. It made her feel angry and forlorn.

"I, however, am quite adept at figures and facts," Bartholomew said, taking a sip of tea. "Although I feel far less comfortable with visual projections, an area in which you seem to excel." He set his cup down and looked at her steadily across the small table. "If you are serious about desiring my help with your venture, Cousin Allegra, might I suggest that you allow me to oversee the accounting while you attend to the production?"

A surge of excitement chased away the moment of melancholy that Oliver's image had evoked. "I am *very* serious about desiring your help, Cousin Bartholomew," she responded, meeting his gaze. "And I think your suggestion is, as they say in this country, capital." They sealed the agreement with broad, affectionate smiles.

As they began to discuss the perceived problems of the business and their plan of attack, their affection blossomed. They had always admired each other's qualities; now their relationship developed a new warmth and closeness. They stopped calling each other cousin and more fondly began using just their first names. As the days went by, they became companionable, more like brother and sister than transatlantic relations.

According to the arrangement they agreed to in the tea room, they set about learning every aspect of Stellar Confections. While Bartholomew closeted himself in the office, poring over the books, Allegra donned an apron and participated, as she had at L'Etoile, in all other activities. She hammered the heavy slabs of chocolate liquor into bits for the conching trough, measured out peppermint oil and essence of vanilla, wiped out the heavy, already emptied, molds, and glued together cardboard to make boxes.

At first, out of politeness and a sense of what would be politic, she tried to enlist Albert Baker's aid, but the more she learned, the more nervous and vague her manager became until she avoided him altogether. Feeling frustrated, she knew she still hadn't gotten to the heart of the operation. She still lacked the information and experience necessary to give the stagnant concern a boost. She needed a better grasp of the business than she had gained stuffing bonbons in boxes, but she was hesitant to take the next obvious step. It meant confronting Bruno Pavese. If chocolate was the key to Stellar Confections, the gruff chocolatier was the only one who knew how to turn it.

For several days she merely watched him, hoping she would somehow magically be inspired to brave his testy manner. Bruno paid her almost no attention as he barked at uncaring workers and scrutinized the candy. Allegra finally got tired of standing for endless hours at the long table, cramming confections into cartons. It wasn't as much fun in reality as it had been when she had fantasized about it. Nor, as she had also imagined, was each candy chipping away at her debt.

"Mr. Pavese," she said one morning when he walked by, "I'd like to talk to you please." She shoved her half-filled box at the gloomy girl standing next to her, wiped her hands on her apron, and moved determinedly toward the bent-over Italian.

Instead of treating her to a barrage of bad temper, Bruno responded graciously. "Certainly, signorina," he said. "It would be a great pleasure to talk to one as *bellissima* as you." He looked left and right, aware of curious ears, then beckoned toward an unoccupied area beyond the racks of chocolate stars waiting to be boxed. "Your eyes are *magnifici*," he told her as they walked slowly away from the incessant racket of the machinery.

"It's very kind of you to say so," Allegra replied, starting to worry that he might have the wrong impression about her request for a conference. "I really wanted to talk to you about other matters, however."

"I see in them the same *spirito* as in your papa's," Bruno continued in his heavy accent. He stopped by an unused table and leaned gratefully against it. "He was a rare man," he went on. "His eyes saw more than what was in front of them. They were connected to his heart and to his *imaginazione*, like the chocolate machines are connected to the boiler in the basement.

"Do you know," he said, wagging a crooked finger in her direction, "that Signor Pembroke gave me this job when no one else in London would give me work? Those others, those peasants," he flicked a disgusted hand over his shoulder, "their eyes had curtains. They could not see beyond my arms and my legs." He snorted. "As if my knowledge of chocolate were here," he said, shaking both curled hands at her, "instead of here." He tapped his head with its covering of thick, black hair. "Only your papa could see that I was still a *bravissimo* chocolatier."

"*That's* what I wanted to talk to you about," Allegra interrupted eagerly. "About the wonderful chocolate that you make."

"Ah, *grazie, signorina*," he murmured dramatically, bowing low. "The moment I saw you, I knew you would appreciate my chocolate. I rejoiced when you came into this room. I knew you would be the salvation of Stellar Confections, that you would see more than the *scifoso* way that these *porcini*, these pigs, keep this place."

"It wasn't easy at first," Allegra started to admit.

"But after you tasted the chocolate *stelle* I gave you, you knew!" Bruno cried, raising his hands in the air in jubilation. "Like your papa, you can see with *fantasia*, with *eleganza*. But even Signor Pembroke, *Dio* bless him, did not take advantage of all my talent. I am *un maestro*, an *artiste* of chocolate. He did not have me make a fraction, not *un piccolo percento*, of the exquisite creations I am capable of." He kissed his bunched fingers for emphasis.

"You must tell me what else you make," Allegra responded excitedly. "No, no," she corrected, waving her own hands in the air. "*Show* me what else you make. I must taste them. I can't wait. Make me some samples."

"*Sì, signorina*," Bruno answered, equally ecstatic. "I will make you a delicious selection. Your tongue will sing with pleasure. I just knew it," he added, almost to himself as he turned to go back to work. "I knew it. This beautiful woman and her cousin, *molto serioso*, will save my chocolate."

Allegra could scarcely contain herself. She wanted to race around the table and leap in the air. Nothing had significantly changed in the past ten minutes. Stellar Confections was still a filthy factory, a debt-ridden business, but Bruno's extravagant confidence was catching. She didn't know why or how, but she was suddenly certain that this conversation was exactly the inspiration she had been waiting for. With a whoop of joy she ran the length of the long factory to tell Bartholomew the news.

The tiny office in the front was empty when she arrived, so she flopped down in the spring-balanced chair behind the desk to catch her breath and to wait for her cousin's return. While she sat, bent comfortably backwards, her toes dangling off the floor, she folded scraps of paper into odd-looking birds. Footsteps, faintly audible above the squeal of the belts, made her look up in anticipation, but the happy message died on her lips. The person who appeared in the doorway was not Bartholomew.

He was a stranger. A tall and extremely handsome man in his early thirties with stylishly groomed brown hair and arresting golden green eyes. His caped cashmere overcoat hung casually open, a silk muffler draped around his neck. A top hat was tucked under his arm and a silver-knobbed walking stick was held in his gloved hand. "May I know whom I am addressing?" he asked in a confident voice with the well-born, well-educated lack of accent that was evident in Bartholomew's speech. His infinitesimally raised eyebrows reflected refined horror at Allegra's relaxed posture.

Her face flamed red as she brought the chair down with a bounce. He was quite the most sophisticated gentleman she had ever seen, and yet there was something about him that made her vaguely uneasy. "I am Miss Allegra Pembroke," she said, struggling to recover herself. "I am the proprietress of Stellar Confections."

His eyebrows rose in silent comment to her claim, but his controlled tone didn't alter. "Then it is you I seek," he said. "I am Mr. Roland Hawkes." He looked at her as if his name should have some meaning.

It didn't, but the authority with which he announced it mad the color rise in Allegra's face again. "Would you like to s down, Mr Hawkes?" she managed to stutter, pointing unnecessa ily to the only other chair in the crowded room.

Mr. Hawkes sat down with a graceful sweep of his cape making the dismal office seem more inadequate than ever. "A you seem to be unfamiliar with my name, perhaps my busine can best be explained by showing you this," he said, unfolding sheet of foolscap and placing it in front of her while not releasir it from his grip.

Puzzled, Allegra glanced down at the paper, her heart su denly pounding when she recognized the handwriting as her f ther's. She leaned over the desk more intently, her attention fixe on the words. Although Mr. Hawkes's elegantly gloved finge blotted out some of the message, enough of it was visible to mal her feel sick and cold. It was a note for a loan from Mr. Rolar Hawkes. For fifteen hundred pounds. With L'Etoile pledged collateral.

All the enthusiasm and optimism that her session with Brur had aroused drained away to nothing. She felt dazed and wea She barely heard Mr. Hawkes explaining the circumstances of tl loan. Just the fact of its existence was overwhelming enough. was dated 10 July 1893, more than five months before the no she had signed to her uncle. This loan predated Sir Gerald's clai to the cocoa estate. The news was devastating.

"I met your father at my club over a year ago," Mr. Hawk said. "I presume, in all events, that Cecil Pembroke was yo father. Am I correct?"

When the silence in the room made Allegra aware that he ha asked a question, she forced her attention back to Mr. Hawke "What?" she asked a bit blankly, then answered. "Yes. Yes, was my father."

Nodding a chilly acknowledgment, Mr. Hawkes proceede "He had an engaging manner, a rather delightful air about hir He was able to make the dullest incident seem like an adventur When he described the chocolate factory he had started, I w most intrigued. Obviously, he was aware that he had captured n interest," Mr. Hawkes went on, his tone getting harder, mc accusing. "He approached me several weeks later asking for loan to buy some machinery. Something about shells, as I recall

"The conching machine." Allegra sighed.

"Quite so," Mr. Hawkes concurred crisply. "He made it seem like a rather casual request, saying he was temporarily short. I was led to believe the money would be repaid in several months' time. Naturally, since we met at my club, I had no reason to doubt his sincerity. I assumed we were all gentlemen and that his word was good."

Allegra nodded, her stomach knotting uncomfortably. This scenario was beginning to sound all too familiar.

"When eight months went by and not a penny nor an apology was offered, I tracked your father down and obtained this note." His finger tapped on the foolscap. In an increasingly cold voice, he concluded, "I've been more than patient about waiting for repayment, but my patience has been abused. I must insist on immediate settlement of this account."

Allegra didn't know how to respond. The folded paper bird in her hand fluttered to the floor. It had taken all her powers of fantasy and rationalization to arrive at this point. And to pull Bartholomew along with her. She had managed to convince herself and her cousin that success was attainable, that Stellar Confections could be made healthy and profitable, able to stave off Sir Gerald while it was accruing capital and clearing her father's reputation. Now, she didn't know what to think. This final obstacle seemed insurmountable, beyond even her energy and enthusiasm.

Through the haze of her shock, she became aware of Mr. Hawkes's questions and of her own listless answers. "May I assume, by your silence, that you recognize the authenticity of this debt?" he asked her. When she only nodded again, accepting her father's improvidence with spiritless resignation, he asked, "May I also assume, therefore, that you are prepared to honor it forthwith?"

This time she shook her head slowly, picking up another scrap of paper and shaping it, mechanically, into a top-heavy swan. The sharp rapping of Mr. Hawkes's walking stick on the floorboards made her fingers abruptly cease folding and brought her eyes up to his. Anger had narrowed them and choler mottled the fine skin of his cheeks. "Really, Miss Pembroke," he snapped, "I fear you are not giving this matter your serious attention. Do you realize I am now entitled to foreclose on this Caribbean estate of yours?"

"I'm sorry," Allegra apologized, consciously sitting up

straighter. She crumpled the swan and tossed it in the rubbish bin, then set her empty hands in her lap. "Yes, I realize it," she said quietly, pain piercing her trance as she uttered the words.

"I have been told that it produces cocoa, is that correct?" Mr. Hawkes continued more calmly, mollified by her effort to collect herself. He draped his hands over the knob of his stick.

"Yes, that's correct," Allegra answered briefly, visions of the tropical groves filling her mind.

"I have also been told that your father was not the sole proprietor of the estate, and that you, as his heiress, share the ownership, as well," Mr. Hawkes said, probing further.

Allegra started to nod again, but caught herself in time. "Yes," she said even more softly. "Yes, I share the ownership with Mr. Oliver MacKenzie." It was the first time in weeks that she had said his name out loud, and under the circumstances, it nearly brought tears to her eyes. She couldn't bear the thought of the fresh peril she had placed him in. She and her father. "He's such a capable man," she said, more to herself than to the polished gentleman across from her. "He doesn't deserve to be trapped in the middle of this.

"He runs L'Etoile so well," she explained earnestly to a very interested Mr. Hawkes. She could see Oliver in his faded frayed shirt, sleeves rolled up above the elbows, whacking open a cocoa pod with assurance and authority. She could see his hand shielding his remarkable blue eyes from the sun as he knowledgeably examined the drawers of drying cocoa. She could see him in the office or at the wheel of one of his schooners or patrolling the groves or prowling around the boucan, confident in his abilities, content with the life he had chosen for himself.

"L'Etoile is really part of him," she said fondly. Never one to successfully camouflage her emotions, Allegra's face shone with the love and longing that images of Oliver evoked. Wrapped up in her musings, she didn't see Mr. Hawkes's golden eyes narrow as his mouth hardened in a frown.

Any reply Mr. Hawkes might have made was preempted by Bartholomew's return. "Oh, I do beg your pardon," Bartholomew said as he walked without knocking through the door, an open account book held out in front of him. He started to back out again, but Allegra stopped him.

"This is Mr. Roland Hawkes," she said, her voice defeated, the memories of Oliver receding. "I think you ought to see this

Bartholomew." She turned to face her visitor. "Would you be so kind, Mr. Hawkes," she asked, "as to show my cousin Mr. Bartholomew Pembroke the note you have just shown me?"

"As you wish," Mr. Hawkes replied, rising and extending the sheet of paper. As before, he did not let it go. Feeling dwarfed by the two tall men in the tiny room, Allegra felt compelled to stand, too.

Bartholomew's eyes quickly scanned the note. Unlike Allegra, he had a lifetime's practice at hiding his feelings. He now did an admirable job of disguising the dread that made his heart sink to his stomach. "May I be apprised of the circumstances in which this debt was obligated?" he asked, his voice even and controlled.

"I have just explained all that to your cousin," Mr. Hawkes replied with a touch of irritation.

There was something about his tone, some indiscernible quality in his expression, that made Bartholomew take an immediate and distinct dislike to him. His tone remained extremely civilized, however, as he murmured, "Having had the misfortune to be absent at the moment of that explanation, I must ask your indulgence in repeating it."

Although Allegra vaguely marveled at her cousin's capacity for politeness, Mr. Hawkes was of the same upbringing as Bartholomew, and he had no trouble detecting the suspicion and distaste behind Bartholomew's refined facade. His own tone changed drastically. "It is I who must ask your indulgence," he said soothingly. "I fear I have been a trifle harsh, but perhaps you can sympathize with the ticklish position I am in. Mr. Cecil Pembroke's tragic demise has left me rather betwixt and between."

For Bartholomew's benefit, he repeated the story he had told Allegra. In this telling, it sounded more like a misunderstanding on his part than an evasion of honesty on Cecil's. "Of course, I would rather have this sum repaid than to foreclose on anyone's home," he concluded, seeming to be horrified at the very idea. "I can see now that I am amongst honorable people, and I have no doubt but that the situation will be resolved satisfactorily.

"In all events," he decided, a gay note dismissing the solemnity of the discussion, "it is too trivial an amount to fret about overlong. Let us, as all sensible people ought, toss this piddling problem in the laps of our accountants and let those tedious individuals sort it out. Surely our time would be better spent in pursuit of more illuminating pleasures."

Hands still resting on top of his walking stick, he bowed low in Allegra's direction. "Most particularly, such a beautiful lady should not be troubled by these annoying matters. You must allow me to redress my reprehensible behavior and prove to you that I am not at all the Tartar I first portrayed myself to be." He flung one end of his muffler over his shoulder with dramatic elegance. "One is forced, rather against one's inclination," he added confidentially, "to be a bit heartless on occasion, don't you find?"

"Oh, yes," Allegra agreed readily, and with such tremendous relief that her knees went weak and she collapsed into the chair behind her. It tipped back precipitously, and she found her feet flailing in the air before the spring recoiled and she regained control of both the furniture and her composure. "I perfectly understand your trepidations," she said, almost eagerly. "After all, you had no way of knowing if I would honor my father's debt or ignore it. But I *assure* you, it shall be settled. If you will only grant me some time, I would be most grateful. It is all the proof I need of your good nature."

"You are too kind," Mr. Hawkes said, modestly inclining his fine head. "I simply cannot permit you to forgive me so easily. My conscience will not allow me to sleep tonight if I do not make amends for my atrocious manners. It is I who will be in your debt if you, and your cousin," he bowed graciously toward Bartholomew, "would be my guests this evening at the Globe Theatre. I have engaged a box for Mr. Thomas's play, *Charley's Aunt.* Please say that you will accompany me."

Allegra could scarcely restrain a gasp of excitement. "With pleasure," she exclaimed without even thinking. If the situation had been any different, she would have demurred no matter how tempting the invitation. But her defenses had been weakened by the powerful scare she had just experienced. For a few terrifying minutes she had seen herself on the thin edge of ruin, taking Oliver, Bartholomew, and her father's reputation down with her. It had been too awful to comprehend.

Then, miraculously, she had been granted a reprieve. The sudden release from doom made her react in a way she normally wouldn't. She failed to wonder what accommodation the "boring" accountants could possibly contrive, given her financially overloaded situation. Nor did she dwell, as was her usual practice, on the new evidence that tarnished her father's bright image.

Most telling of all was the fact that she accepted at once the invitation of a total stranger, a man who ten minutes earlier had made her vaguely uneasy, and who three minutes later had paralyzed her with horror.

"It shall be a delightful treat," she told the handsome Mr. Hawkes. "I'm sure I speak for my cousin as well when I thank you for your generous offer." As a sudden qualm struck her, she turned to Bartholomew. "Don't I?" she asked anxiously.

Allegra's instant acceptance left Bartholomew in an awkward position. Although he was not wholly convinced by Mr. Hawkes's change of tone, he couldn't begin to contemplate letting his cousin go to the theater alone. She was well past the debutante stage, not requiring the hovering presence of a mother or an aunt, but it still wouldn't do to have her appear by herself in public with a man she had just met, whatever his pedigree.

Knowing her impetuous personality, Bartholomew was also a little worried that she might make some rash promises concerning either Stellar Confections or L'Etoile. He was amazed to discover he cared so much about their fates, and equally amazed to realize that the unquestioning awe he'd once held for Allegra had mellowed with closeness to a more realistic affection. Given those circumstances, he could hardly refuse. "Of course, you do," he answered. "I should be most pleased to attend."

Chapter
Fifteen

"Bartholomew," Allegra said decisively as soon as she arrived at the factory the next morning, "we are going to close everything down next week."

"You can't mean it!" Bartholomew exclaimed, aghast. His pencil fell from his fingers and rolled off the edge of the desk. "But why? I thought you were convinced this business was salvageable. It was my understanding that you were determined to make it prosper. You said yourself that the key to success is chocolate, and that the chocolate Signor Pavese makes is of incomparable quality. What has happened to make you revise your decision?" He stopped and looked at her more shrewdly. "Did Mr. Hawkes say something to you last evening that I didn't hear? There were those few moments when Hugh Norton engaged me in conversation about our school days. Did Mr. Hawkes take advantage of my distracted attention to press you for repayment of the loan?"

"No, no," Allegra said reassuringly. She stuck her coat on the hook behind the door and sat down, wiping snowflakes from her fur-trimmed hat with her handkerchief. The raw weather had put roses in her cheeks and a few flakes gleamed in her curls. She looked anything but defeated. "I had a lovely time last night. The Globe Theatre is magnificent, and Mr. Hawkes was the perfect host. He never once mentioned the debt. I thought he was extremely attentive. Imagine, being served champagne and oysters during intermission by that stone-faced butler. I've never seen anyone stand so straight before, have you?"

Bartholomew, for whom stoic butlers and entr'acte champagne weren't in the least unusual, dismissed her thrilled observations with uncharacteristic impatience. "May I ask then what has caused this change of heart?" he said, offended that he had been excluded from such a momentous decision. He thought they had grown close. "By what process of reasoning did you arrive at the conclusion that Stellar Confections is no longer a tenable prospect?"

"What?" Allegra asked, pulling her mind away from the intoxicating grandeur of her evening at the theater and returning to the business at hand. "Oh, no, Bartholomew, you've misunderstood me," she said, tossing her hat up toward the hook. It caught briefly on the collar of her coat, then slid down its sleeve to the floor. Allegra shrugged and turned to her cousin. "I haven't given up on Stellar Confections at all," she said, leaning across the desk to give him her earnest attention. "I never meant to imply that I wanted to close down the factory forever, only for a few weeks. Possibly even less. It needs a thorough cleaning before we proceed any further.

"While it may be true that the end result is all that matters, I can't believe the chocolate isn't affected by the slovenly condition. Even Mr. Pavese has commented on the lax attitude that allows it to exist. Just think, Bartholomew," she concluded, resting her chin on her palm, "if the chocolate is so delicious now, it will be positively divine once it's properly produced."

"I daresay," Bartholomew replied, relief releasing his breath in a rush. He hadn't even realized he had been holding it.

True to her word, Allegra had the steam engine shut down as soon as the last box of chocolate hearts went out the door on St. Valentine's Day. When her employees assembled again on Thursday morning, they were given buckets and brushes and gallons of bleach. Issuing orders through the reluctant and obviously confused Albert Baker, Allegra had every inch of the vast area swept up and scrubbed down. The walls were whitewashed, the copper vats were polished, all the aprons were boiled, every moving part in every machine was oiled or greased. She even sent a particularly fearless boy up on the roof to scour years of accumulated grime from the skylights. With the freshly whitened walls and the newly washed glass, the factory gleamed. Spirits rose.

While Allegra coaxed and cajoled, insisted and assisted until the old building practically shone, Bartholomew led a major attack on the paper work. He reorganized the filing system and restructured the accounting. He made a detailed inventory of everything from spare parts for the boiler to glue for the boxes, not to mention slabs of chocolate liquor and pounds of chocolate stars. He examined expenditures and totaled up sales. He made charts and graphs, plotted ratios and compiled lists. Not even the remotest corner of the operation was overlooked. Stellar Confections was all but turned upside down and shaken out.

Although her days were full, Allegra rarely rested in the evenings. Two mornings after the production of *Charley's Aunt*, Mr. Hawkes stopped by the factory with a bouquet of red roses and an invitation for them to join him at Daly's Theater. "They are doing *Twelfth Night*," he told them gaily. "Miss Ada Rehan has the part of Viola and is reputed to be extraordinary. I know you won't want to miss it, so you must allow me to take you. We can have supper afterward at Simpson's on the Strand." He was out the door again before Allegra, her eyes wide with excitement, could protest his generosity, or before Bartholomew, his nostrils flaring slightly, could decline.

The following evening they attended a recital at St. James Hall, and two nights later the ballet *Don Quixote*. Then they heard a lecture by an African naturalist, the London Symphony in concert, and saw Wulffs Great Continental Circus, featuring sixty horses and the world's greatest equestrienne, Signorina Dolinda de la Plata. Allegra fairly floated. Everything she had ever wished for was coming true. There was no gainsaying the enormous satisfaction she felt from seeing Stellar Confections take shape. The daily progress offered a rewarding fulfillment of her ambitions. The evening activities were the realization of her dreams. She couldn't count how many hours she had spent fantasizing about just such a sophisticated existence.

After the fourth invitation, Bartholomew politely bowed out, leaving Allegra on her own. He no longer had the heart for social pleasures, either in the company of his cousin or with his old friends. He preferred the solitude of his rooms and the comfort of his memories. He was no fonder of Mr. Hawkes than he had been during the first minute of their meeting, but he could see no overt reason to fear for his cousin's reputation. Indeed, their host seemed the perfect gentleman, well-turned-out and impeccably behaved. Bartholomew shrugged off his initial hesitation, attributing his unfavorable opinion to his own peevish state of mind.

Allegra and Mr. Hawkes made an unusually handsome couple. He hoped she was happy.

Allegra found Mr. Hawkes to be the ideal escort on almost every occasion, accommodating, amusing, and eloquently admiring. He constantly commented on her courage and capability, listening with flattering fascination as she described her rehabilitation of the factory.

"You are an unusual woman," he told her over a late night plate of mussels after a performance of *The Second Mrs. Tanqueray.* "Any other female of your beauty and breeding would be more than content to capture the wealthiest, most titled bachelor available, but you persist in carving out your own destiny. My compliments, Allegra." He paused with a spoonful of broth halfway to his lips. "You will grant me permission to address you by your first name, won't you?" he asked. "Perhaps it is unforgivably forward of me, but I feel we have grown comfortable in each other's company in recent days. It seems only natural."

Allegra smiled her acceptance, not knowing how to respond.

"Splendid." He beamed back. "And you must call me Roland."

The smile remained stretched across Allegra's face, but something inside her wrenched. She wasn't sure she'd feel comfortable calling him Roland. It seemed to put him on an equal footing with Oliver. Oliver. For a moment, she had a flash of yearning for Oliver, wishing so hard he could be here with her that her heart ached. She wanted Oliver to accompany her to the theater, Oliver to sit across a fashionable supper table from her, to share her excitement about the restoration of Stellar Confections. It saddened her tremendously to think there was an ocean between them, an ocean and a stubborn argument keeping them apart.

Puzzled by her silence, Roland asked anxiously, "Is something wrong? Are the mussels gone bad? Really, they can be so careless with food sometimes. I'll speak to them at once."

"No, you mustn't," Allegra said quickly, reaching to stay his raised hand. "The mussels are fine. It was just a passing thought." Tossing her head defiantly, she willed away her melancholy, telling herself that Roland's chivalry and cultivated manners were a welcome change from Oliver's blunt behavior. She launched into an animated discussion of the play they had just seen, but to her annoyance, a grinning Oliver leaned casually against a corner of her mind, his arms folded across his chest.

In the carriage on the way home that night, Roland took her hand and pressed it to his lips. "You are enchanting, dear Allegra," he murmured. "Beautiful and bewitching." Before she could recover from her shock, Roland pulled her into his arms and kissed her.

"No!" Allegra gasped, yanking away, reflexively wiping her mouth with the heel of her hand. She shrank against the side of the carriage, clutching her reticule in front of her protectively. "Please don't," she said, her heart pounding with something very like horror. "Please."

Roland retreated at once. "Forgive me," he begged. "It was outrageous of me, but I momentarily lost control. It won't happen again, I promise you, but you must say you'll accept my apologies."

"Yes, of course," Allegra replied nervously, just to end the discussion. She made herself even smaller in the seat. The taste of his lips was still on hers, the smell of his cologne clogged her nose. She didn't know why she found it so distressing, but she didn't want to think about it, only to forget it had ever happened. For the rest of the ride home, she stared out the window, watching the gaslights reflected in the puddles.

Apparently Roland wanted to forget it, too, because he stayed away for several days. When he returned with a huge bunch of pink tulips and tickets for the Royal Orchestral Society, he acted as if the incident had never taken place. Gradually, Allegra regained her ease with him, but somehow their evenings together lost their glamour. Maybe because she was increasingly preoccupied with the course of her business, she no longer had much energy or attention to devote to superficial entertainment.

Had anyone asked her, she would have vigorously denied that Oliver had anything to do with it. She would have refused to consider that the memory of his kisses, so sensuous and intimate, made Roland's caress seem unsavory. She would have scoffed at the thought that the busy, gay life she led had an element of emptiness. She would have argued convincingly that Roland was an utterly desirable man: attractive and attentive, able to offer her whatever she wanted. No one asked her, however. Still leaning casually and confidently against a corner of her mind, Oliver haunted her.

When Stellar Confections started conching chocolate again on the last day of February, Allegra felt strangely let down. After the bustle and purpose of the last two weeks, business as usual was unsatisfying. Now that the factory looked bigger and cleaner, even sounded minimally quieter, she expected grander results. Although the taste of the chocolate was as smooth and sublime as ever, the variety was limited, the boxes were drab, and the orders all in all didn't match the potential of the plant.

"We need more than just a thorough housecleaning," she told Bartholomew as she restlessly drummed her fingers on the desk. "We need an entirely new approach if we are to survive."

"Mmmm," Bartholomew replied, scratching his head with the point of his pencil. "I wonder why four hundred lots of peppermint oil were ordered. Surely, forty would have been sufficient." He looked up from the ledger with an ironic laugh. "At the present rate of production, even four would do nicely."

"You see?" Allegra pounced, jumping up from her chair. She took a small step around the tiny office, realized its limitations, and plunked herself down again. "Business is just terrible. We aren't selling half, not even a third or a quarter of the chocolates we could make every day. Moreover, I'm not sure that merely increasing our output is the answer." She slumped in her chair, her hands folded over her stomach, her legs stretched out in front of her.

Bartholomew had long ago stopped being startled by his cousin's lapses of ladylikeness. He didn't even notice her unrefined sprawl as he responded. "An increase in production, assuming there is a corresponding increase in sales, might not be the answer you have envisioned. But judiciously managed, it would unquestionably reverse Stellar Confections' declining fortunes."

"No," Allegra disagreed, lolling her head over the back of the chair and shaking it pensively. "It isn't enough. It's only more of the same. Bigger, more volume, but still boring. Bartholomew, it isn't, isn't . . ." She sat up abruptly, finding the right word, and looked at him. "It isn't *spectacular*," she finished, spreading her hands outward to encompass the glorious image she had in mind.

"Business is seldom spectacular, Allegra," Bartholomew answered uncritically. "It isn't like the theater, where there are splendid costumes and brightly painted scenery. Business is simply the tedious compilation of pennies and pounds. When the sum of the revenues exceeds the sum of the expenses, the business has succeeded. It's most often a very dry, sober activity, more apparent on paper, than anywhere else."

Sighing, Allegra returned to her meditative slump, not saying anything else, but not relinquishing her idea, either. Regardless of what Bartholomew said about business not being theater, she was sure it was possible to make both a brilliant impression and a respectable profit.

I know *you* would agree with me, Papa, she thought. I'm certain you meant for your chocolate concern to be beautiful as well as lucrative. I'll wager you even had some wonderful scheme in your head for accomplishing exactly that end. Well, you needn't worry, she promised loyally, I'll make sure that Stellar Confections becomes every bit as grand as you conceived it.

She heaved herself to her feet and wandered out into the factory. But couldn't you give me just a tiny hint of what that concept entails? she added.

Not surprisingly, Roland was much more receptive of her vision than Bartholomew had been. "I agree wholeheartedly," he told her, tapping his walking stick on the floor for emphasis. "Too often business is perceived as dull because the people engaged in it are so frightfully tedious. There is no reason why it can't be both charming and successful. There are those firms which gracefully combine both qualities."

"Which ones?" Allegra demanded, eager for confirmation of her theory.

"Well, uh," Roland hedged, for once caught off-guard. "Well, none come immediately to mind," he finally admitted, regaining his blitheness. "I don't generally concern myself with such matters, but I feel confident that they do exist."

"Perhaps I need to see how other chocolate businesses are run," Allegra said thoughtfully, rubbing her chin between her thumb and her forefinger. "Perhaps I should go around to all the chocolate shops and see how they differ from Stellar Confections. Perhaps I could get some useful ideas."

"Espionage!" Roland cried delightedly. "Chocolate espionage! The very thing! Oh, yes, Allegra, I do believe you have hit upon it. What delicious fun. You must allow me to accompany you. I shall be thoroughly dejected if you say no."

"Of course you may come with me," Allegra said, laughing at his boyish glee. "In fact, I shall be grateful for your company. Bartholomew is too caught up in his charts and projections to spare me much time, and I'd feel awkward going alone."

They spent the next three days making the rounds of the chocolate purveyors in London, from the awesomely refined Charbonnel et Walker to the cozy Cocoa Bean in Chelsea. Allegra saw much to admire. With her usual enthusiasm and ever-active imagination, she found one feature after another that she longed to incorporate into her own operation.

"Wouldn't it be wonderful to make cocoa as well as candy?" she sighed, taking a satisfying sip of hot chocolate from a Royal Doulton cup decorated with rosebuds. "Cadbury and Fry are both known for their cocoa. It could almost be a trademark. After all, everyone drinks cocoa." Warming to her subject, she continued excitedly, "We could even blend it the way the Aztecs did, with bay leaf and spices. And then we could put it into tins shaped like the Mexican pyramids, painted the beautiful burnt colors of the ancient tribes."

"Yes, you must!" Roland agreed, leaning across the table and clasping her hand encouragingly. "What a perfectly marvelous idea."

Whether because of Roland's oddly unwelcome touch or because of the practicality Bartholomew was instilling in her, Allegra quickly came out of the clouds. "Quite impossible," she said lightly, pulling her hand away and picking up her cup. "Such a scheme would require vast amounts of money. We would need to buy special machinery to press the cocoa liquor. And the tins would probably be prohibitively expensive. More than likely we would even have to replace the boiler, as I'm sure that poor old furnace could not take further strain. I simply can't afford any of it. I must repay my current debts before I can incur new ones."

"Nonsense," Roland scoffed with a snap of his well-manicured fingers. He seemed not to notice the way she avoided his contact. "You cannot expect to make great gains without great investments. The timid are doomed to tiny successes, while the bold see impressive rewards. I know you are not one of the timid, dear Allegra."

"I don't know whether that is a compliment or an insult," Allegra replied, laughing again. "But whatever the case, who would possibly lend me the money? I have nothing to offer for collateral, and Bartholomew says that bankers are rather sticklers on that point."

"Another painfully unimaginative group of individuals," Roland said, dismissing the bankers with a shrug of his finely tailored shoulders. "You needn't waste your time with them. I am more than willing to lend you whatever sum you wish. Just figure up your expenses and I shall draw you a check immediately."

"But I owe you so much already," Allegra answered. His generosity made her uneasy. She tried to tell herself that he was only making the offer because it would amuse him to see her succeed, that it was an insignificant price for a few moments' diversion. She told herself that his nonchalance came from never having to worry about money, but it still made her uncomfortable. "In fact," she continued cautiously, "we have never settled the question of the money you lent my father."

"You mustn't fuss about that," Roland said. "I should feel dreadful if I knew it was causing you even one moment of anxiety. I feel sure that you will be able to repay it someday. I am happy to await your convenience."

"That doesn't seem very businesslike," Allegra said, still vaguely disturbed by his casualness.

"Poof," Roland replied, waving his slender white hand through the air. "You know how I am. Hopeless at business matters. Would that I had even a fraction of your keen instinct, my dear. Are you going to finish your cake? I can't say I blame you. I think I've consumed more sweets in the past three days than in all of the last three months. A plate of oysters would do nicely just now. Did I ever tell you of the time I made a special excursion to the Belon River in Brittany just to eat oysters?" With a shake of her head and a smile, Allegra allowed the subject to be changed.

She had enthusiastically embraced then restlessly rejected dozens of ideas for revitalizing Stellar Confections before it all came into focus one early March morning. Weak sunshine was making pale shadows on the factory floor as Allegra wandered from station to station, idly inspecting production and hoping, as always, for inspiration. It arrived, preceded by an Italian command. "*Signorina*," Bruno said as she stood mesmerized in front of the conching trough watching gallons of rich liquid chocolate being slowly churned to silky smoothness. "*Signorina, viene con me, per favore*."

Allegra shook herself loose and dutifully followed him to the back of the building where he had constructed his own private workshop by surrounding an unused table with tall racks of trays. With grand ceremony, he led Allegra into the enclosure, seated her on a rickety stool, and held out before her a rounded platter draped with a white damask cloth. When he was sure he had her full attention, he whipped away the cloth with a dramatic flourish, revealing small chocolate treats beautifully arranged on a lace doily, each confection more exquisite than the next. "For you, signorina," he said, his gravelly voice even hoarser with emotion.

"They're gorgeous," Allegra breathed, not removing her eyes from the platter Bruno held in his gnarled hand. Her mouth watered at the sight of the tempting chocolates.

"*Mangia*," he urged. "Eat one."

Her hand darted out then hung in midair as she tried to decide which one to select. Her first inclination was to take a cherry swirled in chocolate, its stem curving gracefully from the top. Then she was intrigued by a nut-encrusted medallion, then a milk chocolate dome with a dark chocolate peak. Finally unable to deliberate any longer, she snatched up a smooth, round bonbon, the plainest on the plate. She took a bite. Elegant dark chocolate met delicate raspberry creme. Her eyes closed in rapture.

"It is very good, no?" Bruno said, beaming at her ecstatic expression.

"It's more than very good," she answered, almost reverently, putting the rest of the candy in her mouth and letting the pure rich flavors and the thick smooth textures melt on her tongue.

Bruno nodded happily. "Its taste is *eccellente*," he agreed, "though it is an ugly little orphan, right now. If we had the right mold, perhaps in the shape of a raspberry, it would be as *bellissima* to look at as it is to eat. Now, please, try this one." He pointed at a tiny dark chocolate log, decorated with white chocolate stripes.

Willingly, Allegra picked it up and took a taste. The tang of moist candied ginger mingled with the semisweet chocolate coating. It was bracing and brisk. "It's wonderful," Allegra said, surveying the platter in awe. "They are all wonderful." She looked up at Bruno. "I don't understand why we aren't making them now."

"Bah," Bruno responded, jerking his head toward the workers beyond his barricade. "They are *cretini, idioti*. They are not capable. They know nothing of these arts. This *zenzero, per esempio*," he said, nodding at the chocolate ginger, "it is hand-dipped. It must be moved through the chocolate bath just so." He illustrated the exact motion with his free hand. "And for the cremes, the molds must be filled with precision, then shaken, then the excess must be poured out so the center remains hollow. It is work for *artigiani*, craftsmen, you call them, not for these clumsy fools."

"But couldn't you teach them?" Allegra asked anxiously, desperate not to lose these delectable treats. "Or find a few people who already know?"

The chocolatier's disgusted frown faded into a hopeful smile. "*Sì*," he said, nodding vigorously. "*Sì. Sì*, it is possible. Here, *signorina*, this one next." He nudged a powdery ball toward her.

She set down the half-eaten ginger, and picked up the truffle. Even as she carried it toward her mouth, the aroma of chocolate and rum filled her nose. With her first little nibble those flavors flooded her senses. The center was thick and creamy and intensely chocolate, tinged with fine, aged rum. Outside was a coat of unsweetened cocoa, dry and bitter in contrast to the heavy, sweet middle. It sent shocks of pleasure down Allegra's throat.

And it instantly evoked memories of Grenada. Of cocoa beans sweating beneath banana leaves and curing under hot blue skies to produce their flavor. Of Elizabeth's serene face as she stirred a pot of cocoa tea in her open-air kitchen and of Jamie's sunburned one as he sipped a glass of rum punch under an arch of brilliant bougainvillaea. Of Oliver, handsome and humorous as he slung an arm around her and hauled her close to him, the faint smell of cocoa clinging to his warm, tanned skin.

"That's it!" she exclaimed, suddenly grabbing Bruno into a hug. "That's it! I've got it! I've got it!" She planted a large chocolaty kiss on the Italian man's cheek, then pulled him through the opening in his barricade and across the factory to the office.

"Bartholomew, I've got it!" she cried, bursting in on her startled cousin. She dragged Bruno into the minuscule room, pulled the platter from his hand, and plopped it down on the pile of papers in front of Bartholomew. "Look!" she commanded. "I've got it!"

Bewildered, Bartholomew obeyed. "They look quite delicious," he said, pushing the platter ever so gently off the graph he was charting. "But I'm afraid I don't know what it is that you've got."

"Everything," Allegra answered, sweeping her arm through the air to indicate the vast scope of her discovery. "I've got everything, Bartholomew. I know exactly what to do to make a grand success, no, a *magnificent*, a *glorious*, success of this business."

"You do?" Bartholomew asked incredulously, looking from his animated cousin to the pretty plate of chocolates. "What?"

"Oh, Bartholomew, listen to this," she responded, practically stuttering in her excitement and her desire to describe the vision crowding her mind. "We are going to do away with Stellar Confections entirely." Flinging both hands from her, she banished the offending factory. "No more ordinary chocolate hearts and chocolate bunnies in shabby little boxes. No more uncouth salesmen in garish suits traipsing around the countryside selling a boring line of candy to rural shops and middle-class spas."

"But Allegra," Bartholomew started to protest.

"No, no," Allegra cut him off, waving a finger and shaking her head. "Listen to me. We aren't going to stop making chocolates, but we are going to stop making *common* chocolates. From now on, we are going to make wonderful, unusual, *luxury* chocolates. From now on, every candy that we produce will reflect the quality and the beauty, even the romance that has been associated with chocolate all through its history."

Bartholomew put down his pencil and sat back in his chair. "Go on," he said quietly, totally attentive.

Allegra leaned over the desk as if to physically draw him into her enthusiasm. "It's the only way," she said with utter certainty. "We can't hope to compete with Cadbury or Fry or Rowentree. They make chocolates that everyone can afford and can easily find. And they make them very well. There is nothing we can add to what they are already doing. They have huge factories. Cadbury even started its own village, for heaven's sake. They own well over three hundred acres outside of Birmingham where they've built immense production buildings and homes for their foremen. In fact, they've just broken ground for three hundred more houses for the rest of their workers. They've got cricket fields and garden swings and kitchens for heating up lunches. They have machines that make ours seem like toys. No, there is no way we can compete with them. Nor do I even want to."

Allegra straightened up. "What I want to do," she said slowly, almost dreamily, spreading her hands out to hold her idea. "What I want to do is make chocolate that will feed people's imaginations as well as their bellies. Like what Papa used to tell Elizabeth about her cooking: It not only fills the stomach, it nourishes the soul.

"I want to appeal to people's desire for opulence. I want them to feel, when they are eating our chocolates, that they are in the same enormously elite and privileged class as Montezuma and Mme. du Barry and the Spanish princess Anne of Austria who brought chocolate as a wedding gift to her future husband, Louis XIII of France. For the price of a pound of chocolates, I want our customer not only to satisfy his craving for something sweet, but also to purchase a place among generations of royalty, both American Indian and European."

"I see," Bartholomew murmured, steepling his hands under his chin.

"No, Bartholomew, you don't see yet," Allegra corrected, refocusing on her cousin. "We are going to make a dazzling assortment of chocolates, and we are going to put them in beautiful boxes, and then we are going to allow only lovely shops to sell them. But the real attraction, the jewel in the crown, will be our very own shop in some appropriately elegant part of London."

Bartholomew's eyes widened, but he didn't say anything. Allegra continued unbidden. Her hands floated across the air as she described the décor of their shop. "It's going to be beautiful," she said positively. "I know you think that business isn't theater, Bartholomew, but our shop is going to be like a stage setting. It's going to seem like a magical place, somewhere far from the fog and the soot of London. People are going to come as much for the atmosphere as for the candy. When they walk in the door, they are going to feel all the wonderful qualities chocolate evokes.

"They are going to feel the tropical sun beating down on the cocoa groves, and they are going to smell the rich, red soil that makes them grow. They are going to sense the vivid colors, the wide, velvet night skies, the warm trade winds against their skin. Without ever leaving England, they will know what a little donkey looks like when it is laden with heaping baskets of cocoa beans, and they will know what the inside of a boucan smells like when it's stacked high with stenciled burlap bags filled with cured beans.

"And finally," she said, her voice softening, "they will see how that sunshine and jungle lushness is transformed in the hands of an artist into sumptuous confections, each one a delicious gem, a delectable prize to savor with the eye as well as with the tongue. Each candy, a culinary masterpiece, will be like a ticket to this extraordinary play, to this sublime fantasy. Our shop will be the royal box of all chocolate theater."

When she finished her announcement, there was a moment of stunned silence, broken at last by Bruno's emotional cries. *"Brava, signorina!"* he exclaimed, tears of happiness running down his cheeks. *"Bravissima!* It is as if you had gone inside my head and found my dreams and set them on your lips. Had I planned it myself, I could not have made it more perfect."

He clutched one of her hands in both of his and said fervently, "As soon as I saw you, saw the *spirito* in your beautiful eyes, I knew that you were *simpatica*. I knew that you would understand the soul of my chocolates. That is why I gave you a box of the very best ones that I am now allowed to make to show you what is possible. Never did I dare to hope, though, that such a *meraviglia*, a miracle, would happen. *Grazie, signorina, grazie mille.*" He pressed her hand to his mouth and gave it a grateful kiss, then, drying his eyes on the hem of his apron and muttering prayers of thanks in Italian, he went back out into the factory.

Rising to her tiptoes with pleasure over Bruno's response, Allegra looked expectantly at her cousin. "What do you think?" she asked.

Bartholomew finally found his tongue. Part of him was affected by the flush of excitement on her cheeks, by the inspiration in her voice, by the very grandeur of her scheme. But part of him was pragmatic. "It sounds truly marvelous," he said honestly. "And if anyone could create such an ambience I have no doubt it would be you, Allegra. But at the risk of sounding curmudgeonly, I must inquire as to your method of financing this dramatic theater of chocolate."

Allegra faltered a bit at this thought, her heels coming down to the floor with a thump. Her plan had evolved so quickly, her ideas flying so fast, she hadn't had time to concentrate on the dreary detail of financing. She didn't allow it to bother her for long, however. Still buoyed by her enthusiasm and by Bruno's demonstrative approval, she answered, "I'm sure you'll think of some way to arrange things, Bartholomew. You are so clever when it comes to figures."

In acknowledgment of the compliment, Bartholomew inclined his fair head but gently persisted. "I may be clever," he said, "but I am not a genie. Would that I could, but I cannot rub a lantern and produce the capital."

Throwing herself into the chair opposite Bartholomew, Allegra asked, "How much money do we really need?" She leaned on the desk and ticked off items on her fingers. "We have the machinery, we have the chocolate, and we have Bruno—the three most essential elements. The other ingredients, the nuts and oils and candied fruits and the like, shouldn't be that dear. Really, the biggest expense will be the shop and the new boxes."

"Ummm," Bartholomew said, taking up his pencil and chewing on its end. He was letting himself be persuaded that his cousin's plan was feasible. "I've gone over the books quite carefully in the past few weeks," he said somewhat tentatively. "And though my eye is inexperienced, I have found what appears to be a great deal of ineptitude. There are duplicate expenditures, unbilled accounts, and uncollected accounts that have been billed. There is some rather expensive equipment sitting in the cellar, idle and unused, collecting dust and interest on indebtedness. By my estimate, at least a third of the employees are unnecessary, given the current volume of production."

He rested his elbows on the arms of his chair, folded his hands across his waistcoat, and regarded his cousin seriously. "If you would be willing to consider some fairly drastic personnel cuts, divesting yourself of unneeded inventory, and initiating a new regime of scrupulous frugality without compromising quality, of course, it may be possible to accumulate some working capital."

Allegra practically dove across the desk to throw her arms around him. "I knew you would help," she said, giving him an enormous squeeze before settling back in her chair. "I knew you would find a way to make it happen. I'd be absolutely lost without you, Bartholomew."

"Yes, well," Bartholomew said, straightening the collar her impetuous hug had disarranged. He was a bit embarrassed by her unquestioning confidence in his abilities and not nearly as certain as she. "Let me ask you this, then," he said, turning the subject away from himself. "If you intend to give your company an entirely new appearance, do you intend to give it a new name, as well?"

"Yes, I do," Allegra answered. An enormously happy smile spread across her face as the last part of her plan, the last free-floating idea fell into place. From out of her memory came

Oliver's words spoken during her first hour in Grenada. "It sounds like a genteel little business or an elegant shop," he had said.

Her voice echoing with pride, Allegra announced, "It's going to be called Pembroke et Fille."

Chapter
Sixteen

Allegra wasted no time in turning Pembroke et Fille from fantasy to fact. Once she realized the effect she wanted, she fairly tripped over herself finding the materials to make it happen. She woke every morning, her mind whirling with ideas, and spent the day in exhausting but tremendously satisfying execution of those ideas. She hunted for the prospective shop space, conferred with Bruno on production, met with the artist who was designing the boxes and with the artisan who was making the molds. She was everywhere, talking, tasting, examining, deciding.

As much as she had enjoyed the rehabilitation of Stellar Confections, she found the creation of Pembroke et Fille to be more exhilarating. In the moments she could spare from business, she marveled at her abilities. She was turning her daydreams, and those of her father, into reality. Not so very long ago she would scarcely have acknowledged their existence. You see, I told you I could do it, she boasted to Oliver in her mind. He didn't answer, but gave her a slow, heartwarming grin.

Bartholomew also seemed to blossom in the new atmosphere. Better than anyone, he knew they couldn't afford to dawdle or make mistakes. Their limited budget demanded that they move quickly and confidently. Because Allegra relied on him in all economic areas, he couldn't let his cousin down.

When the work force of the factory was honed to efficiency, when the past-due accounts began to drift in, Bartholomew was both amazed and proud. He hadn't thought he possessed any practical skills, but he was continually proving to himself that he did. The realization put purpose in his routine, and made him face each day a little more eagerly than the day before.

Allegra was elated, Bartholomew was well-pleased, Bruno was beside himself with joy, and even the remaining employees seemed caught up in the optimism. The only person who was not wholly enthralled with the new plan was Roland. When he called at the factory to invite Allegra to hear works of Rossini and Gounod at the Royal Albert Hall, she put him off with a flurry of activity and an abbreviated description of her intentions.

"What an interesting notion," he commented, though the cool blankness in his tone implied anything but. His golden green eyes narrowed and his finely drawn lips tightened as he said, "It seems a rather extravagant scheme for a debt-ridden business. I hope you know what you are doing."

Allegra's own eyes narrowed at the unfriendliness of his tone. It was on the tip of her tongue to defend her position, but a wave of uneasiness topped her. Instead she replied, shortly and succinctly, "I do."

Instantly, Roland's manner changed. "Of course you do," he said gaily. "I'm positive you mean to be the Chocolate Queen of England, Allegra dear. And I am equally positive you will accomplish your goal. But this time you absolutely must allow me to help you. Come," he said, drawing a blank check from his breast pocket. "I know that you are admirably cautious about incurring further debts, but your magical transformation will require serious funding. I shall be truly devastated if you won't allow me to be of assistance. I want desperately to be a member of your court. Tell me how much you need. A thousand pounds? Two?" He started to fill out the check with a gold pen. "You know that I am completely at sea when it comes to business matters, so you must tell me how much your renovation will require. Name the amount." He looked at her inquiringly, his pen poised above the check.

A smile softened the suspicion on Allegra's face, but her inexplicable uneasiness remained. It would be so simple to give Roland a figure, deposit his check in her account, and proceed with the work unhindered by the need to find money. She heard herself saying, though, "You are really too kind, Roland, but however much I appreciate your generosity, I can't accept your offer. We'll manage as is."

Roland gave a shrug in response, his annoyance just barely

concealed. "As you wish," he said with forced lightness, slipping the check back in his pocket. "But you must remember I stand ready to give you whatever help you need."

After Roland's departure, Allegra tried to understand why she was so uncomfortable with the idea of allowing him to help her. She wandered along the lines of chocolates, arguing that her reaction made no sense at all. Although Roland had little interest in the day-to-day details of doing business, he was certainly whole-hearted when it came to moral support. Despite his lack of practical knowledge, he was convinced she was going to succeed, and he was willing to give her whatever sums of money she needed to achieve that end. He believed in her and was eager to back his belief with a tangible show of encouragement.

Unlike some people I could mention, she thought darkly as she poked her finger through a box of candied orange peel from Spain. All I ever got from Oliver was a lecture on my foolishness and an ungracious reminder that I make a muddle of the account books. That and an obstinate refusal to accompany me to England. She gulped back the sadness suddenly surging up her throat. Oliver. No matter how hard she tried to sweep him out of her head, he remained firmly lodged in her mind.

Often she found herself carrying on conversations with him, triumphantly pointing out her achievements, grudgingly admitting her failures, even asking his opinion on subjects, then pausing to listen to his patient, sensible, unvarnished advice. It's no good comparing him with Roland, she mused.

No, it isn't, she imagined Oliver's wry voice interrupting. And if you have something to say about me, Allegra, tell me directly.

Oh you! she thought in exasperation. Always barging in. Roland would never be so tactless. His manners are absolutely elegant.

I thought we had agreed that it was no good comparing us, she heard Oliver pointing out.

Allegra sighed. "We had," she said out loud. As handsome and debonair and socially smooth as he was, Roland was no match for the strong, healthy man she remembered in a mist of rainbows under a tropical waterfall.

She was nibbling on a piece of peel when Bartholomew approached. His usually composed face was scowling as he banged his omnipresent pencil against a sheaf of papers. "This is the last straw, Allegra," he said angrily. "Albert Baker must be dismissed."

Jolted abruptly from her memory of that euphoric afternoon in Grenada and back to the noisy factory in London, Allegra didn't have time to collect her thoughts. Reacting only to the irritation in her cousin's tone, she snapped, "I think you are exaggerating your program for cutting expenses, Bartholomew. It's become almost a purge. However strict our budget, we simply cannot dispense with a manager. Not only is it bad for morale, it will wind up costing us more than we save if we don't have someone overseeing the daily production, with its countless little problems." Drawing herself up dramatically and shaking the half-eaten orange peel at him, she added, "And if you think *I* am going to fill the position, you're quite mistaken. I'm already working every waking hour, and I can't possibly be expected to do more."

"I hardly expect you to assume the manager's position," Bartholomew replied, with considerably less sympathy than was his wont. Responding to Allegra's high dudgeon, he continued sharply, "Nor do I expect the post to go vacant, but Albert Baker is not the man to fill it. I have unearthed a pattern of misjudgments and mistakes that are exceedingly costly. I've spoken to Mr. Baker on several occasions, questioning the reasoning that led him to make such errors. Each time he has replied with obfuscation, inadequate excuses, and disingenuous promises to be more careful in the future. Yet once again, he has behaved negligently.

"See here." He again banged the pages he was holding with his pencil. "He has submitted full wage cards for two employees. One left the company long before we arrived, and the other was let go last week."

"For heaven's sake, Bartholomew," Allegra retorted, still in a bad humor, "everyone makes mistakes. There have been so many changes lately he probably just got confused. Not everyone is as perfectly organized as you. We must be prepared to be a little forgiving if we wish to retain our employees. Roland particularly noted that Mr. Baker is an able manager, and pointed out the difficulty in finding someone with such a thorough knowledge of the chocolate business."

Bartholomew lowered the papers. In a very tight voice he said, "Mr. Baker may know the chocolate business thoroughly, but I have seen no indication that he is applying his knowledge to the advantage of Pembroke et Fille. Nor am I impressed with Roland's expertise in this matter. May I inquire why you seem to favor his opinion over my own?"

Allegra's mouth opened with a sarcastic reply, but just in time she swallowed it unspoken. Her cousin's undeniable loyalty and logic broke her bad mood. Her face heated with remorse. "I don't favor his opinion over yours, Bartholomew. You have given me nothing but sound advice, for which I am truly thankful. If you say that Albert Baker must be dismissed, I am sure you are correct, and we'll do so at once."

When Bartholomew still stood stiffly before her, his offended pride not completely soothed, she rummaged absently in the box of orange peels and added more gruffly, "I'm sorry if I've acted crankily. You don't deserve such treatment, and I really didn't intend it for you. You just caught me in a moment of homesickness for L'Etoile and I lashed out without thinking."

For a moment there was only the incessant whirring and clanking of the steam-driven machinery as Allegra toyed with the citrus curls, too embarrassed to look Bartholomew in the face. Finally he spoke, his voice soft and sad, the wounded pique completely gone. "I understand," he said. "I, too, have spells of almost unbearable longing for Grenada that quite ruin my ability to concentrate on any other subject."

Allegra's head shot up in astonishment. "You do?" she asked dumbly. She hadn't expected him to believe she could miss a place she had lived in for only a few months so much it would affect her temper, yet here he was, shoulders slumped, admitting to the same feeling after having been there only a few weeks.

Conscious of her curious gaze, Bartholomew could feel his cheeks heat up with embarrassment. He hadn't meant to let such strong emotions slip out, but sometimes he felt as though he would burst with the feeling bottled up inside him. The forlorn look on his cousin's face and the mention of L'Etoile stirred memories and made him confess, "I was extraordinarily happy there."

"So was I." Allegra sighed, thinking again of Oliver and that afternoon at the waterfall. Knowing that it was a person, as much as a place, that was responsible for her happiness she was still incredulous that Bartholomew also felt so strongly.

"No, wait," she said suddenly, staring at her cousin with fresh mazement. "It's not just Grenada you miss, is it?" she demanded. Out of the recesses of her memory came a moment in Matthewlina Cameron's cafe, a moment when she emerged from the kitchen to find excitement and color brightening the faces of Bartholomew and Violet.

She remembered the luster in their eyes and their hands scooting back across the table, and she remembered her own dismissal of the incident. At the time she had thought her English cousin too stodgy to be attracted to Violet, and Violet too lively to be attracted to Bartholomew. Now she knew that behind his correct English exterior was a man of uncommon gentleness, generosity, and appreciation for life. "You miss Violet, too, don't you?" she asked more quietly.

Nodding briefly, Bartholomew started to turn away. Then he turned back and blurted out, "I miss her terribly. I'm in love with her." He glared at his cousin as if daring her to object.

"That's wonderful!" Allegra exclaimed, clapping her hands together delightedly, thinking only that two of her favorite people had found each other.

Relief shot through Bartholomew, weakening his legs. He leaned against the worktable, grateful to Allegra for her immediate and unquestioning approval. It unloosed all the fears and feelings he had locked up inside, and he now poured them out to his sympathetic cousin. "It's not as wonderful as it would seem," he told her, "because there is nothing that can be done about it. Violet must remain in Grenada, while I must live my life in England."

"But why must you?" Allegra asked, dismayed by this unhappy ending. "I thought you said you loved her. Doesn't she return your love?"

"Yes, she does," Bartholomew answered miserably. "As deeply and as profoundly as I love her. I can't tell you, Allegra, just how marvelous I feel when I am with her." His hands sketched the air in an uncharacteristic attempt to describe the magnitude of his passion. "Being with her makes everything else seem unreal, almost trancelike, as if I am only truly alive in her presence." His hands dropped again in defeat, and he leaned more heavily against the table.

"It's an illusion, though," he said wearily. "Being with her is the dream. My reality is in England. It is my father and Pembroke Hall and people of select birth and breeding. It is a way of thinking and living that has been unchanged for generations, with no possible place in it for a beautiful, spirited, cocoa-colored woman from Grenada."

"Surely not everyone in England would reject her," Allegra protested. "There must be some people who would be thrilled to call her a friend."

"Undoubtedly," Bartholomew agreed without enthusiasm. "But unfortunately, my father is not among their number. Sir Gerald would never accept my marriage to Violet, and I am ultimately the sorry product of my upbringing. I am utterly dependent on my father for all practical concerns. I am helpless and defenseless when removed from his protection."

"That can't be true," Allegra objected. "You are so intelligent and serious. You know so many things. I should think you could make your way anywhere in the world."

"Useless information," Bartholomew scoffed. "I have a vast store of useless information. I haven't your innate knowledge of life, Allegra. If I married Violet, I would destroy her."

"No," Allegra said. "No." She was confused by his astounding admission, by this upsetting reversal of their roles. "You have your love for each other," she said. "That's the most important thing of all. If you love each other, everything else will sort itself out." Only after she spoke the words did she realize she was addressing herself as well as him. The realization distracted her.

Shaking himself, Bartholomew returned to his normal composed state. "That's a sweet thought," he said. "But I fear it is not a prudent one. It takes more than love to make a successful marriage, just as it takes more than money to make a successful business. There are so many imponderable elements that can erode the original investment until nothing is left but a bankrupt business. Or a broken heart."

"No," Allegra said again, suddenly overcome by a wave of unbearable longing for Oliver. This time she couldn't deny it or bury it under a flurry of work. She missed Oliver more than she could say. "Love is still the most important element," she insisted, as she finally accepted that idea herself. "Nothing else is as important. Nothing."

She reached absently for another orange peel and took a tentative bite. As she moved slowly away, she gave her cousin a last bit of advice. "Don't let your upbringing stand in the way of your

ove, Bartholomew," she said, then added almost wistfully, "Or
n argument. Or an ocean."

Puzzled by her tone, Bartholomew watched her drift off. He
cratched his head with the pencil he was still holding, made a
ew notes in the margins of his papers, and turned to go back to
he office. Before walking away, he turned again and stared at
Allegra's retreating figure.

She was in a quiet mood several days later, still mulling over
er conversation with Bartholomew. She was trying to come to
erms with the inescapable truth she had discovered under layers
f assumed sophistication and professional preoccupation: Oliver
was a permanent part of her life.

He's a part of me, she thought. Despite that nasty argument
we had on the beach at Gouyave when he insisted that I should
tay at L'Etoile and I demanded that he come to England. Despite
he icy silence between us when I sailed away. Despite the thou-
ands of miles of open sea that separate us now. I'm incapable of
ismissing him no matter how adamantly I insist that I am better
ff without him.

Allegra toyed with the array of foil wrappers and crenellated
aper cups she was supposed to be deciding on while thinking
more intently about Oliver and L'Etoile. About Grenada and
cocoa and love. He's a part of me, she thought again. As much a
art of me as my hands or my heart. Or my dreams.

"What's this I hear?" came Roland's voice behind her,
isrupting her musing. His usually modulated tone sounded
rill. Turning around, Allegra saw his fine, pale face mottled
ith suppressed anger, his golden eyes glittering with fury.

"What do you hear?" she asked, bewildered both by his ques-
on and by his rage.

"Don't pretend such wide-eyed innocence," Roland snapped,
ashing his walking stick through the air in front of her. "You
now very well I am referring to Albert Baker's sacking. I
ought I had made myself quite clear when I praised his abili-
es. Weren't you listening to what I said?"

"Of course I listened," Allegra replied, backing away from his
ick, but not from his wrath. "I just came to a different conclu-
on about Mr. Baker."

"Drawn, no doubt, with the aid of your meddling cousin,"
oland practically shouted, waving the walking stick in her face.

Allegra swatted it aside. At another time she might have at-

tempted to defuse the situation, to mumble an apology or t
stumble for an explanation that would satisfy everyone's injure
feelings. Today she was having none of that. "I'll have yo
know," she retorted sharply, "that Bartholomew meddles, as yo
phrase it, at my request and with my complete approval. An
anyway," she added, her suspicion now aroused, "why are you s
upset? Surely it can't be that you're so worried about Mr. Baker'
employment. You showed no such concern for the welfare of th
other employees we released."

Visibly jarred by Allegra's sharp rebuttal, Roland becam
aware of his own behavior and sought to collect himself. With a
unconvincing laugh, he backtracked, putting a softer facade o
his harsh statements. "I assure you, I didn't mean to criticiz
anyone, my dear," he said placatingly, tucking his threatenin
stick underneath his arm. "I know that you are all working bru
tally hard, devoting every bit of your energy without a trace c
complaint to the good of the business.

"However," he said casually, adjusting his perfectly knotte
tie. "As an investor, despite myself, in Pembroke et Fille, I tak
an interest in its economic health. You can understand, I am sur
that I am most anxious to protect my investment by ensuring th
company's success. Forgive the simple reasoning of an admitte
amateur, but it does seem to me that Albert Baker's long years c
experience in the chocolate business bode better for the prospe
ity of our little firm than Bartholomew's earnest and well-mea
ing, but sadly unproven theories."

Allegra felt her heart freeze at his insidious reference to th
debt he had so often urged her to forget. Nor did his self-depr
cating words deflect the familiar uneasiness revived by his pr
sumptuous pronoun when alluding to Pembroke et Fill
Nonetheless, she would not let Roland intimidate her. "I, on th
other hand," she said, standing up very straight and speakir
very firmly, "prefer to put my trust in Bartholomew's unprov
but honest opinions rather than in Albert Baker's unscrupulo
ones, however seasoned. It would seem that Mr. Baker's exper
ence extends not only to chocolate, but also to lying, cheatin
falsifying records, and mismanaging expenses. There is no pla
for him in *my* firm."

With another laugh, Roland threw up his hands in defeat.
had no idea that was the case," he said. "You know how tru
hopeless I am at business matters. If indeed Mr. Baker is th

villain you portray, then we are, most certainly, better off without him. It's a good job that you and your cousin have found him out. Good riddance, I say."

He slipped his arm through hers and strolled with her the length of the factory floor. "Now you must permit me to tell you how becoming I find your gown. I'm quite convinced that shade of lavender blue is your best color. It makes your magnificent eyes even more extraordinary."

"Yes, well," Allegra said, trying to appear appeased but still feeling agitated and uncomfortable.

"And in all this silly uproar, I've neglected to mention the purpose of my visit," he continued, affectionately patting the arm he was holding. "I've engaged a box for this evening at the Savoy Theater. D'Oyly Carte is doing *Utopia Limited*. It isn't acclaimed as one of Gilbert and Sullivan's better efforts, but by all accounts it is amusing. Shall I call for you at seven?"

"Uh—" Allegra suddenly stuttered. "No, I don't think I can, I mean, I'm not able. No, that is. I must work late this evening." If Roland's reference to the debt she owed him was disturbing, his reference to Gilbert and Sullivan was positively unnerving. In her mind, those operettas would forever be associated with Oliver. The merest mention of their work conjured up that blissful afternoon at the beach in Carriacou when he had held her securely in the warm sea and had sung, "I am a pirate king . . ." while sitting cross-legged and bare-chested on the white sand. Even if she weren't still annoyed with Roland, she could never bring herself to attend this particular performance with him, especially not now, not after so recently acknowledging her undiminished love for Oliver.

"That's it," she said, seizing on an excuse. "I promised Bartholomew I would stay late this evening and review some invoices. It's quite important."

Roland's eyes narrowed marginally, but his tone remained light. "It sounds unspeakably dreary to me," he said. "But I'm sure you know what you must do. Don't think, however, dear Allegra," he added with mock sternness, "that because I accept your demurral this time, I shall do so forever. I shan't allow you to bury yourself in this gloomy factory indefinitely."

He touched a gloved finger to her smooth cheek and gently tapped one of the faint freckles on her nose. "I would be overcome with grief if your lovely face withered in this dismal atmosphere and if your graceful body became stooped from overwork. You may rely on it; I intend to be most vigilant about prying you loose from your pots of chocolate, and refreshing your spirit with pleasurable outings."

True to his word, Roland appeared at the factory every few days with extravagant bouquets of spring flowers or beautifully bound novels aimed at distracting Allegra from her demanding routine. Having finally found a shop to lease, she was continually dashing between it and the factory, orchestrating not only the chocolate, but the showroom now as well. Although Roland extended invitations to the theater and to concerts and to fashionable suppers, Allegra made the excuse of being too busy or too exhausted to attend.

After a while, the suspicion and apprehension that Roland's unfathomable wrath had aroused receded to the back of her mind. She didn't have time to wonder about his strange behavior. It also escaped her notice that Roland avoided coming face to face with her cousin following the less than kind remark he had made about him. If Bartholomew were aware of the slight, he didn't object; he was just as happy to have Roland keep his distance. He was every bit as occupied as Allegra, racing to open the shop and officially launch Pembroke et Fille by April eleventh, her birthday.

As the damp chill of winter gave way to the sweet-smelling days of spring, as primroses and forget-me-nots bloomed in patches of lush green grass, Allegra occasionally allowed Roland to persuade her to spend an hour or so in the balmy afternoon air. They would drive along the Serpentine or Rotten Row in Hyde Park, chatting amiably and letting the welcome sunshine warm them.

"I am convinced these little excursions do you all the good in the world," Roland told her one day. "The air has put a sparkle on your cheeks that is irresistible. You look more tempting than one of your beloved confections."

Allegra gave a happy laugh, not as bowled over by his flattery as she once was, but not totally immune to it, either. It was very nice to be always admired, and today particularly she was very receptive to praise of any sort. The opening of the shop was less than a week away, and everything was going remarkably well. She was proud and pleased.

"You are probably right," she admitted willingly. "I do feel restored. It's so delightful to just sit still for a while, especially out of doors."

"You work entirely too hard," Roland admonished, flicking his whip above his bays' backs. "You'll wear yourself into a state of illness."

"Perhaps," Allegra conceded with a careless shrug. "But I am enjoying myself immensely. I don't believe I could stop now if I wanted to." She gave another laugh. "It's almost as if the business were controlling me, rather than the other way around. It's never out of my mind, even when I sleep. I woke up at two o'clock this morning, my head full of another scheme. And I had such a good time imagining it, it was after dawn when I fell back to sleep."

"Good heavens!" Roland exclaimed. "It sounds like a frightful way to pass the night. What could possibly be so amusing as to be worth one's sleep? Did you invent a new chocolate candy?"

"Something like that," Allegra answered easily, but abstractedly. She knew that however admiring Roland was of her spirit and enthusiasm, he found the details of her business tedious. She didn't want to bore him or to deflate herself by sharing her idea with an unappreciative audience. "Look at the mother swan and her babies. Aren't they lovely?"

Roland was not to be put off, however. "You must enlighten me," he demanded. "I am curiosity itself."

"No, no," Allegra responded, laughing again. "It is only a feather-brained notion, as Oliver would say. Totally impractical."

"Oh?" Roland kept his eyes on the horses, but managed to inject immeasurable interest into that single syllable. "You must not keep me in cruel suspense another moment. I am longing to hear the idea of which Oliver would so colorfully disapprove."

Wishing she hadn't let Oliver's name slip off her tongue to be misinterpreted by Roland, Allegra said simply, "I just thought it would be intriguing to have a line of chocolates made solely from L'Etoile's cocoa." After a minute's reflection, she sat on the edge of the carriage seat, caught up in the idea.

"Can't you imagine it?" she asked excitedly. "Each bonbon would be wrapped in a beautiful tissue that has a sketch of the estate and a bit of its history written on it. Perhaps Bruno could even flavor it with some of the spices we grow there. Don't you think it would be fascinating to know exactly where the candy came from? That it would infinitely enhance its appeal? It would be like buying a wine from a particular chateau. And if the L'Etoile chocolates were well-received, we could find other distinctive estates and do the same thing. We could develop a whole line of estate chocolates."

"It's brilliant!" Roland cried. "Thoroughly in keeping with the image you are creating, capturing the aura of chocolate. I don't know why you permit Oliver's vastly distant opinion to convince you that it is impractical."

"Because it is," Allegra answered ruefully, wishing again that Roland would stop referring to Oliver. His name didn't sound right in Roland's mouth. She settled back in her seat. "It's the same problem as with making our own cocoa powder: We haven't the machinery. In fact, it would probably be an even more costly proposition. We would have to buy a roaster and a cracking and winnowing machine, then a crusher, and probably a new boiler to drive them all. More than likely we would even have to lease an additional building to run the operation, as we would need storage for the bags of cocoa. It takes up considerably more space in its unprocessed state than as slabs of chocolate liquor, you know."

"But it's such an inspired idea," Roland protested. "Literally flying into your dreams in the middle of the night. It would be a pity to have it go for naught because of a simple lack of funding. You must let me loan you the capital to finance this scheme."

"We've been over this a dozen times before," Allegra said, regaining her lighthearted mood. The whole thing was too improbable to take seriously, though it was fun to fantasize about and it was rewarding to see Roland respond so positively. "I can't possibly borrow any more money until I have repaid the debts I already have. Besides, I have no collateral."

"And each of those dozen times, I have told you that your word is your collateral. Your word and your wonderful imagination. It's all the surety I need."

"No, no," Allegra answered, as she always did, blithely brushing her hand through the air. "I can't let you take the risk. It's too much money, and you have no assurance when, or if, I will pay you back."

Roland suddenly reined in the horses, coming to a halt beneath a budding elm. He turned on the seat to give Allegra his full attention, his expression intent, his tone, for once, sober. "You think I am a frivolous fellow," he said. "And perhaps I am.

But I am not so absorbed by my idle life and pleasures that I do not recognize your rare gifts. I am in awe of your ambition, of your invincible determination. Would that I possessed even a fraction of your zeal, dear Allegra. Were it so, I might spend my time doing other than amusing myself. As it is, I can only beseech you to accept what is so easy for me to give, that I might imagine myself some small part of your inevitable success.

"I have great faith in your 'feather-brained notions,'" he said. "And I think this recent one is the most credible idea yet. How much better that my money is spent underwriting a line of 'estate chocolates' than on my usual tailor bills and gambling markers. Truly, Allegra, it would be a privilege and an honor to assist you in your remarkable endeavors."

Allegra gulped, her heart beating very fast. This earnest speech was more than just glib adulation, more than tea table magnanimity. Roland made it seem as if she would be doing him a favor by taking his money. She had never seen him so sincere. It was tempting, achingly tempting. She could almost taste the chocolates, rich and as exotically spiced as cocoa tea. She could see the pretty tissues, each one waiting to wrap up a delectable bit of tropical flavor. Most of all, she could feel the pull of L'Etoile, feel the tie binding her closer to Oliver. Until now, this had only been a dream, entertaining to imagine, but completely out of reach. Suddenly it was attainable, the full circle Cecil intended only inches from closing. All she had to do was tell Roland yes. A giddy euphoria filled her as she opened her mouth.

"I say! Young Hawkes, isn't it?" A leather and tweed gentleman with a sweeping white moustache and ruddy cheeks hauled his magnificent mount to a stop next to their carriage.

Annoyance at the interruption made Roland's eyes narrow. He turned abruptly to confront the intruder. "Yes, it is," he said in a tightly controlled voice. "How do you do, Sir Harold. Sir Harold Grimsby, may I present Miss Pembroke?"

"Miss Pembroke." Sir Harold bowed his head, but did not tip his hat, instead keeping both hands on the reins of his nervous thoroughbred. "Don't mean to detain you," he said apologetically. "Just wanted to ask after your father. Haven't seen him in ages. Is he well?"

"Very well, thank you," Roland replied with the necessary civility.

"Splendid. Splendid. Well, I must be off. Thunder doesn't

suffer these social interludes lightly. Miss Pembroke. Hawkes."
He nodded his head toward them again and barely loosened the
reins. His horse sprang forward. "Do give my best to your father," he shouted over his shoulder. "Tell Lord Fenwick I was
inquiring after him."

Allegra's mouth clamped shut. Cold horror cut off her breath.
Her heart seemed to stop and icy shock socked her stomach. Lord
Fenwick. The man who had won Argo estate in a hand of cards
and had turned it over to his arrogant son, Oliver's archenemy.

Lord Fenwick's son was the man who had allowed his schoolboy jealousy to escalate into an adult vendetta. Who had started
Argo Shipping to dominate the West Indian cocoa trade. Who
was responsible for the vicious raid on L'Etoile's cocoa and the
malicious attacks on its reputation. Who worked hand-in-glove
with the repellent Frederick Smart. Lord Fenwick's son was Roland Hawkes.

The man whose avowed goal was the humiliation and destruction of Oliver MacKenzie was Roland Hawkes, and she was sitting next to him on a carriage seat in the spring sunshine. For the
last two months she had laughed with him and confided in him,
had accepted invitations to share his private theater boxes and his
late-night suppers. She had found his handsome face attractive
and his smooth, sophisticated manners appealing, even imagining
that they were a welcome change from Oliver's blunt honesty.
And she had come within half a second of sinking irrevocably
into his debt. Her breath came back in a gasp and her stomach
rose to her throat.

"Allegra, what has happened?" Roland asked in alarm.
"You've gone deathly pale. Is there too much sun? A chill
breeze? Speak to me." He clutched the reins in one hand and
reached out the other to brush her white cheek.

Allegra cringed away from his touch, repulsed. "You lied to
me," she said, her voice hoarse with the pain of betrayal. "You
never told me you were Lord Fenwick's son."

"Ahh," Roland said, withdrawing his hand, his tone considerably cooler as understanding set in. "I see you know *that* name. I
did think it rather odd that, intimate as you seem to be with our
mutual acquaintance, you were unfamiliar with my name. Apparently he prefers to refer to me by my future title. He is more
properly awed by nobility than he would pretend to be."

"He isn't," Allegra retorted, defending Oliver. "He loathes

snobbery. He never referred to you by your title. In fact, he never referred to you at all. I only learned of your existence through his solicitor."

Angry color rose above Roland's collar as he heard how little an impression he made on his rival. "Obviously you didn't learn your lesson very thoroughly if you only now realize who I am," he said nastily. "But you are a silly little chit, given to emotional flights as an excuse for avoiding good sense. You accuse me of being untruthful to cover a lapse in knowledge you ought to have had. If you did not acquire it in Grenada, you or your plodding cousin ought to have acquired it here."

It was Allegra's turn to color with mortification at her own ingenuousness. Not only had she failed to discover his background, she had willingly swallowed all his fawning praise. She had ignored her instinctive uneasiness and had allowed herself to be persuaded by his admiration, admiration now revealed to be utterly invented. "I took you at your word," she said brokenly. "I believed you were my friend, that you had only my best interests at heart. If not an outright lie, then your behavior toward me was a deception, for what reason I do not know."

As soon as she said the words, she did know the reason. Her heart raced in agitation as the pieces fell rapidly into place, as vaguely disturbing incidents and inexplicable actions were suddenly explained. "You planned it all," she said, aghast at her discovery. "From the very beginning. It's all part of your wicked scheme to bring Oliver down. My father never approached you in your club, did he? It was you who approached him, enticing him into debt with your unctuous flattery, pretending to be completely ignorant of business, just as you did with me. You probably told him the same things. How much you admired his ambition, how honored you'd be to play a small role in his success. Isn't that right?" she demanded, outraged at his actions and ashamed at her own gullibility.

Roland raised his eyebrows in reply, a sneer frozen on his face. There was no trace of the affable gentleman, no sign of the carefree cavalier who had wooed her these past weeks. "You fascinate me," he said coldly. "Pray continue."

"Once he'd taken your money and spent it on the factory, you pressured him into signing a note, with L'Etoile as collateral," she went on, describing the scene that was becoming clearer to her as she spoke. "You never cared about helping Stellar Confections, you only used it and my father as a pawn to get closer to Oliver, to take half his estate, to wreak your mad revenge.

"You even made sure Stellar Confections would fail, didn't you." She didn't ask, but stated it bitterly. "Knowing my father hadn't the patience for details, you put Albert Baker in as manager. At your instructions, he unbalanced the books, making unnecessary payments and not billing accounts. You wanted Stellar Confections to fail so you would have an excuse to foreclose on L'Etoile. That's why you were so irrationally angry when we sacked Mr. Baker, and why you dislike Bartholomew's careful scrutiny of the books. Can you deny it?"

"Should I?" Roland returned mockingly.

"It won't work!" Allegra suddenly shouted, furious with his smugness. "We are going to make Pembroke et Fille succeed, and we are going to repay all the debts. You won't get L'Etoile. Your machinations are useless." She turned quickly away from him to climb out of the carriage, unable to bear his proximity another moment.

"Not so fast," Roland said sharply, seizing her arm and yanking her back on the seat. "I have a few things to say now myself. I think you will find that you are not in quite the independent position you imagine." He snapped the whip at his horses, sending them rapidly out of the park and rendering it impossible for Allegra to descend.

There was a feral light in his golden green eyes and a dangerous note in his voice as he spoke. "My machinations, as you call them, have not been useless," he told her, driving at breakneck speed through narrow streets. "My strategy has been quite sound. Despite the efforts of your wearisome cousin, and despite your own baseless boasts to the contrary, L'Etoile is very much within my reach. You seem to forget that I hold a note for your foolish father's share. I can, at any moment, demand payment of that debt, and unless you have the funds to honor it, you must forfeit the estate you inherited."

Glancing sideways, he seemed to take satisfaction from seeing Allegra's face go from white to gray as her eyes opened wider with fear. "It amuses me to refrain from calling in the note at this time," he said with false geniality. Then the whip cracked again, and so did his voice, making Allegra jump. "From now on, however, you will follow my wishes. There will be no more fiddling managers and no more crusading cousin. It will be quite simple elemental enough for even you to understand. I will tell you what to do, and you will do it."

"I won't," Allegra whispered, protesting weakly, her self-assurance battered but her dream still faintly flickering.

Roland pulled smartly to a stop in front of the house where Allegra lived. He turned to look at her. "You will if you want to save your precious few acres of jungle," he told her in an ugly tone. He nodded his dismissal, let her descend from the carriage unaided, and set his team in motion almost before she was clear of the wheels.

It seemed an interminable distance from the curb to the steps. Allegra's legs barely responded to her command. As she started up the brick stairs, the hem of her skirt caught on the wrought-iron boot scraper, tugging her off-balance. She stumbled and fell hard to her knees, the palms of her gloves splitting as she thrust her hands forward to protect her face. The impact jarred her both physically and mentally. It had been a long time since she had tripped like that, clumsy from lack of confidence.

What was worse, there was no one to catch her. There was no Oliver to grab her securely around the waist and set her squarely on her feet. For a moment she remained as she was, on her hands and knees, tears streaking down her cheeks, too demoralized to stand up. Her eternal optimism was extinguished, her vivid imagination was blank. She had failed. All her grand plans of success, all her glorious visions of triumph had come to this. She had lost her money, her business, her estate, and her pride. And she had lost Oliver.

Never mind that they had had a chilling argument when she left Grenada, or that she had repeatedly sworn to put him out of her mind. Ever since the day she had discovered she couldn't stop loving Oliver, a fantasy had formed in her mind. She had romantically imagined sailing back to Grenada, the profits from Pembroke et Fille bulging her purse, the luster of Cecil's restored reputation reflecting on her. She had dreamed of that day, of debarking on the pier at Gouyave and being scooped into Oliver's arms.

Now the dream was over and reality was the cold, damp bricks beneath her bruised knees and scraped hands. There were no profits, no esteem, and no Oliver. How could she ever face him again knowing how foolishly, how naively, she had allowed herself to be taken in and manipulated by the one man on earth who was bent on destroying him? And how could he ever forgive her for her stubborn stupidity, the mistake that would cost him the life he loved? Her dream was over. Just moments before she'd thought she had achieved her goals, but now she found that instead, she had failed on all counts.

With tremendous effort she forced herself to stand up and climb the stairs. Once in her room, she shut the drapes, then slowly she undressed her aching body and crawled into bed. She pulled the covers high to ward off the chill penetrating her bones and her spirit. She felt so worn out. She had set out from Connecticut six months before to make something of herself, to twine her fate, brilliantly, with her father's. "Pembroke et fille," she said. The pillow smothered her bitter laugh.

We're a likely pair, you and I, Cecil, she thought, barely aware that she had stopped called him Papa. She'd lost the reverent respect for the image of him she'd invented. She'd lost her self-respect as well.

All we've ever cared about is the impetuous pursuit of our feather-brained ambitions, she thought miserably. Between the two of us, we've managed to alienate everyone who's ever trusted us. And we've both betrayed Oliver. Father and daughter. The pillow, wet with her tears, was cold against her face. "Pembroke et fille," she repeated.

Chapter
Seventeen

While the peak harvest period continued through the end of January, Oliver managed to keep himself busy enough not to have time or energy left over for thoughts of Allegra. But when the pace slackened, her absence was all too obvious. Where once he had cherished precisely this privacy and solitude, he now found himself feeling lonely and out of sorts.

He missed discussing the day's events around the dining table and going over the accounts in the office. He missed seeing her dashing across the lawn or the cocoa yard, blond curls springing wildly around her head. He missed watching her bring smiles to the faces of the workers, and extra effort to their production. He missed her laughter, her never ending, often inspired, sometimes absurd, but always amazing string of fantasies and ideas. He missed her all-consuming optimism and her occasional exasperating attempts at staid behavior. He even missed catching her when she stumbled and tripped.

He missed very much the feel of her soft body in his arms, the clean scent of her smooth skin, the closeness of her expressive face. A wonderful warmth filled him, knowing he was able to save her from harm. He had never felt so needed before. And so needing. He missed being able to love Allegra.

Although he missed her, he refused to admit it. The irresistible images of her that cluttered his memory were banished, the tender feelings were brushed away. Usually not one to bear a grudge, he found it hard to forget their argument on the rocky beach in Gouyave. It wasn't because she had clung to nonsensical illusions about the debt-ridden chocolate factory her father had half-formed. It was because, given a clear choice between it and him, she had chosen Stellar Confections.

Asking him to accompany her to England didn't compensate for her decision. She knew perfectly well it was against all his principles ever to step foot in that country again. If she loved him, as she had so joyously claimed that afternoon at the waterfall, she would have offered him more than an impossible compromise. If she loved me, he thought, she would have accepted who I am.

Normally, Oliver treated his disappointments with cool common sense and after a brief blowup maintained his even temper. Now, however, he was unusually ill-humored, unbearable to be around.

"Well, I mean to say, you acting like you stood under a machineel tree in the rain," Elizabeth scolded him as she thunked a plate of conch fritters on the kitchen table. "Like the sap drip drop on your head and make it itchy and crazy."

"Just because I told you the sorrel tea has too much ginger in it?" Oliver responded contentiously. "It tastes as if you dumped the whole root in to steep. Am I supposed just to ignore it? Just sit here and choke?"

"I been feeding you sorrel tea for twenty-five years," Elizabeth retorted, unfazed. "You never choke yet. Something else making you choke."

Jamie was equally disgusted with his friend's belligerent mood. He arrived at L'Etoile looking forward to a weekend's retreat and was ready to leave again after an hour. "Your behavior has reached new heights of barbarity," he informed Oliver. "You have all the social grace of a treed cat. You've been living alone too long, I fear."

"I *like* being alone," Oliver growled in reply.

Jamie didn't answer but studied Oliver shrewdly. Finally, he shook his head, muttered, "Och," and went up to his room, his valise in one hand, a glass of rum punch in the other.

Although Oliver was aware that he was acting insufferably, the knowledge only irritated him further. He was annoyed with himself for allowing thoughts of Allegra to affect his disposition, to distract him to the point of surliness. Seeking to put some distance between himself and the site of his memories, he left L'Etoile in Septimus' hands and went back to sea. He sailed with his schooners from Grenada to Trinidad, Trinidad to Venezuela, Venezuela to Barbados, to Tobago, St. Vincent, St. Lucia, St. Kitts, Martinique, and Montserrat. He wound up in Carriacou more than a month later, salty and sore, in need of a fresh bath and a soft bed, and no less troubled than when he had started.

With the launching of his new schooner only days away, Oliver was determined to immerse himself in the traditionally festive event, to forget about Allegra, to recover his equilibrium amid the comfort of his family. That resolve lasted one afternoon. The big aloe plant by the side of the porch reminded him of how Violet had soothed the sunburn Allegra had gotten during her swimming lesson at Sabazon. And that reminded him of how it had felt to hold her in the sea, to sense that exquisite moment when her fear had fled and she had put her trust in him totally. His abrupt and humorless manner returned.

"Everyone is so cross these days," Lily wrathfully declared, stomping out the door. Accustomed to her adored big brother's unstinting affection, she was stung by his rebuff when she attempted to joke with him. She stopped on the hard-packed dirt path in front of the house, put her hands on her hips, and shouted at the occupants inside. "First Violet comes home from Grenada with her chin around her knees, and now you are acting like an attacked sea urchin, Oliver. It's not fair!" Her braid swinging indignantly, she turned and marched down to the beach.

Emerging from his self-absorbed state, Oliver looked across the tea table to Violet. He was surprised to see Lily's observation was true. His sister, indeed, looked very sad. There were shadows under her luminous brown eyes and a defeated set to her shoulders. Attuned to his own feelings, he imagined that Violet was missing Allegra and life at L'Etoile, too. Almost immediately, he dismissed the idea. While he didn't doubt that Violet felt her friend's absence, something about her expression told him the misery went much deeper. Her face seemed suddenly more experienced and mature, as if she had found a center for her young life.

When the cups and cakes were cleared, he guided her outside to the bench beneath the frangipani tree, just beginning to flower. "What is it, Violet?" he asked quietly, pulling a fragrant blossom from a branch and brushing it under her chin.

"What is what?" Violet answered, halfheartedly avoiding his question.

"What is weighing you down so?"

Violet shrugged and squinted through the waxy white flowers to look at the turquoise and purple streaks of sea.

"Do you feel ill?" Oliver patiently probed. When she shook her head, he went on. "Are you unhappy in Carriacou? Are Angus and Rose too strict? Is someone bothering you?" When still she said nothing but only gave another slight shrug in reply, Oliver crossed his arms on his chest, leaned back against the tree, and stared at her speculatively. It suddenly occurred to him he had been right to interpret her feelings according to his own. He'd simply miscast them. It wasn't Allegra she was pining for, but someone she loved as much as he loved Allegra.

"Have you found someone?" he asked gently. "Have you fallen in love?"

Violet finally turned her head toward him, her eyes brimming with tears. "Yes," she said softly.

"Who is it?" Oliver demanded, a shade more roughly, caught between his sympathy for her obvious heartbreak and his brotherly concern. Taking her chin in his hand, he repeated more urgently, "Who is it? Do I know him? Is it LaMont Bristol? He was hanging around last time I was here."

Violet sucked her tongue against her teeth in an exclamation of disgust, dismissing that hopeful suitor. She pulled her chin free and looked back at the sea. After a moment of silence, she spoke a single word. "Bartholomew."

"Bartholomew?" Oliver repeated, astonishment nearly rendering him speechless. "Bartholomew Pembroke? Allegra's cousin?" He liked him well enough, probably because of his physical resemblance to Cecil, but he hadn't considered him at all able to win over his sister.

Apparently Violet thought otherwise. "You think he's dull," she said, turning toward him again. "But you are mistaken." She stared hard at him, as if daring him to defy her, but Oliver was still too shocked to protest. "He takes an interest in everything. He's inexhaustibly curious, and though he has a quiet way of putting things, his feelings are deep and true."

"If you say so," Oliver murmured, not wholly convinced.

"I do," Violet insisted. "I've never met anyone with a keener appreciation for life. You would see that yourself if you gave him a chance."

"Mmm, perhaps," Oliver conceded dryly, recovering his balance. "Tell me, then, if he is such a paragon, why are you sitting here moping while he is in England?"

Violet's shoulders slumped again. Little by little, she admitted the problem, explaining how Bartholomew was dependent on Sir Gerald for support. She spoke candidly about her birth, her breeding, the color of her skin, and about Bartholomew's inevitable disinheritance should he marry her. "Love isn't always enough," she concluded with more wisdom than Oliver imagined her to possess. "The world can present too many obstacles for love to overcome."

It was on the tip of Oliver's tongue to retort that an immoderate number of life's obstacles seemed to emanate from England. His usual disdain for the hypocrisy of the British social structure increased with Violet's revelations, and he would have condemned Bartholomew's part in it if he hadn't realized, in the nick of time, to do so would only make his sister feel more wretched and alone. He was familiar enough with those feelings to keep silent out of sympathy for her. He contented himself with slipping the frangipani blossom into her shiny curls and squeezing her small hand.

He was considerably less diplomatic in his conversation with Jamie, several evenings later. Never one to miss an opportunity for enjoyment, the redheaded lawyer had arrived on the weekly steamer for the boat launching the next day. They sat on the beach watching the full moon edge over Gun Point, a bottle of local white rum set companionably between them.

"Life can be so pleasant," Jamie sighed in satisfaction. He stretched out in the sand, his shoulders propped against the half-buried ribs of a long-abandoned boat. "Mankind gets so exercised about such trivial matters. What a waste of precious time." He reached for the bottle of jack, wrapped his fingers around its neck, then stopped, adding philosophically, "Although I suppose this cantankerous proclivity does supply me with a living."

"Uhn," Oliver responded noncommittally, taking his turn at the bottle.

"Uhn?" Jamie questioned lazily. "Does that mean you agree or disagree with me?"

"It doesn't mean a damned thing," Oliver replied, a trifle more testily than he had intended. "It was just to let you know that I am listening to your gabble."

Jamie cast a sharper eye on his friend. He didn't say anything for a moment, then quietly commented, "Still in a foul mood, eh?"

"And if I am?" Oliver answered, glaring his defiance.

"If you are, it's your own bloody fault," Jamie said with very little sympathy. He rolled over on one elbow and glared back at Oliver. "Do you think I don't know what is gnawing away at you? Do you think I don't know you are in love with Allegra? You're a fool, Oliver MacKenzie," he said, shaking a finger at him. "You are a stubborn, unromantic fool. You drove away a magnificent woman, the only woman who could ever possibly tolerate your beastly behavior. You let her slip away."

"Rubbish," Oliver snapped, reaching again for the rum. "You have no notion of what you're saying. Morever," he added angrily, pointing the bottle at Jamie, "it is absolutely none of your concern."

"Of course it's my concern," Jamie replied, his indignation forcing him upright. "When my best friend goes around acting like it is three days to Armageddon, how can I not be concerned? A fine friend I'd be if I didn't care. Your happiness is an important matter to me." Nodding his head righteously, he added, "As is Allegra's."

More touched by this admission than he wanted to acknowledge, Oliver responded gruffly, "In any event, I did not drive her away. She went by her own choice. She had it fixed in her mind that she could make a success of that chocolate factory of Cecil's, despite all the sane and sensible advice I gave her to the contrary. My opinion was of no interest to her, so I'm forced to wash my hands of the whole affair."

If he thought that explanation would end Jamie's attack, he was mistaken. "I thought you were in love with her," the Scotsman said scornfully. "It's a poor sort of love, by my measure, that lets you abandon Allegra just when she needs you most. If it means so much to her to make a success of Cecil's business, then you should be helping her to put it on its feet, not prophesying its failure. I don't wonder that she chose to go to England without you, considering your gloom-and-doom attitude."

Stung by Jamie's continued offensive, Oliver retorted with asperity, "I said she chose to go to England. I did not say she chose to go without me. At the last moment she asked me to come along, even though she knows it's against all my principles ever to set foot on English soil again."

"Allegra asked you to accompany her and you *refused*?" Jamie was aghast. "Oliver, you are a bigger fool than I first thought. You rejected the love of a beautiful, lively, imaginative woman, an extraordinary woman, for the sake of some pig-headed principles?" He shook his own head in disbelief. "Och, man, wake up. Don't you know that principles make a cold, empty substitute for Allegra? For once in your life, you should put aside your damned logic and just follow your heart." He soothed his outrage with a swallow of jack, passed the bottle across the sand, then asked, "You do have a heart, don't you?"

"Don't talk nonsense," Oliver replied in a subdued voice. "Of course I do."

He refrained from saying anything else, but the conversation was far from forgotten. By the end of the evening, and the bottom of the bottle of jack iron, Oliver's attitude was changing. Lying in bed that night, images of Allegra swimming on waves of rum, the last of his obduracy vanished. Jamie was right, he admitted, stretching his arm across his forehead. So was Allegra. "If I love her, I should be with her," he said out loud. "And I do love her."

Confession of that simple fact released him. The dozens of self-serving excuses that had been distorting his perspective disappeared, replaced by his usual straightforwardness. He had demanded that Allegra accept who he was, respect his wants and needs, without ever returning the favor. Instead of accepting who she was, he had insisted she conform to his standards. Instead of accepting that he loved her precisely because she was impetuous, impulsive, spontaneous, and unpredictably alive, he had expected her to behave with a prudence of spirit he would have found dull.

He had, indeed, abandoned her when she needed him most, as Jamie had so unceremoniously pointed out. Despite her proud declarations of independence and her staunch assurances that she would succeed, she did need, if not his practical help, then his moral support. This time she had needed not swimming lessons nor lifesaving, not a strong arm nor a mathematical mind. This time she had needed his love, and he had let her down.

Oliver rubbed his hand across his forehead, wishing he had not drunk quite so much rum. He wished also that he had not spurned Allegra's invitation quite so adamantly. After all, what was so difficult about going to England? He was no longer a schoolboy at the mercy of his upper-crust classmates, no longer an unproven youth, still vulnerable to the effects of condescension. So what if England were home to untold numbers of hypocrites and snobs? It was also home to Gilbert & Sullivan. And to Allegra. He finally drifted off to sleep, relieved to have realized his mistake and resolved to remedy it. As soon as his schooner was launched, he would unearth his tweed jackets and take passage on the next steamer bound for England.

Despite his late night and the quantities of rum he had imbibed, Oliver was up at dawn the next day, attending to the details of the launching. Over the years and after hundreds of boats, a certain ceremony had evolved for setting them safely in the water. It was part African, part Anglo, but mostly West Indian. Whoever owned the vessel, black, white, or some combination of each, followed the same time-honored ritual.

In the early hours, observed only by Oliver and its builders, the new schooner received its first blessing. To ward off evil spirits, a "libation" of rum was poured on the white cedar deck and grains of rice were scattered about. Five chickens were killed in the galley, in hope that the larder would always be full. A ram was slaughtered over the stern, so the schooner would be butted along by favorable winds, and a sheep was butchered on the bow to ensure an easy helm. After more libations were poured over the sacrificed animals, they were passed down to the huge "coppers", or cauldrons, to be cooked for the afternoon feast.

A second blessing took place a little later in the morning. Watched by a gathering crowd and accompanied by ten serious "godparents", an Episcopal priest climbed to the deck and intoned prayers and benedictions. He, too, sprinkled liquid on the deck, though his was holy water, not rum. Finally, and with a great deal of flourish, he performed the most eagerly anticipated act of the entire ceremony. Pulling a loosely tied string, he unfurled the ship's burgee, revealing its name for the very first time. While the crowd cheered in general jubilation, and Jamie grinned in specific glee, a hastily stitched banner reading *Stella Confections* fluttered free in the breeze. Oliver felt a surge of warmth at the sight.

Gods supplicated and spirits appeased, the actual work of the launching began. Axe men armed with finely honed hatchets and directed by Angus chopped away at the poles that propped up the schooner. "Cutting down" the supports from the bottom barely above sand level, they gradually lowered the boat to its side, until it rested on a bow plank nailed in place especially for this purpose. Block and tackle, rigged between a big anchor buried at sea and the boat on shore, inched it slowly over log rollers laid on the beach. To the rhythm of sea chanteys and the encouragement of the crowd, and lubricated by vast quantities of jack, the *Stellar Confections* was hauled to her home in the water.

Oliver threw himself into the work, sweating and straining and feeling hopeful for the first time in weeks. When the schooner finally floated upright, a feeling of exhilaration filled him, as if he had launched not only a new boat, but also a new phase of his life. By midafternoon he was in high spirits, hungrily eating the spicy hot stews being ladled from the coppers and joining the dancing taking place on the beach.

"Oliver," Violet said, tugging his sleeve to get his attention when he stopped to catch his breath and joke with Claude Baptiste. "Oliver, please come and talk to me."

"What is it, sis?" Oliver asked happily, laying an affectionate arm over her shoulders. "I haven't seen you dancing today. Still too sad?"

"Please, Oliver," Violet said more urgently. "Please, I must talk to you."

"Yes, yes, I'm coming," Oliver said, not moving from where he stood. "Do you remember Claude Baptiste, Violet? From L'Eterre? He's the mate on my freighter and has just three days ago returned from a trip to England. In a week's time, he'll turn around and head back."

"Of course she remembers me," Claude answered for her. He was a short sturdy man whose amiable smile was missing a few teeth. "I brought her a package only today, all tied up in string like a Christmas pig. A very fine gentleman in England gave it to me."

Oliver looked quickly at Violet for an explanation of this surprising news. Her cheeks darkened a shade, but all she said was, "Please come."

Curious now, Oliver willingly followed her away from the boisterous crowd around a bend of the beach. Under a palm tree by an immense pile of cured conch shells, they stopped and perched on an upturned dory. "What's this about?" he asked. "Is that the package?" He tapped the swath of brown paper Violet had laid in her lap.

Blushing again, she reached inside the wrapping and withdrew a pink and white oval box whose lid was beautifully painted with ribbons. Almost reverently, she opened it up, revealing in a nest of Swiss lace and pale green satin a picture-perfect chocolate Easter egg. Spun sugar vines swirled around its dark middle, pastel posies sprayed over its top. A tiny card, tucked under its edge and tied with a gold satin bow read, "I love you."

"It's from Bartholomew," Violet said unnecessarily.

"So it is," Oliver said, laughing in delight. "And it's starting to melt. Claude must have stored it in the ice box or else it would have been chocolate syrup by this time. It's a good thing Easter is only a few days away. You can gobble it fast before it turns into a puddle."

"I couldn't eat it." Violet was horrified. "It's too beautiful."

"You'd best eat it," Oliver said practically. "It won't be beautiful for long. If you have trouble, I'm sure Iris and Lily will gladly give you a hand. It is a pretty thing, though, I will say." His tone grew more more meditative as he stared at the egg. "It would seem that she's doing a good job, wouldn't it?" His question was addressed more to himself than to Violet, as it occurred to him he might have waited too long, that Allegra might no need him after all.

"That's what I wanted to tell you," Violet said, shoving the lid back on the box and sticking it back in its package. She folded her hands on top of it and looked anxiously at her brother "Bartholomew wrote me a letter, too," she said almost tentatively.

"Good news?" Oliver forced his mind back to Violet.

"Well—" She hesitated, not knowing how to phrase it.

"Don't tell me he's cutting you off, after that lavish declaration of his feelings," Oliver asked, misinterpreting her hesitation "Surely, he's given you some sign of encouragement."

"Oh no, no," Violet answered quickly. "I mean, yes, he has Somewhat. But that isn't what I wanted to say."

"What is it, Violet?" Oliver asked quietly, a flash premonition sending a chill down his spine.

"It's Allegra," Violet finally blurted out, looking at Oliver with pain in her eyes. "Bartholomew said that almost as soon as they arrived in London, they discovered Cecil had borrowed another sum of money." She gulped, then added, "And secured it with his share of L'Etoile."

As her brother stiffened, she reached out a sympathetic hand nd set it on his arm. "The creditor has been very generous, hough," she went on, a quaver in her voice. "Not only has he not alled in the loan, he's offered unlimited additional amounts to efurbish the factory. Bartholomew said he comes by every day or wo to see what they're doing and to invite Allegra out to the heater and concerts. He said he's quite charming."

Her eyes dropped and so did her hand. "Oliver," she said nhappily. "He's Roland Hawkes."

Oliver stood up abruptly and stalked down the beach, his fists alled up and jammed in his pockets. He was furious. Not pee-ish and prickly, not irritable from self-pity, but truly and purely urious, a rare and awesome state. The elation that had buoyed im a short while ago was gone as completely as if it had never xisted. In its place burned a sense of bitter betrayal, a jealousy ade all the more venomous because he hated himself for feeling , because Allegra didn't deserve it.

Not only had she forgotten about him in a matter of weeks, ut she had replaced him with the one man in the world he most espised. Roland Hawkes. She had turned misfortune into musement, another of Cecil's debts into revenge. She was re-aying him for rejecting her plea to come to England. She was nowing him, clearly and cruelly, that she could manage without m. Although his lips were clamped grimly closed, a steady ream of oaths shouted through Oliver's mind. He called Allegra very name he could think of, cursing the moment she had ap-eared in Grenada, turning the pain of his hurt into a wrathful tack.

When he couldn't think of any other epithets to hurl at her, he arted in as mercilessly on himself. He had been a fool to trust er, an idiot to fall in love with her. He whirled in the sand and rode back the way he had come, still storming inside. How lossally stupid of him to have been taken in by those wide olet eyes, by that ingenuous air. How blind of him not to see e was cut from the same selfish cloth as Cecil.

He kicked out savagely at a derelict fish trap, sending it flying to a dozen bamboo shards. He was unspeakably disgusted with mself for being swayed by the sentimental rubbish Jamie had poused last night. Allegra's deceit was all the more devastating cause of the hope he had allowed to build. That's what came of serting his principles, he castigated himself, of backing down

on things in which he believed. He'd learned a hard lesson, but
would never happen again.

"Where are you going, Oliver?" Violet asked worriedly
struggling to keep up with him, her package clutched to he
chest. "What are you going to do?"

Oliver didn't answer her, he scarcely heard her. He was to
intent on finding Jamie among the festive throng on the beach
He had to inform his solicitor that his half of L'Etoile was for sal
to the first bidder.

It no longer mattered who would eventually win the battle fc
the other half: Roland Hawkes or Allegra or her snobbish uncle
One prospective partner was as intolerable as the next. He didn
want anything more to do with Cecil's estate. Or with Cecil
daughter. It was time, past time in fact, to cut his losses once an
for all and be rid of Pembroke et fille.

Chapter
Eighteen

At ten in the morning on Allegra's twenty-sixth birthday, she opened the door of Pembroke et Fille. Despite the heavy sense of gloom that had been hanging over her since that afternoon in the park, this particular moment brought an air of celebration that even thoughts of Roland couldn't mar. The shop was just as she had imagined it, an exact rendering of her ideas, a perfect execution of her goals. She had wanted to create an atmosphere evocative of chocolate, of the vibrant tropics where it began and of the opulent palaces where it was considered precious. She had wanted to convey a sense of its rich taste, its intriguing history, its magical appeal. Looking around with swelling satisfaction, she knew she had achieved her objective.

The walls were painted a gradually lightening shade of rose, the color of a Caribbean dawn. Clouds crowded the ceiling and drifted into corners. Huge potted palms and a hibiscus in full bloom stood on the thick green carpet, the same muted hue as the jungle floor. On small round-topped tables and lace-draped stands sat artfully arranged tableaux. On one, a sepia-toned photograph of L'Etoile in a silver filigreed frame leaned against an exquisite porcelain chocolate pot surrounded by delicate cups and saucers. Atop another, aromatic and highly polished cocoa beans spilled out of a crystal jar and scattered across an embroidered linen napkin.

Along the marble counters and in the glass cases at the back of the shop was the crowning display: the chocolates. Endless shapes, sizes and varieties of chocolates. They sat in meticu-

lously straight rows or piled into heaps, in careful circles o
silver trays or rolling out of overturned bowls. They were stacke
in boxes, set in pleated paper cups, placed daintily on doilie:
and perched on tall-stemmed epergnes.

There were butter cremes and coffee cremes, rose, orang
vanilla, and violet cremes. There were chocolate-dipped cherrie
and caramels and candied citrus peels. Molded chocolates in th
shapes of feathers, fans, shells, flowers, and fruits. There we
chocolates studded with hazelnuts and walnuts and almonds, ha
moons filled with toffee, truffles drenched in champagne, choc
late bottles holding liqueurs and chocolate cups holding hothou:
strawberries. There were dark chocolates, white chocolates, ar
creamy fresh milk chocolates. There were pyramids, squares, ar
medallions. There were chocolates with smooth surfaces, choc
lates with textured surfaces, chocolates decorated with squiggle
lines, leaves, horses, and fleurs-de-lis. And there were the trad
mark, star-shaped chocolate mints.

Allegra's delight grew as customers came in, cautious a:
faintly curious when they stepped through the door but increa
ingly enchanted when they saw and smelled what was insid
They trailed back and forth in front of the cases, tantalize
tempted, totally taken. They pointed to their choices, more irr
sistible than the rest, and pretty clerks, wearing lace aprons ov
pink-and-white-striped dresses, lifted them into boxes or ba
and tied them up with bows. They went back out the door full
compliments and praise for Allegra, carrying home a few ounc
of the atmosphere, a sample of the chocolate spell.

Allegra was flushed with pleasure. No matter what else ha
pens, she thought, no matter what the future brings, I'll alwa
have this moment. Nothing can diminish it. I'll always know th
I started from Connecticut with only a few silly notions I
learned from novels and a hazy desire to somehow make a mar
and that for at least one moment, I did.

Gazing around the enchanting shop, she was overcome by t
same sense of pride that had filled her when she had mastered t
art of curing cocoa at L'Etoile. I took Cecil's inheritance a
turned it into this, she thought, standing very straight. From
encumbered cocoa estate and a failing chocolate factory, I creat
Pembroke et Fille. That is to say, she quickly amended, I did
with Bartholomew's help.

The thought of her cousin punctured Allegra's bliss. Po

Bartholomew wasn't here to see the culmination of their labors. Using one of his many imagined illnesses as an excuse, Sir Gerald had summoned Bartholomew to Sussex five days ago, selfishly robbing his son of the joy of seeing the shop successfully opened. And Bartholomew had gone. Not as compliantly as he once would have, but he had gone, nonetheless.

The luster lost from the day, Allegra moved away from the door. She picked a leaf off a palm tree and absently twisted it around her finger, staring out the window. Bartholomew was all she had left, congenial cousins bound together by their efforts in the chocolate business and by similar experiences of love found and lost on a lush island fifty-five hundred miles away.

We both should have stopped there, Allegra thought wearily, discarding the leaf. We should have stayed in Grenada, where we were happy and in love, instead of chasing after illusory ideals. Rubbing her hand across her forehead, Allegra wondered how long she would retain even this one last relationship, how long Bartholomew would remain her friend when he found out about Roland. He had left for Sussex the day before she had made the dreadful discovery, so he was still in the dark. But she couldn't keep it from him indefinitely.

While Allegra continued staring vacantly out the window, a carriage pulled smartly to the curb and Roland stepped out. She instinctively drew back, as if she could hide behind the hibiscus. The last thing she wanted right now was a confrontation with him. Ever since she had learned of his identity, Roland's respectful courtesy had vanished. It was as if he held the mortgage not only to her property, but also to her soul. While his manners remained smooth in public, in private he dropped all pretense of decorum.

"Allegra dear," Roland cried as soon as he entered. "My congratulations! What a splendid little shop."

The loudness of his voice made Allegra shrink in embarrassment; its underlying condescension made her shrivel. "Thank you," she managed to mutter and tried to make her way to the protection of the counter.

"You've worked a miracle, I'm sure," Roland continued, casually taking her arm. While one kid-gloved hand held her captive, his eyes swept around the shop. "Quite impressive," he said, his cold tone not matching his compliment. His gaze fastened on the steady stream of shillings and pounds being passed to the cashier. "Quite impressive," he repeated, more speculatively.

His fingers suddenly biting into her arm, he turned her to face an unoccupied corner. "I shall come around to the factory on Friday," he said, his voice considerably lower and completely stripped of all agreeableness. "I should like to introduce you to a man I think very well suited for the position of manager. Once you have met him, I am sure you will concur. See that you are in attendance at three."

"I won't," Allegra hissed fiercely, yanking herself free. A spark of her old spirit flared up as she answered him without thinking. "I won't hire another Albert Baker to run the business into bankruptcy."

"Tut tut," Roland said mockingly, taking a menacing step toward her. "What a naughty display of defiance. Must I remind you that I hold an overdue note, with your beloved cocoa estate named as collateral?"

"But I could repay you, if I just had some time," Allegra said desperately. "You can see how well the shop is being received. I should be able to raise the money for your loan in no time at all."

"'No time at all' is not the same as right now," Roland said more harshly, running out of patience. He took another step toward her. "Either you follow my advice, or I will foreclose on L'Etoile. Do you understand me?"

Defeated, her momentary resistance overwhelmed by cold, hollow failure, Allegra could only miserably seek escape. Her confidence destroyed, she stumbled awkwardly backward, colliding with the carved mahogany umbrella stand behind her. In an attempt to avoid knocking it over, she twisted quickly to catch it but, in righting it, lost her balance. She fell sideways, her arm flailing the air as the moss green carpet rose closer.

Then, suddenly, she was standing firmly on her feet and a strong arm was circling her waist. Oliver. She knew it instantly, even before she turned. As she had that day at Argo estate, she sensed him, caught the tropical scent clinging to him, felt the West Indian sunshine soaked into him. She whirled to face him, her heart pounding with joy, all else forgotten but the single fact that she loved him.

Whatever happy greeting was in her head never had the chance to spill onto her lips. Oliver did not seem to see her. Although one hand remained lightly under her elbow to steady er, his dark gaze was fixed intently on Roland's face. Allegra's ubilation changed quickly to anxiety as she looked from one man o the other.

She had often wondered, in the past few days, how she had ever found Roland attractive. Seeing him now in contrast with Oliver, her wonder and her worry increased. Though both men could rightly be called handsome, Oliver's cleanly cut features and straightforward expression were infinitely more appealing than Roland's pale, chiseled cheeks and narrow, tight mouth. The eyes, though, showed the difference.

While Oliver's dark blue eyes were unyielding, they were steady and calm, softened perhaps by some inner joke he was enjoying. In contrast, the golden green light in Roland's eyes shone with neither humor nor composure, but rather with an almost frenzied irritation at Oliver's intrusion. Allegra found herself holding her breath, afraid Roland would make an irrational move.

Oliver, however, seemed not to share that fear. In fact, his manner was detached and casual, as if his presence in the shop, indeed in England, were completely unremarkable. "My compliments, Miss Pembroke," he said pleasantly, withdrawing his hand and glancing her way. "Most lovely. Delightful."

Allegra's mouth dropped open in amazement, but he only nodded briefly and made his way up to the counter. She recognized him less now than when she had only sensed him. This well-mannered Oliver, wearing a waistcoat, a wing collar, and a necktie, was a stranger. He acted as if they were the most formal of acquaintances, as if his only interest in being here were to purchase a pound of chocolates.

If Allegra watched in astonishment as Oliver made his selection and paid the cashier, Roland watched in growing agitation. Already irritated that Oliver had interrupted his satisfying session of intimidating Allegra, he became further incensed that his former classmate had actually snubbed him. Oliver MacKenzie, the tradesman's son, had deliberately ignored the future Lord Fenwick, walking past him as if he were a lackey.

Unable to endure such a cut, Roland responded in kind. On Oliver's return, he arrogantly extended his silver-knobbed walking stick, effectively bringing Oliver to a halt. Oliver glanced down at the stick, then lifted his gaze to Roland's face, but other than raising his eyebrows in faint curiosity, he made no comment.

It was finally Roland who was forced to acknowledge his rival. Seething with fury, his voice just missed carrying the upper-class nonchalance and condescension he sought.

"My, my," he said. "You are the very last person I eve thought to see in England. I had supposed the colonial back waters had reclaimed you forever. Indeed, I never suspected yo capable of appreciating London's charms."

For a long moment, Oliver continued to stare at Roland When he finally spoke, his tone was mild, almost conversational "I find it quite fascinating," he said, "to discover how greatly w have misjudged one another. I, for example, never suspected yo capable of robbing a candy store." He calmly brushed Roland' stick aside, nodded again at Allegra, and walked out of the shop the dainty box of confections tucked underneath his arm.

Roland's pale cheeks turned an ugly, mottled red. It had bee years since he had come face to face with Oliver, years in whic' he had imagined his schoolboy rival grown slothful and stupid besotted with rum in the stagnant life of the colonies. Anythin but that had happened. Oliver seemed to have flourished in th Caribbean air, maturing into the man he had shown promise o being, still besting Roland at every turn.

And still winning the hearts of beautiful women. Perhap Oliver had missed it, but Allegra's reaction hadn't escaped Ro land's notice. Her face had been illuminated by Oliver's pres ence. He had seen that radiance before, the first day he had me her, when, lost in memories, she had described her partner i L'Etoile. He had guessed then that she was in love with Olive today's reaction confirmed it. His frustration mounted when h remembered how she had cringed in disgust from his kiss.

"This changes nothing," he spat angrily, wishing it were s "Do not think your darling Oliver will save you. I guarantee you'll both regret it if you go sniveling to him. We have a appointment for three o'clock Friday. See that you keep it. Barely restraining the desire to roughly push her aside, h stormed from the shop, slamming the door so hard an uneas moment of silence stilled the happy babble of voices.

Unable to cope with the moment, praying it would pass, All gra shut her eyes until the murmuring resumed. When she opene them again the shop's atmosphere had returned to normal, but h mind was still filled with confusion. It got no better as the afte noon wore slowly away. Although somehow she managed to m chanically smile, to accept felicitations, to answer questions, to offer samples, all she could think of was Oliver and Roland, Roland and Oliver.

She was genuinely frightened by Roland. Remembering the suppressed violence of his manner, the wild gleam in his eye when he was thwarted, she wondered to what dangerous extremes he would pursue his obsessive quest for revenge. She worried that he would not be content just to take L'Etoile, but that he would harm Oliver, as well.

She gulped again, thoughts of Oliver bringing her near tears. Though at first she had been puzzled by his seeming disinterest in her, then hurt by his indifference to the unequivocal love she longed to offer him, she now mercilessly admitted that she deserved such treatment. Why should he pay any attention to me when I betrayed him so vilely? she thought. Why should he want my love when I managed to jeopardize, in a few willful weeks, what he has spent long years building? I'm a jinx, she thought glumly. A Judas. Cecil and I, both.

All afternoon her thoughts went back and forth between Roland and Oliver, between fear and self-recrimination. By the time she closed the door on the last enchanted customer and dragged herself home, Allegra was physically exhausted and emotionally drained. As she climbed the brick steps of her lodgings, studiously careful not to catch her hem on the bootscraper, she wanted only to get into bed and pull the covers over her head. She wanted to block out this day, to find refuge from her haunting reflections in the oblivion of sleep.

Her landlady, Mrs. Callahan, intercepted her in the front hall, an almost girlish blush brightening her withered cheeks. "There's a gentleman to see you, Miss," she said, smiling and cocking her head toward the parlor. "A handsome gentleman he is, too. From the West Indies, he said."

Oliver. Allegra felt her heart first soar, then sink. She wanted to see him, but didn't have the courage to confront him. "Please make my excuses," she said hurriedly. "Tell him I have a headache." The next instant she put out her hand to stay Mrs. Callahan, saying nervously, "No, don't tell him that. I'll go in."

Oliver rose when she entered the parlor, his tall body and outdoor aura at odds with the fussy, overcrowded decor. A tender smile filled his face at the sight of her. "I've missed you, Allegra," he said without ceremony.

"Oh, dear," she replied, keeping a tiny table with three separate skirts and a goldfish bowl between them. If he had said that when she had first seen him, she would have thrown herself into his arms, heedless of anything but how much she loved him. Having had the afternoon to brood over his tepid greeting, to blame herself for the peril she had placed him in, her response was more inhibited. She felt bewildered by the warmth in his direct words.

Oliver frowned at her restrained reaction, concerned by the change he suddenly saw. Although her face was as lovely as he remembered it, and framed by a golden fluff of undisciplined curls, her eyes were different. Still wide and nearly violet blue, they no longer shone with innocent optimism, with impetuous enthusiasm for life. They seemed sad, her magnificent spirit dampened. She looked almost lost.

"I don't want to be separated from you anymore," he told her, trying to reach beyond her despair. "Either by the Atlantic Ocean or by a silly quarrel. Or by a fish in a jelly jar." He rounded the table to be near her.

"No," Allegra said quickly, holding up her hands as if to ward him off. She dodged behind a gilded birdcage so precipitously its yellow-feathered occupant chirped in alarm. For a fraction of an instant his brief speech had inspired her, his familiar, frank affection made her pulse pound, but that moment faded. "No," she repeated more severely with a certain touch of tragedy. "No, don't deserve such devotion. I'm like the Ancient Mariner's albatross. I've only brought you trouble and grief." Unable to look him in the eye when she said it, she added, "You are better off without me."

"Why don't you let me be the judge of that," Oliver answered relieved to see, at least, that her sense of drama was unaffected even if it was propelling her in the wrong direction. He started to circle the birdcage, but when she hastily backed up, he stopped afraid she would trip in this bric-a-brac jungle and break her beautiful neck before he could intervene.

"No doubt you are referring to Roland Hawkes," he said standing deliberately still. "I know all about it. I know about the debt, about the money Cecil borrowed from him, mortgaging his share of L'Etoile. I know that Hawkes has continually offered you additional loans, hoping to get you more deeply obliged to him. Allegra, I know that he has charmed you, as he is quite capable of doing, and taken you about town."

Allegra looked at him again, put off-guard by this announcement, and by the matter of fact way he made it. "You do?" she asked incredulously.

Oliver nodded and took a trial step toward her. When she stepped back again, he stopped once more. "Bartholomew wrote to Violet and told her everything. When I first heard it, I was bloody furious," he said honestly, remembering his rage on the beach. "I thought Bartholomew was a pompous little telltale and that you were . . ." He stopped himself before he repeated exactly what he had thought of her in that awful moment. "Well, that you were behaving in a less than honorable manner," he finished, smoothing over the matter with a small gesture.

"You were right," Allegra said in a small, stricken voice, clenching her hands together. "At least about me, you were. Bartholomew has no notion of any of this, even now. I'm sure he was just reporting things as accurately and factually as possible, which, you may remember, is the way he is."

"I remember," Oliver said wryly, folding his arms across his chest. "Although, at the time, it took Violet's pleas and all of Jamie's considerable skills as a solicitor to make me realize your cousin had probably never heard of Argo or of Lord Fenwick or even informed of the sorry history of this absurd feud. Once I could be made to understand that, it was a relatively easy step to deduce that you probably didn't know who Roland Hawkes was either."

"But I should have," Allegra said mournfully, not willing to let herself off so easily. "I should have checked on his background. It was stupid and careless of me not to have done so."

"Probably so," Oliver agreed, with his usual candor. "But it doesn't really matter. It was obvious by your expression in the shop this afternoon that you are now aware of his identity and you are no longer chums. Whatever it is that Hawkes is doing, or has done, is incidental. Unless he has changed since school, which I doubt, he is only a minor irritation, which we can eliminate handily. I'll help you."

"Why should you?" Allegra asked, questioning not Oliver's chivalry but her own worthiness.

"Because I want to," Oliver answered simply. "Because I came here precisely to do so."

"You did?" Allegra was thrilled at the thought. The idea th[a] he had come to England against all his principles, just to be wi[th] her and help her, almost swayed her, as did his powerful pre[s] ence. It was hard to resist his healthy, handsome face, his humo[r] ous blue eyes, his full mouth, tender though twitching to gri[n] But she did.

"I can't let you," she said, moving another step away fro[m] him for good measure. "I can't expect you to be responsible f[o] my predicament." She was so convinced she had betrayed hi[m] so sure she had done him an unforgivable wrong, even Oliv[e] himself couldn't change her mind. The same force that made h[e] so relentlessly positive, when she seized on an idea, was no[w] working in reverse. Though her heart soared at the mere sight [o] him, solid and sure, though it pounded happily at his no-nonsen[s] declaration of feeling, she was too wound up, too firmly set [o] her present course, to alter her direction.

Then, too, there was another force at work. Way down at t[h] bottom of her thoughts, stubbornly resisting both Roland's da[rk] threats and Oliver's entreaties, there was a spark of her origin[al] ambition. Fanned by the sense of pride and accomplishment s[he] had felt in the shop this morning, it refused to be extinguishe[d] She still wanted to prove, despite Oliver's and William's a[nd] Jamie's ideas to the contrary, despite Roland's efforts to sabota[ge] her, that she could make a success of Pembroke et Fille. She st[ill] wanted to prove that with only her loyal cousin's assistance, s[he] could redeem her father's name and establish her own. "I can't l[et] you," she repeated.

"Allegra," Oliver said, perturbed that she was moving furth[er] away from him, "you must. You forget that I *am* responsible f[or] your predicament. After all, it's not you that Roland Hawk[e] wishes to hurt, but me. You are just a convenient means for hi[m] to achieve that end. Whatever difficulties he has created for y[ou] are more my fault than yours, and I want to help you resol[ve] those difficulties."

Seeing again the almost mad look in Roland's eyes when [he] warned her against running to Oliver for help, Allegra didn't da[re] allow herself to be persuaded. "No," she said, shaking her hea[d] "I may only be the means to his end, but I didn't have to be [so] foolish as to let him use me for that purpose."

Oliver stared at her, not sure of how to proceed. He was exa[s] perated by her obstinacy, but he wasn't aware of the irony of all. Not so long ago, after accusing her of foolishness and lack of caution, they had argued because he wouldn't give her any help. Now, while he was excusing those very same qualities, they were arguing because she wouldn't accept any.

The longer they stood there in fidgety silence, the more frustrated Oliver became. He was sure she loved him. He had seen it in her face earlier today. He knew that she needed him. Roland Hawkes wasn't her problem alone. But he didn't know how to reach her. "Well," he finally said, a bit more astringently than he intended, "I certainly didn't come over five thousand miles to stand in an overstuffed parlor looking at a bird in a cage and a fish in a dish. I left prettier ones, free, in Grenada." He waited one more second to see if she would respond. When she only studied the floor, he left.

As soon as Oliver was out the door, Allegra lifted her eyes in pain. As awful as she felt in his presence, sure she had ruined his life, she felt more miserable alone. She stifled the urge to run out in the street and beg him to come back. For his sake, she couldn't. Instead, she dragged herself up to her room and buried herself in her bed, more wretched than she could ever remember. It was hard enough to have Oliver leave her because she had acted unpardonably. It was worse to have chased him away. Even if it were for his own good.

Chapter
Nineteen

Despite her weariness, Allegra did not sleep well that night. With the utmost reluctance she dragged herself from bed late the next morning. Having missed breakfast, indeed, most of her meals the day before, she stopped at a corner tea shop, lingering a long time over a few slices of toast. Finally forcing herself to confront business, she left six pence on the table and stepped out onto the street. The April sun was shining and the air was balmy but they neither threw a light on her problems nor warmed the chill in her spirit.

A detour to her shop was more beneficial, giving her another flush of satisfaction. A little more optimistic, Allegra continued on to the factory, hoping that Bartholomew had returned, released from Sir Gerald's selfish tyranny. She needed desperately to talk to him, to lay her problem on his desk so he could patiently pick it apart, line up all the pieces, and reduce them to unintimidating ratios and graphs.

Bartholomew was still away when she arrived early in the afternoon, but Bruno accosted her before she was halfway to the office. "Signorina," he said, holding out a small plate with some chocolate treats, "tell me what you think of these." It was an indication of how far they had come, from that first tray of samples; Bruno had dispensed with silver platters and lace doilies. He didn't even wait in anticipation while she tasted one but hurried off to test the fondant, confident that she would appreciate his creation.

Allegra carried the confections into the office and hung her

oat behind the door. Sitting on the edge of the desk, she picked
p a chocolate and took an appraising nibble. It was delicious.
Alternating layers of whipped hazelnut nougat and frothy choco-
ate creme were dipped in dark chocolate and topped with a sprin-
le of hazelnut dust. Bruno had done it again.

She was licking her fingers and eyeing the other five candies
vhen she became aware of someone standing in the doorway.
Looking up quickly, she saw Oliver leaning on the doorframe, an
mused expression on his face. Confused, she set the plate down,
wkwardly wiping her hands on her skirt. She started to rise, but
Oliver, seeing signs of incipient clumsiness, stopped her.

"Don't get up," he said, straightening rapidly, ready to spring
orward if needed. "You look quite content as you are. Besides
vhich, I won't stay long enough to interrupt your feast. I have an
ppointment at half one with Cecil's solicitor. I only came by to
ring you a caller."

Allegra's hands flew to her hips and the demand to know what
usiness he had with her father's lawyer was on her lips, but she
ound her indignation aimed at empty air. Oliver was gone. Her
nger was barely subsiding when another face peeked around the
oor. "Violet!" she cried, leaping to her feet, her pique and all
er problems forgotten.

"Hello, Allegra," Violet said, a smile wiping the tentative
ok from her face. She stepped into the office and into Allegra's
mbrace. "I'm so glad to be here," she added, more softly.

Allegra heard the quiet fervor in her friend's words and under-
ood at once what they meant. She gave Violet an encouraging
g, then held her off, saying, "Bartholomew is going to be
rilled to see you." Her intuition was rewarded by a positively
eatific glow.

"Will he really?" Violet asked anxiously, grabbing Allegra's
ands for assurance. "I've been so uncertain. Is he here now?"

"Oh," Allegra answered, reality coming back with a kick.
No," she admitted, giving the small hands holding hers a con-
ling squeeze. "He's in Sussex with his father. But he should be
ck any day now."

It was Violet's turn to say, "Oh," as she dropped her hands,
sappointment clouding her face. "No matter," she said, forcing
rself to brighten. "I came to see you, too, Allegra, and we shall
ve a good visit, you and I."

Impressed by Violet's composure, Allegra quickly pulled her

own thoughts together. "We'll send him a telegram this minute,"
she said decisively. "I'm sure Sir Gerald doesn't really need him
We'll tell him to come at once." Another radiant smile mad
Allegra glad the idea had occurred to her.

Waving Violet into the spare chair and pushing the plate to
ward her, she said, "Sit down and have one of these chocolate
while I write the telegram. I'll send one of the boys with it imme
diately."

Violet dutifully sat where she was told but leaned forward, he
anxiety returning. "Do you think it's the right thing to do?" sh
asked, her eyebrows knitting in doubt. "Perhaps he'll be angry
upset that I've come."

"Angry?" Allegra asked, astonished. "Bartholomew? Don't b
ridiculous. He is going to be beside himself with joy. The onl
time he is truly happy is when he is with you. He told me s
himself."

That made Violet sit up straighter, another smile smoothin
her brow. "Yes?" she said happily.

Allegra nodded vigorously. "Absolutely," she said. "Why, l
is miserable without you, only half alive. Sometimes I'll catc
him just staring into the air, a lonely look on his face." Sh
nodded again and turned her attention back to the telegran
"You'll see. This will be the best thing that ever happened f
either of you."

Sighing in relief, Violet finally settled back in her chai
"That's what Oliver told me, too," she said. Reaching for a cho
olate, she failed to see Allegra's head shoot up in sudden interes
"He said that it's a terrible thing to have to face each new d;
when the person you love is thousands of miles away, when y
are kept apart by senseless conventions and hollow principles."

"Oliver said that?" Allegra asked, thoughtfully tapping a pe
cil against her chin. It sounded like an echo of her own advice
Bartholomew, the advice that made her realize her love for Oliv
was greater than an ocean or an argument. It also sounded li
what Oliver had said to her yesterday, words she had been t
wound up to hear. Repeated now, in a less emotionally charg
atmosphere, they made a definite dent in her obstinate refusal
let him forgive her. Her spirits lifted.

"Um-hm," Violet answered, her mouth full of chocolate a
her mind put at ease. "Allegra, this is delicious! I'm sure it's t
best thing I've ever eaten."

Despite wanting to ponder her discovery, and ask Violet for more news of Oliver, Allegra responded to the compliment. "It's the best chocolate in England," she said proudly. "Maybe in all of Europe." She jumped up, saying, "Come. I'll show you how it's made. The process is positively fascinating. And I'll introduce you to Bruno Pavese, our chocolatier. You can't believe what wonderful chocolates he invents. And later we'll go to the shop so you can see how beautiful it looks." Her words came tumbling out. Life was back in perspective; her indomitable optimism was restored.

Violet jumped up too, not the least bit surprised by Allegra's infectious enthusiasm. This was as it had always been. She did, however, cast a glance at the telegram lying on the desk, more interested in seeing it dispatched than in anything else. Allegra noticed her covert look and snatched up the paper. "Alfie Lewis is sweeping the storeroom," she said. "We'll send him over to the telegraph office." Violet smiled, ready for the chocolate tour, the only obstacle to her complete attention removed.

Despite Allegra's declarations to the contrary, Violet was not wholly fascinated by the giant machines that paddled and stirred cauldrons and troughs of rich, liquid chocolate. But she was impressed by her friend's knowledge and zeal, and most of all, by Bartholomew's considerable contributions. The realization that Pembroke et Fille had been as much a part of his life these past months as it had been of Allegra's kept her interested. She nodded and murmured as Allegra explained over the noise of the churning equipment about conching and tempering and filling and shaking and dipping, as she described the new methods they had instituted, the costs they had cut, the unnecessary machines they had sold, the necessary ones, like the steam boiler, they had patched and repaired.

It wasn't until they reached the packing area that Violet's eyes really lit up in appreciation. Racks and racks of exquisitely tempting chocolates sat perfuming the air, waiting to be slipped into beautiful boxes. Allegra laughed indulgently, very familiar with the rapturous daze that came when confronted by this tantalizing array. "Try whatever one you fancy," she urged. "Try more than one. They are all equally delicious."

"I'll just pick out one for now," Violet said without taking her eyes off the candies. "But perhaps I'll take another one for tea." She trailed up and down the rows, deliberating long and hard.

"Violet," Allegra said, interrupting her careful review, "let m
introduce you to Bruno Pavese, who is responsible for the
treasures. Perhaps he can help you choose. Signor Pavese, this
Miss Violet MacKenzie."

Violet tore her eyes away from the chocolates long enough
meet their creator. "*Molto piacere, signorina*," Bruno said, bov
ing low in her direction. "It is a pleasure to be acquainted wi
the young lady for whom I made the Easter egg. Now I can s
why Signor Bartholomew was so demanding. For *una donna be
lissima*, only *una bellissima* confection will do."

His extravagant compliment brought a confused blush to Vi
let's cheeks. "Thank you," she stammered.

"*Perfetta*," Bruno murmured, staring at her face and claspi
his gnarled hands together in enchantment. "You are the pictu
of tropical beauty, like an orchid flower. Let me suggest to y
the seashell filled with coconut and rum, inspired by your *isola*
the sun. There is a tray that has just come from the hardeni
room."

"Oh yes," Violet agreed immediately. "I must have one
those. They sound wonderful." She followed Bruno's finger
the end of the line of tables where an apple-cheeked girl w
arranging the chocolate tritons in boxes. For a moment, she j
stood watching in mouth-watering admiration.

"Take one," Allegra said, and Violet reached out her hand.

In that instant a tremendous sound exploded through the air
deafening, heart-stopping noise. Almost simultaneously came
shriek of tearing lumber, of thick floorboards being viciou
ripped apart. A metal valve from the old steam boiler, wicke
mangled and twisted, came shooting up from the basement. W
terrifying speed and intensity, it slashed through a foot-wide r
ber belt running from the drive shaft to the shaking machine. T
belt whipped across the room, missing Violet's head by inch
but whacking into the cabinet next to her with such sudden fo
the commode tilted forward, its doors flying open and its conte
hurling out.

Allegra screamed in alarm and stretched desperately tow
her friend, but too late to avert disaster. Dozens of lead molds
bunnies and roses and half-moons and hearts spewed out of
cabinet and fell exactly where Violet was standing, her hand s
extended toward the shell-shaped chocolate. There was the si

ning sound of a bone snapping, then Violet lay unconscious on
he floor.

The next instant it was all over except for the hiss of escaping
team and the chug of belts and shafts as the machinery ground to
halt. In the eerie quiet, Allegra could hear her own sobs of fear
s she tripped over heaps of dented molds and fell to her knees
eside the deathly still body of Violet. Blood was pouring down
er face, no longer the color of toasted coconut, but now an
minous shade of gray. Her right arm, the arm that had reached
ut toward the candy, was twisted at an odd angle, the skin very
ut.

The frightening sight filled Allegra with dread, completely
aralyzing her. She sat on her haunches, unable to act. A circle of
unned workers gathered around them, standing equally as dumb
nd useless. Fortunately, Bruno was not as immobilized by
ock. He lowered his crooked body onto the floor, and, with the
lge of his apron, wiped the stream of blood from Violet's eyes,
acing it back to a rapidly swelling wound near her hairline.
oking his bent fingers into Violet's neck, he felt for a pulse.
hen he nodded.

"*Non si preoccupa, signorina*," he soothed Allegra. "Do not
orry. She is still very alive. The head, it always makes much
ood."

His words, puncturing the silence, seemed also to break the
sabling spell. Allegra's enormous sigh of relief was lost in an
cited babble of voices, but her quick commands a moment later
se above it. The wits that had so totally deserted her came
shing back as she snapped out orders.

"Mrs. Dalrymple, fetch me a blanket from the cloak room.
ey Godwin, run and get a doctor. There's one I've seen on
rlyle Street. Tell him to come right away. Signor Pavese, let
e have your apron, please."

While she was making a clumsy bandage around Violet's
ad, she said, "Oh, yes. Someone had better go down to the
sement to see what damage has been done. Good God!" Chills
nt down her spine as another appalling thought came to mind.
he stoker! He's always down there." Torn between this fresh
ar and her reluctance to leave Violet for even a moment, she
d, "Mr. Bradford, you'd better take some men and go have a
k. Hurry!"

It was dark, damp evening when Allegra climbed back into

the bed she had left so unwillingly hours earlier. She was ex
hausted in every bone and fiber of her body, weary down to th
bottom of her soul. But, as it had last night, sleep refused t
come to erase the horror of this day. She had moved through
admirably, and, except for that one frozen moment, with assu
ance and authority, doing what had to be done. Now that it wa
over and she was all alone in her dim room with no one depend
ing on her for comfort or courage, she could assess the situatio
And succumb to the bleakness of its consequences.

Violet would heal quickly enough. Though she had broken h
arm and suffered a concussion, they were clean, uncomplicate
injuries that her young body, full of West Indian sunshine, cou
easily conquer. Jeremy Jones, the stoker, had, by another mir
cle, been visiting the W.C. when the boiler had blown. Thoug
pasty-faced with fright, he was physically unharmed.

It was Allegra who was irreparably hurt. There were no vis
ble bruises, but she was deeply wounded. Once the heiress to
tropical estate, once the creator of a brilliant business, once,
least, a comfortable and secure American woman, she had lc
everything. Now she had to look for any employment, a job as
shop clerk or a servant, whatever it took to put a roof over h
head and food on her plate.

If there had been even a glimmer of hope that she could m
neuver her way around Roland, that he might possibly be pe
suaded to give her time to pay back her debt, that hope had be
extinguished today. Time was no longer enough. She need
money. And she had none. The old boiler could be patched
more; it needed to be replaced. The floor needed to be repaire
new belts needed to be bought, the molds needed to be reca
She had no money for any of it, and without the boiler that r
the machines that made the chocolate, she had no way of raisi
it, either.

Sir Gerald would take whatever capital could be gleaned fr
the sale of the chocolate-making equipment as partial compens
tion for his loan. Roland would take L'Etoile. She would ha
nothing. And no one.

Undoubtedly, Bartholomew would find little time for her n
that Violet was in London. His attention would be taken up w
the woman he loved. No longer having the factory as a comm
goal, he would drift away from Allegra, disappointed that l
ability to survive had been only an illusion.

And Oliver. Bitter, hot tears streaked down her cheeks and soaked her pillow as she remembered how he had looked this afternoon when he had returned to the factory and found his sister lying on the floor. His suntanned face had been stern, his full mouth grim. He had lifted Violet into his arms and had carried her to the waiting ambulance, hardly glancing at Allegra as he swept past her. Now he would wash his hands of her, disgusted with her on two accounts. His philosophical musings about love would be overwhelmed by his fury at finding himself with Roland for a partner and by her carelessness where Violet was concerned. This time, for sure, she had lost him.

The only one she had left was her father, the made-up memory of a man she had never met. Cecil, in whose adventurous and exciting footsteps she had longed to follow, whose imaginative and impulsive personality she had inherited, whose reputation as an impractical and irresponsible man she had wished to clear. She still had him left, she was still his daughter. And now they were both dismal failures.

Chapter
Twenty

With a reluctant sigh, Bartholomew handed the reins of his horse to the groom and steeled himself to reenter the house. The April afternoon was balmy and bright, but the air inside Pembroke Hall would be stuffy, the light dim. He had ridden into the village to retrieve a new bottle of pills for his father. It was an errand any one of the servants could have done, but he had used it as an excuse to have a few hours to himself.

He had been here almost a week, and the days had been long and tedious. No longer accustomed to sitting idly about, he had needed an outlet for his energy. A gallop across the greening downs before turning his horse's head toward the apothecary had served nicely. Nor was he as stoic as he had once been about spending endless afternoons and evenings listening to his father's list of ailments and complaints. The solitary sound of his horse's hooves on the spring grass had been welcome.

As he crossed the foyer and headed for the stairs, Hodges intercepted him. "A telegram has arrived for you, sir," the butler said, holding out a silver salver bearing a single envelope.

"Thank you, Hodges," Bartholomew said, picking up the cable. He opened the envelope as he went, only mildly curious. Its message arrested him in midstep.

"Come at once," the telegram read. "Violet is here in London —stop—Allegra."

The words seemed too unbelievable to be real. Then, with a leap of his heart, he accepted them. Violet was in London, only a few hours away. He took the stairs two at a time and ran down the hall and into his room, where he hauled his portmanteau from his closet. With a highly unusual lack of order, he stuffed it full of shirts and ties and toiletries. If he hurried, he could make the 6:45 train and be on Violet's doorstep in the morning. As he feverishly grabbed garments from his drawers, his mind kept singing the same joyous refrain. Violet was in London. Violet was in London. In less than a day he would see her and hold her again.

"Excuse me, sir," came Hodges's imperturbable voice from the doorway. Bartholomew whirled to see the butler holding out another envelope on the silver salver. "This has just arrived for you, sir." With the same gladness of spirit Bartholomew seized the second telegram, sure it was an impatient reminder from his cousin. There was a fond smile on his face as he ripped open the envelope and unfolded the paper within.

"Shall I send Henderson in to finish packing for you, sir?" Hodges asked, professionally assessing the situation. His eyebrows rose fractionally as he scanned the haphazard pile of clothes. When a few seconds went by and there was no answer to his question, he glanced back to Bartholomew and was startled to see that his face had gone white. "Sir?" he asked, showing only the appropriate amount of concern.

Raising anguished eyes, Bartholomew stared unseeing at the butler. He held his hand to his forehead, as if physically coralling his wits. "Yes, please," he finally said, suddenly springing into action. "Yes, have Henderson come in at once. And please tell Thompson to bring the carriage around immediately. I must make the 6:45. I'm just off to see my father."

Pulling the bottle of pills from his pocket, he dashed down the hall to his father's room. Not caring if he woke him from a nap, he rapped loudly on the door and entered. "I've brought your medicine," he announced when he saw that Sir Gerald was awake, sitting up on his chaise with the newspaper. Ignoring the glare his father gave him for his unceremonious entrance, he said, "I've also come to tell you that I am leaving within the hour. I must return to town at once."

Already irked by Bartholomew's abruptness, the thought of his son's desertion further annoyed Sir Gerald. "What could possibly be so urgent as to tear you away from your infirm sire?" he demanded waspishly. "Is my suffering of so little consequence to you that you can blithely abandon me?"

For the first time in his life Bartholomew rebelled. "Your 'suffering'," he answered with little compassion, "is far more taxing on those seeking to ease it than on you yourself. But in all events, you are scarcely left to bear your dolors unattended. You are surrounded by staff employed to fulfill your every whim. My presence is unnecessary. Indeed, it might almost be considered superfluous."

Shocked but not subdued by this uncharacteristic exhibit of defiance, Sir Gerald peevishly remarked, "However many servants there may be in my hire, their ministrations can hardly be compared with those of my own flesh and blood. It is a sad pass that you place more importance on the diversions of town than on your filial duty. Your pursuit of pleasure has grown to reprehensible proportions, and if I am not mistaken, this unbecoming trait is directly attributable to your cousin's influence."

"You are *quite* mistaken," Bartholomew replied coldly, "on two accounts. Firstly, Allegra's influence has been of the most favorable nature, and secondly, it is not pleasure that calls me to London, but calamity. There has been an accident at the factory, a boiler explosion, and I must attend to it."

"Ha!" Sir Gerald pounced. "I predicted as much. I told that flighty girl of Cecil's that it was a hopeless proposition, an ill-advised operation doomed to failure. But she would have none of it. She has a head full of the same impractical rubbish that possessed her father.

"And you," he looked at his son accusingly, "for some unfathomable reason, have taken her part, encouraging her irresponsible fantasies. I fear she has you bewitched." He resettled himself on the chaise, rattling his newspaper irritably before adding, "I daresay it is the best thing for all concerned to have that benighted factory blow up, although I don't know how I'll ever get my money now."

For an instant, Bartholomew opened his mouth, an angry defense of Pembroke et Fille already formed, but he closed it again without saying a word. It was a futile exercise, and one he did not have time for. He turned and headed for the door.

"Was anyone hurt, by the by?" Sir Gerald called after him, suddenly realizing that Bartholomew really was leaving.

Bartholomew halted with his hand on the doorknob. "Yes," he answered stonily. "One person." He opened the door, stepped out, and closed it behind him. *One person*, he thought, as he raced down the hall. *Violet*.

Allegra's second wire hadn't said how seriously Violet had been injured, only that she had. All the long drive to the station and the interminable train ride to London, Bartholomew went through agonies imagining what might have happened. He endured nightmarish visions of Violet, torn and bloody, the vibrant life blasted out of her exquisite body. Memories of her taunted him, memories of her sweeping across the dance floor; moving efficiently around the breezy kitchen; lying naked and indolent by the lily pond, her slim body hot and gleaming in the sun.

He was terrified that Violet's injuries would take her away from him forever. No matter that they had been separated by thousands of miles and by social barriers, just knowing that Violet existed had sustained Bartholomew since the day he had met her. As long as she was alive, so was he.

It was late evening when he arrived in London, but heedless of the time he went straight to the address Allegra had named in her telegram. It was a small hotel, but one whose thick carpet, overstuffed lobby chairs, and polished mahogany panels spoke of comfort and elegance. "There is a Mr. Oliver MacKenzie in residence here, I believe," he said, approaching the desk clerk. "May have his room number, please."

The clerk, a slender fellow with a long nose and spectacles, gave Bartholomew a measuring stare. "It is past the hour for guests to receive callers in their rooms," he said priggishly. "If you would care to leave a message . . ."

"His room number!" Bartholomew roared, his patience snapping, his fist unconsciously balling on the blotter.

The clerk glanced nervously at the fist, then back at Bartholomew's expression. "Mr. MacKenzie is in suite number seven, on the second floor," he said grudgingly. "But there has been an accident and . . ." He found himself talking to Bartholomew's back.

When Oliver opened the door to suite number seven a few moments later, Bartholomew was immediately overwhelmed by a sensation of Grenada. Everything about the tall man in shirtsleeves standing in front of him reflected that tropical island, its vividness, its heat. He was reminded so sharply of Violet, he could scarcely keep from shoving his way into the room to find her.

"I apologize for the lateness of my call," he muttered, tripping over the stiff manners that had been bred into him. "I came straightaway, you know. As soon as I received the wire. The train was a bit delayed. Engine difficulty of some sort." He bit off his words and drew in his breath, willing himself to stop babbling.

"I came to inquire after Miss MacKenzie," he said, starting over. He could contain himself no longer. "How is she?" he blurted out.

For a long moment, Oliver just stood giving Bartholomew an assessing look, weighing, it seemed, his own impressions against his sister's opinion. Reaching a conclusion, he swung the door wider and beckoned Bartholomew into the sitting room. "She's broken her arm," he said, coming directly to the point. "And is slightly concussed from banging her head on the floor when she fell. There is a cut on her brow that bled quite profusely, no doubt weakening her, but it is actually superficial. Other than that, she has a few bruises that look nasty and probably feel worse, but are in no way grave."

Relief flooded Bartholomew so rapidly he felt momentarily dizzy. He set down his portmanteau to give himself time to recover, arranging it in the entryway until his pulse beat more normally. When he straightened again, he returned Oliver's steady gaze, understanding the other man's scrutiny, but feeling oddly unthreatened by it. Rather, he was strengthened by Oliver's frankness, refreshed by his lack of stultifying formality. "May I see her?" he asked, neither stuttering nor stumbling now.

"She's asleep," Oliver replied, nodding his head toward the door to her room. "The doctor gave her a sedative to help her through the shock. It's been quite effective." Seeing the disappointed look on Bartholomew's face, he added, "I suppose there's no harm in you looking in on her. Just don't wake her."

"No, I won't," Bartholomew promised, already halfway across the room as he spoke. He opened her door and stepped inside.

It was a large room with a big four-poster bed made up with white linen sheets and white lace pillow shams and a plush white satin duvet. Lying right in the middle of it, very small and very still, her right arm covered in a heavy plaster cast, a bandage taped to her forehead, was Violet. The only light in the room came from the open doorway, but it was enough to illuminate her. Despite Oliver's reassuring prognosis, she looked so frail that

Bartholomew's heart gave a lurch at the sight of her. Tears filled his eyes.

He sat down on a chair by her bed, his elbows on his knees, his chin on his hands, his eyes fixed on her face. A cloud of black curls was spread over the white pillow, giving her face a dramatic frame. Silky lashes fringing over smooth cheeks made it seem fragile. With a sudden gasp, Bartholomew buried his face in his hands, overcome by emotion. Five hours ago, he hadn't thought he would ever see her again. She had been a memory, a daydream, an impossible wish. Now, he swore he would never let her go. Not as long as she lived.

He raised his face again, wiped his eyes, and resumed his vigilant watch. Hoping the intensity of his thoughts would penetrate the awful barrier of her unconsciousness, he sent her silent messages. "You must recover," he told her. "You must." There were so many moments still to share with her, so many things they hadn't yet said. He couldn't lose her now. Not after he had finally found her.

He felt a hand on his shoulder and saw a shadow across the bed. Oliver was standing above him, motioning him away. Reluctantly, Bartholomew rose. He gave Violet one last glance and telegraphed her one last plea. Wanting to run his fingers over her delicate face, but afraid he would wake her, he smoothed a wrinkle from her sheet before walking quietly back into the sitting room.

As Oliver closed Violet's door behind him, he said gently, "Don't be overalarmed. She looks dreadfully stricken, but it's because of the sleeping draught, I'm sure. When it wears off, he'll appear infinitely more vigorous and will proceed rapidly with her recovery. She may have some pain for a few days or a week, but she'll mend completely, you'll see."

Though Oliver's unexpected show of kindness caught him by surprise, Bartholomew remained unconvinced. "She seems so vulnerable," he said doubtfully. "I do hope you are right, Mr. MacKenzie."

"Of course I am right," Oliver said firmly, folding his arms across his chest. With more customary bluntness, he added, "But whatever the case, you are not doing either of you a favor by sitting by her bedside, gazing forlornly at her. You are only working yourself into a state of high drama, a habit acquired, I suspect, from your cousin." He shook his head ruefully before concluding, "I sympathize with your anxiety, but I believe it's misguided. What Violet needs most is uninterrupted sleep. And what you need most is a stiff brandy."

Oliver crossed to the side table and filled a snifter from one of the three decanters sitting on a tray. As he extended the glass, he commented wryly, "Considering our circumstances, Bartholomew, may I also suggest we dispense with the misters and misses?"

Bartholomew flushed with resentment at Oliver's remarks, then recognized the sense in them. "I am sure you are being very wise. Oliver," he said somewhat sheepishly, accepting the brandy and taking a welcome warming sip. "However, I daresay it is unjust to blame my agitation on Allegra."

"Probably so," Oliver agreed instantly, a grin catching at the corners of his mouth. "Having known Cecil, I think it would be more apt to consider it a peculiarity of Pembrokes in general."

Bartholomew flushed again, this time from uncertainty. "Well, I couldn't say, precisely," he mumbled.

"I could," Oliver responded, his grin widening. He waved at the settee and said, "Sit down. You look exhausted. Are you hungry? If you've just come up from Sussex, have you eaten?"

Sinking obediently onto the settee, Bartholomew realized that he hadn't had anything to eat since breakfast. Under the steadying effects of the aged brandy and Oliver's rock-hard realism, the usual orderliness of his mind began to reassert itself. "Yes, I am hungry," he said in surprise. "Ravenous, actually."

Oliver nodded his approval of this return to rationality. "I'll go down and rouse the kitchen," he said. "I'm sure they can scare up a morsel or two."

While Oliver was absent, Bartholomew leaned back and collected the rest of his thoughts. In less than a day, his life had completely changed course. Up until now, he had drifted back and forth with the tide, leading an aimless existence. He had invented excuses not to confront reality, burying himself in books. Even his work at the factory, however rewarding it had turned out to be, was a way of avoiding hard decisions about his life. Now, however, he had a definite purpose. Now he had the direction that had always eluded him. Now he had Violet.

His life no longer belonged to his father, or to stifling social dictates, but to himself. The murmurings and gossip of "polite" society were no longer of importance. From now on what mat ered was Violet, her happiness, her health, her comfort.

Bartholomew toasted his resolution with a gulp of brandy, still not certain how he was going to make this brave pledge actually happen. Unlike the past, however, he felt optimistic that he could. Unlike the past, he now felt confident.

Before he had time to trace the source of this new assurance, or even to bask in its glow, Oliver returned to the room. He was followed, almost immediately, by a waiter bearing a huge tray laden with bread and cheese, a cold game pie, potted crab, and a basket of fruit. "The grills have all been turned off for the night," Oliver explained as the waiter set the tray on a table, "but this should keep you going for a while."

"Is it only for me?" Bartholomew asked, taken aback. "Aren't you going to eat as well?"

"I had supper hours ago," Oliver answered, poking around in the fruit basket. "But I will have some Stilton with a pear. I hate to admit it, but I've missed eating Stilton almost as much as I've missed seeing Gilbert and Sullivan. We simply can't keep decent cheeses in Grenada."

He maintained a hospitable silence, enjoying his snack, while Bartholomew devoured his meal. When the last scrap of pheasant and the last flake of pie crust had disappeared, Bartholomew sighed contentedly, setting his napkin neatly on the tray. Considerably revived, he felt ready to face whatever lay ahead.

Oliver rose and went over to the table holding the decanters, where he poured out two glasses of port. He came back and handed one to Bartholomew. "Now," he said, sinking into a wing chair and draping his leg over its side, "tell me all about Pembroke et Fille."

The decanter was empty, and Bartholomew was growing hoarse when Oliver finally yawned, putting an end to hours of questions and answers about Allegra's chocolate business. "It's too late for you to be trudging across London with your valise," he said, standing up and stretching. "And I doubt you'll be able to find a hack, either." He nodded toward the settee. "Why don't you sleep here tonight," he casually suggested. "You shall only be back in the morning."

"Yes, I shall be," Bartholomew agreed, dithering only an instant over propriety before accepting the invitation. Although he had answered Oliver's questions at length and had been interested in the discussion, his eyes had kept straying to Violet's door.

Socially correct or not, he'd prefer to spend the night here, as close to Violet as he could get. "Thank you," he said, no longer surprised by Oliver's blunt kindness or by his uncanny perception. "I should be most grateful."

Despite his worry about Violet, and despite the discomfort of the settee, especially for someone as long as he, Bartholomew fell asleep almost immediately. It had been a very draining day. He slept deeply and solidly.

When he woke early the next morning, he disengaged himself as soundlessly as possible from the couch, carefully folded the blanket, then fished in his portmanteau for his shaving kit and a clean shirt. Those items under his arm, and a towel over his shoulder, he went down the corridor to make his morning ablutions.

When he returned, his tie properly knotted and every hair in place, the suite was still silent with sleep. For a few minutes, he paced noiselessly about, then skimmed the front page of yesterday's *Times*. Finally, he could restrain himself no longer. Going over to Violet's door, he slowly, with painstaking quiet, turned its knob. He cracked the door open a few inches and peeked into the room. Violet was propped up against the lacy pillows, wide awake, smiling straight at him. With a gasp of joy, his heart pounding furiously, he went in.

He was across the room in three strides and leaning over the bed. He told himself not to touch her, that she was bruised and sore and not recovered from yesterday's trauma, but when she turned her innocent, lovely, exotically colored face toward his, he couldn't resist. His hands cupped her chin, his lips brushed over hers. She felt so warm and vital, his heart took another bound, his breath was cut off. All the brilliant sensations he associated with Grenada surged up.

He kissed her again and again, on her lips, on her cheeks, burying his cleanly shaven face in her shiny black curls. He savored her taste, her silky texture, the scent of tropical flowers in her hair, remembering, discovering, until, afraid he was hurting her, he forced himself to ease away. He sank down onto the edge of the bed, grasping her good hand in both of his. Smiling back at her, he was happier than he had ever been before in his life.

Despite the bulky bandage on Violet's forehead and the cumbersome cast on her arm, despite the disinheritance that was in the offing, despite the devastation of Pembroke et Fille, Barthoomew was utterly, entirely, heart-swellingly happy. He was happier even than he had been that day at the lily pond, or riding the donkey home from eating soursop sorbet. Then, Violet had been just a wish, a desire, someone he had desperately wanted, but had been helpless to keep close. Now she was here. She was alive. And she was his. Forever.

"I love you, Violet," were his very first words. "I always have and I always shall."

Violet's smile increased, crinkling the corners of her deep brown eyes. She pressed her palm against his, reveling in his response as he raised her hand to his lips and laid a kiss across her fingers. "Oh, Bartholomew," she said, "I love you, too."

There was just a hint of hesitation in her words, a slight shadow of reservation. It wasn't because she didn't cherish his love or because she didn't return it with equal feeling, but because she longed to know where it would lead. She remembered their last night together, in the library at L'Etoile, when he had told her that his father would never approve of their union. She remembered selflessly relinquishing him to the castle he was bred for, bravely bidding him farewell as he returned to his fairy tale existence. As thrilled as she was to see him by her bedside, her handsome prince with china blue eyes, she couldn't help wondering how long he would remain.

"Always," Bartholomew answered, hearing the question in her husky voice. He squeezed the small hand he was holding and set another tender kiss on its fingers to seal his promise in place. "I want to be with you always. I want never to leave you again," he said earnestly, keeping her hand against his cheek. "Dear Violet, would you do me the inestimable honor of marrying me?"

In reply, Violet propelled herself off the pillows and into his arms, ignoring the pain her abrupt movement caused. "Yes, I will! I will! I will!" she said, punctuating each exclamation with a excited kiss. She was aware only of Bartholomew, of his cool, clear skin, of his clean, correct scent, of the devotion and adoration on his face. She was aware only of Bartholomew and of being incredibly happy, happier than she had ever been before in her life. She was alive. She was in London. And he was hers. Forever.

Although overjoyed at her response, Bartholomew was conscious of Violet's injuries. With a gentle hug he lowered her back against the pillows. "You mustn't overtax yourself," he admonished. "The most integral element in a complete convalescence is rest. The less you stress yourself, the more rapidly you will mend." He placed a fond kiss on her forehead, pressing it in with the tips of his fingers. "Undoubtedly, I am to blame for unduly disconcerting you," he added remorsefully. "I ought to have tendered my proposal at a more propitious moment."

"Oh no, Bartholomew," Violet protested. "It was the perfect moment. I can't tell you how much better it has made me feel." But she had a more urgent question, and she asked it immediately in the straightforward MacKenzie manner. "How did you manage to make your father change his mind?" she demanded.

For a moment Bartholomew looked startled, as if he had forgotten all about his formidable sire, then he broke into a laugh. "My father's mind is quite unchanged," he said with a lightness that surprised them both. "Most probably, nothing short of a petition from the Queen could make Sir Gerald change his views. I however, have changed mine."

Violet didn't answer, though she sucked in her breath and her eyes grew wider as she waited to hear more. Bartholomew didn't keep her in suspense for long. In a more serious tone, he explained, "I have discovered, in recent times, that I am not as helpless as I once assumed. It is no longer essential that I receive quarterly stipends or be dependent on my father to maintain respectable living standards. I am quite able to make my own way, and it needn't be in a barely sustaining position at a mediocre boy's school. You see, my proclivity for details and my collection of facts have very useful applications in the world of commerce.

"I am indebted to Allegra for this discovery," he added, with proper appreciation. "Thanks to her, and to the unwavering faith she has placed in me, I have gained an immeasurable amount of confidence. I am no longer daunted by the simple skills of survival. While it is true that I am still unable to boil an egg or press my suit, I am quite certain I shall be able to acquire these abilities, handily, should it become necessary."

"I am quite certain you shall, as well," Violet replied staunchly. "I have always felt you are capable of accomplishing anything you decide upon. You are the cleverest person I know. And you needn't trouble yourself about boiling eggs, because do that surpassingly well. Besides, they are far tastier poached with hot pepper sauce on top."

Bartholomew laughed again, a gentle, happy sound that ro

rom his heart. He leaned over and touched her lips with another iss. "My sweet Violet," he said softly. "My dear, sweet flower. Ve are going to have a wonderful life together. I am looking orward to every single minute." He drew a line around her eart-shaped face with his finger, marveling, as always, at her eauty.

"I promise you one thing," he solemnly swore. "I shall never t you live in wretched surroundings. I shall not let you be cold r hungry or wanting in any way."

"I believe you, Bartholomew," Violet said fervently. "I be- eve you, absolutely."

"Mind you," Bartholomew warned, smiling at her unquestion- ig loyalty, "I don't know, yet, how I am going to attain this ate, but I do promise you I shall find a way."

"As it happens," came Oliver's voice from behind them, "I ave one or two thoughts on that subject."

Startled by the interruption, both Bartholomew and Violet oked quickly around. Oliver was standing in the doorway, his irttails out, his face unshaven, a tray of hot chocolate and sweet lls in his hands. Indifferent to their obvious intimacy or to their tonished expressions, he crossed the room, set the tray on the d of the bed, and poured out three cups of frothy cocoa. Hand- g them around, Oliver calmly began to outline his ideas.

Chapter
Twenty-one

If it had been difficult yesterday to get out of bed, today it was nearly impossible. It was almost noon before Allegra could force herself to crawl out of the cocoon of bed clothes that kept the cumulative catastrophes at bay. Inside the warm, safe bundle of blankets and sheets, she could succumb to the lassitude creeping over her body and her mind. With the covers pulled securely over her head, she didn't have to confront her colossal failure.

It was finally habit, more than a sense of duty or guilt, that made her emerge. She dressed automatically, routinely selecting a skirt and a clean shirtwaist, running an obligatory brush through her unruly curls, buttoning on a linen topcoat mechanically. Today when she stepped out on the sidewalk, the weather was more in tune with her mood, foggy and bleak, the air full of its usual soot. Although she'd missed yesterday's meals, she made no stop at the corner tea shop. Today she had no interest in eating.

Nor did she stop at her shop. It would open or not open without her. It didn't much matter. In a few more days, all the chocolates would be sold, then the doors would close permanently. It would be just a pretty room, empty of merchandise, mocking her efforts and ambition. She had no interest in viewing the scene of her imminent defeat.

As concerned as she was about Violet's condition, she didn't go to the hotel either. She hadn't the courage to face Oliver or to bear witness to his scorn and disgust while he recounted the full scope of the Pembroke betrayal. Though she couldn't bear face him, she could scarcely blame him. He had gotten much more than he bargained for when he purchased half of L'Etoile. Not only had he bought part of a cocoa estate, he had also brought down on himself the problems of all the Pembrokes, their foibles and flaws.

She went straight to the factory, walking the whole way, in part to save tuppence on the omnibus, in part because she was in no hurry. The building was silent when she entered, its stillness adding to its chill. For a few moments she stood in the open door, half inclined to yield to an urge to turn and run from it all. In the end, she sighed and stepped forward. Although she had no idea what possible purpose she could serve in this deserted hall, she had nowhere else to go and nothing else to do.

Swinging the door shut behind her, she started slowly down the length of the room, her footsteps sounding small and insignificant on the wooden floor. She stopped at each station, as she had on her first tour of Stellar Confections two months before. In her mind, she recited the function of each piece of equipment, as Bartholomew had done that day. Her explanations were longer, more detailed and thorough, a result of the knowledge she had proudly acquired for herself since then.

Pausing and looking wearily around her, Allegra reflected that it was just so much useless information now. The factory already seemed derelict, a long-dead business. Dull-coated chocolate was hardened in globs and drips, clogged on paddles and rollers, puddled in troughs. Resuming her walk, she skirted the ragged hole punched through the floor, toed the lifeless rubber belt severed from its shaft, and eyed the mutilated metal valve responsible for its destruction.

Only when she wandered by the racks of unwrapped candies did a certain resolve overtake the aimlessness that had gripped her. Losing the machines and the equipment, the bricks and mortar, so to speak, was one thing, but she couldn't stand to see the chocolates go to waste. They were Bruno's creations, each one a work of art. They had a life, a reason, they were meant to be appreciated. She would sell them in the shop or give them away in the streets, but she wouldn't have them lost to rats and neglect. Taking off her coat and pushing up her cuffs, she set about packing the confections.

More than an hour had gone by, an hour in which the steady rythm of setting chocolates in boxes had an almost calming effect on Allegra's nerves, when she heard the sound of heels thumping on the floorboards. The accompanying tap of a walking stick on the wood told her, without looking up, that it was Roland. Though she kept on working, her illusory contentment vanished, replaced by anxiety and dread as he drew closer. With her head bent to her task, her hands slightly fumbling, she tracked his approach until he stood only a few feet from her.

Her throat was very dry, her pulse abnormal as she waited for the axe to fall. For some reason, she was having trouble making a lid fit its box. She was tense, her thoughts in turmoil. She waited to hear him gloat, to gleefully demand settlement of his loan, and then to triumphantly claim L'Etoile when she admitted she couldn't pay. She knew it was going to happen, knew it was only moments away, knew that in a second she would lose everything she owned or loved. With every inch of her being she prayed it would somehow be postponed.

"Please allow me to express my deepest regrets, Allegra," Roland said in his smoothest, most civilized tone. "It was a ghastly accident, even more unfortunate because success was in sight. Were I in your shoes, I would be utterly devastated, simply paralyzed by the cruelties of fate. Yet, here you are, sorting bon bons as if nothing had happened. You are indomitable, my dear, indomitable."

Allegra's head shot up at this astonishing speech, her mouth hung open in amazement. This was the Roland she used to know, charming and agreeable, an admiring smile lighting up his face. This turnabout in attitude rendered her speechless.

"I can see you are surprised," Roland acknowledged, folding both his hands over the silver knob of his stick. "Not that I fault you. I confess that I have behaved very badly. Poor Allegra. You are an innocent victim of my quarrel with MacKenzie. You have been valiantly playing against a stacked deck, but your indefatigable determination puts me to shame, my dear. It has jolted me awake."

His face very serious, his voice very sincere, he said, "You must allow me to make amends for the problems I have caused you. I am convinced you would be prospering by now if it weren't for my fiendish scheming. Do you think you could begin to forgive me if I tore up that troublesome note of your father's?"

Allegra swallowed hard and blinked. These were the miraculous words she had hoped against hope to hear, but now that it had said them, she was having difficulty believing it. It was too good to be true. "Would you really?" she asked. But her voice was such a scratchy whisper, she had to clear her throat and say it again. "Would you really tear up the note?"

"I would, my dear, gladly," Roland said, smiling. "Moreover, I insist on lending you the funds to put your factory to rights. This time, I won't permit you to refuse me. If you won't accept for your own sake, you must accept for mine. My conscience will torment me if I know I have not helped reverse the damage I have done."

It was on the tip of Allegra's tongue to exultantly accept, to shout her ecstatic relief at being granted a reprieve. It would be her salvation, her release from doom. Her spirits soared sky high. A happy smile of agreement spread across her face as she opened her mouth to speak. In the next instant, she saw behind the apologetic expression Roland had fixed on his face. She saw the obsessive gleam in his eyes, the predatory cast to his pale features. In that horrible moment, she knew that this was just another trap. Her stomach twisted in a sickening knot. Her spirits plummeted.

To hide the tears suddenly sprung into her eyes, she turned her attention back to her work. With hands that were trembling now, she jammed the chocolates into boxes, unstrung by this dizzying seesaw of hope. She knew that borrowing money from Roland would not be a solution to her problems, but a way of making them worse. "No thank you," she said in a shaky voice.

For a moment, Roland made no reply, fighting to control his rage at her refusal. Blotched color covered his cheeks, turning his handsome face ugly. He could not contain himself. "You stupid little fool," he snarled, taking a menacing step toward her. "You will soon learn that such sanctimonious pride is a costly luxury. Your precious integrity commands a high price."

He rapped his walking stick ominously on the floor. "Now, Miss Allegra Pembroke," he said. "Now is the time to settle our accounts. You owe me fifteen hundred pounds. Kindly pay me."

"I can't," Allegra said weakly, backing away from his unleashed anger. The dreaded moment had arrived, after all. "You know I can't. You know I haven't the money."

Roland's laugh held no trace of humor as he took another step toward her. "If you have no money, then you shall have to offer me some other form of payment. One way or another, you shall pay. I am uninterested in the money; that paltry sum is meaningless to me. I would gladly spend twice or thrice that amount for the satisfaction of taking from MacKenzie something that he loves, to humiliate him, as he humiliated me. Once and for all time, I shall teach that colonial rube a lesson."

Her heart in her throat at this maniacal threat, Allegra backed up some more. Her retreat was abruptly blocked when she bumped into the table stacked high with boxes of chocolates. In a panic, she looked around for a new route of escape. The instant she took her eyes off Roland, he closed the distance between them and seized her by the front of her shirt.

The shock of contact made Allegra's frayed nerves leap in fright. She pulled out of his grasp so precipitously, the pearl buttons on her blouse popped off and bounced on the floor. The suddenness of her release unbalanced her, and in seeking to evade Roland's renewed assault, she crashed into the tall columns of boxed confections behind her. Chocolates went flying everywhere.

"Minx!" Roland shouted, mashing the beautiful candies underfoot as he closed in on her. "Miserable baggage! Don't think you can evade me." He grabbed her arms and pinned them to her sides, pulling her closer to him.

His grip was brutally strong for one who presented so pale and refined an appearance. Allegra struggled in vain, twisting so hard his hands burned her wrists. She tried yanking and kicking, but succeeded only in losing her balance again. This time, she fell fast and hard to the floor, and Roland fell on top of her, never relinquishing his vicious hold.

The force of his fall smashed her back onto the chocolate strewn floor and crushed the breath from her chest, but he never eased his mad attack for a moment. With cold, dry lips he cut off her gasps for air, keeping his mouth cruelly clamped to hers no matter how desperately she tried to wrench free. He rubbed himself on her heaving body, sending waves of revulsion and disgust on top of the pain.

Rage and loathing were rapidly replacing her fear. She felt totally helpless beneath his bruising weight, a rag or a toy for Roland to use for his own deranged purposes. With every ounce of strength she could summon, her lungs begging for breath, Allegra tried to push him away, but her frenzied efforts only resulted in more punishing pressure. Frustration at her helplessness grew with abomination of his power.

Suddenly he was gone, torn from her with extraordinary force. As air poured back into her seared lungs, as grateful relief made her limbs limp, Allegra saw Oliver toss Roland around like a burlap bag of cocoa beans, throwing him to the floor, then yanking him back up. His face wild with fury, his fists moving rapidly, Oliver smashed him right below his watch chain. When Roland squealed and doubled over in agony, Oliver smashed him again in the mouth.

Propelled by the blows, Roland staggered back and sagged against the packing table for support. His pale face was green with pain, his suave appearance ruined. Blood oozed from swollen, split lips, and from a black gap where a front tooth had been. His clothes, custom-tailored on Savile Row, were crumpled and torn, blood and chocolate smeared across the fine fabric. His breath was ragged, his eyes were glazed, his arrogant assurance was destroyed.

Without taking her eyes from the scene before her, Allegra slowly raised herself to a seated position, then inched as far away as she could get, stopping only when her back hit the racks of unboxed chocolates. As she watched, half-awed, half-appalled by Oliver's ferocity, she was overcome by a feeling of déjà vu. It was like the night of the cocoa raid, when Oliver had savagely ripped an attacker away from her.

Oliver moved almost on top of his defeated enemy, his long, braced legs and broad, bunched shoulders the epitome of threatning power. When he spoke, his voice rang with the same cold precision as it had at Argo estate, with the same bleak authority that had subdued Frederick Smart and Cyril Joseph. It was a tone that had sent a shiver down her spine that day, and was doing so now.

"I have had a surfeit of you," Oliver told Roland, clearly enunciating every syllable. "And I have had a surfeit of your game of vengeance. Up until now, you have been setting the conditions and dealing the cards, a very one-sided arrangement. But now it is my turn. Listen carefully, Hawkes. These are the new rules.

"One—" He thrust an iron index finger under Roland's nose. "You will send, by tomorrow's post, a check of sufficient sum to over the cost of a new steam boiler for Pembroke et Fille.

"Two—" A second finger shot up with such force, Roland jerked back involuntarily. "Within very short order, I expect to hear that Lord Fenwick has, for reasons unknown, elected to dissolve his West Indian holdings and to invest his money and his attention in some other part of the globe. He shall refuse no reasonable offer for either of his enterprises.

"And three—" A third finger rose, and Oliver's voice became even more deadly. "If ever Allegra or I or anyone we are fond of meets with inexplicable hardship or harm, I shall consider you to be responsible. In that happenstance, not only shall I finish the dental adjustment I have just started, but I shall create such a scandal, you shall never be able to show your toothless face in public again."

"I don't believe you," Roland mumbled, trying to shrink away. He coughed weakly and clutched his stomach, trapped between Oliver and the table. "I think you are bluffing. Everyone knows that boiler was worn out. Why should I pay for it?"

"Because you are to blame for its explosion and for the damage it caused," Oliver retorted harshly. "And you will find out who is bluffing when the signed affidavit of Jeremy Jones is reprinted on the front page of all the papers. How long do you suppose that snobbish society you revere will continue to embrace you when it learns the truth: That you paid the stoker five pounds to loosen the old valve enough to blow? How many invitations to debutante balls and elegant suppers do you suppose you will receive when your esteemed peers realize that you, and your diabolical scheming have directly caused the injury of one innocent young woman and the financial ruin of another? Society will brand you for the pathetic coward that you are, anathema to proper Englishmen." Oliver gave him a contemptuous stare before concluding, "You have no choice but to comply with my rules."

Roland didn't deny bribing Jeremy Jones, but he desperately tried another tack. "I still hold a note against your cherished estate," he said, his words whistling ineffectually through the gap in his teeth.

"You hold *nothing*!" Oliver roared, grabbing Roland by his collar. "You are a liar and a cheat, as well as a bully! Cecil raised that money last September by selling the contract for L'Etoile' crop to your crony Smart. He repaid the loan immediately, and his solicitors have the canceled check to prove it. In typical fashion, he failed to retrieve the note, but fortunately he had the sense to demand a receipt. It hasn't been out of magnanimity that you've continually offered to invest in Allegra's business, but out of a desire to establish a genuine lien on L'Etoile. One that would eplace the worthless piece of paper you've been waving at her."

Allegra's mouth dropped open at this revelation. Pure outrage prought hot color to her cheeks. Furious words came spilling to her tongue. Before she had a chance to spit them out, Oliver was moving again. Still holding the beaten Roland by the collar, he dragged him upright and gave him a shove toward the door. "Out," he said icily. "Get out, but remember all three rules."

As Roland shuffled across the wooden floor, his heels no onger making a confident thump on the planks, Oliver stooped and retrieved Roland's silver-knobbed walking stick, his fallen cepter. At the door, he waited until Roland had stumbled down he steps, then he tossed the stick out after him. He swung the loor shut, slid the bolt decisively in place, and started back cross the room with slow, deliberate steps.

Both Allegra's awe and her outrage evaporated, replaced by larm as Oliver approached. Subconsciously trying to make herelf invisible, she pressed tighter against the racks of chocolates. Now it was her turn to receive Oliver's wrath. He would recite er follies and mete out her fate. He would enumerate her failres, starting with her foolishness in thinking she could run a usiness by herself and progressing through her laxness in invesgating Roland and the alleged loan. Now she would hear him ay that he never wanted to see her again, that she had heedlessly eopardized L'Etoile and, worse, Violet's life.

As Oliver came to a stop a few feet from her, she looked ervously at her hunched-up knees. It crossed her mind that this asn't unlike the scene played out just a short while ago when, ith averted eyes, she had waited for Roland to announce her oom. As the quiet seconds ticked by, the hollow dread in her omach hardened into resentment. Allegra suddenly felt battered nd bruised and tired of having her future decided by the actions nd opinions of others. The streak of rebellion rose from her omach and lodged itself in her jaw.

Oliver saw the rapidly evolving emotions flash across her ce, saw them change from anxious to obstinate. The last of the inding rage that had possessed him faded at the familiar sight of r defiant chin. He chuckled. Startled by this unexpected reacon, Allegra looked up quickly.

"May I?" he asked lightly, nodding his head at the empty ace next to her, as if asking permission to sit on a damask-cov-

ered divan in her private parlor while making a polite afternoon
call.

She looked at him, suspicious of his everyday tone. Finally
she shrugged and looked away.

With the toe of his boot, Oliver brushed aside the smashed
chocolates, then, with uncharacteristic concern for his uncharac-
teristically well-kept clothes, he dropped his handkerchief over
the residual stickiness. "It's quite a mess, isn't it?" he commented
conversationally, sitting down on the floor and leaning his back
against the racks.

Allegra glanced at him sideways but still made no reply, her
mind racing to decide what he really meant. He was only inches
away from her, and though he made no move to touch her, she
found his nearness distracting. Provoked though she was, he
made her pulse pound.

In the same conversational vein, Oliver continued to chat. "I
had an interesting talk with Bartholomew last night," he said
casually. "I was better acquainting myself with my future
brother-in-law."

"Your what?" Allegra gasped, instant excitement temporarily
replacing her pique.

Oliver grinned at her delight. "My brother-in-law," he repeated. "He and Violet are determined to be married as soon as
she can hold a bridal bouquet. I wish them well," he added sincerely. "I do think they'll be happy. Which is not to say they
won't have some sizable obstacles to overcome, Sir Gerald coming most immediately to mind. He'll cut Bartholomew off without a farthing."

"It's not the least bit fair," Allegra said warmly, sympathizing
with her cousin. "But I'm certain Bartholomew will find a way
around it. He is far more clever and capable than he imagines. I
don't think he needs his father's largesse to survive, or even to
thrive."

"I don't think he does, either," Oliver agreed. It was his turn
to look away. "However," he said, carefully studying the ceiling,
"I'm afraid your relationship with Sir Gerald is more vulnerable.
Without Bartholomew to act as your buffer, I doubt your uncle
will continue to let your loan lapse. I'll wager that he sends his
solicitors around to collect on the note within twenty-four hours
of Bartholomew announcing his nuptials." He turned his gaze
back to Allegra's horrified face and said, "It would seem that

ven without Roland Hawkes to plague you, you're still in a spot
f trouble."

Allegra swallowed, her throat suddenly dry. The good feeling
roused by her cousin's engagement to Violet was gone, as was
he earlier relief she'd hardly had a chance to acknowledge.
he'd regained and lost everything so many times today, her
nind was growing numb. "Yes," she said hopelessly, staring
ack at him. "It would seem so."

"I wonder, Allegra," Oliver said, with as much delicacy and
aution as he could summon, "I wonder if you would be inter-
sted in listening to a proposition of mine, one that might remedy
he situation."

Despite his mild, well-mannered approach, his suggestion
iggered a reflexive response. Thrusting out her jaw again, and
eturning her gaze to her lap, Allegra grunted. Now it was com-
ng. It didn't matter whether she wanted to hear his proposal or
sten to his advice, she knew she was going to. Just as her
nother and her grandfather had always prefaced their scoldings
ith polite phrases of concern for her, she sensed that Oliver was
ading up to another lecture on her incompetence. Maybe she
as incompetent. Not maybe, probably. But she was tired of
eing told so.

Oliver interpreted her noncommittal grunt for assent. He was
ell aware of her fierce scowl of annoyance, but he would much
ather see that than the blankness that had preceded it. He was
sed to her stubbornness. In fact, he expected it, and despite the
xasperation it caused, he actually welcomed it. It was when she
ave up that he worried.

"On more careful consideration," he began blandly, picking
p a chocolate-covered caramel and juggling it in his hand, "I can
e that my initial criticisms of Stellar Confections cum Pem-
roke et Fille were a trifle exaggerated, hastily drawn, as it were.
ow that I have had the opportunity to review the business more
bjectively, I admit that your faith in the company was not as
nwarranted as I once thought. Though it's still in straitened con-
itions, I think it has potential for success." He paused, dropped
e chocolate, drew in his breath and plunged recklessly ahead. "I
ould like to buy Pembroke et Fille from you," he said, looking
irectly at her. "I am prepared to offer you three thousand
ounds."

Slowly, Allegra lifted her face. Slowly, she brought it around toward his. "No," she said succinctly, her scowl deepening.

Oliver bit back the blunt remark he was about to make, ironically reminding himself that he enjoyed her obstinance. "Be reasonable, Allegra," he said calmly. "It's a fair offer considering you own neither the factory building nor the shop, and that you are not yet really established. It more than covers the worth of the equipment and the inventory, minus, of course, some outstanding bills, with a decent sum left over for goodwill. With the money you receive, you will be able to pay your uncle back and be free of debt, while still retaining your share of L'Etoile. Otherwise, i proceed on your present course, you will most certainly lose the estate, and most probably lose the chocolate business."

"Oh?" Allegra said coldly. "I seem to have held onto it until now."

"Yes, you have," Oliver agreed, nodding his head. "And give you tremendous credit for turning a shabby enterprise into shining jewel by sheer force of will. But unfortunately, it will take more than that to keep it in operation. Even after the boiler i replaced, there are other repairs to be made, and there are, inevitably, slow seasons like the coming summer to muddle through. I takes a certain amount of capital to get a business on its feet Allegra, you haven't got sixpence to rub together."

Allegra's mouth twitched as she grudgingly accepted his assessment of her expenses. She had calculated them herself already. It in no way meant, however, that she was prepared to give in. "In the first place," she said testily, crossing her arms over her torn blouse, "your analysis overlooks one fact. I won't be 'free of debt', as you claim, because I still owe you fifteen-hundred pounds for the money you gave Frederick Smart. Money, as happens, that went to pay back Roland. So, even though you don't hold an actual written note, I am doubly bound to honor this loan."

"Mmm," Oliver commented, crossing his own arms and leaning back, waiting for the rest of her argument.

It wasn't long in coming. "In the second place," Allegra continued more strongly, "I've already told you I won't accept charity. And your purchase of the factory would most certainly be charity since you hate living in England and, therefore, couldn't genuinely want to own the business. If Pembroke et Fille has as much potential as you say, then I should be able to find a true

nterested buyer, an *English* buyer if it comes to that. Perhaps
ven someone who will pay me a bigger price."

"Perhaps," Oliver conceded. "Although you might only find a
uyer who would pay you less." He thought about it for a minute,
veighing the possibilities, then dismissed the subject as irrele-
ant. "In either instance," he said, moving on to a more interest-
ng topic, "I would not be the ultimate owner, thus my residence
1 England would not be a factor. I would immediately resell
eventy-five percent of the company to Bartholomew, postponing
ayment for five years, and giving him some working capital as a
vedding present.

"You must admit, Allegra," Oliver said coaxingly, leaning
orward and resting his arms on his upturned knees, "other than
ou, Bartholomew is the ideal proprietor of Pembroke et Fille.
'o one knows it better or will run it as well. And even the name
appropriate. Well," he retracted, "perhaps the 'Fille' doesn't fit
ow. But he and Violet ought to be able to rectify that situation in
me."

Allegra's arms uncrossed too, and she let them fall wearily in
er lap. He was right, of course. Bartholomew was the perfect
roprietor, but she was not yet ready to admit it out loud. She
ound herself unaccountably annoyed by Oliver's neat solution to
veryone's problems. With her factory as the sacrificial lamb.
ers and Cecil's. "I suppose," she said peevishly, "that removes
ir Gerald's threat and provides for Bartholomew and Violet, but
y first objection still stands. I owe you fifteen-hundred
ounds."

Realizing she was finding his magic wand more upsetting than
oothing, Oliver was hesitant to continue. "I'd like to be able to
ll you that in my generosity I forgive the debt," he said warily,
ut the plain truth is that L'Etoile made an unprecedented profit
is year. The final tallies of this year's crop far exceeded expec-
ions, especially since Cecil's new acreage started yielding.
'ith the price of cocoa at a record high, we did very well. Your
are should make a large bite in that fifteen-hundred pounds,
d next year's crop should eliminate it altogether."

So that was it. Her problems were over. Why didn't she feel
lieved? Rubbing her forehead with the palm of her hand, Alle-
a told herself that she ought to be pleased with the way things
orked out, grateful for Oliver's intervention. But she still felt an
ational resentment.

"It's not just a building, you know," she finally burst out. "It's not just some candies." She scattered a few of the chocolates by her feet in illustration. For a moment, she was silent as she tried to assemble her flying thoughts, then she turned to him, imploring him to understand. "Pembroke et Fille isn't Bartholomew and his baby," she said intently, all trace of sulkiness gone from her voice. "Cecil is the Pembroke and *I* am the Fille. Me." She jabbed her chest with a clenched fist for emphasis. "It's . . It's . . ." she broke off in frustration, unable to articulate her feelings.

How could she explain to him that Pembroke et Fille wasn't just a business she had inherited, but a symbol of a more important legacy? How could she explain to him that only by making a success of the chocolate factory, by clearing her father's frivolous reputation, by proving that his romantic schemes were realistic only then could she prove her own worth too?

All her life, she had been reprimanded and ridiculed for nature she had tried in vain to repress. All her life she had been nagged by ambitions and dreams she didn't dare express. It wasn't until she discovered her father's existence that she realized, with joyous relief, where her undesirable character had come from. Now, only by showing everyone who'd ever doubted it that Cecil wasn't a hare-brained, half-witted, improvident fool could she show them at long last that she wasn't either. And more importantly, she could show herself the same thing. How could she make Oliver understand that?

She didn't have to. Oliver heard it in her voice, saw it in her desperate expression. Most of all, he just knew it. He knew because he had known Cecil and because he knew her and because he knew how the world worked. He reached over and very tenderly ran a finger down her cheek. "You aren't your father, Allegra," he said. "You are not Cecil."

When she looked at him, wondering what he meant, he brushed her cheek again and gently elaborated. "You are your father's daughter in many ways, but you are enough of a person to stand on your own, apart from him. In fact, you would be better off if you separated yourself from him.

"Cecil was impulsive and imaginative, and so are you. He was amusing, attractive, full of life, and so are you. But Allegra," he said more urgently, "in the end, Cecil was a selfish, spoiled child, and you are not." He took her cold hand in one of his warm ones, wishing he could somehow soften the words he was about to say.

"Don't misunderstand me," he told her, "I liked Cecil. He was my friend and, by choice, my partner. But I wasn't blind to his faults. He was an interesting man whose primary interest was himself, an extremely talented man who used his talents for his own gratification and ease, blithely ignoring those who cared for him the most. He took advantage of his father, he abandoned your mother, he cheated me, and, Allegra, he forgot about you."

With a sharp intake of breath, Allegra withdrew her hand from the comfort of his grasp and folded it with her other on her knees. Resting her head on them, she painfully accepted this last cruel blow. She didn't resist the rest of Oliver's assessment of Cecil. She'd already come to the same conclusion herself. But it was one thing to admit her father had betrayed someone else, quite another to admit he had betrayed her.

"Perhaps it was for the best that you grew up in your grandfather's house, Allegra," Oliver mused, trailing his finger down her arched neck and winding a golden curl around it. "As confining as I'm sure it was, it probably set a stronger example than life with your father would have.

"Cecil was famous at starting things, but he was notorious for never finishing them. He had wonderful ideas, truly marvelous schemes, and he plunged into them with enviable enthusiasm. But he always fell short of seeing them through to fruition. The fact that you have resurrected this business, that you have taken on assets and liabilities alike demonstrates a sense of responsibility and determination Cecil never exhibited. You have, by far, exceeded his best efforts."

Although his touch sent a shiver all the way through her, Allegra didn't look up. Her voice was muffled by the folds of her skirts as she responded, "That isn't what you said before. You've told me often enough that I have a hopeless head for doing business. Just like my father."

With her face still turned down, she couldn't see Oliver's eyebrows rise in chagrined acknowledgment of her accusation. With his usual unvarnished honesty, he said, "I have to admit, I still think you have a hopeless head for doing business." He felt her neck stiffen beneath his fingers. "But I also think you have a rare genius for seeing that it gets done."

When Allegra turned her head slightly and peeked at him out

of one eye, he smiled and continued. "You were right the time that you told me I didn't take you seriously. I underestimated you. We all did. Me, Jamie, the solemn apple farmer from New England. I saw only that you were Cecil's daughter with the same impetuous enthusiasm and distinctly hazy grasp of arithmetic, and I looked no further. I matched the dismal state of Stellar Confections with your inability to add a column of figures and decided it was an impossible proposition." He untwined his fingers from her curls and waved his hand around the room, encompassing the entire operation. "You have shown me that I was wrong," he said simply.

Allegra turned her head a little more and looked at him harder, not quite believing the words she was hearing. Although she didn't answer, her heart was hammering.

Oliver didn't seem to expect a reply. Setting his hand back on her shoulder, he said, "You have done a remarkable job, Allegra, one Cecil would never have done, no matter how long he lived. If you don't carry it personally through to prosperity, it is irrelevant. With diligence and adherence to your ideas, it can be made to happen. Leave it for Bartholomew to do. You would only be bored with the day-to-day details. You have already proven your point."

Absently rubbing his thumb down her spine, he continued, almost as much to himself as to her. "I should have realized it all along," he said sheepishly. "I should have seen it those months at L'Etoile when you had everyone doing cartwheels with your calico competitions." He stopped rubbing and gave her a little shake. "You have a knack for making people do what you want, whether it's picking cocoa pods or packing chocolates. Or figuring the finances.

"If I hadn't been so stubborn, I would have seen that it isn't necessary for you to balance the books or calculate your costs, because you attract people who will do it for you. You command their indelible loyalty, their utter devotion." Gently yanking on another curl to get her attention, he asked, "Do you know why, Allegra?"

This time he waited until she said, in a very anxious whisper, "No."

He ran his finger under her chin and lifted it until her face was level with his. "Because you inspire them," he said. "You are a

spiration to everyone around you. Your ideas, your imagina-
on, your wholehearted interest make people try harder than they
ormally might. You make them find qualities inside themselves
ey didn't know they possessed."

This time he gave the chin he was still holding a little shake as
e asked, "Do you think Bartholomew would have found the
ourage and the confidence to defy his father without your inspi-
tion? To help you with the factory? Or to marry Violet? Do you
ink Bruno would have created the confectionary masterpieces
at he has? Or that the painters and carpenters and sales clerks
uld have assembled that shop in a month?" He paused a mo-
ent before asking, more pointedly, "Do you think Cecil could
ve inspired them to the same ends?"

Oliver shook his head in answer to his own question, then
ked another. "Do you think Cecil could have inspired me to
me to England? To realize the idiocy of my refusal to even
ntemplate such a trip?"

Glad tears filled Allegra's eyes and made a lump in her throat,
oking off her voice. Instead, she shook her head in reply.

"No," Oliver agreed, catching a tear on her cheek with his
umb. "No, he couldn't have. Cecil charmed people, he amused
em, but he didn't inspire them. I liked Cecil, Allegra, I liked
n very much. But I love you."

She blinked back the rest of her tears, her heart practically
rsting in her chest. She hardly knew which thrilled her more,
 declaration of love, or her own acceptance of what he was
ing. Then she realized that the two were inseparable.

Once, standing on her veranda in the sweet, warm breeze, she
 decided that it wasn't enough just to love Oliver, she had to
fill her ambitions first. Later, sorting orange peels and paper
appers, she had realized that somewhere on her journey from
nnecticut to England, by way of the West Indies, Oliver had
ome a permanent part of her life, that nothing else was as
portant. Now, sitting on the chocolate-littered floor of her fac-
y, she knew she needed both to achieve the satisfaction she had
n seeking. It was impossible to separate her head from her
rt, and impossible to separate Oliver from the life she had
ays longed to live.

In the next instant she let go of Cecil, stopped using him for a
tch. She gave him a shove and he drifted off, leaving Allegra

on her own. No whistles blew, no guns went off, nothing cat
clysmic happened. She didn't stumble awkwardly or trip and fall
The beautiful chocolate business she had built didn't disappea
Oliver didn't fade away. And she didn't love her father any les
She was still his daughter, they were still Pembroke et fille, b
now she was entirely Allegra.

Before she could tell Oliver of her extraordinary discover
before she could put her elation in words, he slipped his ha
around the back of her head and pulled her toward him. For
fraction of an instant, she saw him coming closer, saw the hum
hiding in the corners of his mouth and the improbably long lash
fringing his eyes. His lips pressed against hers, his cheek graz
her face, and all her racing thoughts faded.

In their place came memories of places and moments, of se
sations and smells, of brilliant colors and exotic tastes and spe
tacular emotions. She remembered the feel of Oliver's hands
he held her in the sea at Sabazon, or cradled her among t
burlap bags in the boucan, or helped her steer the big wheel o
schooner. She remembered his salty kiss in the waves
Gouyave and the ones that cooled her hot skin as they lay in t
wildflowers and watercress. She remembered the sky and t
stars and all the feelings that were flooding her now, the de
pleasure, the intense desire, the love. Her hands unfolded fr
her knees and slid around his neck, her fingers buried in his ha

"I accept your offer," she said when she stopped to catch
breath, leaning back and looking into his eyes.

Oliver smiled in delight. "Excellent decision," he told h
pulling her toward him again.

Her lips were almost on his, she was almost lost in a k
when another thought snuck in and struck her. "Wait," she sa
setting both hands on his shoulders and pushing him an ar
length away.

"Wait?" he asked, apprehension suddenly gripping him.

Allegra nodded, her brow wrinkling. "You said you w
going to sell Bartholomew seventy-five percent of Pembroke
Fille. What are you going to do with the other quarter?"

"Oh, that," Oliver answered, relieved that it wasn't some
possible objection. "That is a wedding present for you." Wh
the quiet seconds ticked by and she didn't respond or remove

ands from his shoulders, he gently prompted, "I'm asking you
· marry me, Allegra."

A smile of her own unwrinkled her forehead. "Yes, I know,"
1e said. "I am becoming quite adept at recognizing your pro-
osals, despite your best efforts to disguise them." More reflec-
vely, she added, "I can't help thinking, though, that if we
1arry, my half of L'Etoile will become yours, and I will be left
ith nothing."

For an astonished instant Oliver only stared, then he burst out
.ughing. He pulled her hands from his shoulders and held them
. his, laying an emphatic kiss on her fingers. "On the contrary,"
· said. "To paraphrase an old saying, you won't be losing half
. estate, but gaining a whole one." He dropped her hands and
·rapped her in an embrace, his tone becoming more serious. "I
.n't imagine running L'Etoile without you," he said. "It would
· a wholly spiritless exercise. I need your help, your inspiration.
.eed an equal partner."

His lips brushed over hers and touched each cheek, his breath
ffled her hair. "What do you think, now?" he murmured in her
.r.

"Well," Allegra answered earnestly, squirming back to a more
.actical position, "I think we should reconsider L'Etoile's sole
.pendence on cocoa. There was a good crop this year, but what
excessive rains should ruin the blossoms or drought should dry
· buds? We should think, too, about the cocoa estates being
.rted in Africa. They have the backing of Cadbury Brothers and
·wentree and Fry. With that type of sponsorship, the West In-
.an trade might suffer."

Ignoring Oliver's amazed expression and the glorious glow
.t being in his arms created, she continued, her excitement
.ilding. "I have the idea that we ought to give bananas a
·ught. After all, we grow them already to shade the young
.coa trees. And I was talking to William before I left. We
·reed that bananas might make the ideal supplement to his apple
.siness . . ."

Oliver cut off the rest of her comments with a kiss quivering
.th laughter. "Not only would L'Etoile be boring without you,"
. said, when she was effectively silenced, "but my life would be
.erly empty and dull, as well." He dropped another kiss on the
.dge of her nose and brushed a few curls from her face. "How-

ever, do you think you could defer your thoughts on bananas for few moments while you answer my question about marriage?"

"Of course I could," Allegra responded agreeably. Then she smiled and twined her arms around him again. "I accept that offer, too," she said.